TO HUNT A SUB

SUB

A Novel

By J. Murray

Other books by Jacqui Murray

Rowe-Delamagente Series
To Hunt a Sub
Twenty-four Days

Dawn of Humanity trilogy
Born in a Treacherous Time

Crossroads trilogy
Survival of the Fittest *(Book 1)*
The Quest for Home (Book 2—coming Summer 2019)
In the Footsteps of Giants (Book 3—coming Summer 2020)

Non-fiction
Building a Midshipman: How to Crack the USNA Application

Education
Over 100 non-fiction resources integrating technology into education available from Structured Learning LLC

Praise for *Rowe-Delamagente*:

A blistering pace is set from the beginning: dates open each new chapter/section, generating a countdown that intensifies the title's time limit. Murray skillfully bounces from scene to scene, handling numerous characters, from hijackers to MI6 special agent Haster. ... A steady tempo and indelible menace form a stirring nautical tale. – Kirkus Reviews

***

... a satisfying read from a fresh voice in the genre, and well worth the wait. The time devoted to research paid off, providing a much appreciated authenticity to the sciency aspects of the plot. The author also departs from the formulaic pacing and heroics of contemporary commercialized thrillers. Instead, the moderately paced narrative is a seduction, rather than a sledgehammer. The author takes time rendering relatable characters with imaginatively cool names like Zeke Rowe, and Kalian Delamagente. The scenes are vividly depicted, and the plot not only contains exquisitely treacherous twists and turns, but incorporates the fascinating study of early hominids, and one ancestral female in particular who becomes an essential character. – Goodreads reader

***

A fusion of technology, academics, and archaeology make "To Hunt a Sub" a thrilling ride. The stakes are high as a PhD student and an ex-Seal risk all to stop terrorists from stealing American submarines carrying nuclear weapons. The writing is clipped and crisp, fitting well with the genre—there's little fluff. The author's expertise in technology shines through. A quick read I finished in just a few days. Solid debut novel. – Amazon reader

***

So last night I couldn't sleep and finally got up about 3 o'clock in the morning and thought I would just read for a while and maybe I would get to sleep unfortunately, I read your book. Needless to say I was only halfway done when I started at 3 a.m. and by 6 a.m. I had finished the book! too good to go to sleep. Excellent book. Can't wait for the next one. WOW – Amazon reader

***

This is a complex layered story that successfully blends well researched archaeology and cutting edge technology, with a high stakes terrorist plot to steal nuclear submarines. It's got characters to root for, and villains to loathe. –Amazon reader

***

I loved the way the author combined vulnerability and strength in her main characters. I loved where the macho character 'Rowe' takes Kali's hand even though she pulls away. And there is this beautiful raw, insight into what it can cost you to be a mother. Otto is very cool too. – Amazon reader

Published by Structured Learning LLC

Laguna Hills, Ca 92653

This is a work of fiction. Names, characters, places, and incidents either are the product of the author's imagination or are used fictitiously, and any resemblance to actual persons, living or dead, business establishments, events, or locales, is entirely coincidental. The publisher does not have any control over and does not assume any responsibility for author or third-party websites or their content.

Design and layout for cover: Paper and Sage Inc.
Printer: Quality Instant Press

Printed in the United States of America

ISBN 978-1-942101-46-8

My sincere thanks to the following people for their support and knowledge. CDR Matthew Carr for his passionate discussions about submarines, my brother CDR John MacCrossen who shared what he could from his days hunting submarines, Dr. Philip Ender of the University of California Los Angeles for savvy insights into computers and an alternative approach to thinking, Mike Merrifield for inspiration, Roxane Teboul for her tips about being a Columbia grad student, my husband for his constant belief in my ability to tell this story, John Rowe for allowing me to use his son's name, my daughter's cerebral friends for their humorous approach to all things complicated, my anonymous friend for his anecdotal insights into radical Islam—providing a personal face to the terrorists' goals, Donald Johansen and the Leakey's for nurturing my abiding love and respect for our ancestors, and the talented members of my writing group and blogging community—thank you for unselfish hours of editing.

Please know that, while these individuals assisted in this book's development, all mistakes are my own. In some cases—particularly with Columbia University and parts of New York—I adjusted reality to reflect the needs of the script. In other cases—such as submarine protocols and other government-based details—I purposely strayed from reality to insure my story never got close to resembling national secrets.

Table of Contents

Praise for the Rowe-Delamagente series
Other Books by Jacqui Murray
Introduction
Prologue

Chapter 1
Chapter 2
Chapter 3
Chapter 4
Chapter 5
Chapter 6
Chapter 7
Chapter 8
Chapter 9
Chapter 10
Chapter 11
Chapter 12
Chapter 13
Chapter 14
Chapter 15
Chapter 16
Chapter 17
Chapter 18
Chapter 19
Chapter 20
Chapter 21
Chapter 22
Chapter 23
Chapter 24
Chapter 25
Chapter 26
Chapter 27

Chapter 28
Chapter 29
Chapter 30
Chapter 31
Chapter 32
Chapter 33
Chapter 34
Chapter 35
Chapter 36
Chapter 37
Chapter 38
Chapter 39
Chapter 40
Chapter 41
Chapter 42
Chapter 43
Chapter 44
Chapter 45
Chapter 46
Chapter 47
Chapter 48
Chapter 49
Chapter 50
Chapter 51
Chapter 52
Chapter 53
Chapter 54
Chapter 55
Chapter 56
Chapter 57
Chapter 58
Chapter 59
Chapter 60
Chapter 61
Chapter 62
Chapter 63
Chapter 64

Chapter 65
Chapter 66
Chapter 67
Chapter 68
Chapter 69

Epilogue

About the Author
Preview of *Twenty-four Days*

Prologue

Two weeks before present

Every day, desperate people pushed through the wide glass doors of 111 North Hill Street, hoping the justice delivered within these hallowed walls would solve their problems. No matter his mood, Alfred Zematis offered a warm smile, sometimes listening to their sad tales, other times simply nodding encouragement. He took pride in the sparkling tile floors, the immaculate sinks in the bathrooms and the trash bins he never allowed to overflow. This grand old courthouse had been his home for thirty years.

Musai Alland changed that.

Today Alfred swished his broom back and forth in practiced steady sweeps, knowing this would be his last time. He mopped his brow with a faded kerchief. The air conditioner was broken—again. By the time it was hot enough his bosses asked him to bring up the big box fans stored in the basement, he would be under arrest. He winced. Every breath hurt his chest. It could be the illness. Or nerves. Probably nerves, but it made no difference anymore.

He checked his battered Timex. One fifty. Time crawled when a man outlived his children. God never intended that.

He peered into Room 22. The man who wasn't Gegham Keregosian stood in the back, head down, lips moving. His cocoa-colored skin, as smooth and unlined as a teenager, was dry in spite of the ninety-degree building. The low rumble of voices and the crinkle of food wrappers muffled his words, but he must have felt Alfred's presence. He stared at the janitor with those empty eyes before continuing his quiet prayers.

Alfred turned away. It was not yet time.

Alfred didn't mean to learn Gegham Keregosian's real name. A week ago, Alfred had been asked to remove black drag marks from the floor. He blocked the hallway with cones, excited about the prospect of working without interruptions, doing the job he was hired to do and doing it well. Around the corner, out of sight, a voice he recognized as Keregosian whispered to someone Alfred couldn't see. The unknown man called Keregosian 'Salah'. There was a crack followed by a hissed warning from Keregosian: '*Do not ever use my real name*'. Alfred fumbled headphones over his ears and hummed loudly to his silent music as the two men came into view. The only noise as they passed was Alfred's wet rag and Keregosian's hollow footsteps.

Alfred had no idea how to end another man's life, but a father must avenge his daughter's death. In exchange for Alfred's now meaningless savings, Keregosian would kill Musai Alland and allow him—Alfred—to claim responsibility. Alfred felt no regret. God understood why he must break the sacred Commandment.

One fifty-two.

In the reflection off the mirrored elevator doors, Alfred saw himself as the TV cameras would. A clean, pressed uniform bagged on an emaciated frame. Shoes, old and cracked, shone with polish. His sparse grey hair lay neatly against his freckled skull. A thin gold band, scarred from years of labor, shimmered on his parchment skin, the sole reminder of the stunning exotic dancer who stole his heart, leaving him with a child he named Angel who thought her daddy could do no wrong.

He gave Angel's cat away this morning. She had found it in the alley, left eye blind and bloody with a deep laceration from his stomach through his haunch. She nursed it back to health and loved it so completely, Alfred worried what would happen to his Angel if the animal ever disappeared.

He should have worried about the reverse.

One fifty-five. The jury's decision had been expected twenty-five minutes ago. Why so late? They must see the defendant was guilty.

Two o'clock. The courtroom phone trilled and the guard

pounded the gavel.

All rise…

Alfred Zematis' personnel file called him dependable, friendly, and a hard worker. He had taken only three sick days in thirty years. The first was for the birth of his daughter, Angel. Alfred had proudly shown off pictures of a pink bundle of squirming limbs and satin skin. His finger, thick as a sausage, nail grimy with embedded dirt, hovered over her cherub cheeks as he promised: *No evil will touch you, whatever it costs.*

His next sick day came when a neighbor left an urgent message with Alfred's supervisor. One-year-old Angel had been crying all morning. Alfred's boss drove him home where they found a farewell note from Alfred's wife pinned to Angel's yellow-and-white patchwork blanket. He hugged the infant, changed her diapers, and assured her nothing in God's glorious world could hurt them. From then on, until the County's onsite daycare center had room, he mopped floors, swapped out light bulbs, and cleaned bathrooms with Angel tied to his chest in a homemade sling, Alfred's heart beating against hers.

Alfred took his third and final sick day when seventeen-year-old Angel died. She had been so excited about the new job. The money meant *Dosuna*, her pet name for him, could stop working overtime. She gave him a web address, a password, and kissed him for the last time.

When his shift ended, he went to the library and logged into the website his daughter had given him. It was a webcam in a well-lit room with no furniture or windows or decorations of any kind. A striking, dark-skinned male introduced himself as Musai Alland. He wore conservative pleated slacks, a dark turtleneck and a heavy gold chain around a muscular neck. When the camera panned out, Alfred could see that he stood by a rugged trestle table holding what Alland called an avatar—a caricature—of a naked girl, five wide leather straps securing her limbs, trunk, and head. Blood oozed from hundreds of cuts in her youthful skin and the grisly remains of nail beds where fingernails should have been.

Alland assured the audience the pathetic creature was fictitious—her pain the result of high-tech wizardry. As he tortured the girl, he asked if viewers felt contempt for his treachery or pity for her misery.

Alfred felt shame that mankind considered this being with her cracked voice, tangled filthy hair, and wild eyes entertainment. She squirmed and pleaded while the man named Musai Alland brushed a soothing hand over her frightened face. Alland leaned forward to inhale her fear with a narrow, aquiline nose and then watched her wretchedness with wide-set, soulless eyes. He selected a squat cylinder from a shelf under the table, like the mace canisters people carry for protection. He smiled as he showed it to the creature. She pulled back, feral eyes wide, but the heavy straps held her firmly. She begged for mercy until her sobs became hysterical hiccups, and then sprayed her mouth. She howled in pain, writhing from the chemicals. He squirted her pixie ears, button nose, terrified eyes, and vagina. Primal screams vibrated against the room's walls, her fingers clawing at the wooden bed, leaving bloody streaks under her hands. Her neck cords bulged and her back arched. As tears sprang to Alfred's eyes, he wondered how this horror involved his Angel.

Until one word soaked through his senses: "*Dosuna!*"

Alfred blanched. No one used that name but Angel. He called her his angel and she called him her Archangel, or 'two A's—*Dosuna.* Now he saw it, in the curve of her blood-spattered neck and the swell of her tortured cheek. The crazed eyes—that last week overflowed with the fullness of life—searching for a savior who would never arrive. Through blinding tears, he stabbed at the library's pay phone, but got only the website's answer machine. He dialed the police, told them between sobs what he was watching and implored them to hurry. They asked him to bring the website address in and tell his story to the on-duty detective. The operator sounded bored or tired, or both. When Alfred got back to the computer,

Alland was handing Angel a jagged piece of wood. She grasped it in shaking hands and slashed her wrists over and over until they were but a gory sludge of tissue. Alfred forced his eyes to remain on his baby, hot tears rolling down his face and chest heaving in agonizing sobs. He could not let his Angel die alone.

When the screen went dark, Alfred called the same policeman and told him Angel was dead.

His next call was to a New York number Angel had given him, a woman with a robot she said could track anything. At least, that was her claim to Angel's high school tech class. He told the woman about Angel and Alland and asked for help. They talked for ten more minutes, and then Alfred took a taxi to the police station.

The next morning, an email awaited him. He called in sick, shined his dress boots, donned his church clothes, smoothed his hair, and appeared at the office of the District Attorney. The golden letters over the door said he sheltered the innocent. The janitor rocked side to side as he talked, head bowed, coarse hands clutching his work cap, trying to describe what he saw and why he knew it was murder. The Great Man splayed tapered fingers across the cluttered desktop, intelligent eyes taking in Alfred's ragged words before responding.

"One of our detectives visited Musai Alland early this morning. He admitted to making the tape, but said he used a simulacrum, not a real person. He says he desires to attract Hollywood's attention, not the police."

Alfred brushed a tear from his cheek. He didn't know what a 'sim-yoo-*lay*-crum' was. He dropped out of high school when his mother died and worked sixty hours a week to raise five siblings. He opened his mouth, but found his throat too tight to speak.

The District Attorney softened his voice. "Torturing a simulated human is not illegal. We have no crime scene or body. Without new evidence, we have no case." He waited, as though hoping Alfred could offer more.

With a shaking hand, Alfred nudged the email he'd

received this morning across the District Attorney's desk. "This is from an expert at Columbia University. She says these numbers give you the address of the video. They also prove the—what did you call it? Simulation?—was my daughter. She asked to remain anonymous."

The man thanked him and Alfred left. The next day, Musai Alland was arrested.

When strangers passed Salah Mahmud Al-Zahrawi, aka Gegham Keregosian, in the Courthouse, they saw an attractive well-dressed man with dark foreign looks who could be Italian or Middle Eastern, maybe Spanish. He always adopted the slightly bemused expression and humble visage of an immigrant eagerly exploring the ways of his new country. They knew nothing of his mission to avenge the deaths of all Muslims killed by the infidel in the fight for Allah.

Today would bring him one step closer to his goal.

As he traversed the wide Courthouse hall with its faded tile floor and barren smudged walls, he prayed:

"I desire nothing but reform, and with none but Allah is my direction to the right and successful path. On him do I rely and to him do I turn."

Despite performing daily sacred ablutions, Al-Zahrawi had not felt clean since arriving in the unholy city of Los Angeles. The scent of animals slaughtered in names other than Allah, the noxious aroma of cologne blaring carnal pursuits, and the stench of their sweat leeched into Al-Zahrawi's being until he feared it would destroy him.

SubhanAllah.

He shoehorned his slim form into a narrow spot along the back wall of Room 22. All around him, the profligate sinners whispered among themselves. They insulted Allah, the women side-by-side with their consorts as though equals and the men obedient to their lust. None in this unholy land understood duty. The desire to rid the world of these heathens grew like a desert flower under spring rain.

But they were not who Allah instructed he kill today.

"All rise…"

An hour later, the media reported, "*In a surprise verdict, Musai Alland was found innocent. Despite electronic footprints chased by Columbia grad student, Kalian Delamagente, that led to blood and DNA evidence, the jury agreed with the defense that the video simulated a human…*"

Al-Zahrawi approached Alfred Zematis, filled with excitement at the part the old janitor would play in bringing peace to this servant of Allah. Soon, the man would be reunited with his daughter and his God.

"Do not despair, my friend. I bring good news," and Al-Zahrawi led Alfred into the stairwell.

Alfred shook with anger. "He was supposed to be thrown in prison where you could kill him. Now what will we do?" Alfred's voice cracked as the heavy metal door slammed behind him.

"That is no longer your concern, Alfred. *JazakAllah.* May Allah reward you."

Alfred did not resist when Al-Zahrawi wrenched his neck until there was a satisfying snap and then tossed the carcass over the railing. It bounced once off the wall before thunking to the ground below. Pulling a piece of paper, a heavy hammer, and a four-inch spike from his pocket, Al-Zahrawi pounded a note into the dead man's sunken chest. The police would not identify its importance, but by the next dead civilian, and the next after that, they would remember.

He paused before leaving. The old man was at peace for the first time since they had met.

…they who are slain (in Allah's way) live, finding their sustenance in the Presence of their Lord. They rejoice in the Bounty provided by Allah.

Al-Zahrawi dove into the rush of pedestrians. The key to his jihad's success now had a name.

Kalian Delamagente.

Three days before present

Ten hours and thirty-seven more minutes and the crew of the USS *Hampton* SSN 767 would be home. Seasoned submariners, the six-month covert intelligence-surveillance-reconnaissance tour down the eastern seaboard of South America had gone flawlessly and silently. The Atlantic is a large ocean and the *Los Angeles*-class sub's noise footprint small. Once the boat cleared Cuba, the crew would relax.

The Captain sipped the morning's fourth cup of burned coffee when the hair on the back of his neck prickled. He glanced around, trying to identify what bothered him.

"Captain," the Watchstander's gaze bobbed from the Executive Officer to his watchstation. "Navigation is non-responsive." Confusion tinged his words.

That was it. A change in the deck's subtle rumble. Before the Captain could react to the impossibility that guidance controls had crashed, every monitor in the sub's nerve center shut down.

He hadn't seen this in twenty years of driving subs. All personnel made a hole as he rushed toward the Control Center, shadowed by the XO.

"Sonar readings?" The Captain called to Sonarman Second Class Andy Rikes in the compartment just aft of Control, barely larger than a broom closet but elbow-to-elbow with operators, fingers flying across keyboards and eyes locked onto screens that blinked a dull grey.

Rikes answered, "Negative, Sir. The hydrophones are working, but aren't sending raw data, like someone pulled the plug and flushed everything out to sea. Trying to fix it." His voice was hopeful.

If the screen had worked, Sonarman Rikes would have seen the ping, a final gasp before everything electrical collapsed.

The COB—Chief of Boat—interrupted, "Captain. Reactor Scram!" The sub's nuclear power had evaporated. "Nuclear technicians isolating the problem. Battery back-up is being attempted."

"Shift propulsion from main engines to EPM," an auxiliary electric motor that could turn the propeller.

"Negative, Captain. Non-responsive." Fear leaked from his voice.

The depth meter no longer worked, but the XO guessed that the sub was angled downward at 10 degrees

"Blow main ballast tanks!"

"No response, Captain."

"How deep is the ocean floor in this sector of the Atlantic?"

The Sonarman answered, "It varies between 1,000 and 16,000"

16,000 feet was well below the sub's crush depth.

"There are seamounts and ridges spread throughout. We could get lucky and land on one. Or not."

"Inform US Strategic Command of our situation."

"Sir, comms are down."

"Release the message buoy," though all that told the world was they were in trouble. It could quickly drift miles from their position.

The Captain continued, voice calm, face showing none of the worry that filled his thoughts, "I want all department heads and Chief Petty Officers in front of me in five minutes. I want the status on every system they own and operate. Wake up whoever you need to." He had a bad feeling about this.

"Gentlemen, solutions." The Captain looked first at XO, then COB and finally NAV, the Navigation Officer who turned to the senior chief of navigation.

"It's like an electromagnetic pulse hit us, which can't happen underwater..." then he shrugged as though to say, *I have no idea, Sir.*

They practiced drills for every sort of emergency, but not this one. No one considered a complete electrical shutdown possible.

"We're checking everything, but nothing is wrong. It just won't work."

"Where's CHENG?" The Chief of Engineering.

"Troubleshooting, Sir." COB's voice was efficient, but tense.

The Captain didn't wait. "Condition Alpha. Full quiet—voices whispers, all silent, no movement not critical. Defcon 2," the second-highest peacetime alert level.

No one knew who their enemy was or why they were under attack, but they had one and they were.

"XO, get lanterns up here."

Within an hour, the massive warship had settled to the ocean floor like the carcass of a dead whale. It teetered atop an ocean ridge, listing starboard against a jagged seamount, and the gentle push of an underwater current from a cliff that plunged into a murky darkness. Every watertight door was closed. As per protocol, the oxygen level was reduced to suppress a fire hazard. Without climate controls, the interior had already reached 60 degrees. It would continue dipping as it strove to match the bone-chilling surrounding water temperature. Hypothermia would soon be a problem. For now, though, they were alive.

The hull groaned as though twisted by a giant squid.

The Captain peered into the gloomy waters that surrounded the sub. "Thoughts, XO?"

"We're stable for the moment, barring a strong underwater current."

Based on the creaking protests from the hull, they were at or beyond crush depth. Any deeper, the outside pressure would snap the HY-80 outer hull and sea water would roar into the living compartments. Everyone would be dead in seconds, either drowned or impaled on the ragged remains of the sub by a force in excess of a Category Five hurricane.

"We're beyond the depth of the Steinke Hoods," escape equipment that included full body suits, thermal protection, and a life raft. Budget cuts had eliminated funding for more advanced solutions.

XO pointed toward a darker expanse of black just yards

from the sub. "No telling how deep that crevice is."

"Gather the crew in the Forward compartment. Seal all other compartments. Ration water. Start O2 candles when levels reach 50% normal. Did the message buoy launch?"

"Yes, sir."

That was a relief. The Deep Submergence Rescue Vehicle (DSRV) deployed in emergencies from shore couldn't assist if it didn't know they needed help.

Chapter 1

36 hours before present

The sturdy navy blue Land Rover caught his attention, old but well-maintained with clean windows and enough tread on the tires to be serviceable in this remote African village. The tall slender Kenyan driver talked with friends while awaiting a customer, bare feet layered with dust, clothing worn but washed, a charismatic smile stretched from ear to ear to inspire trust in visitors looking for a ride. His unlined face told the man with the briefcase he was young enough to test fate. The wide ragged scar covering his left cheek said he was not afraid to take chances.

Still, when the man with the briefcase told him where he wished to go, the Kenyan refused. *No one will go to there*, he insisted with a toothy grin, waving his arm to include the four other men offering their services in the dusty roadside lot, *because no one returns*. Of course he needed the money—*this generous amount will pay my bills for a month but who will support my family when I am dead?*

He shook his head, laughing, and turned away.

Until his phone rang.

Thirty seconds later, sweat dimpling his blue-black forehead and long slender fingers knotted into panicked fists, the Kenyan driver and the man with the briefcase departed.

The directions were simple: Proceed west-northwest keeping Mt. Kilimanjaro in his rear view mirror, Lake Natron to his right and Ol Doinyo Lengai to his left. When he passed the two-trunked baobab, he would be close.

Do that or never see his wife and five children again.

Dense dust choked the battered car as it labored across the burned scrubland. The blistering midday sun moved a hand at a time through the cloudless sky, sucking hidden moisture from the parched land. The driver said nothing. The only sounds were the gravelly soil bouncing up from below rattling around in the undercarriage and the Kenyan's occasional sigh.

The man with the briefcase coughed again. The windows would not close and dust coated his throat and lips, even his teeth. The water bottle lay abandoned at his feet, emptied an hour ago of the last drops. He stared out at the flat, dry, and limitless terrain. There were no landmarks or relief of any kind, save the bleached bones of animals who had succumbed to the savage habitat. Not even the Bedouin tribes, traveling south to Arusha or north toward the shores of Lake Victoria, would risk this passage. If the vehicle broke down, both men would die from exposure.

Still, the man with the briefcase felt no fear. He brought news to Salah Mahmud Al-Zahrawi, number three man to the infamous Osama bin Laden's successor.

Just as the passenger decided the driver was lost, a broken-down hovel appeared, fortified by two hulking grey-black figures pointing AK-47s at the dusty vehicle. The driver waved timidly to a rough, muscular thug who scowled and motioned them forward.

The car rolled to a stop a meter from the building. The passenger unfolded himself from the back seat, stretching his legs, seeing nothing but emptiness as far as the eye could see. He ran a hand down his wiry black beard and ducked through the muddy cloth flap that served as a door. The driver remained outside. He greeted the guards as Cousins, passed around his khat, then chewed slowly, eyes moving over the landscape, alert and frightened.

Inside, cross-legged on a pillow, sat a handsome man dressed in a pure white dishdasha. His eyes were clear and intelligent, skin smooth for one raised in the desert wind. Though a small man, his presence filled the room. A tray of fruit, a teapot, and one cup were arranged carefully at his left elbow. The visitor bowed and sat across from his host on a threadbare but handwoven carpet.

"You bring good news." Salah Mahmud al-Zahrawi's voice was cultured, with a quiet intensity. His smile carried neither welcome nor warmth. There was but one reason the man with the briefcase would arrive in person.

The guest dipped his head in obeisance. "I am pleased to see you, Salah," he offered with an air of suppressed energy. "The virus made contact."

"Which means what?"

"The ping activates as the last action before communications terminate. At this point, we can assume all electrical systems are down."

"Where is the submarine?" Al-Zahrawi asked, voice softer, tone somewhere between hope and disbelief.

"Midway between Cuba and Florida. In three days, the crew will suffocate from lack of oxygen. In four, the virus will restart the submarine's navigation and propulsion and it will sail to Cuba. An *Akula*-class Russian sub will pick it up forty miles offshore and guide it to port. "

"What if the Americans find it?"

"Yes, they might, but we do not think they will." He spread his hands palms up. "The Atlantic is vast. The submarine—it is as a grain of sand in the desert. We will find it only because it comes to us." He cocked his head. "Of course, the ocean there, it has depths in excess of 10,000 feet. If the submarine finds those, even we will not be able to retrieve it."

"But we know the virus works."

Al-Zahrawi felt excitement tingle through his shoulders and down his fingers. This success moved him that much closer to his final goal: Incapacitate the fourteen American Trident subs that roamed the world's oceans. The destructive force carried by just one exceeded five thousand Hiroshimas. He would sink them or sell them.

Al-Zahrawi blinked in his excitement. How much would America's enemies pay to rid themselves of these weapons? The money would fund the Holy *jihad* for decades to come.

Chapter 2

Present day, Friday

Fatigue smothered Bobby James like his last girlfriend's endless, meaningless chatter. His flight had been delayed at both ends, the onboard meal stale, and the taxi driver rude. He closed his apartment's solid core steel-reinforced three-hour fire-resistant door and did a one-eighty. The thin film of cornmeal just inside the threshold was undisturbed and the area rug remained forty-five degrees to the coffee table, two feet from the wall. Reassured, he dropped his bags and headed to the kitchen for some ice. He needed a drink.

His brain felt limp, like a plant that's been soaked in saltwater. Crypto-this and cyber-that—none of it made sense, but his FBI bosses assured him this was the future. Cyberspace had become the fourth domain of modern warfare—like land, sea and air—but without geopolitical boundaries. For three days, he gamely tried to understand how to find the enemy using what the instructor termed 'digital footprints'. These were virtual breadcrumbs that chronologued a persons' journey. Sometimes, they were easy to follow, especially via social media sites like Facebook, Twitter, and a site James had never heard of called Instagram. Other times, they were less public, but still obvious for those who knew how. With billions of people uploading data from cellphones, computers, and tablets, invisibility was an arcane concept. The instructor demonstrated simple searches of each student accessing only public domain information. One FBI veteran was caught kissing three women not his wife. Another photographed handing an envelope to a known gang leader. In fact, twenty-five of the twenty-six class members ended up stuttering through explanations of why 'it's not what it seems'.

"But you, Bobby James, are an enigma. You were a star fullback in high school, in national news forty-seven times by my count, but passed up a scholarship so you could serve your country. According to the local paper, this broke your mother's heart and inspired your girlfriend to dump you."

James smiled at the memory—the first time in his life he'd been in control.

The teacher tapped a few keys on his iPad and continued. "You spent three years as an MP, reported to be firm but fair. You retired after your second overseas tour and got a BA in criminal justice while working for the Los Angeles Police Department."

"OK, I get it—" It was time to short circuit this romp through his personal life, but the teacher barreled on.

"When cameras caught you rescuing a child from kidnappers, tears running down your face, a bloody knife in one hand and her stuffed bear in the other, Hollywood called. Their profile of you read 'chiseled body, a frisson of danger, and a photogenic presence make Robert 'Bobby' James the perfect hard-bitten but damaged detective.' This earned you," he paused, eyes widening, "a high five-figure side-income."

"Nothing says authentic like a camera phone at a crime scene. We done—" but there was no stopping the teacher.

"Until one horrific case where a right-wing militia group kicked a teenage girl to death for sharing food with a stray dog."

James' thoughts turned inward. She had bled out before he could save her, sheltering the shaking mongrel in her arms. A week later, James walked out on his Hollywood career and the LAPD, haunted by memories he couldn't control. Within a month, he had three job offers.

"Six months after joining the FBI, you got your own team." The teacher's eyes appraised James. "Your bosses and subordinates alike say you don't play politics and they would walk through fire with you."

James glared. "We done? Or is this an intervention?" James struggled to smother what had always been a hair-trigger temper.

The instructor held his hand up. "That's it. There's nothing else online."

Was that a compliment or an insult? James couldn't have been happier when New York called him home. Sitting there, everyone taking notes on tablets and laptops while he used his trusty pen and notebook, he felt old.

He loosened his tie and poured a Black Label neat. Just one. Tomorrow required a clear head and steady hand. An American sub had missed three call-ins.

He sipped his drink and logged into the secure FBI server. As he retrieved updates, he half-listened to his voicemail—one from his mother, two from a neighbor about a lost cat, and then a friendly voice from his past: *Bobby. Something you might be able to help with.*

Curt Sauvain. They had been partners at LAPD. James yawned. 9:27 in Los Angeles. Curiosity got the better of him.

"Bobby! Glad you're working late. Something good I hope?"

"According to Churchill." The British Prime Minister had famously proclaimed that success was going from failure to failure without loss of enthusiasm. "Congratulations by the way, on your promotion." Last year, Sauvain became LAPD's Chief of Detectives.

Sauvain chuckled. "Enough about me. You read about the Zematis case?"

"It was all over the news."

"What the press doesn't know is the murderer pounded a note into the old man's chest threatening more deaths if our Trident subs don't return to base."

"The fourteen SSBN submarines—"

"—the most powerful offensive weapon platforms on the

planet, armed with enough ballistic missiles to destroy our enemies ten times over. Yeah, those Tridents."

James' instincts pinged. Zematis' murder was about two weeks ago. Now the Navy had a missing sub. James had never met a coincidence he trusted.

He said nothing because Sauvain had no need-to-know. His ex-partner continued. "The Navy says docking the Tridents is non-negotiable regardless who might be killed, though they put Kings Bay and Bangor—the two primary home ports—on alert."

James fidgeted with his glass. "Have there been more deaths?"

"Not yet. I have one loose end I hope you can help with. D'you know a Columbia student named Kalian Delamagente?"

James had dated a few grad students, but not from Columbia. "No. Should I?" He tapped *'Zematis'* and *'Delamagente'* into the FBI's Criminal Justice Information Services Division Next Gen ID system. It could identify suspects by DNA, fingerprints, palm prints, or at least a dozen other methods and then used a subsystem called 'Rap Back' to cross-reference them to crime scenes and suspects. The only connection between these two names was the Zematis case.

Sauvain continued, "Delamagente provided police with the physical address where Angel's torture/murder occurred and proof the simulacrum was juxtaposed on her body, to make the suffering look fake and real at the same time. Double jeopardy prevents us from retrying Alland, but we could go after who bankrolled his defense."

A story popped up. "Delamagente will be at a DARPA— Defense Advanced Research Projects Agency—competition this weekend in New York City. I'll see what I can find out."

James hung up and clicked open his address book. He knew just the guy for the job.

Chapter 3

Saturday

Close to a decade working together and Zeke Rowe had never received three calls in thirty minutes from Bobby James. It was either a concerted effort to say hello or—more likely—he needed help, neither of which Rowe had time for.

Among other things, he had to do something with his front yard. Right now, it was all weeds and brown cracked dirt, but had great potential—according to the real estate agent who'd sold it to him. *Throw around grass seed, water it. Soil is perfect.* That was just one of a long and growing list of deferred maintenance mentioned in the latest official letter from his homeowner's group. Yesterday, he promised them he'd fix the sagging, weather-beaten, warped eyesore-pretending-to-be-steps before leaving the country for a three-week archaeologic dig. Today, he had to admit, he needed a Homeowner 101 course.

He'd been sanding for close to three hours, with ample breaks to drink beer, watch a spider spin a web, and review plans for his field study. As sawdust floated through his fingers, a sense of giving new life to damaged wood warming him, he thought back to that Joint Task Force where he and Bobby James met. A Pakistani cell based in France had been selling American weapons out of Los Angeles. He was with Naval Intelligence at the time, sure he knew more than the civilian police and angry with Bobby James for wasting his time. James was in charge because it was LAPD turf. Rowe had been warned to play nice while offering what he could to assist.

He got there early, eager to start, finish, and head home. James arrived late. One look at the man's chiseled face, bull neck, wide shoulders, and seven percent body fat on a 250 pound six-foot frame was all it took. Rowe knew the type, good looking man's man with a big personality that covered a paucity of skills. The fact he brought donuts did nothing to assuage Rowe's simmering anger, though he ate four.

Rowe spent the next eight hours arguing with everything James said, but the man refused to engage. At five p.m., James invited the team to dinner. Rowe tried to beg off, but James clapped him on the back and said it would be fun. He'd even drive.

By half way through the meal, Rowe had slipped into a sullen silence, ignoring the buzz of friendly chatter, waiting for the first opportunity to leave.

"Your turn to share, LT Rowe. Friends call you Zero. Is there a story there?" James found Rowe's eyes, head tilted slightly, a half-smile playing on his lips.

Rowe said nothing, but was impressed despite himself James had dug deep enough to come up with that closely-held nickname. When the silence became uncomfortable, James continued softly, "You're intelligent, knowledgeable on this subject, with a reputation for connecting the dots with scary accuracy. How do you see this playing out?"

Rowe waited a beat, but James remained motionless, face benign, eyes steady. Rowe decided to answer the question.

For ten hours, as the other task force members listened, yawned, and finally lumbered off to bed, the two men verbally sparred, blew holes in theories, discussed evidence, and researched options. They moved from the restaurant to the hotel lobby and to the conference room when night turned to dawn. By the time the team reconvened at 8am, Rowe and James had a plan. It took less than a month to arrest the ring leader.

When the courts released him on a technicality, James

quit in disgust.

Rowe had started sanding the last step when his sat phone rang again. He squinted at the blazing sun, still two hands above the horizon, took a gulp of beer, and answered.

"You want me to attend a grant competition? I'd rather go out with your ex-girlfriend, the one who dumped you for a woman."

Rowe wiped his palms on a tattered t-shirt. The slogan—*SEAL: Often mistaken for the wrath of God*—had faded, but he owned ten more like it. Some days, his favorite was *I don't need a weapon. I am one.* Other days, *If I weren't supposed to kill people, God wouldn't have made me so good at it.* It depended on his mood.

Instead of one of James' signature quips, he got empty air. "Bobby. I'm close to unraveling the mystery of man's African exodus. Don't come to me with a problem only I can solve. I don't have time."

"Can't a friend buy a friend lunch?"

Rowe checked his watch. He could take a break. Why not? They agreed to meet at a local Mexican cantina.

The sharp tang of peppers saturated the air as Rowe popped another tortilla chip into his mouth. James swatted a handkerchief over the booth before sitting. No surprise he was late.

"Zeke, buddy! Good to see you. You never call. Never write."

The years since they'd last seen each other had been good to James. He was fit and tan with the presence of a man used to being listened to.

"I ordered. Figured it would save time." Rowe lasered in on James' suit. "Is that red in your jacket the same as the shirt? Who does that?"

"Magenta." James corrected. "My personal shopper picked it. Not too much, right?"

Rowe had no idea, so kicked James' shoes. "What

happened to the Blahnik's?"

"You like these?" James flapped his foot. "*GQ* gives them better style marks."

The only magazine Rowe read regularly was the *American Journal of Archaeology*, and it didn't cover fashion. He fumbled for a rejoinder. "Do they get you where you're going?"

The adobe walls and overhead fans provided a welcome chill from the New York heat. The lunch crowd had left and dinner guests were still in the bar. Dishes clattered in the background, punctuated by Spanish. After the waitress delivered their food, James got down to business.

"I only need you for one day. You're the only guy I know with a Ph.D. in—what's it called?"

"Paleoanthropology. How I pay my bills."

When SEALs and the fast-moving drama of Navy Intel ended, Rowe reverted to a subject he loved: the study of man's roots. He became renowned for both his research-intensive field studies and his well-evidenced articles written in words the armchair scientist could understand. His prose were said to do for ancient man what Margaret Meade's did for anthropology. The zeitgeist of life was subtle, but satisfying. Rowe had no intention of returning to the snake pit.

"Where are you going this time?"

Rowe patted his pockets for a cigarette before remembering he'd given them up about the same time he quit doing stuff he didn't want to do.

"Israel, to research a theory about early man's exodus from Africa."

"Isn't that what you got your Ph.D. in?" When Rowe nodded, James added, "I thought our predecessors left via the Arabian Peninsula."

Rowe perked up. "That's the conventional theory. I think their exit was the Rift Valley. With this field study, I hope to put a fork in the argument."

Rowe's eyes flicked to a neighboring table, a family celebrating what looked like a birthday party. Both parents wore uniforms—the dad for a security company and mom a local pastry shop, faces tired but happy. The man's blue-black hair was sprinkled with gray, but his eyes sparkled. Despite the faded look of hand-me-downs, the children's clothes were spotless, the youngest in a frilly yellow dress and paper crown with crayon stars along the edges. When she caught Rowe staring, she broke into a beatific smile.

Rowe turned away. Happiness depended upon who traveled with you. This nameless man was living Rowe's dream.

"What's so important about this conference, Bobby?" His voice was gruffer than he intended.

"One of our subs missed three call-ins."

Rowe masked his surprise. That kicked in an automatic protocol that would either find the sub, end the Captain's career, or both.

"The last position was west of Florida, almost home. We're hoping to find it with comms and engines incapacitated, but that's a big patch of ocean to search."

James stalled, like he ran out of words, but Rowe knew he was deciding how much to say.

"Why involve you, Bobbie? The Navy has plenty of resources—" He stopped short. Unless they thought it was terrorism.

James caught Rowe's eye. "NCIS was tasked with background. They're worried more subs are in danger. I know a guy there and he knows my experience. He asked me to get involved."

Rowe's neck muscles tensed, but he kept his face a mask. "Again, why me? The FBI has its choice of prominent paleoanthropologists. I've been out of Intel for too long to be of any help, even if I wanted to be."

"NSA picked up chatter about a DARPA presentation. They don't know the connection and neither do I. That's where you come in. The presentation is by," James pulled a notebook from his breast pocket and thumbed through it, "Kalian Delamagente. Something about tying 'paleoanthropology' to submarines. You may be the only intel guy alive who can understand the connection, maybe find a thread to our missing sub and its crew. I'm only talking a day. Surveil. Take pictures. Enjoy yourself."

Rowe eyed James, not satisfied at all with his friend's explanation. "What aren't you telling me?"

James sipped his coffee, scanned the room, and checked his phone before answering. "Odd coincidence. I got a call from a buddy in Los Angeles. That murder trial that was all over the news—*Zematis vs. Alland*. Somehow it also connects to this Delamagente lady. She didn't do it, but maybe she can lead the LAPD to whoever did." He dipped his head and then eyed Rowe. "That old man didn't deserve to die, and his daughter didn't deserve what Alland did to her."

Rowe had seen the story. He remembered thinking no way was the torture in those images fake. "I can't spend more than a day, Bobby."

James grinned. "That's all I need. Just show me the slope. I'll bring the skis."

Chapter 4

Saturday night

Kalian Delamagente pawed past half-used tissues, spare change, and AA batteries. *I really need to clean out my purse,* she thought, choking down the reflex to vomit. She closed her eyes against the fluorescent lights and fumbled blindly.

"OhthankGod."

She teased the headache pill from a fold at the bottom of her bag, bit it in half and dry swallowed, then pressed her palms against her eyelids. Fifteen minutes and she'd be good.

She'd had headaches since high school. Aspirin did nothing except churn her stomach. Normally, she went home to sleep it off, but tonight that wasn't an option. She had only until Monday to convince a hunk of circuits with a god complex to help her.

Technically, Otto was an AI—artificial intelligence—programmed to collect data and draw conclusions based on an objective interpretation of facts, immune to the prejudice of human emotion and experience. Though intrinsically capable of speech, facial recognition, lip reading, interpreting emotions, and game-play, she lacked funds to activate those functions.

She built Otto for her early man research. He would collect billions of megabytes about the era's flora and fauna, paleoclimate, and paleogeography, evaluate them and present his conclusions as a video—a movie with ancient man the star and his life the plot. Half-way through her research, as her funding came up for reconsideration, her Ph.D. advisory committee reclassified Otto as 'paleoanthropology'—early man—where grants required an archaeology background. To get around this, she unveiled Otto's intriguing research skills at local schools where he was an instant hit. In seconds, he could provide answers to everything from 'Who's the leader of Luxemburg' to 'What noise does a tree make if it falls in an empty forest?' Because many schools lacked the robust infrastructure required to run Otto, she operated him off a network of slave computers called 'zombies', similar to what was used by the Search for Extra-Terrestrial Intelligence—SETI.

Despite these successes, funding continued to elude her. Monday's DARPA presentation could change that, thanks to Catherine Stockbury—Cat—Kali's best friend and office mate. Calling Cat smart was like calling Shakespeare a playwright. Besides a 188 IQ and a passion for reading, Cat had a caustic attitude and no patience for arguments lacking logic or evidence. Where those traits drove most people away, Kali liked the challenge and invariably came up with a new twist to the Gordian knot of her friend's thinking.

Months ago, Kali had been watching a video Otto created about man's primeval world when Cat blurted, "I smell red oats grass..."

Kali took a bite of the tuna sandwich she brought from home. "That's from Otto's sensory ports." She indicated a tiny window on the front of Otto's CPU. "He has access to millions of olfactive files to incorporate in whatever scene he displays, to provide more authenticity. Red oats were common in East Africa during this time."

"Proustian memory. Clever, but this comes and goes, like on a breeze."

"Otto stitched the paleobiology of the area into a 360-degree four-dimensional panorama—"

"You include time."

A tingle washed over Kali, her sandwich frozen in midair. "Yes, of course. This," she poked an elbow toward her screen, "is as close as anyone will get to Plio-Pleistocene Africa without a time machine. Let's take the pothole the female hominid stepped in. The equatorial heat spiderwebs the savanna with crevices, but I might forget to add it. Otto wouldn't."

Cat tossed a file to Kali.

"*Funding for Strategies in Support of Trident Submarines*. Fascinating." Where was this going?

"Go online and apply."

"But Otto is an educational tool."

"You described an *intelligence* tool, Kal. Every day, US agents try to detect threats to our country based on millions of intercepts. The sheer volume overwhelms the effort. Connecting those dots—as Otto does—is what they seek."

"I know nothing about submarines."

"Ask Otto for the connections. We'll go together."

Riverside Church's seventy-four bells chimed ten pm. If she leaned just right, she could peer out the tiny slit that was her view of the outside and find the cross atop the twenty-four story Gothic structure.

Tonight, she barely had time to use the bathroom. Thirty-four hours to show time. Two thousand forty minutes. Thrice as much time wouldn't be enough. No matter how she refined Otto's programming, he still wouldn't listen. He treated deadlines and rules as suggestions. Qualitative attributes like 'team player' meant nothing to him. An hour ago, she had given up and told Otto to do what he thought best as long as it met her—*their*, he pedantically corrected in a typed message that appeared on her screen—goals. If he failed, they'd both be deactivated.

It got worse. Her son Sean wanted to attend college next year. Kali struggled to keep him in peanut butter sandwiches and clothes much less class credits and textbooks. She needed this funding.

"I'll make it work, Sean." For years, her promise was meaningless. Now, it was their bond.

Her stomach growled, which happened when she missed lunch and dinner. As Otto rendered the next scene, she grabbed a handful of change and an empty plastic cup, and headed for the vending machines. Her senses pricked at the crack of a door slamming. When her name had been revealed during the trial of Angel Zematis' murderer, a man named Salah Al-Zahrawi had offered to fund her research if she would use Otto to find something he had lost. She refused, explaining Otto was an academic tool, not a gun for hire. Al-Zahrawi didn't like her answer.

She shivered. Why did she remember him now?

The rattle of her coins dropping into the machine and the clatter of the chips tumbling to the tray reverberated around her. She filled her cup from the fountain and started back, shoes clacking on the tile floor. As she turned onto her hall, footsteps echoed at a distance, stopping and starting as though the owner was unsure where to go. She ducked inside her office as a figure rounded the corner. She stood for a long minute, stomach in knots, back to the wall, hands gripping her water and chips. When the steps faded, she nudged the door closed. Why would anyone be on this wing? It was all grad student offices.

The building once again drifted into silence. She chided herself for worrying, opened the chips, but set them aside. She'd lost her appetite.

A few jabs at her keyboard and a Pleistocene landscape appeared, complete with the primordial primate who had become a familiar figure in Otto's movies. The AI was programmed to provide the big picture, not focus on an individual, but he always returned to this female. Was he trying to communicate something?

She had grown fond of the creature. She was curious and friendly with sophisticated communication—albeit non-verbal—Kali wouldn't have dreamt existed when mankind was young. In this scenario, the female trotted across the African savanna, a grace to her movements thanks to the long slender legs topped with the round firmness of mankind's first *gluteus maximus*. Her thorax was already raised to draw the deep breaths required for extended jogging. Kali jogged five miles a day, but this female did four times that. Even with her truncated forehead, prognathic snout, and negligible chin, she would be invisible on most New York sidewalks.

"Who are you?"

Her shoulder length hair hung like exploded cattails, the color of dusty obsidian. A bulge broke the flat plane of her lightly-furred stomach. Dried dung covered her face and shoulders. Slender digits of well-formed hands snatched vegetation as she ran. Every movement bristled with equal amounts of caution and confidence. Her head swiveled side-to-side.

Until she stared straight into the face of her twenty-first-century observer. Coffee-brown eyes, the same variegated shade as Kali's, sparkled with intelligence.

And something else. A desiccated trail of tears etched the female's face like an African wadi, but Kali saw no cuts or bruises. Did early humans feel emotional pain?

A paleo-horse nickered off screen. The female jerked toward it. Was she frightened? Kali dredged up the jingle she learned in second grade. *Eyes in front, they hunt. Eyes to the side, they hide.* Primitive horses—Hipparion—were vegetarians.

A voice barked 'Lhoo-sih' as the movie ended.

"Lucy." She had a name.

Kali pushed F7 to refresh the video and wondered how Otto picked his geo-temporal locations. Sometimes a young Lucy brachiated through the jungle canopy, arm over arm; other times she crossed the dry savanna with a baby in tow. If Otto had a plan, he wasn't sharing it.

Kali massaged her temples and pondered whether Lucy got headaches. She tugged at her tiny diamond earrings, all that remained of her mother, and her eyes settled on a framed photo of Sean in the science lab at his school—goggles on, eyes intense, the bare trace of a smile tugging at the corners of his mouth, surrounded by applauding teens.

She couldn't afford to fail.

Otto burped. Another video was ready.

Chapter 5

The phone dragged Kali back to the twenty-first century. "Hello?" She heard soft breathing and then a dial tone.

"Jerk." Only faculty and students had access to this number. She tried to forget the call, but fear nibbled at the edges of her concentration. She appraised her defensive options. She could throw books to distract an intruder while she escaped, or record everything through Otto so the police would know how she died. No chance Cat would arrive to frighten off an attacker. She was already in a posh DC hotel, resting up for her presentation.

Kali forced herself back to work, stomach churning over the mountains of analysis that still remained. Numbers careened across the screen as Otto culled through thousands of encyclopedias, online libraries, databases, historic records, weather charts, maps, primary documents, searching for his next scenario. When he finished, he would create a movie using an open source program called VripPack to infill the pixels.

"Excuse me."

Kali jerked and stabbed a shortkey to hide her screen. A tall, muscular man filled her door. Bushy blonde hair surrounded a tan face. A smile hovered over full lips. He jangled a key at his side.

Kali tugged her earring. "Did you just call?"

His face scrunched in confusion and Kali began again, "Can I help you?"

"I'm looking for Faith Saunders. She's a history

professor. I'm taking her to dinner."

He wore stylish black-rimmed glasses, a pressed Polo and khakis, and carried a bouquet of roses. The scent of Old Spice distracted Kali as he fingered a wayward thatch of hair from his eyes. The expensive gold chain around his neck and diamond-encircled Krugerrand ring said he wasn't a struggling academe. She frowned at the pale band on his left ring finger.

"You want 1180 Amsterdam." Kali pointed left.

"Oh! Silly me. I could get lost in a… one way… street," he sputtered with what he no doubt considered a friendly grin but came out more of a smirk. Clearly, charisma wasn't part of his make-a-friend toolkit. "Name's Fred." Kali took his hand. It was soft and damp. "I'm proposing tonight." His eyes glowed with childish enthusiasm like he wanted her approval. She wanted him gone. She offered a tight smile, which seemed enough to keep him talking. "Is Tom's romantic?"

Asking Kali for dating advice was like expecting fashion tips from Phyllis Diller, but Tom's was a perennial favorite. "If it's crowded, try Café Lalo. They're popular for celebrations."

He bobbed his head as he took in the clutter. Despite his boyish innocence, something about him was off. "Were you here a half-hour ago?"

His eyes widened. "No. I just got here," and with the flash of toothy whiteness, he left.

Kali watched him pull a phone out as he disappeared out the door. Why lie about when he got here? And why didn't he call for directions earlier? Nothing about Fred made sense. Still, an intimate dinner, the heady aroma of fresh flowers, and the question that changes lives. Kali had never given any male the gift of her time. Fletcher, her son's father, had been a moment of weakness. The more he wooed her with his enthusiasm, attentiveness, and kindness, the harder she pushed him away until he gave up on her—but not on their son.

When Sean left for college next year, she'd have only Sandy and her research. She should accept one of the awkward invitations regularly stuttered out by fellow grad students, but they frightened her. Kali could tick off every early man artifact and where it was found, but she couldn't answer questions like, 'How was your day' over a dinner table.

Hector's eyes narrowed as the *guerro* exited the building, tossed a bouquet of flowers into the trash with one hand and held his cellphone to his ear with the other. A middle-aged man with more bling than common sense spelled trouble. Whatever he heard on the other end brought a scowl to his synthetically-tanned face. He didn't even try to keep his voice down.

"She looked frazzled." The man folded an arm over his chest and pawed the ground with a shoe. "Of course she never suspected. I'm good at this undercover stuff. Leave the money where you always do," and he shoved the phone into his pocket.

Hector waited until the man melted into the nighttime shadows, and then re-checked the doors to Schermerhorn and the Computer Science building. One light remained, the same one every evening for the past two weeks, He made a note in his log and continued his rounds. The lady professor sure did put in long hours. He'd come back and check on her later.

Kali gasped. Next to Lucy was a hominid who shouldn't exist in this era. Thick hair-fur shrouded a broad face with jutting brow ridges. A protruding muzzle projected almost as far as a chimpanzee's. Simian arms dangled halfway down the bandy legs. Dull fuzz covered her body as she stood frozen at the edge of a primeval forest. The almost-human eyes were wide and her breath came in shallow pants. Pre-humans survived by avoiding danger, but this creature exhibited enviable courage as she slapped herself on the chest and mouthed 'Boah'.

"Boah? Is that your name?"

A bear-sized bandog padded onscreen. Lucy barked what sounded like 'Ump' and the proto-dog plopped to the ground, massive head nestled between filthy paws, without taking his liquid brown eyes off Boah. He resembled a feral version of Kali's Labrador Sandy, but bigger, uglier, stronger, and dirtier. A heavy red tongue hung out and the cheerful up-down bob of his tail sent dirt billowing into the air.

"I can see why Lucy calls you 'Ump'."

Ump's dewdrop-shaped ears perked as Boah moved forward. With her squatty torso exposed, Kali saw 'she' was a 'he'.

The scene stunned Kali. No scientist would put Boah, Lucy, and Ump in the same geo-temporal location, yet Otto, with his logical connections based on available facts, did. This was what she needed.

An hour later, she packed up Otto with a satisfied grunt, locked her office and left. She'd finish tomorrow, in plenty of time for Monday.

It was well past midnight, but inside the campus borders, the bustle of industry and the sizzle of hope buzzed on. Students giggled and flirted on the steps of Lowe Library. A pizza delivery person swerved around her as *Passacaglia in C Minor* erupted from the 5,000 pipes of the chapel organ. The chiseled buildings were soft grey contours limned against the horizon.

"Hello, Ms. Delamagente."

Her adrenaline spiked and then she recognized the voice. "Hector. I didn't see you in the shadows. Hello."

"Everything OK with the *guerro*?" He said 'guerro' like he found half a worm in an apple.

She nodded. "Though he lied to me. Odd." She offered a wan smile. "Thanks for checking."

Hector grunted and melted soundlessly into the darkness.

Kali pulled her jacket tighter around her body and hugged her briefcase closer as she hurried off, glancing over her shoulder every few seconds. Hector had been at Columbia longer than Kali. He never worried about security, but Fred caught his attention. *Come on—you're over-reacting,* she chided herself. Angel's murder, Al-Zahrawi's call, and now Fred's unexplainable visit shook what used to be a resolute faith in the fairness and goodness of the universe.

She reached her apartment building in record time. It was squashed between two high rises and backed up against a cluttered alley. She entered the lobby, a generous word for the unmanned foyer no larger than a good-sized broom closet. The linoleum floor was scarred and beige walls chipped, but Kali knew she was lucky to have it. Columbia subsidized it while she pursued her Ph.D. As she fumbled with the lock, a sharp yip greeted her. She didn't want Sandy to smell her fear, so she took deep breaths to calm herself before opening the door.

"Shh! You'll wake Mr. Winters!" She said without anger as she rubbed the front of Sandy's neck. Kali preferred dogs to people. They were honest and straightforward, without ulterior motives or hidden agendas. They always gave you a second chance, and a third, which wasn't Kali's experience with people.

Sandy was best friends with Kali's next-door neighbor, Mr. Winters. His perfect white teeth and abundant gray hair made him look fifty rather than seventy despite what he called a 'botched autopsy' scar from last year's quadruple bypass. She met him the day she tried to sneak Sandy into the no-dogs-allowed building. Instead of righteous anger, he winked.

"Dogs taught me a lot, like how to leave room in my schedule for a nap."

Since then, Sandy had become his daily visitor; the only one as far as Kali knew. If she worked late, he took Sandy on his evening walk. Tonight, the leash was rolled into a careful circle, Mr. Winters' sign they'd exercised. "What would we do without Mr. Winters, pup?"

She tossed her briefcase onto the counter and poured a glass of lemonade. Something troubled her about Fred's visit, but she couldn't quite pull it from memory. As she stuffed her keys into the drawer next to a credit card she used for emergencies, she got it. He shouldn't have a key to her building. She concentrated on the mental image of his key ring, jangling in his fingers. It was the right shape, but she couldn't bring up the number. She chewed on it for a while and then gave up, collapsing into a scruffy second-hand couch in an uninspired plaid that had long ago lost its support. Someday, she'd buy a newer used sofa, but today, it's what she had.

Sandy laid his head across her lap and she inhaled the fragrance of home, forgetting about keys and Otto and Monday's presentation. In minutes, her lids drooped and the sweet waves of oblivion began to wash across her consciousness.

She jerked herself up and announced, "Bedtime, Sandy."

The dog sprinted to her tiny bedroom, jumped on the bed, took a couple of turns and settled, nose dangling over the side as Kali washed her face, brushed her teeth, checked the doors, and dropped into bed. As she reached for the light, she paused as she always did at a tuxedoed picture of Sean performing Dragonetti's *Concerto for Double Bass*. His neck was arched, eyes slits, wrist taut as the bow flew over the strings, his passion evident even in the stillness of the image.

"If I lose Monday, I'll find another way to send you to college, my son."

Chapter 6

Monday

If he had met Kalian Delamagente under different circumstances, they might be friends. Like her, Salah Al-Zahrawi, his parents, and siblings were learned people forced by events to follow unusual paths. His father was a college professor and his mother well-educated with a bibliophile's joy of words she passed on to her three sons. When Al-Zahrawi was young, his family moved to Canada as directed by their imam. There, Al-Zahrawi led a happy childhood filled with friends, brotherly fights, and fantasies about a girl in class who smiled at him.

Everything changed when the American Federal Bureau of Investigation placed his father on the Suspected Terrorists List. The family fled to Afghanistan where his parents were murdered by American mortars and the life of Salah Al-Zahrawi took a dramatic turn.

The Qur'an ordered those who killed Muslims must themselves be killed. Salah Al-Zahrawi's elder brother died attempting to carry out this duty in a failed attack on an American outpost. Omar, the next in line, tried to clear the family obligation by tossing a grenade into a vehicle loaded with U.S. servicemen. A quick-thinking Marine tossed it back and Omar's battle ended.

It was left to young Salah Mahmud Al-Zahrawi to revenge his parents and brothers.

One August morning in 1999, an eighteen wheeler

crashed through the rear security of an American embassy. When the driver breached the wall, he blew himself up with forty pounds of C4 taped to his chest. With the truck's full tank of diesel fuel and trailer of explosives, the complex was heavily damaged and dozens killed. It fulfilled Salah Al-Zahrawi's responsibility, but he did not stop. Hate for the Great Satan had become a way of life for the angry boy who used to love school and dream about his first date. Now, his purpose was Allah's. Like a whale snagged in a fishing net never stops fighting, even as it is dragged under and can no longer breathe, the only event capable of stopping Salah Al-Zahrawi's fight would be his death.

Alhamdulillah.

The guard checked Salah Al-Zahrawi's credentials, ticked off his name from the list of attendees, and briskly waved him through. He found a seat with good visibility and turned on his camera. *Insha'Allah,* Kalian Delamagente and her Otto would be the final piece of his jihad.

Chapter 7

The DARPA presentation room looked more like a school cafeteria than where America's premiere minds would unveil the future. It had indoor-outdoor carpet, faded curtains on the lone window, and was decorated with the vanilla colors designers called calming—and annoyed Zeke Rowe. A dais stood in front for the presenters bordered by an eight-foot judges' table. Folding chairs for public seating filled the balance of the space. A robust air conditioner kept the temperature close to freezing.

Rowe had dressed in his professor uniform—casual slacks, deck shoes, a navy polo shirt and an old faux-leather attaché. With calculated disinterest, he swept the crowd for Kalian Delamagente. There was no way he could miss her fresh-faced beauty amidst the putty colored, too-skinny/too-fat scholars who populated the room.

A harried last-minute competitor almost knocked him down in her haste to enter the crowded room.

Kali Delamagente bumped open the door with her hip while juggling a briefcase, two portfolios and Otto's accoutrements. She almost missed her plane and then couldn't find a taxi from the airport. Somewhere along the way, she splashed coffee on her baby blue suit. She hoped no one would notice.

"You spilled coffee on your skirt."

"And you have bad manners," she retorted, tugging at her jacket as she glared into the first friendly face she'd seen since

Sandy's this morning. The sturdy compact man had the disarming looks of a jock lost at a Princess House party, nothing like any scientist she knew.

"I was warned mail-order Emily Post classes wouldn't work." His voice was deep, like rich mahogany. He cocked his head, studying her with russet-colored eyes behind dark-rimmed glasses. She fumbled to smooth her imploded French braid.

"I hope your name doesn't start with 'Judge'."

"Zeke Rowe. Call me Zeke." He stuck his hand out. "I like confident women. Who says you need all that stuff?" He waved a hand over the array of laptops, hard drives, cables, and minions of undergrads assisting other competitors.

"Mine're still at the airport," Kali lied, but felt a prickle of trust for this stranger with his crooked smile and missing fingers. "Does everyone feel this way around you, Mr. Zeke Rowe?"

A loud murmur prevented him from answering as the next presenter approached the stage.

Chapter 8

Kali gave Cat a thumbs up as she stuffed herself and her baggage into an empty seat at the back of the room. No last minute flights or coffee stains for Cat. A tailored navy blue suit trimmed in white piping snugged her body, her flaxen hair knotted into a braid and secured with a pearl clip. She stood on the dais, just Cat and an oversized screen. The lights dimmed and animated waves appeared on the monitor as she began to speak.

"An important part of America's national security is a policy called Mutually-assured Destruction—you attack us, we destroy you with submarine-launched nuclear missiles. Other than that, the sole mission of these submarines, as declared by the Joint Chiefs of Staff, is strategic deterrence. They can remain submerged for up to six months because they make their own air and water. Their reactors can run for decades without refueling. 24/7/365, loaded with half our national stockpile of warheads, they troll the oceans. Each nuke can split in flight and hit over a hundred targets— thousands of people—with more destructive power than the sum of WWII's Little Boy and Fat Man.

"Without firing a shot, they have convinced our enemies an assault on America will be Armageddon.

"That changes today." Stockbury held up a glass tub holding a blob of dark viscous goo. "Meet NEV, the computer virus that cyberexperts can't stop. Unlike traditional data-based malware, this one is built with DNA." She waggled a finger. "This DNA. I have millions of weaponizable cells on my fingertip."

"Excuse me, Ms. Stockbury." The judge's lips were pursed, voice stiff and surly. "This is a field I have some expertise in. A Trident computer network is shielded by a high-tech firewall."

Stockbury locked onto her.

"Designed to shield it from the most advanced viruses, yes yes, but it has a fatal flaw: It searches for a script with zeros and ones, not the six organic bases in DNA. This allows NEV to sneak undetected past the gatekeepers and into the living heart of the network."

"But," the judge sniffed, "it would still identify NEV as foreign to the system. It won't let anything through that doesn't belong."

This time, Stockbury sighed loudly. "Then you know the Sysadmin accomplishes this by looking for irregularities—the dent made on active system processes that are other than those commanded. NEV doesn't leave one because it's organic."

She turned away and was again interrupted.

"Excuse me, Ms. Stockbury." This time it was Dr. Fairgrove. "How does it get in?" His well-established reputation made every word he uttered seem charged with import and authority.

Cat wiped her index finger through a tiny tub. "I smear this goo on either the Ethernet cable or the computer's WiFi antenna. It is stuffed with nanorobots so small they slip through the atoms of the cable and then probe for an open port. When the computer calls out, NEV enters with the legitimate traffic—a wolf in sheep's wool." A sub materialized, gliding mutely through the black waters. An hour glass tumbled twice, replaced by a green circle. "Once inside, NEV awaits the trigger to unleash its programmed instructions." Without warning, the sub rumbled to a halt, dead in the water.

A muted rumble of questions engulfed the room. The lady judge next to Dr. Fairgrove shouted over the noise, "Ms. Stockbury. How can DNA—an organic compound—talk to a silicon-based computer?"

Her tone was smug.

"Think about the pacemaker installed in a human body to help the heart, or deep brain stimulators and cochlear implants—mechanical devices that function symbiotically with living body parts. They are expected to communicate effortlessly and effectively with your body though one is DNA-based and the other isn't. NEV operates on the same principle."

Stockbury waved off the rest of the waving hands, her face now rigid, stance wide, eyes piercing. "I neutralized this $2.4 billion key to national defense for the price of a stamp—using one of the most freely-available molecules on earth. The only tricky part is believing it will work. Once the bad guys make that intellectual leap, America is at grave risk. Public Enemy #1 isn't the suicide bomber or the warrior with an AK-47. It is this virus."

With that, Catherine packed up her computer and left the platform

A cold shiver ran down Rowe's spine. Is this what happened to James' missing sub? He scanned the room. Two individuals sat frozen in their seats, faces flushed. One was a youthful man, Spanish or Italian, probably a student, eyes wide, knuckles white where they gripped the chair back. Another was a journalist Rowe vaguely recognized, a glisten of perspiration on his brow, shoulders so tight Rowe thought they would crush his ears.

Rowe ran the reporter's photo through a visual recognition program and Carston Devore's name popped up, a reporter with the *New York Times* Science section. Worth a chat when the presentations ended. The other, he emailed to James. He slipped into the hall, phone to his ear.

"Bobby. Look at Catherine Stockbury. Her invention may explain what happened to your missing sub," and he gave a quick rundown on NEV.

James listened in stunned silence. "*Is* it possible?"

Rowe's intel training included chemistry, biology, and a myriad of other scientific disciplines. He understood Stockbury's logic, but it sounded too simple to be true. "All cell walls are permeable to varying degrees. Wires and cables are just a different sort of cell wall, penetration dictated solely by the particle attempting to breach the barrier. The right make-up would allow the nanobots in the goo to do exactly what Stockbury postulates."

"We may need her. Tell me if I trust her," and James disconnected.

A ping announced the arrival of James' file on Stockbury. She earned straight A's in high school despite a penchant for living on the edge. Daddy's deep well of money bought off several youthful indiscretions. After graduating summa cum laude from Brown University, she toured Europe with one of her professors, but dumped him in Italy when Columbia's grad program called.

When he looked up, Stockbury's penetrating gaze was fixed on him.

Chapter 9

"Cute, in a bad boy macho way." Cat lasered in on Zeke Rowe. He stood along the back wall, feet spread, hands in his pockets, gaze fixed on her but made no effort to get through the mob jostling for her attention.

"Excuse me. Ms. Stockbury." A hand tugged her sleeve. "My name is Carston Devore, with the *New York Times*—"

Cat shook off the grasp. "I'm not talking to journalists." Her tone could freeze hydrogen. She turned back to Kali.

"But keep your attention on that silver-haired judge."

Where other men his age thickened around the chest and upper arms, he retained the athletic build of a field researcher, but wrapped in an Armani suit. Bangs spilled artfully over furrowed brows almost hiding his crystal blue eyes. Whatever he was saying to the pinched-face grey-haired woman next to him pulled her mouth into a chuckle, muscles Kali was pretty sure she rarely used.

"Who is he?"

"Dr. Fairgrove. Talk about bad boy. He oozes mystery like a bachelor's bedroom."

"*Wynton* Fairgrove?" Every article Kali had read about Dr. Wynton Fairgrove described an earnest intellectual who accepted with grace the ups and downs of a research career.

As though he heard Kali, he caught her eye. She flushed and fumbled with Otto's drives, displays, speakers and scent ports. She felt like an insect under a microscope—until he winked.

Delamagente stood on the platform, hands folded in front of her body, one leg straight and the other bent. She made eye contact with no one and the only people displaying undue interest were the same two entranced by Stockbury's presentation.

Rowe skimmed his notes on her. Pregnant at fourteen, Delamagente's parents raised the baby while their daughter continued her education. Her Mom taught music on a secondhand piano while Dad did odd jobs. They got by—no arrests, no credit card bills, income tax filed on time. By all accounts, the family seemed happy. When her parents died unexpectedly, her grandparents stepped in to raise mother and toddler. Delamagente graduated high school with honors and Columbia three years later with a double major in Evolutionary Biology and Computer Science. When her grandparents died too, she disappeared, foregoing a prestigious research stipend and a privileged academic future. It wasn't until Sean entered ninth grade that she reappeared as a grad student at her alma mater.

One oddity: The grandparents filed several police reports about an unknown male stalking their granddaughter. The officers assumed it was Sean's father and made little effort to find the man.

Kali was worried. Cat had left in the company of two men wearing dark suits and bored faces. Her best friend wouldn't miss this presentation for any reason other than an emergency.

"You may begin."

Kali smoothed her skirt nervously after one final glance at the door, and started.

"Intelligence services—HUMINT, ELINT, and SIGINT—collect information in the hope they can safeguard our nation. The problem is, there's too much. Mountains of it every day. Individuals generate over 5.6 zettabytes—that's five hundred sixty *trillion* terabytes—of emails, websites, documents, blogs, photos, and movies every day. How does an analyst sort, understand, and ultimately extract clues from that haystack?"

A picture materialized of a serene meadow. "Meet Otto." An earthy scent wafted across the room. Unseen insects buzzed and a bird's mournful call swelled and waned.

"His job is to collect, analyze, and share information. Lots of it. He excels at pinpointing abnormalities the human eye would miss."

A stream of black and white text replaced the meadow, single-spaced in a Times New Roman font, size twelve, rolled endlessly down the screen.

"What's anomalous in this text report? To determine that, traffic analysts would eliminate disinformation, highlight repeated words, phrases, patterns, and compare findings to other intelligence agencies. They would use the subjective process of 'experience' to decide if, say, a downturn in communication indicates a delay in plans, a lack of them, or a finalization."

Kali dipped her head thoughtfully, giving credit to proven protocol. "Otto's approach is different. He begins each event as John Locke's *tabula rasa,* a blank slate unaffected by experiences or emotions or a hoped-for goal. Upon command, he executes a common AI function called 'grokking': He sends web crawlers, bots and spiders to collect information— everything, not just what a human agent considers important— sorts and examines, then delivers his report as a movie including the visual, tactile, olfactive, and acoustic elements that informed his deductions.

"Let's say I want to write a biography about Dr. Fairgrove." She approached the surprised judge with slow, measured steps. "I might read articles and interview his colleagues to find out about his research and incendiary rise to fame. I could collect intimate details from a friend he's dating like restaurants he frequents and movies he's seen."

Dr. Fairgrove leaned back in his chair with an engaging smile. By now, Kali stood in front of him as though this conversation included just them.

"Does this mean I know you? Am I coloring my

conclusions by my respect for what you've accomplished in a treacherous field?" There were a few nods among the judges and audience and she stepped back a pace.

"Otto never does that. He takes everything at face value and in the process, may uncover a hidden secret you shared with no one. A digital detective like Otto reads the electronic footprints marking your passage around our world. He'll find every receipt ever entered into a database, every image taken by surveillance cameras or doting fans and uploaded to YouTube or Facebook. He'll grab every internet-based email with your name in it, even if they're deleted. Then, he'll make reasoned, logical deductions from these facts."

To Kali's surprise, Dr. Fairgrove went rigid, his smile tight and his face pallid. She turned away, back to the other judges.

She punched a few keys and the text became a village street with crude shacks spaced along the rough edges. To the casual observer, they were alike, but Otto zoomed in on one.

"A well-trained intel agent would mention the two windows in the front of this house, but not that one was an inch higher. Since he failed to relay this fact, analysts on the other end missed the local militia group's headquarters."

She shook her head. "This is not the agent's fault. Human beings are hard-wired to reject inconsequential details—which they may or may not be—and concentrate on what experience and agenda underscores. Otto, though, doesn't."

"Let's consider a second example. If you walk through a pitch dark room, sealed to preclude the slightest wisp of light, Otto can still record your passage as though brightly lit. His acoustic skills exceed a dog's and his vision beats any night owl out there. He collects data from the contents of the room—their mass, the scent of the materials they were made of…"

Kali swiped a finger across the judges' wood desk and snuffled in the fragrance of oil.

"…their ability to absorb and desorb heat. He gathers odors—smoke, perfume, food you ate—expelled through your pores. He creates a probable phenotypic representation from the DNA of skin cells or hair shed. He determines your height and mass by the air displacement as you walked through the room and your slight gravitational pull against other matter in the enclosure."

Kali took several steps. "He would decipher the impressions of your feet as they hit the ground, your body as it brushed objects, your hand on the doorknob. In the end, he would have a complete delineation of you and your journey."

Her fingers flew over the keyboard as she prepared her coup de grace. "My final video shows a revolutionary conclusion Otto reached based on readily-available data. His analysis will upend the scientific world. If you fund my research, Otto can do the same for American intelligence services."

Gray snow popped and flickered like tiny fireflies, covering the screen. "Otto is honing in on space-time coordinates I provided."

The graininess cleared to show golden grass bordering an archipelago of volcanoes. Kali gritted her teeth, trying to tamp down the panic that threatened to swamp her confidence. This wouldn't be Boah and Ump and their miraculous story. Otto had dropped her somewhere else.

"I'm... glad... this happened," she stuttered as she fidgeted with Otto's commands, "because it highlights the differences—the difference between my project without funds—sufficient funds—" she flashed a banal depiction of three migrating hominids onto the screen, "—and this."

Surely the judges heard the bass drum that boomed in her chest as she paraded a color print of Boah and Ump and Lucy in front of them. They squinted and started writing on their tablets. It took one question to defeat her: How did she authenticate the picture?

Chapter 10

Monday, late afternoon

Rowe sat on his still-unfinished steps and absorbed the last of the day's warmth. A lawnmower purred and the rich scent of loam filtered through his subconscious as his brain browsed the details of Stockbury's virus. Instinct told him there was more here than a simple prototype. Somehow, this research had gotten Alfred Zematis killed.

His satphone jangled. He gulped the last of his coffee and answered. "Hey, Bobby. I'm leaving in a few days and wanted—"

James interrupted. "We found the sub."

Rowe exhaled. The tightness in his shoulders loosened a turn. "How?"

"Someone banging Morse Code on the hull. One of our Cruiser's on the way to Haiti picked it up. We were just in time. They were down to their last O2 candle.

A couple of hours. "Do you know what happened?"

"The Captain says there were no malfunctions, no warnings. One moment, everything was fine, and then the power vanished and the sub sank."

"That's why you pulled Stockbury out of the meeting."

"Pretty suspicious her virus can disable a sub. We thought it might be a stunt, to get our attention. When we confronted her, she became hysterical, said she warned us a year ago but no one listened. She told them she could fix the problem if it was a DNA virus, just take her where she could contact the sub."

"I hope you took her up on it."

James snorted. "Either that or tow a 10,000-ton 550-foot block of iron to port. If that's even possible. We gave her a lab, a computer, and babysitters to keep her legit. In ten minutes, she built a program to quarantine the virus—if it exists. Our scientists tested it successfully on a mock-up. A SEAL team delivered it via a Rescue Bell. The sub should be underway in a few hours."

Before Rowe could get beyond a surprised grunt, James added. "There's more.

"Once the patch was installed, Stockbury could study the installation remotely, to make sure there would be no surprises. She said the code is primitive. It was programmed to restart select systems and send the sub to pre-ordained coordinates."

Rowe locked down the fear building in his chest. "Like Cuba."

James grunted, "But it wouldn't have worked. One piece of luck. If our Cruiser hadn't been there or the sub sank into an ocean trench, we never would have found it."

Rowe's stomach heaved. He swallowed. "Does whoever did this know they succeeded?"

"Stockbury says the virus sent a ping just before everything shut down."

Rowe jumped up off the steps and started pacing, head down. "So someone knows they can disable our subs—"

"Ships, fighter jets, anything run by computers. Stockbury says the virus isn't selective."

Rowe paused a moment, let the silence sit, and then asked, "How do we stop it?"

James barked at the word 'we', but Rowe ignored him. This virus was as dangerous as any he'd encountered. The only edge the US had right now was surprise. Whoever was behind this didn't know Stockbury had decloaked them.

"We're combing through everywhere and everyone with access to a sub's network. Problem is, that could be cables, satellite communications, repair facilities, or thousands of contractors. No one's ever considered Vaseline-type goo dangerous."

"But locations are tightly guarded and highly encrypted?"

James flared. "So is everything about a sub, and still..."

An idea bounced up, unbidden, as so often happened for Rowe. "Maybe that's why the student-looking man was at the presentation. Now he knows Stockbury's work is more sophisticated than his."

Rowe paused, thinking through how to use this. "What if we made it easy for him to steal her research, but she defanged it, added a backdoor, and a tracker."

James answered slowly, "Yeah. That could work."

"Will she do it?"

James grunted. "I get the feeling if we don't involve her, she'll do it on her own."

"She'll be putting herself in danger. Get one of your—"

"You know I don't have anyone who could fit in that academic environ," James interrupted, and then said nothing more.

Rowe's mind went back to the submariners, most of them just kids, signed on to the Silent Service because they loved their country. Desperate, freezing, down to their last O2 candle, probably thought they were doomed until that cruiser found them.

"I have a few days." He'd already forwarded his personal tools—a spade used on every dig he ever worked, the four-inch hand trowel from a mentor, and an old set of dental picks donated by an Uncle when he upgraded his office—to Israel and arranged for the expedition vehicles, tents, and provisions, which included a generous supply of chips, Twinkies, trail mix and the other snack foods grads loved. He was as ready as he could be.

"What about Delamagente?" Rowe asked.

"What about her?"

"Her Otto is smart, like Tony Stark's house robot in *Ironman*—JARVIS. Otto can connect the dots, extrapolate from data, and track anything. She made a persuasive argument at DARPA about its importance to submarine security."

Rowe admired Delamagente's tenacity. Even when her experiment collapsed, she didn't give up.

James harrumphed. "Keep an eye on her, too."

"OK. Shouldn't be difficult. They share an office. Maybe I talk her into coming to Israel with me and you cover Stockbury while I'm gone."

"This trip of yours can't be cancelled?"

Rowe ignored his question. "Dig around in the background of a Wynton Fairgrove, too. He was one of the judges."

James grunted. "Dr. Fairgrove has a worldwide reputation. Why judge a grad student competition?"

Rowe would like that answer, too. "Probably looking for a new idea to steal."

"What's that mean?" And then, "You know him?"

"Like a rat knows a snake. The last time I ran into him was when his wife died under suspicious circumstances."

Carston Devore, dressed in what he considered non-descript but professional—blue button-down shirt, black trousers, and loafers—took a seat in the middle of the audience. Devore would have ignored the caller, but when 'Delamagente' was plugged into the *Times* database, it came up with an unsolved Los Angeles murder. Devore emailed his LAPD contact who said a note found on the victim mentioned nuclear submarines, but that wasn't released to the press. Did Devore have information? The journalist promised to get back to him.

Devore listened to two presentations, one by a six-foot blonde who sneered at the judges and another by a nervous raven-haired woman who turned out to be Delamagente. She couldn't even get her equipment to work. As he waited, a gruff young man tapped Devore's shoulder and motioned he should follow him. Something in Devore's hindbrain whispered a warning, but he ignored it. As usual. Reporters would miss a lot of good stories if they worried about safety.

Once outside, he asked, "Are you the one who contacted me?"

Without turning, the man said, "Come."

Devore didn't hesitate. This story was Pulitzer material. He called to his cameraman, Nelson, and they climbed into the soiled back seat of a gray Volvo. Thirty minutes later, they stopped in front of an abandoned warehouse in a neighborhood Devore only read about in the obituaries. The driver jumped out and disappeared through an opening in the concrete tilt-up building. Devore did a quick once-over and then turned to Nelson, the man who had been part of every big story Devore had ever written. They'd been in much worse places, but for some reason, this time, Nelson looked green.

"Garbage is an improvement over the stench of the driver's body odor, right?" He slapped his colleague on the back. "Get ready to be famous, friend."

They'd just entered when a searing pain exploded in the middle of Devore's back. As he collapsed, someone thunked to the ground behind him. Powerful hands hauled Devore to a wall and propped him up next to Nelson. Out of the corner of his eye, Devore saw blood pouring down the younger man's face. Nelson made no move to staunch it.

It didn't take long for Devore to figure out he too was paralyzed. He tried to ask what his host wanted, but nothing came out. All he could do was soundlessly scream as a nail was pounded through his breastbone. When the stranger repeated the procedure on Nelson, the cameraman gasped, sucked in the stream of blood rolling down his lips, and then his chest stopped moving.

The man who had promised Devore the scoop of his life slit the journalist's wrists and left.

Chapter 11

Monday

Wynton Fairgrove walked with what he hoped was the relaxed gait of a man with no worries. That was a lie. Kalian Delamagente and her truth-seeking robot had shaken him. If she knew the unconventional steps he'd taken to advance his career, she could cause him difficulties.

Well, technically, everything illegal had been committed by Salah Al-Zahrawi. Fairgrove rolled this around in his brain, thinking how to spin it, and then shook his head. Al-Zahrawi could smell disloyalty. They'd been dining one evening at the Russian Tea Room in New York when a man rushed up, sweating and nervous. He left his daughter's birthday party to warn his boss of a mole in the organization. Al-Zahrawi thanked him and asked one of his bodyguards to walk the man back to his car. *I set the trap and this man fell for it like a skydiver without a parachute. Never give a liar a second chance.*

Fairgrove eased into an empty meeting room and punched in Al-Zahrawi's number. "I didn't expect to see you at the presentation."

Silence greeted him and the judge flushed. "Of course, you have wide-ranging interests—"

Al-Zahrawi interrupted. "I have another job for you."

Fairgrove bit his tongue. He was tiring of Salah's demands. He had to buy his way onto the DARPA panel and then Al-Zahrawi had been there anyway. What would the next chore cost?

"What Catherine Stockbury calls NEV provides unexpected opportunities."

"Yes, of course. I too was fascinated." In fact, when Stockbury explained how simple NEV was to create, he turned her off. He never wanted 'simple' and 'Fairgrove' in the same sentence.

"In two weeks, you will receive an invitation to join the Columbia faculty as a visiting professor. Once there, you must keep tabs on Catherine Stockbury for me. You will start by creating a distraction that offers me access to her lab."

Fairgrove preened. Teaching at a reputable university was an honor he hadn't enjoyed in a long time.

Before Fairgrove could respond, Al-Zahrawi asked, "What did you think of Kalian Delamagente?"

Fairgrove choked back his surprise. "She has potential. I believe with my influence and assistance, she can become an adequate researcher."

"Her invention—Otto. Will it work, Dr. Fairgrove?"

Here was his opening. He must sound objective, but collegial. "I'll make sure it does."

Apparently, he sounded frightened because Al-Zahrawi said, "If this is difficult, I have other ways to persuade her. She has a son, true?"

"Leave him out of this!" Fairgrove hissed.

"Never tell me how I must act." If Al-Zahrawi's voice had been a cornered rat, it would have bit Fairgrove.

The scientist wiped his brow. "You misunderstand me, my friend. I've worked with many young researchers. I know how to get what we need."

"I will give you everything you require. Find out if her Otto will work. If the boy is important to you, do it quickly."

Fairgrove hung up to the sound of a dial tone. Despite Al-Zahrawi's derogatory attitude, Fairgrove was energized. It had been far too long since last his name lit up the scientific leaderboards. Former colleagues who gossiped he'd become irrelevant would soon eat their words. The glamorous and connected Dr. Wynton Fairgrove would befriend grad student Kalian Delamagente, study her notes and whatever Al-Zahrawi could collect, come up with dazzling insights to gain her trust, and then create a problem only he could solve. He would become her white knight.

Al-Zahrawi's spies reported that US Navy helicopters and ships were searching an area of the Atlantic half the size of Iran, most likely for the sub. Al-Zahrawi cared nothing for the outcome. His plans had changed. If the AI Otto could do as Ms. Delamagente promised in her presentation, maybe with the proper data, he could track US Trident submarines, the crown jewels of the American military defense.

Catherine Stockbury, though, bothered Al-Zahrawi. If America realized his virus was like hers, they might come up with a way to inoculate their weapons. He called Aleksei Borodnoi. The Russian did not take the *jihad* seriously, but in this errand, being a true believer was less important than sex appeal.

Alhamdulillah. Praise be to Allah for showing how to carry out his wishes and for guiding him in the path of patience.

Chapter 12

Monday evening

Back home in the seclusion of her lab, Kali fiddled with her diamond studs and talked to Lucy.

"They misunderstood you today."

The ancient primate's arms pumped and legs churned, sweat pouring from her steaming body, huffing past an endless panorama of primeval grassland and scrub. The projecting brow ridge did little to cool her. The male she traveled with set a torrid pace, muscles rippling across a hirsute body, but Lucy kept up. Her smooth brown face no longer looked pained, just resigned, but to what?

Lucy mouthed a word—'Rah-zah'—and sniffed.

"Raza." Kali replicated the movement of Lucy's lips, the slight raising of the tongue. "Now I know your name."

Lucy pointed to a male silhouetted against the dusky sky. His head fur billowed and shoulders arched back, legs spread. He clenched his fists so tightly, Kali could see the white of his knuckles beneath his hair-fur.

The scene evaporated.

The solitary male's raw emotion haunted Kali as she gathered her materials. The tension in his muscles, the fear in his eyes, the desperation—all were so human.

As she left, she asked the night guard about Fred's key.

"No one gets one without authorization." He checked his list. "No 'Fred Kaczynski'."

"Did a Professor Faith Saunders work Sunday evening in

the History building?"

He didn't even check this time. "No one named 'Faith Saunders' in any position in any department. Are you sure of the name?"

Kali smiled inwardly. Even if she wanted to forget, she couldn't. Eidetic memories were funny like that. "I must be confused," and left.

The day's ninety-degree heat had bled off to a pleasant evening cooled by slight breezes from the Hudson River. As an undergrad, she hated Columbia with the same ferocity she now loved it. It wasn't Columbia's fault she had to pick a school close to home, but she took it out on everyone. Over time, the school's cerebral passions seduced her. Schermerhorn, where she devoured anthropology. The authentic bronze casting of Rodin's *Le Penseur* before the entrance of the Philosophy Hall. Low Plaza, built to resemble a Greek amphitheater and used as an urban beach by students. When she graduated, she would miss the ardor of the professors, the fulminations of her classmates, and the sense every student had that they could improve the world. And she would sorely miss the CAVE, the Machine Learning Lab, and all the Computer Science areas.

She greeted several neighbors at the local family-owned grocery as she bought milk. A Persian man she didn't recognize offered a wan smile as though his day too had been challenging. In her lobby, she collected mail and opened the door to the rhythmic slap-slap of Sandy's tail against the narrow entry walls. She scratched his neck as he huffed an enthusiastic greeting, nose twitching at the scent bouquet clinging to her body. That done, he curled up and fell asleep. Someone once said man was a dog's conception of God, but Kali thought they had it backwards.

As usual, nothing in the mail—a Publisher's Clearinghouse notice, a pre-approved credit card, a demand to update Sandy's license, and a letter with no return address. She flipped on the news and thumbed open the last.

"Alfred Zematis' killer is still free," she muttered as the

janitor's homely face appeared on the TV. In her final conversation with Angel Zematis, Kali promised Otto would search for Angel's birth mother. A week later, the girl's father called. His daughter was missing. Otto found the girl, but too late.

While Kali mentally replayed these events, she unfolded a linen page with an embossed heading announcing, 'Gegham Keregosian'.

It contained a check to Kali's research fund for $100,000.

Chapter 13

Wednesday

Within hours of Rowe's acceptance, the Columbia Department of Anthropology published a press release about their coup adding the formidable Dr. Zeke Rowe as a visiting professor to their already prestigious faculty.

Today was his first day. He might as well try the University's coffee. He'd be drinking a lot of it. While he waited for his vending machine cup to fill, he breathed in the intoxicating aroma. Strong and slightly burnt—could be worse. As he took his first taste, Kalian Delamagente showed up. She wore a soft blue tank top that flowed from her bronze shoulders to just below her waist. It had a low neck and narrow straps that offset the healthy glow of her skin. Her off-white shorts accentuated long muscular legs. He fumbled with his hands and ended up sticking them in his pockets.

Her cheeks flushed a beguiling pink. "You must be lost. No one down here but DARPA losers."

"I was looking for a good cup of coffee," and he offered her his friendliest grin.

"You won't find that either." She glanced at his badge. "You forgot to mention you taught here."

"I just signed on. Porter assured me you and Stockbury are indicative of Columbia's talent."

Her eyes hooded and a look he couldn't identify sped across her face. She smiled, a notch cooler than before. "Seventy-three Nobel Prize winners have come from this faculty. Someone has to be the seventy-fourth."

In spite of the dismissive response, Rowe sensed she wanted to trust him. He could work with that.

"By the way, your presentation deserved more than Dr. Fairgrove's pejorative comments. They ignored its significance in the wider framework of human development."

Delamagente's head dipped as color flooded her face. "Since I no longer answer to judges, I've embraced my previous goal—an exploration of mankind's roots."

Here was his opening. "Maybe I can help you, now that we're colleagues. I'm leading a field investigation of the Tethys Corridor—"

"—one of man's possible migration routes out of Africa. You're that Dr. Rowe." Delamagente's full lips parted and her intelligent eyes glittered with curiosity.

"Would you like to join me? A student cancelled so we're short," which was not quite a lie. "It's paid for, but it starts this week." That part was true.

Delamagente opened and closed her mouth several times, but said nothing.

"Think of the new friends you'll meet, shoulder to shoulder exposing our past, removing ossified breccia from fragile artifacts, discussing fascinating topics like horizon layers, sleeping under the Israeli moon." She looked unconvinced so he added, "I'll share my iodine tablets."

She stared into the middle distance and then asked, "Your dig covers the Plio-Pleistocene?"

Rowe nodded.

"Otto keeps throwing me into that era. There's a female habilene he has a crush on."

He touched her arm. A tingle of electricity burst into his chest and up his neck. When was the last time he felt that? She must have felt it too because she said, "When do we leave?"

She loved the way Zeke Rowe never stuttered or stammered, always knew what he wanted to say, every movement imbued with a quiet authority. The only real problem accepting his offer was she knew so little about him. To start with, why was he at DARPA? The presentations weren't in his field. She typed 'Zeke Rowe' into Google search. Sixty minutes later, she'd read enough.

He had a BS in geology and a Masters in paleontology from a Midwestern college. He got his Ph.D. in paleoanthropology at the University of Paris and became one of the youngest professors in the school's history. She uncovered pictures of him teaching in a high-ceiled nineteenth-century classroom, and one walking with a short comfortable-looking woman, sandy brown hair tied back into a schoolmarmish bun, huge eyes fixated on Rowe. A student, Kali guessed. Then he fell off the grid. She fiddled with her earrings and wondered if his disappearance had to do with how he lost the tips of fingers.

Which was none of her business. Everyone had secrets. She certainly did. What she did know was he felt right. She emailed Sean at his music camp that she would be unreachable for a few weeks. Mr. Winters agreed to keep Sandy. The dog loved these sleep-overs in no small part for the food, usually steak and French fries which the ex-Marine called 'Freedom Fries'. The old man set a place at the counter for himself and one at his feet for Sandy. Over dinner, Mr. Winters shared commentary on his favorite TV shows. Afterward, they went for a walk, Sandy to do his duty and Mr. Winters to follow the doctor's exercise routine. At bedtime, they slept together in the old man's double bed.

Kali packed a battered duffel bag, dug her passport from the Sentry safe in her closet, and accessed the State Department's website on international travel.

"*Extreme caution for those visiting Israel.* Consider me warned."

Many 'early man' sites were in hazardous areas—Kenya, Ethiopia, Tanzania. It was *de rigueur* for paleoanthropologists to put themselves in danger for science.

Before tucking in for the night, she logged into her school

email account to let Mr. Keregosian know she'd be overseas for a few weeks. She smiled at his answer: *I will be your fan and silent supporter till the end, Kalian. Bureaucrats must not overpower your brilliant mind.*

He asked if she required more money.

It pained Al-Zahrawi to deal so familiarly with a female, to treat her as his equal. After every email, he cleansed himself thoroughly and prayed to Allah for understanding.

The Prophet's gift was righteous if not at times circuitous.

He pulled a report up on his IPad to view the next puzzle piece that had fallen into place. The report lasted only fourteen lines, but gave Al-Zahrawi the power to identify any American Trident in the world, if he could locate it.

Subs were built of iron. Because the weight and mass of every submarine was different, the size and shape of its ripple through the Earth's magnetosphere was unique. That 'magnetic signature' was top secret and as such, stored on a SIPNet server few could use and no one could copy from.

Al-Zahrawi knew this because he had attempted it. When it failed, he had been forced to recreate the signatures himself. He found the Trident home ports on a public website available under the Freedom of Information laws. The site helpfully explained how the subs required scheduled and periodic maintenance—a wonderful word in the *jihadi* vocabulary. Al-Zahrawi purchased an off-the-shelf Magnetic Anomaly Detector—MAD, aimed it at an incoming sub and waited for the wrinkled fluxes to appear. Nothing.

He realized he needed something more like the MAD devices the Navy hung from helicopters, but customized. Al-Zahrawi found a sufficiently credentialed employee with the morals of a sociopath who provided the manufacturer's name, only to be told he must be approved by the Department of Defense. After countless failed bribes, contributions, and subterfuge, Al-Zahrawi accepted he would have to build his own. That became a reality, thanks to a retired German mechanical engineer still bitter over the Second World War.

Al-Zahrawi rented a hi-rise apartment whose roof offered a line of sight to the Bangor Washington port and instructed his *mujahedeen* to stay until they succeeded. Days passed, and then weeks, before a sub showed up. They aimed the MAD device at the boat and watched as a ghostly shape appeared that replicated the bend in the Earth's fluxes caused by the submarine's presence. This magnetic signature was uploaded to Al-Zahrawi

With that success, Al-Zahrawi sent workers to every submarine base with orders to collect Trident signatures.

Now, he required a method to find the submarines at sea. Delamagente's Israel trip presented an opportunity.

Chapter 14

Saturday

Where was she?

Spending two weeks with Delamagente would be harder than Rowe had thought. He reminded himself this was research, not a date. Besides, he wouldn't survive a third strike, if life after Paulette and Amanda could be called surviving. He unbuckled his tool belt with its trowels, brushes, tape measure, cameras, and canteen, and distractedly massaged the chronic ache in his knee, glancing every few seconds at the edge of the hill he had just crested.

The last few days had been a flurry of inactivity. He settled into his cover as Columbia's newest research star, kept in contact with Catherine Stockbury and Kalian Delamagente from a distance, checked with James for updates, and mentally prepared for the field work that could prove his theory.

He flew into Ben Gurion International Friday to meet with the Israeli Antiquities Authority Director-General, and iron out the political and logistic details inherent to every expedition. Over *café barad*, he described how the excavation's footprint skirted the holy areas thanks to guidance from local religious leaders. By the time he had the permit, Delamagente and the Land Rover full of grad students had arrived. Everyone wanted to settle in and gossip except Delamagente. She said a five-mile hike in the one-hundred-degree heat, ninety percent humidity, sounded great so off they went.

He had begun to worry in earnest when her head popped over the ridge. Sweat poured down her face and plastered her short-sleeved cotton blouse to the curves of her body. She limped to a painful halt and doubled over, gasping.

"I should have broken my shoes in first."

In place of the rejoinder that leaped to mind, he handed her his canteen and politely inquired if she had another pair. She bobbed her head once, lungs wheezing.

"Anyone who can climb as fast as you and isn't Special Forces missed a bet." She grimaced.

He did a double-take. She couldn't know. "You'll get used to it—iodine-flavored water."

"As long as it keeps me healthy, it can taste like raw eggs."

Rowe grimaced. "How do my troops sound?"

"Young and enthusiastic. The four I shared the ride with talked nonstop about the Levantine Corridor and the history of the Dead Sea Fault Zone. I tried to keep up and then gave up."

One hand firmly planted on her thigh, the other gripping the water bottle as though life itself, Kali watched Rowe out of the corner of her eye. He seemed worried about her at first and then shut it down. She hadn't seen him since that day at the vending machine. He emailed instructions for what to bring, how to get her tickets, where to meet the driver at the airport, and how to reach him if she needed to.

She tamped down the queasiness that left her dizzy in his presence. She wasn't here to find a boyfriend. Early man research had been her passion throughout undergrad, one she put aside to raise Sean. Otto's focus on Lucy had resurrected that hunger. The AI never acted without purpose and always charted a logical path. If he was monitoring Lucy, she must play an important part in the research.

In that, Dr. Zeke Rowe could prove useful, assuming his grad students could concentrate. Contrary to what she told him, what they really talked about was *I wonder if he's as cute as his publicity photo.* And *He's single does he have a girlfriend?* And *What are the sleeping arrangements anyone know?* When they found out she worked with him, they peppered her with questions she couldn't answer.

He swept his hand over a swath of arid featureless land. "Hundreds of thousands of years ago, our ancestors followed the Great Rift Valley from the African desert to the abundant lakes of what today is the Dead Sea."

How amazing it must have been. Small bands of roving hominids gathering roots and nuts and scavenging the cast-offs of predators. Did they arrive here by following the grazing animals or had that uniquely human trait of wanderlust already evolved?

"There's Route 90 from Ben Gurion International." Rowe traced his finger down a shimmering silver ribbon in the distance. "North are Ubeidiya and Gesher Benot Ya'aqov with their 1.5 million-year-old remains showing evidence of man's early control over fire."

Delamagente tingled as though an antediluvian breeze had parted the haze, exposing an ancient world. "I can see Lucy with Boah and Ump at her side. She'd stop there," Delamagente indicated the spreading limbs of an aspen, "to rest."

"Lucy?"

"The *Homo habilis* Otto likes. She's an efficient survivalist which leaves time for planning and tool-making. And problem-solving. In the months I've observed her, I've come to respect her decisions."

Delamagente felt Lucy's presence, watching, wondering if the strangers were predator or prey.

Rowe cocked his head. "You talk about Lucy as though she's human."

"*Habilis* is the first human species in the genus *Homo*. Lucy's eyes hold a sadness that never goes away even when she's happy. Her internal strength is formidable. She soldiers forward, seemingly resigned to her destiny."

Kali stopped. She just described herself on a good day. "Not unlike a few people I know."

"Must be a useful trait or evolution would eradicate it."
He turned toward the hill they'd scaled. "Time to head back
for the official welcome to the troops."

As the days passed, Kali lost herself in the organic
pungency of this ancient land. She jogged as the sun rose to
avoid the heat and then relaxed over a cup of Turkish coffee
before beginning the shoveling, chipping, and sifting that was
daily work. Just when she thought she couldn't stand another
scorching minute, the cook's bell clanged, announcing a
hearty meal of fresh bread, cheese, melons, vegetables, and
juice.

After breakfast, in the relative cool of the tents, she
scrutinized the collected bones and rocks, logged in data and
created the meticulous maps part and parcel to every
expedition. The day ended with a light meal and passionate,
scholarly discussions about why a hominid molar had been
found separated from a jaw, or how pig and human skeletal
parts came to be buried together.

Throughout the day, Rowe wandered through the
encampment to review the artifacts, ask questions about a
bone or tooth dug up the day before, and prod his researchers
to understand connections to the bigger picture. He always
joined the evening exchanges, sharing his learned wisdom,
urging the group to think deeper and find what was there, not
what wasn't, and forcing them to put aside personal prejudices
in favor of authenticity.

Every night, he retired alone while the rest of the crew
arranged themselves into favorite sleeping pods. Most
evenings, one of the women would find an excuse to approach
his tent and be invited in. It was clear from the silhouettes
nothing happened but talk. Kali sensed a sadness to Zeke
Rowe. His passion for life stopped with proving his theory.
Someone had hurt him and he hadn't recovered.

Maybe never would.

As Kali hacked at the baked earth of grid twelve, she

couldn't help but envy the snake, his needs nothing more than eating every few weeks and sleeping under a shady rock. Her muscles ached from days of crouching and her eyes burned from the sun's glare off the parched earth. Under the searing Israeli sun, her hat's built-in sweatband proved as useless as a chocolate teapot. She chipped, scrape chipped, scrapechipped, thoughts revolving around whether she would ever again take a cold shower, one ear on the muted voices around her and one on the lunch bell.

But if it rang, she didn't hear it. "Zeke! Over here!"

Rowe jogged over, face pale from the heat, eyes hooded, shadowed closely by several students.

"What d'you have, Kali?"

Zeke had been working as hard as anyone, but had no sweat stains under his arms. She stunk like a pile of dirty socks.

She smoothed her thumb over a round nub protruding from the hardscrabble. "I think this is human."

He knelt, face inches from the artifact. "No, I don't think so. Too narrow." Then his eyes moved left, squinted, and widened. "I'm wrong."

Kali wiped sweat from her eyes. This heat was killing her. "It *is* hominid?"

He indicated a tiny protuberance less than an inch in circumference. "Yes, because that's a human phalange." He tilted his head up and bellowed, "Everyone over here!"

Rowe's eyes glistened, a dirt smudge on his nose. All signs of fatigue had washed from his body.

Heat forgotten, the entire crew went to work. The area was sectioned off and mapped, the location numbered. Students gently chipped loose the bones Kali had located and chiseled away the matrix. Some catalogued the start and stop depth, soil color and texture, and what had been removed around each bone. Others screened organic artifacts from dirt and pebbles. By the time the Sun set, they'd unearthed fragments of a *Homo habilis*, an Australopithecine and a canis, all in a hundred-square-foot area.

Kali straightened, wincing at the machine gun pop of her vertebra. Time to quit. She was more tired than hungry, so gathered her tools, sketched a wave to Rowe and stumbled to her bedroll. She crawled inside after a quick search revealed no hidden scorpions or other crawly creatures indigenous to the Israeli desert. Everything hurt. Her skin burned, joints throbbed, and she had dozens of sand flea bites and tiny cuts from rocks uncovered while excavating.

Rowe's voice filtered through the dreamy haze, happily chattering to a group of students who wanted to talk through every possible outcome of what had happened today. Their voices were a soothing buzz as Kali fell asleep, wondering where Lucy and Boah and Ump were buried.

Hours later, Rowe sat on an overlook at the edge of the camp. Up here, the night drowned out everything. The moon cast a luminescent glow, the stars remote pinpricks. Far down the nocturnal sky, the branches of an acacia traced blue-black against the horizon.

He sorted through today's events as his subconscious rummaged through the sounds and scents of the environ. The thin air reverberated with muted voices, insect chirps, and the occasional canine howl.

And a car, maybe half a mile out. Who would drive here at this hour? They were literally in the middle of nowhere. Rowe had just decided to check when steps approached. He leaped sideways and spun around as a hulking male jerked back, palms out.

"Hold on, friend. I did not mean to frighten you! Please, my name is Evan."

Rowe tilted his head up. Evan towered over him with frizzled hair backlit by the moon's glow. He had shoulders like a ledge under a powerful neck, hair trimmed tight to the scalp, and eyes as flat as pebbles. His body had the tight musculature of someone not afraid to be physical. A puckered white scar interrupted his right brow, probably a knife fight. His accent was Russian.

"What's up?" Rowe kept his voice casual, but inside, he thrummed.

"My car stalled. I saw lights and came to see about getting some help."

He pointed toward the headlights. Rowe instinctively turned toward Evan's finger, but some primal instinct pulled him back. He caught Evan's fist with his palm and squeezed until the fingers caved in. Evan started to say something, but Rowe had stopped listening. He hammered an elbow into the man's knee moments before it reached Rowe's crotch and then slammed a solid, fast punch into the giant's nose. Cartilage crunched and Evan's head whipped back as far as his neck would allow, then forward where it connected with Rowe's head-butt. He howled as Rowe pounded him to the ground and stomped on his good fingers. Bones popped like dry twigs and the man curled into a fetal ball, whimpering.

"What do you want, *Evan*—"

A volley of bullets drove Rowe to cover. By the time they stopped, Evan and the car were roaring away. Rowe inched out of the crevice he'd wedged himself into, did a quick sensory run-through of the area for danger, and then watched the taillights until they vanished behind a tangle of shadows.

"Hey, Dr. Rowe. Is everything OK?" One of the students.

"Just a car backfiring," Rowe answered without looking. "Go on back to sleep."

The student grunted and left. Rowe quieted his mind and body until all he heard were crickets and a soft desert wind. He scanned the terrain, the horizon, the scrub limned against the night sky, but all was normal. Was the target Rowe? Or the camp? He doubted they were after the ancient bones. Only satellite phones worked out here so they wouldn't know about today's discovery. If it was related to James' case, why here rather than New York? Or was it something to do with Delamagente's computer—Otto?

He shook his head. None of those made sense. No, this was a message, but about what?

He called James on the sat phone. "I just had company,"

and he gave a rundown of the last fifteen minutes. Rowe had been out of Special Forces for years and was pleasantly surprised his skills remained intact.

"Have you seen this Evan before?"

"Nope."

"Did you get the make of the car, a license plate, description of the driver?"

"Nope."

"Anyone suspicious in your group?"

"N—" and Rowe paused. He had no idea. "I'll check."

As they talked, he paced off the area, flashlight scanning in neat rows. As he was about to say goodbye, he found something.

"I'm sending you a map Evan dropped. The excavation site is circled in red with GPS coordinates."

As James waited, he asked, "Remember Carston Devore from DARPA? He hasn't answered my call. I think he's kidnapped, or dead. This is more dangerous than we thought."

Delamagente's presentation was a catalyst. Rowe hung up and punched a number in his phone.

"Your so-called gimp almost killed me!"

"What happened?" The voice carried a hint of disgust.

"I surprised him, but it didn't matter. He fights like Spetznaz. I would have died if Aleksei hadn't shot at him."

"Did you get Delamagente's computer?"

"I got nothing but a headache."

Chapter 15

"Otto can make the connection!" Delamagente said, rushing into Rowe's tent as the sun peeked one timid ray over the horizon, and then stopped short. "Sorry. I didn't know you had company."

Last night, Rowe and James agreed Evan's handler would send a bigger crew to accomplish whatever it was Evan had failed to do. Rowe's first call after he and James hung up was to Duck Peters. Though they hadn't talked in a year, it might as well have been yesterday. No small talk, no catching up, just what did Rowe need. In minutes, Duck lined up two retired SEALs who would be there at dawn. He would join them as soon as possible.

Rowe had slept poorly, dreams haunted by subs disappearing, warheads raining down on the US, and Delamagente screaming. When he finally gave up sleeping, Duck's friends were crouched outside his tent, waiting. Both were former SEALs who now did protection details for referrals. Their sturdy, compact builds, intelligent eyes, lean hungry faces threw Rowe back to another world. The perfectly rolled shirtsleeves, faded Levis, heavy boots, and loose jackets in 85-degree heat screamed authority, not disheveled researchers. They needed a different cover.

"Gentlemen. Would you like to explore camp, give me a minute with Ms. Delamagente," he said as he handed them ceramic cups of Kafe Turki, Without a word, the men disappeared.

"What's up, Kali?"

Rowe yawned. He spent most of last night hunting futilely for clues left by his attackers. Delamagente on the other hand, looked fresh and energetic in clean khaki shorts and a crisp white blouse, shining hair plated into a loose abundant braid.

"Have you been up all night?" She peeked over her shoulder at the visitors and blurted, "I can use Otto to see if the bones we found are related. You saw my presentation. He's good at connecting dots."

Rowe turned away. "Not enough time. We're wrapping up today." He tried to sound professorial rather than the besotted fool he felt like around her.

"No problem. All I need is their DNA when we get back to New York." She stepped closer to Rowe, her face earnest, eyes direct. "Otto predicted this trio, Zeke. If he can establish those bones traveled here from Africa, it would prove your hypothesis."

Rowe absorbed the rich odors of sweat, dirt, and soap. They awakened memories from a time when worries were few and learning paramount, before the SEALS, Paulette's death, and the Accident.

"ADNA." A furrow appeared between Delamagente's eyes, so he explained, "Ancient DNA is older than regular DNA." Why'd he correct her? He scratched his head. "None of the traditional reasons—water flow, volcanic activity, scavengers—explain the cohabitation." An idea nudged its way to his consciousness. "OK. I'll singalize the aDNA if you share everything with me, including individuals who benefit from your research." Astonishment swept over her face. "It would be required of any field researcher," he added. "Is someone involved you can't reveal?"

"I... I have to...go... take my turn at... the grid."

Rowe wondered what was going on.

Kali tapped the dental pick lightly against the calcified jaw, little by little separating the cement-like breccia from the bone. The work was tedious and boring, leaving her free to consider Rowe's demand. Mr. Keregosian's only request, in return for his generous donation, was secrecy. Kali suspected he was involved in a Creationist ideology that would object to evolution. She had agreed, never considering a need to divulge his name.

"You look worried, Kalian Delamagente. Is there something I can help with?"

Kali liked Carl Hamar, an eager young grad student on his first dig. He often worked next to her. Today, he wore his usual white hemp drawstring pants with a t-shirt and simple leather sandals on narrow, hardened feet. He exuded a pleasant scent she associated with vegetarians and the calm demeanor of one who took life in stride.

She ignored his question. "I like your slogan, Carl. 'Be patient. I'm still evolving'."

"A gift from an Uncle to honor my acceptance into this program. I am the first archaeologist in our family."

"How do you do that—be patient?"

"Patience, like oxygen, is in plentiful supply and only valuable when it disappears."

Kali laughed. "Such wisdom in one so young. Tell me about yourself."

Carl Hamar, known in his Iranian hometown as Laslo Hemren, offered a wan smile. He liked this Western female who shared her emotions so easily. Lines creased the corners of her eyes when she was happy and framed her mouth when worried. She noticed everything around her, like his sisters before their dreams were dashed, which made him want to tell her the truth.

He was Laslo, son of Latif, himself the son of Shibli. He was born to Muslim parents who, like everyone in his *ummah,* inculcated their children in a religion that shaped their lives but they had not chosen for themselves. He had fond memories of Fridays in the Mosque, sitting cross-legged on the cool tile floor, listening to the imam's stories. Of joining the adults afterward for the meal of lamb, goat cheese, bread, fruit, and a variety of nuts.

As he matured, his beliefs became more fervent and the demands of Islam more numerous. He grew a beard as the Prophet had done, memorized the Qur'aan, and performed the Islamic toiletry etiquette before each prayer. This entailed washing his face, neck, arms, head, nasal cavity, mouth, ears, feet, repeating the process three times, and again if he so much as farted or sneezed. He found the ablutions rejuvenating to body and soul.

Laslo might have remained a believer if not for his sisters. All they wanted from life was to be teachers, but under Islamic law, they were chattel, no different from cars or camels. When Laslo's father died, control of them transferred to Laslo and he devised a desperate plan to acquire their freedom. He requested the honor of becoming a 'sleeper' in America to which his *imam* agreed. When he completed his task here, he would move to the lair of the Great Satan where his sisters would join him. There, they would become loyal immigrants until Allah called Laslo to *jihad*. This, Laslo decided, was a fair trade.

Carl Hamar, aka Laslo Hemren, could tell none of this to Kalian Delamagente, despite how kind she seemed. He dipped his head, listening to the murmur of camp gossip, the smack of tools against the rocky soil, the caw of birds, and his own labored breathing. When he next looked up, worry filled Kalian Delamagente's eyes. That was good. It was time to share the cover story he hoped she would believe.

"I am from Esfahan, Iran. I grew up in a Muslim family, the third of seven children. My parents taught me that Muslims are not on this earth to be happy, but to preserve the values of our Prophet. I believed that until the age of fifteen when a favorite cousin pulled me aside to say goodbye. While his schoolmates embraced the Qur'an's words to *Fight those who do not believe in Allah,* he was leaving for America, the land of opportunity, freedom, and happiness. He invited me to join him.

"To this day, my mother refuses to talk with me."

Carl waited, eyes focused downward, hiding the deception that must be obvious in his eyes. After what seemed like hours, she spoke.

"You've been honest with me, Carl, so I have a confession. I'm not an anthropologist. A computer program I created failed and I'm here to gain perspective on my life."

"Technology I love as much as archaeology. We have much time, dusting and sifting. Please tell me about your work."

Delamagente started with her dream to improve education and the futile struggle to seek funding. The more she opened up, the more he came to like this American. He pushed that aside and remembered his sisters. He managed to get all the information his handlers required without arousing the woman's suspicions.

As they rose for lunch, he took her arm. "We all fail once or more. When I graduate and my day of failure comes, I will remember your strength, Kalian Delamagente, how you recovered and moved on."

Delamagente's elegance attracted every male in the group, but Carl's attention was different. It took seven minutes for Rowe's new security personnel to declare him 'interesting' which inspired Rowe to dig out the man's application. The man pictured was broad-faced with an intelligent honest smile and brown eyes glittering with enthusiasm, but not the person outside Rowe's tent. He Skyped Carl's anthropology professor at Hebrew University.

"My apologies. Our records sometimes fall behind. Yaakov Demsky, the student who signed up, died in a car crash. A tragic event. His professors considered him a promising scientist. Carl Hamar called about the possibility of late cancellations. We select from a waiting list which he wasn't on, but he said his wife contacted us several times. Luck was with him. Everyone else had alternate summer plans. I'll fax his curriculum vitae immediately."

"Who recommended him?"

"I have the letter. Ah, here it is. Dr. Wynton Fairgrove. Surprising an unknown student attracted the attention of such a prominent scientist, yes?"

The judge at the DARPA competition. That couldn't be coincidence.

"Could you email the files to me? And thank you for your time, Doctor."

Rowe wandered over to where Carl Hamar and Kali Delamagente were working. Now that he knew he was an impostor, it was obvious. Everyone wore old footwear on a dig, but Hamar's shoes were new. Where his nails should have been scarred from constant digging in hard soil, they were smooth. Most telling, he lacked the environmental awareness every archaeologist possessed like a second skin.

"Carl. We haven't chatted. Are you learning what you hoped to with us?"

If the boy-man understood Rowe's double meaning, he gave no indication. "Oh, yes. I am blessed to have found a kindred soul in Kalian Delamagente. If I could, I would come to your Columbia University to study."

Rowe tapped his watch and held it up to his ear before returning his attention to Carl. "I understand Dr. Fairgrove referred you to this project?"

"Yes. Dr. Fairgrove. He remembered me from a lecture."

"He is an excellent speaker. Where did you hear him?"

Carl scratched a flee bite on his arm. "Where did I hear him?" His brows knitted and his mouth formed a lipless line. "Max Planck Institute, on a semester exchange program."

Rowe coughed to hide his surprise. Carl's handler should have prepped him better.

"That must have been before you married."

Carl blushed. "I have yet to meet my wife. My *imam* will arrange that at the right time."

Rowe had heard enough. "Well, keep up the good work. Someday, you may solve one of man's important mysteries."

He left, forcing himself not to rush. Carl was young, naïve, and unprepared for an undercover assignment. Duck's friends would find out what he was supposed to accomplish—and if he had succeeded—tomorrow.

Inside his tent, Rowe called James. "See what you can find out about a 'Carl Hamar'. I just sent an audio. Also, find out about the death of Yaakov Demsky in a Jerusalem car crash."

As he hung up, his mind raced. First the gunmen, now a plant in his crew. Why? His only out-of-the-ordinary activity was the favor for James. Rowe gulped half a bottle of water, dumped the rest over his head, and made his decision just as Delamagente entered.

"Hey, Kali. Ready to go home?"

"What's my choice?" He motioned her to sit. "What you asked, about revealing who I share data with. That's standard? Anyone funding me would expect it?"

"Demand it, to avoid conflicts of interest. Requests for anonymity are unreasonable."

She met his eyes for the first time. "OK. Let's do it."

Chapter 16

Wednesday

As the plane taxied to the gate, Kali turned her phone on and found three messages from Sean, all about how much fun he was having. She pecked out a response as she cleared Customs, telling him she was back in the US and couldn't wait to talk to him.

She took a taxi home rather than the bus, taking advantage of Mr. Keregosian's grant. When she saw Mr. Winters' light on, Tears sprang to her eyes. She missed Sandy's wild enthusiasm and unstinting love. She knocked on the door, hugged Mr. Winters, and promised to share all the details tomorrow when she wasn't asleep on her feet. Sandy greeted her, tail wagging like an out-of-control metronome. After a quick tussle, they went home and fell into bed where she slept until the sun blazed through the window.

Sandy popped up with a contented yawn as though pleased to be home. Kali wrapped her arms around his thick neck, kissed the crown of his head, then tossed a handful of kibble into his bowl and started coffee. That's when she realized she didn't have a headache. She could count on one hand the days in any given month she woke without one. So besides the other, Zeke was medicinal.

She showered, threw on a robe and took two coffees to the back stoop. Mr. Winters was already there, dressed in a blue oxford shirt, tan trousers secured by his always-shiny Marine Corps buckle, and slippers.

"What's up today, Mr. Winters? You getting frisky with your Vet friends?"

"Hello, kitten. Just wanted to say good morning. Boy that smells good." He took the steaming mug and inhaled. "No one makes coffee like you, kitten. No, not my friends. I have a doctor appointment, like they do any good."

The arthritis had spread from his hips, knees, elbows, and back to his feet. He'd started wearing slippers during the day and using a cane—'an old man's third leg.'

"A friend of yours stopped by. I got his picture." He patted his camera phone. "And I let the plumber in. The unit above you sprang a leak."

"Oh. I didn't see any problems."

Two lines creased Mr. Winters' wrinkled forehead.

"I'll find them later." She checked her Timex. "Gotta go. Full day!"

She sketched a wave and ran inside, Sandy in pursuit. Too late for a run, she dressed in pleated ivory slacks, a white short-sleeved blouse and navy blue pumps—her meet-the-Dean outfit. He wanted an update on her thesis. After ten minutes of searching, she found her mother's diamond earrings. She didn't remember leaving them on her nightstand, but she had been rushed.

She opened the doggy door, pulled the top off a yogurt, and hurried into the humid New York morning. A short walk, right turn at the bodega, and a straight line to Columbia.

Amsterdam Avenue's eclectic mix of architecture never failed to awe Kali. Grand old buildings with art deco entrances and limestone facades mixed with rundown liquor stores, their blue awnings stark against the brick-and-stone high-rises, a valley like Lucy's African Rift except molded by man. When Riverside Church chimed eight, she broke into a trot.

A Post-it note was stuck to her keyboard when she arrived at her lab.

"From your hunky new boyfriend." Cat waved distractedly, feet on her desk, an icepack over her brow, and an earbud peeking from beneath her hair.

Zeke and his two muscular friends had dropped her off at home last night and still he beat her in.

"Hello to you, too, Cat. Did you miss me?"

She rolled her eyes. "How would you like to face our booboisian colleagues alone?"

"Booboisian?"

"What the French call Americans to denigrate our lack of culture."

Cat's eyes glowed red and were perilously close to shutting. Kali sniffed Chanel 22 trying valiantly to disguise the stale liquor fumes seeping from her girlfriend's pores.

"Where'd you go last night?"

"The Blue Note. A quartet played the oldies. Piano, tenor sax, drums and stand-up bass. Grady Tate's *Multiplication Rock* brought the house down."

By the looks of her, Cat *closed* the house down.

"I met a blonde hunk—cultured, intelligent, gorgeous, and rich. All the requirements. A girl was there with him, but I won him over."

"As though there was any other outcome."

"How was Israel?"

"I met my soulmate." Though Carl's disappearance on the last day left her wondering.

Cat smirked. "Many primitive cultures believed people possess two souls, one for the spirit and one for the body. Which do you mean?" She readjusted the ice pack.

Kali scowled as she sorted through the mail on her desk. "He's too young."

"Yes, Daddy. I'm still here." Her shoulders hunched. "If you want my opinion—"

She stopped mid-sentence and bit her lip. The billionaire's baritone drowned out his daughter's words. He hired yes men for ideas. From Cat, he expected a son-in-law to take over the business. Her forehead wrinkled. "Umhm. OK... Kali, do you have any Visine?"

Kali emptied her purse, found nothing, and moved on to her desk. As she dug through Lifesavers, sugarless gum, a pile of flash drives and a half-eaten bag of chips, Cat grunted and ummed into the phone.

"Anything happen while I was gone?"

"Dean Manfried stopped by. He's at Step Two."

She and Cat rated the Dean's visits. Step One—a rare occurrence—was The Friend. Step Two was The Harridan, flushed cheeks and bouncing jowls as he spouted orders—*You must comply with academic standards*. Step Three, The Termagant, where he lost control and spittle exploded from his mouth like a lawn sprinkler.

No Visine in her desk. She tried the first aid kit by the door. "Why's he want to see me?"

"Daddy says you made waves again."

"Did you talk to him?"

"I'm talking—oh. Don't mix your pronouns, Kali. No. Of course not."

Cat dipped her head and picked at her nails. Daddy must be lecturing. "OK. Call back."

Kali waved a Visine bottle and handed it to Cat. She squirted two drops in each eye and tipped her head back. "Is that box about the skeletons you found?"

Kali nodded. "If they're as old as Zeke thinks, they could validate Otto's findings. Zeke will singalize their aDNA, and I'll digitize it and plug it into Otto. I'll either get better-looking Lucy, Ump and Boah, or three new characters."

"But they're too old to be viable."

"I don't need them alive."

Kali tucked the box under her arm, flapped a goodbye, bought two coffees from the vending machine and wove through the underground corridors to Zeke Rowe's lab. When she got there, she stopped in awe. It was the size of her entire apartment, and unshared.

"Ah. Beware of geeks bearing gifts."

Rowe's voice came from behind a pile of boxes. He was digging through an architect's cabinet, drawers labeled 'Teeth', 'Bones', 'Jaws', and 'Assorted Fragments'. He must use these for comparison pieces in his research. An oversized monitor rose above the clutter like a mechanical philomath.

"Be nice, Zeke, or I'll drink both."

"Geeks with coffee are always welcome," and went back to his phone call.

"Thanks. I'll find my own seat."

The only chair she found not buried in books listed so dangerously, she decided to stand. She scrutinized the polished wood shelves that ran wall to wall and floor to ceiling. They contained everything from archaeology monographs to the Zionist history of Israel. The current issue of *Nature,* corners dog-eared and post-its stuck out like playing cards in bicycle spokes, lay open to an article on dating bones.

"Is this a good time to singalize the aDNA?" she asked, indicating the box still under her arm.

"Give me one second. I'm finishing an expedition update."

"Sounds exciting."

"If you like driving in traffic jams." As she started to open the box, Rowe stood. "Done. How're Sandy and Sean?"

Kali chuckled. "Sandy prefers Mr. Winters' food, and Sean loves Juilliard's summer program."

"And Cat? Your office mate?" He held her gaze long enough to make her uncomfortable.

"Nothing new unless you count meeting the man of her dreams. Again."

Kali gawked at Rowe in dark pinstripe slacks, a white shirt with rolled-up sleeves and a blue paisley tie. "You look so—professional." She wanted to say handsome or sexy, but stopped when she felt her face start to burn. He saved her by briskly moving to the far corner of his lab as though he hadn't seen her blush.

"Let's get started."

He donned a mask, gloves, and lab coat, handed her the same, and gathered disposable tubes, filtered tips, and sterile solutions. He washed the bones with an acid solution, cleaned them with deionised distilled water, drilled out the bone powder, and prepared the DNA singalization and identification.

An hour later, they tossed their lab clothes into an industrial laundry pouch. "Now, we wait. Hungry?" Rowe motioned her to follow him.

He picked the popular Carleton Lounge in the Mudd Building. If Delamagente was like most people, sharing a friendly meal would lower her defenses. James was worried this undercover assignment might be another dead end. There hadn't even been a nibble on Stockbury's research in the two weeks since the conference. Rowe didn't agree. Keregosian's arrival immediately after DARPA was more than coincidence. When James tried to clear him, his emails led back to overseas remailers with anonymous identities, which was tantalizing

Why hide his identity if there wasn't something to hide? And how was that tied to Stockbury?

"Stockbury's a true whiz kid, huh?"

"She has a 4.0 GPA and is one of six GIGA members."

"GIGA's the MENSA of MENSA?"

"The average IQ of the world's population is around 90, which means Cat can accurately tell people she's twice as smart as they are."

"Porter told me about a run-in between Cat and a thermodynamics professor. She disagreed on a minor point, which the teacher declared 'balderdash'. She seemed to acquiesce with grace, but the next day, every time he spoke, his display went black. He fiddled with it, rebooted, and called Tech Support, to no avail. He ultimately replaced the laptop, never realizing Cat hacked it."

Delamagente laughed. "Cat loves a good fight, but you better be ready. She lives for Voltaire's axiom: *'No problem can stand the assault of sustained thinking'*."

He chewed through half his hamburger before nonchalantly asking about Keregosian. Delamagente bubbled with excitement about the man's serious interest in her work, the daily communications, and their shared mutual trust. Rowe was stunned by how quickly Keregosian had wormed his way into Delamagente's confidence for a relatively small sum of money.

"I assume Mr. Keregosian is the man you were concerned about when we discussed sharing the results of the aDNA tests?" He paused and she offered a tight nod. "Have you met him?" If so, campus surveillance might have a picture.

Delamagente took a long sip of sugarless tea and shook her head. "Why would we?"

To eyeball him, HUMINT, see if he's as suspicious in the flesh as digitally, Rowe wanted to yell, but instead asked with all the calm he could muster, "Was he at the presentation?"

James matched sign-ins to attendees, but the only person unaccounted for—and on no security camera—was the young student Rowe identified. If that was Keregosian, he used a fake name, knew how to avoid surveillance, and might be a kidnapper and murderer.

"I have no idea what he looks like. All I know is he's the rare academic."

Terrorists were neither rare nor academic.

"I laymanned my theory at first, but he asked so many questions, I gave him the technical version, which surprisingly he understood."

Rowe struggled to keep his face neutral. As part of the investigation, he read every communication between the two, and the level of detail Keregosian requested made Rowe cringe. Why did he want such minutiae? Rowe chewed his roast beef sandwich to hide his irritation.

No logic connected Keregosian to the attack in Israel, though the possibility tickled like the barometer before a hurricane. James found no fingerprints or trace on the map Evan dropped. It was torn from standard 8.5 x 11 20 pound paper, available anywhere. The car was abandoned in a grocery store parking lot, wiped clean. Israel had CCTV cameras everywhere, but this corner was dark, like the driver knew it.

Until Devore returned, Keregosian was the only lead.

"Does he push you?"

"Who? Boah?" Delamagente focused on Rowe, her sandwich halfway to her mouth.

"Mr. Keregosian." *I guess she changed topics.*

"Nooo. He says he's an amateur scientist thrilled to be on the cutting edge of research such as mine." She nibbled a corner of her sandwich and kept her eyes on Rowe.

"Is his background related to your work?"

Rowe tried to make this sound benign, but Delamagente stiffened.

"I never asked. Is it relevant?" Her words were short and her tone defensive.

"Just curious." His phone hummed. "Time to go."

When they reached the sample tray minutes later, three test tubes showed the distinctive DNA band. Rowe completed the analysis and smiled at Delamagente.

"Congratulations. You have a canis, an australopithecine and a *Homo habilis*."

Delamagente beamed as she packaged the samples to return to her lab, but paused to toss a baggy to Rowe.

"Would you identify this DNA, too?" She left before Rowe could ask questions.

Chapter 17

Salah Al-Zahrawi enjoyed Delamagente's missives. She wrote with an eloquence unusual in Americans. Praise be to Allah for delivering such a useful tool into Zahrawi's hands. He felt unworthy, but if Allah thought him capable, he would succeed.

Masha'a Allah

His project was proceeding well. Soon, he would possess Catherine Stockbury's research, then his scientists would rework their DNA virus and he could re-infect the Tridents with the updated strain. As far as he knew, the Americans had not found the downed sub and did not suspect foul play.

Only three weeks remained before the auction. The website would soon go live. The promise of a Trident would significantly increase interest, but he still did not know if Delamagente's Otto could find them.

He pecked out a reply to her last email. *"I am captivated by the way you anthropomorphize Otto's complex behavior. Is it useful to consider—him—more than the perfunctory result of algorithms and programs?"*

So contradictory to America's dehumanization of the living.

Al-Zahrawi forwarded a copy to Dr. Fairgrove and shut down the connection with ten seconds to spare. His message would be encrypted and bounced around the world. Anyone who successfully traced him got a surprise.

Inshallah. It was time for daily prayers.

A half hour after Delamagente left, James called. "She made contact. We're tracking Keregosian's data shadow—"

"English, Bobby. I don't speak geek."

"I'm linking in Raj Ajit, one of our senior ciphers. He liaises with the other government geeks."

The CIA recruited Raj Ajit, listed as one of 'the top ten hackers in the world', but quit when they wanted him "suited and booted". When James heard that, he drove out to his home with a smorgasbord of snacks Eitan Sun said Ajit would love, and promised he could wear whatever he wanted as long as he kept thinking. Now he worked in the basement of the NSA's Fort Meade complex behind a door with no name on it. Just the way he liked it.

Ajit chimed in, "A data shadow is like your car's GPS map of where you drove. In this case, it includes dozens of remailer accounts spread throughout the world. All I do is follow the trail."

"How long to find him, Raj?"

"Well, it depends... If he logs on again..." Rowe had a feeling Ajit was talking to himself.

"Do you think you'll break this in the next few days or not?" Impatience crept into James' voice, but he bit it back.

The muttering stopped. "Yes."

James sighed. "Well, that's good news. Thanks, Raj."

James picked up his handset. "Never ask a yes-no question when what you really want is a discussion. On a more positive note, your instincts are right about Carl Hamar. His real name is Laslo Hemren. His NCIC— National Crime Information Center—profile reads: *Member of radical Islam groups and minor figure in low-level terrorist activities.* Thankfully, he's not as cyber-savvy as Keregosian. We traced several emails between the two. Plus, every week Hemren contacts someone with the code name 'sisters'. It could be a drop box."

"Any chance Hemren and Keregosian are the same person?"

"According to analysts, both write like non-natives, but

their word choices indicate dissimilar educational and cultural backgrounds."

"Let's assume for now they are different people, Bobby. Hemren emails Keregosian and Fairgrove recommended Hemren for my dig. That connects Fairgrove and Keregosian." Rowe chewed on this for a beat and moved on. "What about Demsky?"

"No record, no radical acquaintances, no missing blocks of time in his background. No travel to suspect nations. Investigators blame his accident on drunk driving, but friends insist he was a tea totaler. Plus, stomach contents include no alcohol. Blood tests found Rohypnol. Our working theory is he was killed to free a spot for Hemren."

Rowe paused as a student poked his head in the office. When he saw his professor on the phone, he mouthed an apology and withdrew to a position outside the door. There, he shuffled from one foot to the other, raked his fingers through his hair, and started bouncing to a rhythm only he heard. Rowe lowered his voice.

"Kali joined only days before the field study began. How'd they find out?"

James humphed. "Who'd she tell about going?"

"Her son, next door neighbor. Stockbury…"

"Keregosian?"

"Maybe."

"Tess! Where's the report on the members of Zeke's dig?"

Tess was James' assistant and a two-hundred-pound force of nature. She could turn an Army General into a quaking bowl of Jell-O if she was in the mood.

"No one tied to anyone suspicious with the exception of Hemren, who knew Fairgrove and Keregosian."

Why would Fairgrove be involved? "Gotta student here, Bobby," and Rowe disconnected. He snatched his briefcase, told the student to come back later, and left. He had an errand to run.

Delamagente spent two hours digitizing the DNA Rowe collected. While it rendered, she replayed her conversation with Mr. Keregosian. He always lifted her spirits. Partly because of his delving questions, he became a sounding board for her project. Today, she asked what he thought about expanding Otto's capabilities beyond research. If Otto could establish a temporal connection between Lucy, Boah, Ump and the Israeli artifacts, it would be huge. Keregosian encouraged her, saying he believed in a strong military and surely this tool would assist the American defense.

Skype bonged and a round, bespeckled face popped up. "Eitan!"

She beamed at one of the few people she considered a friend. Honest and straightforward, he never failed to live up to his surname. He typed on two keyboards at once because no single buffer could keep up with his fingers. He and Otto were in a race to see who could unravel the baffling Birch and Swinnerton-Dyer conjecture. Solving it required a solid mix of intelligence, intuition, and machine computation. Plus, the correct proof won a $1 million prize.

Before she said another word, Sun blurted, "The sensors at your apartment alerted."

Kali's house was connected to his campus security network. Profiles of Sandy, Sean, Mr. Winters and Kali were given a pass, but anyone else triggered an alarm.

"Someone is in your house."

Chapter 18

Wednesday

Kali collided with Rowe as he limped up the stairs, scattering an armload of magazines and documents across the concrete. Her throat was so tight, she squeaked an apology.

"Where are you off to in such a hurry?" Rowe kneeled awkwardly, retrieving the scattered papers with Kali's help.

"Someone broke into my house!" Her voice cracked and tears welled, almost blinding her as she bent to help him. "I'm worried about my dog," she sniffed, shoving handfuls of wrinkled sheets into Rowe's arms before scooting around him.

"Wait." He poked his chin toward a curbside handicap spot. "I'll drive."

She swiped at her eyes and accepted his offer with a nod. Faster was good. She jumped into a big old Mercedes sedan, exterior sparkling, wheels spotless, and dashboard an iridescent black wafting the perfume of Armor All. Before she could give directions, Rowe turned onto her street.

"How did—" A white shape darted into the path of the car and froze. "Sandy!" Kali screamed as Rowe slammed on the brakes.

The Lab stared doe-eyed at the mechanical behemoth, front legs splayed under his shoulders, hackles up like a punk hairdo, tail glued to his one shaking leg.

Kali threw open the door and raced to his side. His head jerked toward her. The flattened ears perked and tail wagged low on his backside as she locked her arms around his trembling neck, breathing in the musky smell of terror.

"It's OK, boy," she whispered over and over. "It's OK."

Rowe pulled over and was guiding Kali and Sandy to the curb when Mr. Winters hobbled over, mouth tight in his kind face. Rowe said something Kali didn't hear and disappeared.

"Don't you worry, kitten. Sandy would never run away. All his hunting's done in our kitchens."

Kali tried to answer, but couldn't focus. Mr. Winters patted her hair as though protecting her. "Did you leave a key for the utility man? He got in with no trouble. Probably who let our Sandy out."

Rowe trotted back. "Hello—Mr. Winters, right? Kali mentioned you. I'm Zeke Rowe."

Kali rose, but kept one hand on Sandy. Mr. Winters eyed her tenderly while Rowe scanned the surroundings, lips set in a hard line.

"Zeke, this is Mr. Winters. We watch out for each other, although he usually carries the heavier load." Tears sprang to her eyes, but she blinked them away.

"We'll be even when the hourglass is empty, kitten." Mr. Winters nodded in agreement with himself.

"Can you describe the man you saw, Mr. Winters?"

"My eyesight's going so I use this." Mr. Winters plucked a camera phone from his pocket. "My granddaughter gave it to me. I take pictures of the neighborhood and check them later. It's how I know what happens all day. This," he tapped the image, "is the same gent from when you two were off in Israel, but he didn't wear his uniform today. See," and he pulled up another. Both showed a medium sized, muscular man with a deep tan. In one, he wore a blousy grey shirt, an Aussie hat and wrap-around shades. In the other, it was tan with an unreadable water company logo, dark brown Dockers, and work boots. "Same guy."

Rowe chuckled. "You remind me of a gunny I served with."

Mr. Winters eyed Rowe. "Yeah, lots of us like that. We figure things out with nothin' but spit and shinola."

Rowe waved at the door. "Wouldn't take much to crack these locks."

Mr. Winters scowled. "If he can write Seabee with two letters, he could break in. Landlord's promised for years to fix them. Morals of a turpitude, that man."

Rowe turned to Delamagente. "Who has a key?"

"Mr. Winters, Sean, me. Cat. University Housing." Her right leg started vibrating.

"Would Cat lend her key to anyone?"

Delamagente shook her head. "She isn't trusting," but Rowe saw something ping.

"What are you thinking?"

"Saturday before DARPA, a Fred Kaczynski showed up at my lab. He didn't enter through security, which means he had a key, but the guard says no."

"Why was he there?"

"Meeting a friend he said, but there's no record of her, either."

"That picture you took—is this him?"

"No. Fred was more doughboy than GI Joe."

"Was Fred tall—six and a half feet?"

"No, about my height."

"Gunny, can you send it to me?" He'd compare it to Kaczynski.

"Yeah, I know how to do that. My granddaughter again. They're smart these days."

"Email it to Eitan Sun, Zeke. He can grab Fred's photo from the onsite cameras." Rowe's stomach tightened, but he said nothing.

Small world. A geek named Eitan Sun had once saved Rowe's life.

As Delamagente called Sun, Rowe considered the intruder. If this was the thug who attacked him in Israel, then Delamagente was the target, not himself. He wished he'd asked Duck's friends to stay.

"Eitan—" Delamagente paused to listen. "I'll explain

later. Zeke Rowe sent a snapshot to you… Can you match it to the man who came to my lab three Sundays ago?" Her face tightened as she listened. "I'm not sure—" She frowned and continued. "OK. Just see if it's the same person. Please?"

Mr. Winters turned to her. "Hey, kitten. Sandy's a touch nervous from all this. We'll eat dinner and watch a show till you get back."

As Mr. Winters and Sandy left, Delamagente called the police and Rowe called James. Rowe waited on hold, enjoying Delamagente's indignant, "What do you mean I can't file a complaint without proof of a break-in? How do you think my dog ran away?" She gave a good argument—"Anyone who belongs in my house knows about Sandy—do you have a pet? ... How would I know what they used—I'm not into B&E." Rowe was sure they heard because she was screaming, but they remained unimpressed.

James asked, "How the hell did you come up with a picture?"

"Old half-blind gunny next door uses a camera phone to keep an eye on the neighborhood. I think this is related to our case. Can you send your people over—and slap one of those anti-theft stickers on Mr. Winters' door? And Kali's." There was something else he needed to ask, and then he remembered. "Did Carston Devore call yet? It'd be nice to know if this is the man he left DARPA with."

"No. *Times* still says he's on assignment."

"He's avoiding me, too. I stopped at his office with urgent information. Got nowhere, but the receptionist was worried."

"I'll send an agent by."

They talked a few more minutes and Rowe hung up. Delamagente was still arguing with the police and he couldn't think of anything to do so he sat on the curb. James's team arrived, a matched triplet in dark suits, white rolled sleeves, blue silk ties, and loafers. They ignored Rowe's insights, so he and Delamagente left. The entire trip back to her lab, she ranted about the cops and would Sandy being hit by a car fit their protocols? Rowe added what he could or nodded sagely.

She finally fell silent when she was back in front of Otto, checking on his activity while they'd been gone.

Time to call Bobby, see what he found.

"My team found four sets of fingerprints. One's probably Delamagente. Another's worn down so should be her neighbor." Age smoothed out fingerprint whorls. "The last two, one'll be her son and the other if we're lucky, our intruder."

Or her ex or a date or Sean's friends, but they might get a break. James kept talking.

"We also found two surveillance bugs. One in the back of a clock in the kitchen and the other in the living room. Ajit is tracing them."

That surprised Rowe. Why bug her home? As far as he knew, Delamagente did all her work at Columbia, but Rowe located no hidden cameras yesterday when he dropped off the note and checked around with a sniffer James swore would find anything.

Thankfully Sean was gone. Not a day passed on the dig Delamagente didn't tell a funny story about him or wonder aloud what she'd do when he left for college. The bond between those two was more Krazy Glue than Elmer's.

As Rowe disconnected, his phone chirped again. It had a Columbia prefix.

"Rowe." He put a gruff edge on his voice. He didn't have time to chat with administrators.

"Zeke Rowe. Eitan Sun. Kalian Delamagente asked me to help you."

"Dr. Sun—"

"Eitan."

Rowe wanted to ask Sun if he ever did work for the SEALs, but decided to wait until they met in person. "I appreciate your help."

"Fred Kaczynski hid his face from the cameras, but I got patches from his ear, neck and temple. He's not Kali's intruder. Skin color, body build, facial structure—nothing matches."

Sun spoke in a soothing, mellow tone without the pauses people use to allow their mouth to catch up with their brain.

"There's an 89%—" He muttered what sounded like *prime number*, followed by a clatter more jackhammer than typing, "...chance this is the man in Mr. Winters' photograph... The apartment's automated surveillance de-activates when a life form included in the pre-programmed parameters enters. When it found Mr. Winters, it shut down. An error which has been rectified."

Neither man spoke. Five seconds passed and ten, before Sun said. "You remember me." A statement, not a question.

Rowe stared into a middle distance, seeing events he struggled daily to bury, as clear as if they happened yesterday. "You flooded a Bedouin camp with sightings of a stranded Coalition unit. That gave Duck Peters all the time he needed to rescue me. If not for you, I'd be dead."

A text came in from James. *Call me.*

"The police—"

"More likely FBI."

Rowe relaxed. "Glad to work with you again."

Chapter 19

"Got something?"

"We're going to update the software that runs Delamagente's webcam. Whoever planted the bugs will have to physically access them for a reset. I lined up an agent-bodyguard for Delamagente who will follow anyone suspicious. Make an excuse for her to arrive this evening."

Rowe tingled with excitement. In the last few weeks, Demsky had been killed, Delamagente tailed to Israel, her home broken into, and Rowe attacked. DARPA was some sort of tipping point, but he had no clue why. This was their first real break.

James continued, voice tighter. "This doesn't make sense, Zeke. They should be after Stockbury's research. Why the interest in Delamagente?"

Rowe paced the narrow University hallway, head down, oblivious to the students who veered around him, the angry stares, or the noise of his shoes on the old tile floor. "I'm not sure. Yet."

In fact, Rowe had been asking himself the same question. Though Delamagente called her AI a research tool, it used the same methods cyberexperts did.

What became clear at her presentation was, this could be applied to submarines.

There was a connection, Rowe just didn't see it yet. He would bet his Ph.D. they were following Delamagente's work with Otto, waiting for her to complete it.

"I'll get back to you," and disconnected. He jumped in his

car, made one stop, and then hurried over to Columbia's Department of Public Safety. He shook hands all around and extended the box of donuts as an ice-breaker. The officers grimaced like he insulted them, so he tucked the pink box under his arm and explained he worked late Sundays, wanted to chat with the man who covered that shift. *That would be Hector Rosado and he's off.* No problem. He'd check back later. Rowe offered to leave the donuts, but they said no one would eat them, so Rowe took his pink box to Delamagente's lab where he found Catherine Stockbury.

"The presentation hunk."

Stockbury wore a black sleeveless blouse that clung to her curves, tucked into grey light-weight capris. Her hair was pulled into a high ponytail that tumbled past her shoulders in a tawny waterfall. She batted long-lashed bedroom eyes as she fingered a flash drive that hung into her cleavage.

"I like your older-man aura."

Rowe didn't think of himself as 'older', but Stockbury made it sound sexy. She placed a finger to her lips. Rowe tightened his grip on the donut box like a life preserver.

Thank God Kali arrived.

"Allow me to introduce Dr. Zeke Rowe, DARPA mystery man, my colleague in Israel and Columbia's newest paleoanthropology professor. Catherine Stockbury, officemate extraordinaire." Her voice shook slightly and her eyes were red and puffy.

"You can call me Cat," she purred. "I feel like we're already intimate friends."

No wonder Stockbury had boy trouble. Rowe turned to Delamagente and cocked his head.

"I'm fine, Zeke. Sandy's fine. He and Mr. Winters are having an early dinner and watching *Evolution of Dogs* on Discovery Channel. What's in the box?"

"Here are the donuts I promised—anything but glazed, right sweetheart?"

Kali glared. "Cat won't believe—" She stopped short as she peered inside and picked an old-fashioned. "We can talk about it later—*sweetheart*."

Stockbury's eyes moved between Rowe and Kali until she seemed to arrive at a decision she didn't share.

"I love love love donuts." Stockbury selected chocolate buttermilk and asked, "What's with your trigger fingers?"

"Got the tips chopped off by some bad guys so I couldn't shoot."

Stockbury grimaced. "And your limp—same bad guys?"

"They didn't want me to escape."

"Was it Dean Manfried?"

"Porter?" That stopped Rowe.

"He can't keep qualified professors."

Kali saved him from finding an answer. "While we were out, Otto completed the DNA integration from your Israeli bones, Zeke. Want to see what changed?" Her cheeks flushed and her eyes brightened

"I do," Stockbury mumbled through a mouthful of donut.

Kali's eyes locked onto a male and female who had just appeared in a bucolic clearing. Both their heads were larger than in prior scenes and their stomachs flatter than a vegetable-rich diet would predict. "I can't believe this is Lucy and Raza." Awe filled Kali's voice. "Lucy's face is so clear, freckles even show."

"All this from adding DNA?" Rowe wouldn't have believed it if he weren't seeing it.

"It's like exploding a zip file," Kali responded absently. "DNA contains all the phenotypic and genotypic data—mental and physical characteristics—to reproduce a species."

Rowe's heart raced as he studied the scene. "The indigenous life and volcanics are African, which means these two or descendants with the same mitochondrial DNA migrated to Israel."

Kali touched a tear dimpling Lucy's cheek. "Lucy and I both have loved ones to defend."

That startled Rowe. "You mean Sandy?"

"The intruder—it must be Fletcher, Sean's dad. He wants to see Sean."

"Does Mr. Winters' photo match Fletcher?"

"No, but I filed a restraining order against him so he would have to send someone."

"Why break in?"

Kali shrugged. "Why does he do anything he does?"

Rowe left to update James, passing a man he'd hoped never to see again.

Cat leaped to her feet. "Kalian Delamagente. Dr. Wynton Fairgrove."

Kali pressed 'screen hide' and Lucy's face dissolved into a binary formula, then turned to face the pedagogue who spear-headed her DARPA failure.

Dr. Fairgrove wore a rugby-striped polo over tailored jeans and white-stitched navy Top-Siders. He should be on the pages of *Gentlemen's Quarterly* rather than in her unkempt lab. He extended a soft hand, not what she expected from a paleoanthropologist. She smelled Old Spice and lemon drops.

"How many?"

"Excuse me?"

"How many computer programmers does it take to screw in a light bulb?" He pointed at the zeros and ones floating in a marquee across her screen.

"Wow. No one's ever gotten that."

Dr. Fairgrove chuckled as he punched buttons on his phone. "I, too, would share my research with only trusted colleagues. If you're wrong, they denigrate you. If you're right, they steal it."

Was he warning her or hoping she'd warm to his honesty? He continued, unfazed by her silence. "I asked Catherine to introduce us. I'm sure you intended a different outcome at the presentation. Do you mind sharing?"

Kali cocked her head to the side. Why not? He would have heard everything at the presentation if Otto had cooperated. She synopsized her research, but left out the new DNA results. "I apologize for using you as an example."

"Ah, and I had hoped you were interested."

Kali blushed. "No I didn't—I mean…" and she sputtered to a halt, not sure what to say next.

"What's your time frame for completion?"

Kali picked her words carefully. "I have acquired backing which will speed the process up."

Dr. Fairgrove snatched a picture from Kali's desk. "This must be your son. A good-looking boy and a musician." A dreaminess softened the scientist's face. Kali started to tell him about Sean, but Cat tugged him to the door. He seemed to resist, as though he wanted to listen, then stuffed his phone into his pocket and shuffled after Cat.

"Join us, Kal. Afternoon Tea is in Dr. Fairgrove's honor."

This Columbia tradition gave up-and-coming researchers a chance to mingle with the era's leading researchers. Fairgrove's warm smile made the invitation personal.

"I'll try," but she wouldn't. Gossiping was as appealing to her as drinking vinegar.

As they left, Dr. Fairgrove whispered, "The answer's one."

"One?"

"It takes one programmer to screw a light bulb in because they count in binary," and he winked.

Chapter 20

It had been too long since Kali felt excited about a man, and now two. She took a deep breath, trying to focus, only to be interrupted by a smiling Fairgrove and a seething Rowe.

She blurted, "Dr. Fairgrove—"

"Please, call me Wynton."

"And Dr. Rowe. Have you two met?"

Annoyance flushed Fairgrove's face and a forced calm overtook Rowe's.

"Hello, Wyn. Can't say I've missed you since our days at Max Planck."

"Of course. Dr. Rowe. It's good to see you again, too."

He offered a cursory handshake. "Excuse me. I need to take this." His fingers stabbed at his phone as he stepped into the hall.

"Why is he here?" Rowe asked in a tone Kali would use to discuss pantry moths. She hadn't realized how childish he could be.

"He's a colleague, Zeke. Is it impossible that you treat him with respect?"

"There are only two things I consider impossible, world peace and a friendship with Fairgrove. If you're as smart as I think you are, you will soon agree."

Before she could respond, Fairgrove returned. "I hope you will join me at the reception, Kalian. I'd like to hear more about your research."

He left without waiting for an answer. Rowe's jaw clenched. Kali stifled a grin.

Fairgrove glanced back at the building, hoping Delamagente had already fallen for his star-power, but instead found Catherine Stockbury. He'd used groupies like Catherine his entire life. He acknowledged her and she turned on a tilted hip and left.

He flipped through the photographs taken before—what was his name? Rove?—interrupted. He zoomed in on Delamagente's monitor, tapped a hi-tech app that adjusted for curve and glare, and brought the corrected image into focus. It showed a fissured graben valley, littered with bleached bones and footprints turned to stone by the passage of time. Atop the precipice, a male stood limned against the moonlight, a *Homo erectus* judging by the vaulted forehead and the graceful upright stance. One hand gripped a staff as his eyes scoured the chasm. Hiding in the shadows was a *Homo habilis* female. Her eyes canted upward at the male. Tension rippled through her neck and shoulders. The hair on her lightly-furred body stood on end and her protruding snout stretched in a tight line across her flat face. She was a beautiful specimen of the extinct species.

But this image didn't exist. He shivered at the thought it might be the result of the AI, Otto. The reception would be a perfect time to ask.

Rowe knew Dr. Wynton Fairgrove as a devious liar and a probable murderer, all prettily packaged with rugged movie-star looks and a skin-deep reputation. Women he got close to disappeared and their brilliant research ended up published under Fairgrove's name. Delamagente and Stockbury of course would catch his attention. They were undergrads, unpublished, unfunded, academically vulnerable, and on the verge of changing the world with the product of their brains.

Rowe sat on top of Stockbury's desk, one foot planted on her chair, the other dangling over the side in an effort to radiate a peaceful serenity he didn't feel. He pulled a pencil from his pocket and tossed it in the air as he spoke. He began this habit after Paulette's death, when his tortured subconscious demanded distraction.

"Fairgrove wasn't talking on his phone." He eyed Kali, curious what her response would be.

"What do you mean?"

Here I go. Rowe flipped his pencil twice before answering. "He lied, but why?" Rowe suspected Fairgrove was buying time to record images of Delamagente and her lab.

"Is it so odd he made up an excuse to talk to me?" Rowe stiffened. He didn't expect this.

"I didn't mean he wouldn't… I meant…" but everything he thought of sounded defensive and petty so he leaned back, scratched a shoulder, and changed the subject.

"If Otto can use data as small as DNA to search—well, that would be revolutionary." He flipped his pencil.

Something flickered through Delamagente's eye.

Rowe cocked his head and said as innocently as he could manage, "For example, the military catalogues submarines, tanks, and other weaponry by magnetic signatures, but these can't be used from a geographic distance, which means their worthless for tracking. If Otto can change that, DARPA will pay attention."

Delamagente's eyes glazed over for long seconds before stuttering, "I don't know," then disappeared into a world that didn't include Rowe. He waited a minute, two, before standing.

"I guess I'll go. Oh—I have a friend, an anthropology grad student, coming to Columbia to finish her dissertation. Can she stay with you a few weeks?"

Delamagente's body turned toward him, but he doubted she saw him. "Kali?"

"Sure. No problem. Where would I be without your ancient bones?"

His phone buzzed saving Rowe from a response. He waved goodbye as he answered.

"Bobby. All arranged."

"Good. She arrives tonight."

"Anyone try to hack Stockbury yet?"

"No, and we better not be wrong about this. It's hell getting those Tridents to call in. Their security depends upon being unreachable."

"Fairgrove was just here, making friends with Delamagente. That puts him close enough to Stockbury's computer to cause all sorts of trouble. As a visiting professor, he'll be inside the firewalls."

"You think he might try to infect it remotely? I don't know. I ran him through NCIC. A few problems, but he's never been involved in illegal activities or any police or federal investigation."

"Go deeper," and he shared the rumors that Fairgrove used grad students to fuel his research. "Delamagente or Stockbury could be next. If we can catch him, we have leverage to force him to turn on his partners. Get me his published writing. I'll look for a pattern." He waited silently as a student walked by. "Has Ajit traced Keregosian's emails?"

"When I ask, he says 'meh', which is half-way between 'Hell yes' and 'No way'."

Chapter 21

Damn Zeke and his dual personality. In Israel, Kind Patient Zeke labored beside her, one of the crew. With that Zeke, Kali imagined a future where they researched a forgotten corner of the world together. No politics. No distractions. No hidden agendas. For Kind Patient Zeke, she'd crawl to the narrow tip of that emotional limb sure the fruit would be worth it.

But lately, all she saw was Preoccupied Distracted Zeke. This automaton always worked an agenda, never noticed her discomfort, asked her advice, or listened to her ideas. For this Zeke, she wouldn't even climb the tree much less reach for the fruit.

Still, there were the rare appearances of Cerebral Zeke which invariably tweaked her imagination and explained his worldwide reputation. After he mentioned magnetic signatures, she researched for hours and decided tracking them was possible with clever programming, unique scripts, and a lot of work. She texted Eitan and sat back to await his answer.

Shouts interrupted her. A crowd gathered below on the Engineering Terrace. Cat wandered into Kali's narrow field of vision, eyes fixed across the patio on Wyn. His back was hunched, arms tight against his body, head shaking as he talked on his phone. Kali was about to turn away when a figure caught her attention. His carriage was familiar, but hair and clothes were wrong. Hands in his pockets, he zig-zagged through the crowd toward Wyn.

Before Kali could make sense of it, an alarm clanged and

the acrid stench of smoke reached her senses. In moments, two firefighters were in her lab, shouting *Leave everything ma'am. Get out!* Kali grabbed her briefcase with the portable version of Otto and fled.

A fireman shouted into his comm device, '*Start with the third floor'*—Kali's floor. Rowe almost raced into the building, but something made him stop. He pulled back, letting his brain automatically sort through the scene. It didn't take long to realize something was wrong. Firefighters in tennis shoes... Non-FDNY uniforms... Carrying equipment like it was their first time.... How'd they get here so soon?

And why was Fairgrove calmly smiling into his phone?

Now he got it. This was the plan to steal NEV. Rowe did a full circle and another, searching the crowd for the contact that must be there. He stopped at a man with coffee-colored skin, a punk cut, blue eyes and a boyish face. The beard was a nice touch, but the gait gave him away. Rowe uploaded the image to James.

Kali's headache rumbled awake. Her purse was up in her lab, hopefully not being destroyed in the fire, so she dug through her pockets for aspirin.

"Does he look familiar?" Rowe nodded toward the figure she'd seen from her window.

"Yes! I feel like I know him."

"Carl Hamar. He dyed his hair, grew a beard, and added colored contacts."

Kali squinted. "Why would he do that?"

"To create a lousy disguise."

Kali started toward the man who a week ago she considered a soulmate, but turned when she heard her name.

"Dean Manfried. Hello."

She had left him two messages since returning from the dig, but he'd been 'busy'. All she knew was he had questions about Otto. The Dean whined chronically about Otto's massive electricity costs. Each time he brought the subject up, she wondered if this was the day his patience ended.

He waved a pudgy hand as he bumped through the crowd. His rotund figure strained at the buttons of his charcoal suit. Perspiration dotted his domed forehead and his neck spilled over the collar like a frosted red donut. He offered Rowe a perfunctory nod, but focused on Kali. Whatever he wanted to say wouldn't be good, so Kali jumped in first.

"I trust you received the check from Mr. Keregosian. I'm assured his support will continue."

The Dean mumbled. "Yes, quite munificent." He tightened the knot on his tie, squeezing another inch of florid neck over his collar, and fingered the thin layer of hair on his freckled dome. "No surprise, though, now that Dr. Fairgrove is working with you. He believes with guidance, you can become an excellent researcher. I hope you appreciate his kindness."

Kali bristled and started to snap a reply, but Manfried dismissed her with a truncated flutter of two fingers and tottered off.

"Kissinger once said University politics made him long for the simplicity of the Middle East," Rowe said as he pulled an envelope from his pocket. "My friend arrives today. This covers room and board. Let her pay whatever else she wants. She has a grant."

"Sure." She took it and turned to find Carl, but he'd disappeared.

Chapter 22

"Mr. Al-Zahrawi would like to talk to you."

Fairgrove glared at the obsequious individual who stood inches from his side. His bleached hair shone with grease. Crumbs of food clung to a scruffy beard. Dirt ringed his cuffs, and an unsavory odor drifted from his body. Fairgrove edged away, fearful it would leech into his $2,500 suit.

"Give me the phone." Where did Salah find such pedestrian help? "Who is this creature?" he hissed.

"He represents me. That is all you need care about."

"How do I know I can trust him?"

Al-Zahrawi laughed. "Ms. Delamagente considers him a friend."

He sighed heavily. "Salah. I worked tirelessly constructing this fire drill. You will own Stockbury's research shortly."

"We need Ms. Delamagente's also. We could not penetrate her firewalls and she took the back-up with her."

"That's not my fault—"

"My people failed three times to steal the Otto she carries so resolutely. I have reprimanded them appropriately. You must retrieve the AI for me. If you cannot, her son will provide the requisite leverage."

Fairgrove cringed. How far he'd fallen. At seventeen, he had everything: movie star looks, charisma, a brilliant girlfriend. When she unexpectedly died, he published her revolutionary research under his name. To his surprise, the work earned him the Presidential Young Investigator Award and a reprint in the *Proceedings of the National Academy of Sciences*. His striking appearance, vibrant youth, and consummate humility made him a favorite on the talk show circuit. They called him the brightest new star in the scientific sky. The glow faded when his next project failed abysmally. Frantic to quell rumors his early success was a fluke, he decided to see if what worked once would again.

It took so little to steal Haddith's heart. Intimate dinners, stories about his sad past. He must have been the first man to love her chunky body as well as the genius of her mind. They became engaged. She excused the omission of her name from their pioneering research because *his* triumph was *theirs*. He ticked off the days to their nuptials, desperate for a way out.

Enter Salah Al-Zahrawi. Fairgrove met the earnest, polite young man at a local bistro. He immediately understood Fairgrove's bright future would be crippled by this dowdy female. He offered to help for free, collect the debt later. Fairgrove bought the man a drink to seal the deal.

Within a week, she vanished. Wherever Fairgrove went, sympathy for his loss found him, until once again, his research failed. He wasted no time selecting another wunderkind grad student, eager to participate in Dr. Wynton Fairgrove's next project. But when he suggested she include his name when she published, she refused. When Fairgrove slapped her (on the recommendation of Al-Zahrawi), she swore to tell authorities her suspicions about Haddith. Al-Zahrawi again solved the problem.

Looking back, that was when power passed. Now, the man was a leech, riding on Fairgrove's notoriety like so many others, sucking life from him bit by bit.

Still, he needed this thug one last time.

Al-Zahrawi interrupted his thoughts.

"I know about your money problems, Doctor."

"They are none of your business." Al-Zahrawi had no right intruding on his finances.

"But I respect a man who lives on the edge."

Fairgrove started to stutter a response, but settled on,

"Huh?"

"One more thing. You must get rid of Dr. Zeke Rowe. People like him, they are bulldogs. Once they catch a scent, they never let go. Do you not agree?"

Fairgrove remained silent. Maybe he'd disagree. Maybe next time. "Yes, I see your point."

"Can you arrange he lose his professorship?"

Fairgrove doubted it. "Of course I can."

He felt power shift back. His firm response put Al-Zahrawi in his place. This spy business was easier than it sounded.

Chapter 23

Rowe edged in front of Stockbury and Delamagente as they approached the lab. The hall reeked of saltpeter and potassium. The closer he got, the tighter the skin on his neck puckered. He picked up a burnt fuse, probably from a candle or homemade smoke bomb and certainly what convinced Delamagente the building was on fire.

He held an arm out like a bar. "I'll go first."

He inched inside, slowly studying every surface, not looking for anything in particular, just whatever caught his attention. Stockbury's side still resembled Martha Stewart on steroids and Delamagente's a mad scientist. Same open books. Same cupboards ajar. The light had been turned off, but Delamagente might have done that as she left.

Something was missing. Rowe mentally ran through an inventory of the room. "Your sweatshirt is gone, Kali, the one you keep on your chair."

Delamagente said nothing as she deposited herself in front of Otto and started typing.

Stockbury wrinkled her nose. "I'll give your regrets to Wyn, Kali. His heart—or ego—will be crushed." She blew Rowe a kiss and left.

"Someone tried to hack my computer." She entered a password, and then stared at a logo in the corner of the screen. "I installed a retinal scanner and a weight sensor. Whoever sat here failed both so Otto loaded a spoof of my desktop, activated a keystroke recorder and taped him through the webcam. If he uploaded malware, Otto will attach a RAT—

Remote Access Trojan to the outgoing message. It grabs the IP address and gives me access to the system." She shook her head. "They're either too dumb or too smart for that. Darn."

Her security page booted up. "Here's the recording."

A masked firefighter sat in front of the camera. Kali checked the log. "He—or she—used the password I hid under my keyboard." She rattled through a series of keys. "He searched 'Otto', 'Trident', 'DARPA', 'research', and the directory. When those came up empty, he gave up."

Rowe whistled. "How do I get this security set-up?"

When Zeke departed, Kali collected her briefcase and left, too. Her head throbbed and she hoped playing with Sandy, watching TV, and going to bed early would ease it. As she approached her building, she found a wholesome twenty-something honey blonde stretched out on the stoop. She wore a lightweight denim jacket, faded jeans and a t-shirt that said, 'I have a Ph.D. in Anthropology. Do you want fries with that?' A duffle back rested on the toe of a hiking boot and a tartan backpack leaned against the step.

And then Kali remembered.

"Annie—Zeke's friend! I'm so sorry."

"No worries—Kali, right? Annie Sams. I'm glad Zeke mentioned me." She grinned as she stuck out a chapped hand. "I'm so appreciative I can crash here. I won't be any trouble—in and out like a ghost."

Kali laughed. "That's two of us, and Sandy—my dog—will love the company. With my son gone for the summer, I think he's lonely."

"They do thrive in a community, don't they? I get furious at people who stash their dogs in the backyard." Annie shared a few choice words about those people and then whooped as Sandy landed smack on her chest when Kali opened the door.

"Sandy! Down!" Kali yelled as she grabbed him by the scruff of his neck. "Allow me to introduce Sandy, Defender Dog, although he has a lot of bed lab in him. No yard dog here."

Annie crouched and let Sandy sniff her hand. "Dogs and wolves have nearly identical DNA, yet a dog would kill a wolf, or give his life in the effort, to save us."

Sandy panted in tempo with the thump of his tail. Kali thought of Ump.

"A dash of gray, huh, Sandy?" Annie scratched his neck. "What is he, eight years old?"

"Nine. The pound planned to euthanize him. I got there just in time."

"I move too much to own a dog. Can I adopt Sandy while I'm here?" The honest enthusiasm in Annie's voice overwhelmed Kali.

"He's all yours, but avoid the landlord. My lease forbids pets." Kali pointed toward Sean's room. "Towels and linens are in the closet. Make yourself at home."

Annie dropped her duffle in the bedroom and poked her head in the bath, then plopped down on the living room floor and leaned forward, straight-legged, grabbing her toes with her fingertips. Kali brought ice water for both of them and asked, "Zeke said you're finishing a Ph.D.?"

"He's being nice. I'm a tenured grad. The ten-year plan. Every time I get close to completion, I start more research."

They talked for a while about the neighborhood and Columbia's library. Kali wanted to ask how Annie knew Zeke, but decided it was too nosy for their first night.

Annie yawned. "I like a bit of exercise before going to sleep. Do you mind if I walk Sandy? Check out the area?"

"Sure." Kali bit her lip. "There's a guy hanging around. He's harmless, just wants info on my son." She shook her head. "Actually, I'm not sure what he wants."

"I'll lock the doors when I return."

Kali walked them out and laughed as a jet of warm air from the sidewalk vent sent Sandy into a frenzied circle. After they faded into the evening, she phoned Sean's father.

"Whoever you asked to spy on me broke into my apartment and let Sandy out, Fletcher. Tell him to leave me alone or I call the police."

She held the phone away from her ear as Fletcher shouted.

"Of course it's you. Who else would it be?" She raked through the mail, not listening to the angry retort. She didn't understand what she'd seen in him.

"I got his picture, Fletch. If you continue to stalk me, I turn both of you in," and she placed the phone back in the cradle.

Annie listened to the conversation. Delamagente was tougher than she seemed. The man sounded like he had no idea what she was talking about. Plus, Annie would bet Fletcher still loved his ex.

To anyone watching, she was just another Columbia co-ed on her phone walking the dog. When Delamagente hung up, Annie lowered her voice and said, "Cloned Delamagente's phone. She called her son's father, Fletcher, at 9:06 pm. He denies being the intruder." She logged into a secure FBI server. "A search for Fletcher bio…" She tapped through several databases. "…turns up no record, no arrests, no legal problems. He's thirty-two, graduated from the same high school Kalian Delamagente attended. He passed up a partial scholarship to work for an Uncle in a garage. Still works there. Taxes filed and paid on time as Single. Excellent credit rating."

Everything she taped was shared immediately with her cloud back-up. If anything happened, her team could access her latest notes on the case.

Annie sauntered onward, cataloging everything—cars parked along the street, houselights, and neighbors taking trash out. She greeted other dog walkers and checked cars trolling by. A deli delivery boy almost knocked her over as he raced to an apartment.

Everything looked fine. It was her job to keep it that way.

That evening, Eitan Sun alerted Rowe to the first overstuffed email. A malware program invisibly attached a piece of Stockbury's research to a note she sent, blind copying a remailer who bounced it around the world before dropping it off a digital cliff in Bulgaria. Rowe told Stockbury. Within eighteen hours, Stockbury sent twenty more emails, each with pieces of her research hidden in the signature. By Stockbury's calculation, the hijackers now possessed the entire revised NEV program with its hidden backdoor. All they needed to do was turn it into goo.

What continued to confuse Rowe was why they would jeopardize their hijacking plan to spy on Delamagente. Laslo Hemren's subterfuge, breaking into her apartment, the attempt to hack her computer—it made no sense.

Unless Otto had become important to their goals.

He rolled it around in his head, testing scenarios. Only one worked: The first submarine was successfully hijacked but the terrorists had been unable to find it. They hoped Delamagente's Otto would solve that. But how? Sure, Otto showed potential, but the skill they required could be months—years—away.

Rowe tracked a smattering of clues that ultimately proved worthless. The burnt wick could be bought on numerous internet sites. The fingerprints from the keyboard weren't in the system. Worse, nothing fit with any other pieces of the case. The only good news was Sun matched the fake utility man's height and build to the Volvo driver last seen with Devore.

While Roe got nowhere, the Navy reached out to the Trident Refit Facilities—TRF—to warn them of the potential breech. The TRFs were tightly-controlled, but populated by dozens of government contractors fixing, repairing, swapping out, and advising. That was a weakness Al-Zahrawi could exploit by blackmailing a freelancer with a gambling problem or a drug addiction, or simple money lust.

Most of the Tridents were deployed, so the Navy sent a message that would download when the sub made a routine contact with the satellite-based Submarine Satellite

Information Exchange Subsystem (SSIXS). Since they couldn't transfer Catherine Stockbury's patch in that way, it instructed they re-install the entire system from back-ups to correct a possible compromise. The problem was the Navy didn't know when they would call in, or if it would be in time.

The FBI's best guess was the virus would go live at a predetermined time. It was James' job to stop it before that happened. If he didn't, America's submarine defense would be at the mercy of whatever ocean terrain they were traversing when the virus shut it down.

So far they had reached none of the deployed boats.

Chapter 24

Thursday

The muggy heat woke Kali early. She shushed Sandy out of Annie's room, filled his bowl with a half-can of Pedigree, and flipped the fan on to cool the apartment. He devoured breakfast, one eye on Annie's door as though worried the new human would eat his food. Kali patted his downy head, changed into shorts and a t-shirt, and went for a run. The sweat rolling from her pores and the burn in her legs felt good. The steady pounding of her feet relaxed her.

As she ran, Kali evaluated the changes to her life. She had never lived with a stranger. She went from parents to grandparents to Sean. She had never lived with a woman her age. Should they eat together? How did they share costs? Would Annie expect an apartment key? Should she worry about waking Annie in the morning or keeping her up at night?

Truth, Kali considered no one a friend except Cat, and Cat was so unlike any human on the planet, Kali didn't think she counted. She heard stories about talking through emotional problems with women who wore concerned frowns, but what did that mean? Should she bare her soul or encourage Annie to? And if so, when? Would she seem cold if she didn't or crazy if she did?

The more Kali worried, the faster she ran until she was sprinting. She decided to skip the rest of her jog, go to work before Annie woke up, and let the questions bubble around in her subconscious for a day.

When she got home, Annie was gone, which immediately dropped Kali's anxiety. She showered, dressed in comfortable lemon yellow crop pants, layered pastel tank tops, and woven sandals, and plopped onto a hardback chair in a splotch of sunlight by her kitchenette. During summer, this was the best place in the apartment. She tucked her feet underneath her bottom and started her second cup of coffee.

If Annie likes coffee, I'll have to make a bigger pot.

Sandy trotted in through the dog door and collapsed at her chair for a postprandial nap.

"Oh hell, Sandy, I'll be myself. If I blow it, so what? She leaves in a few weeks anyway."

She put her cup in the sink, brushed her teeth, gathered her purse and briefcase, then set everything down and returned to the kitchen, washed the mug, dried it, and placed it in the cupboard. That's when she saw a note from Annie suggesting dinner. Kali planned to meet with Eitan late in the day so suggested 7 pm and headed to Columbia, feeling unusually upbeat.

Something about Annie made everything seem like an adventure.

As she walked, she mulled over Mr. Keregosian's motives. She wasn't so naïve to think his assistance was free. The fact Zeke with his Navy Intel background was worried, worried her. How much more concerned would he be if he knew she liked Mr. Keregosian's friendly notes, that often they talked about topics close to her heart like the evolution of culture, the roots of religion, and traits they wanted in friends—and Mr. Keregosian had as much difficulty talking to people as she did. What would Zeke think of Mr. Keregosian's six-year-old nephew who was the center of his world, that Al Qaeda terrorists killed his wife, or that he almost didn't contact her worrying she'd mistrust his intentions. She imagined he was her age with bright optimistic eyes and a quick intelligence, with a love of dogs to match her own. She hoped they never met because she didn't want to find out she was wrong.

And what about Wyn? Cat called the Tea long and boring—'like Wyn'. It cooled her interest and she told Kali to 'go for it' Kali resolved to accept Wyn's next invite, should there be one.

Her head was spinning. No wonder she avoided interpersonal relationships.

Chapter 25

Fairgrove called Delamagente's office at least ten times
with no answer and finally decided to drop in unannounced.
Becoming part of her research required he be seen spending
time with her. He stopped first at the men's room to check his
carefully-selected outfit—an expensive short sleeved silk shirt
with Balenciaga linen slacks and Berluti tasseled loafers
without socks. His hair was perfect, bangs at the rakish angle
he'd been told projected a lighthearted approach to the world.
Overall, he reeked of success and achievement.

After a minute in her doorway with an alluring grin
arranged on his face, he gave up and coughed to get her
attention. He couldn't even get a lunch invite out before she
was claiming too much work, but then surprised him by asking
to bounce a few ideas off him. He cordially agreed and she
started in with a discussion on ancient DNA.

It took five minutes to exhaust the fluff that always got
him through these conversations, but Delamagente seemed to
be just warming up. He pleaded a parched throat and
suggested they get a drink. She led the way to the Engineering
Terrace vending machines where they drank coffee sitting in
plastic chairs. The cheap brew made him gag, but he covered
it with a sneeze.

He needed to move this on. "Our research is similar, my
dear. My 3D geometric morphometrics would render your
geography faster with more accuracy, don't you think?"

Fairgrove considered his timing perfect—a progressive
growth of fellowship resulting in her request they collaborate

on her project. Except, she lapsed into silence, eyes focused on some middle distance. He reached for her fingers. Surely his touch would draw the words from her mouth. She shook her head.

"I tried geometric morphometrics. They made no difference, Wyn." Fairgrove bit back his annoyance. He hated that moniker, but would train her another day.

"Is it a speed problem? My IBM laptop is quite speedy. I use it to manage all my research."

Delamagente's jaw clenched, but she offered an agreeable nod as she stood. "There are few people who understand what I'm doing. How can I thank you?"

Fairgrove jumped at the opportunity. "Join me for lunch. You can tell me what dreams shape your life."

She stuttered, checked her phone, then no surprise to him, agreed. In thirty minutes, they stood in the foyer of a restaurant Delamagente said she had always wanted to go to. The staff greeted Fairgrove by name and guided him to a patio table he called 'my spot'.

She smoothed her hair and hugged her body as the waiter approached.

"Many Columbia professors find this café relaxing." He included just enough condescension to make his point. "You will soon be part of that elite group."

She peered out the window at the people rushing by, phones to their ears, chattering while their eyes saw nothing, arms filled with books. "It gives me perspective, Wyn."

That thought had never crossed his mind. He came here to impress vulnerable young females with the extravagant cost, but Fairgrove knitted his brows.

"Living life for others is perspective enough."

Living life for others is perspective enough. How perfect. He paused so she could marvel at his modern epigram. Just as the silence became uncomfortable, she started.

"When I visited Lucy the other day, she stood on the lip of the Great Rift. A nearby volcano was erupting, spewing columns of fire into the air. Fiery rivers roared down its flanks as though a dam burst. She couldn't have been more than a mile away yet she showed no fear."

Fairgrove didn't understand how this mattered, but he pasted an engrossed expression across his face.

"In the next scene, she and a wolf hunted an Oryx, trailing it up scree slopes and across gullies until the Oryx reached her herd. At that point, Lucy gave up the chase, but the wolf continued."

Fairgrove had been people watching, but when Delamagente's voice dropped to an awe-filled whisper and her eyes found his, he pretended to search for their waiter.

"Water, please!" He motioned toward their glasses

"This is a critical distinction in their decision process, Wyn. Lucy gathered information to make a go-no go on hunting. The wolf did it to inform a hard-wired conclusion he's already reached—*to* hunt. She used free choice and the wolf instinct. The wolf's tenacious way may work, but ours works better or *Canis* would top the food chain."

The waiter dropped off ice water and Wyn took a sip while struggling to convey enthusiasm, but she must have read confusion.

"That's my goal," she reminded him. "To understand."

Now he remembered. He asked about her goals.

She paused, as though listening to herself. "Boy do I sound like a bore."

"To me, you are fascinating." Women wanted to be taken seriously. "By the way, I'm told your security system is excellent. Can you explain it to me? I need one now that I'm part of the Columbia family." He patted her hand. "I'm also curious how Otto works outside of Columbia's network."

Wyn confused Kali. On one hand, they had much in common. When was the last time she talked with someone who read all three volumes in *Baroque Cycle*? They shared an interest in paleoanthropology and children, and he gave off all the signals of wanting to settle down. On the other hand, he didn't ask where she'd like to go for lunch and they ended up in a stuffy and pretentious restaurant—one where he obviously spent a lot of time. When she sarcastically said she always wanted to eat there, he believed her. She found herself jealous of the flood of happy, industrious people who hurried by, outside the window.

In the end, he simply made it easy for her to make the right decision. This year belonged to Sean. The right person would wait.

When they got back to her office, he made himself comfortable on the edge of her desk, a possessive hand on her shoulder, and watched her email populate.

"Another love letter from Porter?"

"Yes. He wants politically-correct research. An oxymoron."

"Don't worry, sweetheart. He'll fall in line now we're working together."

Kali's glare was lost on him, distracted by his own reflection in the monitor. First the Dean, and now Wyn. Where did this come from?

"Which brings up a subject we must chat about." He smoothed his brow while staring into the distance. Kali felt her face pinch, always a precursor to a migraine. She struggled to relax.

"I promised Porter I'd discuss Rowe with you." His tone was weary, but cheerful. "His efforts at Max Planck were spotty at best. Old complaints are resurfacing and I believe your work will suffer from his involvement."

A headache now throbbed behind her eyes. Her doctor said she didn't handle stress well. She placed her hands in her lap and forced her fingers open.

"Why did the school offer him the professorship?"

"They should have asked me first. I could have suggested alternate academes with much more impressive backgrounds."

He knocked on her desk as though that ended the conversation, patted Kali, and left.

On cue, Rowe limped in. He wore a white t-shirt over casual jeans with a Pendleton over it. The rolled up sleeves revealed massive forearms accustomed to physical labor, with a partially-obscured tattoo on the right bicep.

Her jaw unclenched and she swallowed two aspirin.

"You missed Wyn. He complained about you."

He winced as he eased onto Cat's desk. "Someday, I'll tell you the true story of Dr. Wynton Fairgrove." His eyes took on the color of burnt charcoal. There he went again, with his split personality. How did she figure out which was real? If she was going to fall for Zeke, she needed to know what made him tick. "Have you read *Atlas Shrugged*?"

Rowe picked a pencil up and twirled it through his fingers.

"Isn't that a subversive book?"

"Forget it."

"Ayn Rand said, 'Man comes to earth unarmed. His brain is his only weapon.' In *The Fountainhead*. I read it five times." Somehow he got two pencils going, flipping and spinning through the air. "One of my favorite books is *The Poet and the Murderer*, about the notorious forger—"

"—Mark Hofmann." Kali's third-favorite book. "How about the Aubrey–Maturin novels?"

"I started the series while house-bound after knee surgery. I finished eighteen of them before going back to work."

"No one reads eighteen books in what? A month?"

"A week."

Kali giggled. There was a lot more to Zeke Rowe. She took his arm. "You were interested in a security program for your computer? Time to meet Dr. Eitan Sun."

Chapter 26

"Welcome to Eitan's geekosphere." Cluttered didn't begin to describe this room. Trash buried every surface including empty peanut butter jars, soda cans, take-out menus, a tattered burrito, and something green in a pizza box.

"Eitan, Dr. Rowe."

A disembodied voice said, "Yes."

The sole personal touch was a photo of a smiling woman in a floral turban, proudly displayed to the right of Sun's computer.

Rowe asked, "Is this your wife, Dr. Sun?"

There was a muffled gasp from Kali as a round oversized face peeked around the wall of double-stacked thirty-inch monitors. Huge watery eyes peered through tortoise-shell glasses. His complexion was as fair and unlined as a pre-pubescent boy with no hint of beard or mustache. A Giants ball cap covered a thin ragged fringe of hair falling to his shoulders and he wore a stained t-shirt identifying him as *Homo nocturnes*.

Rowe felt at home, warmed by the scruffy disdain for appearance shared by most SEALs.

"Are you OK?" Kali asked, concern tingeing her words.

Sun bobbed his head, more a spasm, like a coiled spring about to pop. Kali caught Rowe's eye and shook her head. He edged forward, close enough to see Sun's fingers flying across two keyboards while he spoke into a wireless headset. Every few seconds, his hands moved across his chest like a choreographed dance.

Rowe turned to Kali. "What's with the hand movements?"

"Those are busy signals in American Sign Language. He says he's almost done."

"I also communicate in Python, Hungarian, Russian, LISP, Visual Basic, SQL, assembly—MIPS and ARM, HTML, XML, and some Bash," Sun added, looking directly at Rowe with the most unusual eyes Rowe had ever seen. They carried the wisdom of generations, the curiosity of a child, and the peace of a man comfortable in his own mind.

"It depends upon the needs of my software friends. Chinese anyone?" Sun offered a carton. "I'm eating orange today."

"Eitan eats by color, which varies with his mood. No thanks," Kali answered. Rowe declined, too, wondering if the fork was to be shared.

Sun rolled toward Rowe. "Cat had a crush on you for a day." His gaze inventoried Rowe's body, not even pausing at the damaged hands as though he, like Rowe, took his handicaps philosophically—a trade-off for some past adventure.

Rowe searched for a jaunty comeback, but came up empty. Kali rescued him.

"Eitan is a polymath with the mental ability to absorb, retain, and reference large amounts of unrelated details."

"Which inevitably find context in later experiences." Sun continued to focus on Rowe.

"Eitan never relaxes. A true stress puppy."

"I don't like others controlling solutions."

"What's your new digital jewelry, Eitan?" Kali pointed to one of the numerous necklaces around Sun's neck.

"Observe." He ran the object over Rowe's head and shoulders and waved it in front of his monitor. A grainy picture appeared and sharpened to a three-dimensional representation as good as any Rowe used in SEAL Intel.

"How'd you get the back of my head," Zeke asked.

"When the face is digitized, the program searches for

online images that include more detail. Somewhere out there are images of the side and back of your head."

Kali got up. "Zeke needs help with security protocols," and she was gone.

Sun continued to focus on Rowe. "I trust you found the analysis of the pictures useful."

"You out-analyzed the FBI."

"They operate with limits I don't. Happy, happy."

"I appreciate the help."

"Kali's webcam, in her house, takes a picture when motion is detected or when the light pattern from her window is disrupted. This morning, a man beamed a device through the window, probably trying to see why the bug stopped working."

Rowe jumped up. "Excuse me. I need to—"

"—notify Bobby James. Done."

Rowe stared at Sun and sat down. Before he could form a question, Sun said, "I never did hear what happened."

From anyone else, that would sound odd, but not to Rowe. He wanted to answer, *Life happened.* He had considered life benevolent until the night it destroyed what he valued most. The SEALs saved him, until they didn't.

It was Iraq, early morning, just before the humidity turned clothing to damp sweaty rags. Rowe and Duck Peters examined satellite photos for clues to where Saddam Hussein kept his Weapons of Mass Destruction.

Duck picked out a smudge. "Those trucks cross into Syria couple times a week. See how the bed sits lower to the ground on the way out? They leave full and come back empty."

"He's sending WMDs out of the country. We just gotta prove that." Rowe tore into a stack of Watch Reports, in search of the next convoy.

Duck's walky-talky squawked. "Hussein is at a farm ten miles south of Tikrit. I'll get him. You find the WMDs," and he sprinted out.

Minutes later, Rowe found them, packed up his gear, and

left.

When Duck returned to base two days later, Rowe was missing. His last communiqué put him in sight of the convoy and then nothing. SEALs often maintained radio silence during an operation, but this felt wrong. Duck made a phone call, refilled his P226, his M16, shouldered an M60 and disappeared. When his hardware ran out, he had his hands.

He traced Rowe to a Bedouin base. Thirty men, all with weapons—machine guns, at least one RPG-7, one FIM-92, a 9mm that looked exactly like Rowe's Sig Sauer, and a couple of machetes. Duck made a phone call, counted down ten minutes, and watched the camp explode with activity as soldiers loaded up trucks and raced out. When they were over the horizon, Duck neutralized anyone left and found Rowe.

"Next time, goddammit, wait for back-up." Duck catalogued the damage to his best friend. His hair was matted with gore, each knee one big festering wound, arms and face streaked with blood. Both trigger fingers dripped crimson, soaking the filthy cloth wrapped loosely around their stubs. His uniform was in grimy tatters.

The dirt floor where Rowe had likely been chained for the last three days was covered in trash, excrement, and three dead bodies—the men Duck assumed who had been Rowe's guards.

Apparently, the SEAL got tired of cooperating.

"They were going for my eyes…" Rowe pulled in a ragged breath, "Couldn't let that happen. I would miss … the sight of… your ugly mug …"

Duck wiped sweat from his eyes. "Who's this?" He nudged a dog who lay at Rowe's side, tail sweeping contentedly across the ground, gaze trusting.

Rowe's SEAL brothers tried to convince him it wasn't his fault, that he did all he could, but Rowe knew it was a lie. He failed his country when he couldn't find the WMDs and spent every day since then terrified he would again come up short when America most needed him. Now, he had a chance to make it right. He could find these terrorists who used innocents as corkboards, who would kill an entire crew of submariners without a thought, who threatened to destroy the US's most fundamental layer of defense. Or he could hide under an academic rock for the rest of his life.

What he wouldn't admit to even himself was this might be about Kali. Failing to safeguard the woman he loved a decade ago was also part of 'what happened'.

He didn't say any of that to Sun, just answered, "I met a dog over there. He trusted me," and he left.

Chapter 27

"An interesting little theory, Kalian."

After relentless prodding, Kali agreed to join Wyn Thursday for a working dinner at his house. She didn't know such a wealthy neighborhood existed so close to campus. Nestled behind wrought iron gates, it overlooked a spectacular panorama of the Hudson River's sleepy progress through the metropolis. They toured all two-thousand square feet, starting in the main room with its solid oak floor and authentic Persian rugs. The walls displayed original oils and watercolors he humbly called 'my little collection'.

The dining room was topped with a gold leaf ceiling from the church of St. John Lateran in Rome. The library—"my favorite room"—was lined with floor-to-ceiling bookshelves and a tile fragment from the Greek ruins of Persepolis. A Waterford chandelier lit circular stairs leading to a master bedroom with a drop-down projection TV, a wet bar and French doors over the garden. When she asked who could live in a place like this, Wyn said she deserved much more.

Now they sat on silk damask chairs beside a stone fireplace, Kali's half-empty wine glass abandoned on a side table. Over the course of the long evening, Kali concluded Wyn considered her research at best creative cobbling and at worst fodder for Star Trek. When she shared her newest accomplishment—the incorporation of DNA—he was dismissive.

"What made you think of that?"

He used this pedagogic tone constantly. Kali was tired

and hungry. The sushi was long gone, leaving only a half-full "exceptional bottle of 1978 Chateau-Lafitte Rothschild Burgundy". Kali didn't like wine, but he never asked.

"You must have read it somewhere? Or talked to a colleague at a conference?"

Did Wyn ever come up with an original thought? Did he know the meaning of 'logical deduction' or 'extrapolation of facts'? She wanted to go home and talk to Sandy, but those lifeless eyes awaited her answer, like the high school teachers when she blew off an assignment.

"DNA perseveres over time, even when the organism dies."

"Of course, dear. Speaking of Otto, we were going to discuss how you get Otto to work remotely. Oh—and how your firewalls operate. I've always been curious about security."

Something about his interest in these subjects stank.

Fairgrove was thrilled she believed him to be—what did she call it?—her Angel. Poverty drove many young women to the arms of wealthy men. He wanted to build on this, but she nattered on so long about herself, there was no time for his insights, and now she seemed tired.

She was brighter and less needy than he expected. She didn't take his suggestions and never confused his comments about teamwork. Still, he would spend enough time with her that Porter would support the addition of his name when she published. The tricky part would be keeping the AI from Al-Zahrawi until that point. Once the research was complete, he preferred Otto disappear to prevent embarrassing technical questions Fairgrove couldn't answer.

Only if Delamagente denied him credit would he involve Al-Zahrawi.

It fascinated Fairgrove how many anomalous conditions Otto found in the lives of early man. Most scientists thought they migrated in groups of ten. Otto showed as few as three living and eating together. And where many experts speculated man's feral ancestors ate where they scavenged, Otto consistently pictured them carrying food back to a home base for mates and offspring and injured group members. Unfortunately, these types of activities weren't preserved in the rocks that provided a history of that time.

Except for one. If the triptych of species—the *Homo habilis* Delamagente called Lucy, the Australopithecine Boah, and the canis Ump—traveling together also died together, it told a story never before postulated by any scientist. That was a find worthy of Dr. Wynton Fairgrove.

"Let's check on Lucy before you must leave." He hoped his tone conveyed disappointment that their time was drawing to a close.

"This isn't good." Delamagente chewed her lip as Otto zoomed in on a huge raptor scouring a vertical rock face. There, rimrocked halfway between precipice and valley floor, clung Lucy and two males. The raptor's great beak opened and its talons extended in a death dive. One male stumbled as he dodged out of the way, but Lucy seized his forearm and hung on until he found a foothold. They hugged the cliff until the raptor left for easier prey.

Fairgrove grimaced his disappointment. If the male had died, Fairgrove could uncover his bones. Maybe next time.

Chapter 28

When Kali got home and saw Annie sitting on a pillow in her pajamas, she groaned. "I forgot dinner."

"You did me a favor. Today's cerebral gymnastics made my head ache so I ordered delivery and curled up to rejuvenate."

Kali handed her a key. "How'd you get in?

"Zeke called Mr. Winters. Lucky they've met. I hope you didn't mind."

Kali waved an unconcerned hand and plopped into the room's only chair. Sandy padded over, but huffed back to Annie when he found no food. This evening definitely destroyed her interest in Wyn. Why did he ask so many questions about her firewall and Otto's remote operations? She didn't answer, which didn't stop him asking over and over.

"Can we reschedule for Saturday?" She kicked her shoes off and wiggled her toes in ecstasy.

"Hmm, my schedule is so busy." Annie's eyes canted up. "OK."

Kali sank deeper into her chair as Bruce Springsteen crooned his blue-collar blues. "How was your day, Annie?"

"Twelve hours in the library without a break except a trip to the vending machines for lunch. When I got back here, Sandy and I walked along Morningside Park—"

"Avoid that area at night," Kali interrupted. "It can be dangerous."

"I'm not sure anything is scarier than guerrillas in

Africa—the gun-toting kind, not the furry ones—but thanks for the advice. Mr. Winters is amazing, and I met the family at the end of the block. How does anyone raise five kids these days?"

Kali massaged her neck. "I try to be at work when they collect for fundraisers."

Annie giggled and shifted in her chair. "Sandy was edgy, probably the new human in his domain."

That could be the reason—no one other than herself, Sean or Mr. Winters walked Sandy—but between Fletcher and Fred Kaczynski, she didn't feel as safe as she used to.

"I ordered pizza if you're hungry. It just got here."

They got plates and sodas and settled into an impromptu picnic on the living room carpet.

"This is a lot more fun than my so-called date."

"Is there a story here?" Annie tucked into the floor pillow and waited.

"One of Columbia's new anthro professors has taken an interest in my work."

Annie made a face. "Nothing to do with your glossy hair or porcelain skin. And those legs!" Annie rolled her eyes. "Yeah, it must be your brains. Girl, the only reason you're not married is you haven't asked anyone!"

Kali blushed. She avoided dates, too often finding them boring and a waste of time, so was clueless how she stacked up against the modern single female. The compliments felt good.

Annie folded her pizza and bit into a slice. "Is he divorced with kids and ex-wives who get all his money, or is he worth the blood test?"

"None of either. I admired him at first, credited him with an intellect because of his research, but he's vapid and boring."

"Wyn's his name? His Mom's a positive thinker. No Matt or Dick for her."

Kali laughed. "So how'd you meet Zeke?"

"He saved my life." Her voice softened. "I'll tell you

about it Saturday." She cocked her head. "He deserves someone wonderful when he vanquishes his demons."

Kali perked up. Despite her best intentions, Zeke had gotten under her skin. She hoped Annie would say more, but she simply sipped her soda, eyes turned inward.

"Why isn't that you, Annie? I've only known you a day, but am quite sure you're worthy of anyone you want."

Annie pursed her lips. "Zeke's a stand-up guy, but not my type. When I finish my dissertation, I plan to settle into a professorship somewhere with my sweetheart."

A weight lifted from her shoulders. "Tell me about him."

"I'll save that for Saturday, too." Her brows arched with intrigue.

"You're fun to have around, Annie Sams."

Rowe sat on a stone bench reading an ebook while professors chatted with colleagues, business people in their collared shirts and khakis rushed home from MBA classes, and students ignored the world as they texted or laughed on their phones.

He picked out Hector from a distance and liked what he saw. Hair combed, uniform clean and pressed and shoes that shined said a lot about his personal pride. When he got closer, Rowe took in the leathery skin pock-marked from teenage acne and the poorly-set broken nose. He saw many like it in battle, soldiers refusing to leave the field so the medics did what they could.

Rowe stuck his hand out as he introduced himself. Hector had a firm handshake, a practiced friendly nod, and eyes that took in everything from Rowe's battered fingers to his functional clothes. They chatted a few minutes before Rowe pulled up the picture of Fred Kaczynski.

"Do you recognize this man?"

Hector needed only a glance. "The *guerro*. He's solidly built, waist going to fat, boyish cuteness that probably works for him. He carried a bouquet of flowers with those frilly white blooms florists mix in. They're expensive. I buy them for my wife's birthday, but he tossed them in the trash as though they were a prop."

"Where'd you serve, Hector?"

"Desert Storm with the 24th Infantry Division out of Fort Stewart, GA."

"Is that where you left your leg?"

Hector pointed with his chin to Rowe's hands. "You too?"

"SEALs. I got myself captured."

"You learn a lot from war. It taught me to pay attention to instinct. I was making sure he exited the campus when I overheard him on the phone."

Rowe adopted a mild expression though he thought Hector would tell him anyway. "Remember any of it?"

Hector pulled a dog-eared spiral notebook from his pocket and flipped to a neatly inscribed page. "I took notes: *She looked frazzled.* The man's face became agitated and he said, *I did my part. Leave the money like you always do.*"

Hector's phone beeped. He glanced down and then stuck his hand out.

"Gotta go teach some college kids how to behave on campus."

Rowe shook his hand. "You bring honor to the uniform and the flag, Hector."

Rowe checked in with James to see if Annie found anything. Nothing yet. He had been furious when he heard the identity of Kali's bodyguard, but when James asked whom he trusted more, Rowe shut up. If anyone could protect Kali, it was Annie. He thought of offering to give her a break on surveillance, but she might take it wrong. Instead, he went home to a rerun of *Man vs. Wild* and enough beer to forget who Kali was dining with.

Home this week was an FBI safe house in Englewood New Jersey, nestled onto a narrow two-lane road that backed up to Flatrock Brook Nature Center. Outside, it matched all the others—well tended lawns, trim greenery, trash curbside on schedule—but inside, the walls were beige, the furniture

Sears, and the curtains lined with copper mesh to prevent eavesdropping.

As he entered, he tripped on a box, a gift from Bobby James. Rowe stripped open the tape to reveal thousands of pages of manuscripts by Fairgrove.

He substituted beer with orange juice, and TV with the first publication, *Analysis of the kinetics of DNA hybridization*, by Mr. Wynton Fairgrove.

Friday

A jangle yanked Rowe from a deep sleep. His phone. He pushed answer, but fell back onto his pillow without a word.

"Zeke. You awake?" James sounded chipper for the middle of the night.

"Hunh?"

"Good. It's 6am, time to arise. Update Stockbury on the TRF search."

"Unh hunh," and he hung up.

He dragged out of bed and through his morning workout, always more difficult on two hours sleep. The scar tissue from the injuries made exercising painful and difficult, but necessary to keep his knees loose. Rowe didn't waste time thinking about pain when there was nothing he could do about it.

When he finished, he took a cold shower, ate a spoon of coffee crystals, and headed for Columbia. By 8am, he'd settled into Stockbury's chair, mulling over last night's reading while he waited for her to arrive. Something felt wrong about Fairgrove's work. He mentally rummaged through the four papers he'd read, all published early in the man's career, but couldn't put his finger on what bothered him.

When Kali arrived, she gave him a passing glance as though people broke into her lab all the time. Just seeing her boosted Rowe's spirits, like the universe's personal rainbow. Today, she wore a sleeveless top over dark bike shorts, hair pulled back in a braid and the omnipresent diamond earrings.

He passed her coffee and a bag of donuts and asked, "Was the DNA analysis helpful?"

She blew on the Styrofoam cup, bit into an old-fashioned, and booted up her computer before answering with a simple, "I haven't checked." Rowe was surprised, but didn't press.

Stockbury arrived, took one of Rowe's two remaining coffees, peered into the grease-stained pink box and chose a donut hole. "Dr. Zeke is jumpy about your date with Wyn."

"He offered to help with my research, Cat, nothing else."

Rowe faced Stockbury. "You don't like Fairgrove."

She crossed long tan legs, adjusting her skirt so it stopped just above the knee. "Wyn can't reach a conclusion much less a decision. Why would I like that?" She flexed her foot in her woven sandals and her lips pulled up the tiniest bit. "I'm happy you went out, Kali. It's exhausting being the only one who dates."

Rowe decided to change the subject. "How's Annie?"

"She feels like a sister. When were you going to tell me you saved her life?"

"When you tell me what's up with Fairgrove."

"Nothing," but Kali blushed.

"Same with saving Annie's life."

"Would you two please do the sex thing and move on? You're perfect for each other!"

Kali kicked Stockbury's chair and Rowe took the opportunity to walk around. He stopped behind Kali. "Your sweatshirt is still gone?"

"The firefighter took it, according to the video."

Why would he want that? Before Rowe could ask, Kali's phone rang.

"Hi, Wyn. Yes, last night was fun. ... Yes, thanks for the help. ... Actually, I'm in a meeting." Rowe mouthed, *I'm a meeting?* "Yes, there is a lot to do. Thanks again."

"Before you include Wyn, check his background," Stockbury ordered and left for class.

Rowe silently applauded. "Hold up. I'll walk with you."

When they got outside, Stockbury started. "I knew you were involved. Bobby James gave me a beeper so he can reach me anytime. The virus must be active before the backdoor opens. That means the moment it pings, I go in and reprogram it. It takes about two minutes. Per sub."

Rowe hurried to keep up with her. "We didn't find any problems at the TRF maintenance facility." He didn't tell her about the ones that had already deployed.

Stockbury exhaled. "Were you searching for a virus with zeros and ones or organic bases?" Rowe tried to keep his expression neutral, but Stockbury shook her head in disgust. "Don't worry. I got this," and she left, head high, eyes straight ahead, oblivious to the rush of bodies around her.

Rowe thanked the Universe that Cat and her devious brain were on the side of the angels, and then called Hector Rosado who had offered to check campus security feeds for Fred Kaczynski. There was nothing other than the one visit. Rowe hung up, with no clear next step. He decided to follow Kali. She still complained about being tailed. Maybe he'd get lucky.

Chapter 29

Friday afternoon

Kali savored a purloined butter cookie from Afternoon Tea as she googled 'Wynton Fairgrove'. Cat and Zeke must be in cahoots. Why else nag her about Wyn's background? She popped the last half cookie into her mouth and typed 'Wynton Fairgrove' into the search engine.

More than ten thousand hits. She refined the search with exclusionary terms and narrowed the number to nine hundred. At seventeen, Wyn burst upon the scientific world with a paper on DNA hybridization dedicated to a girlfriend who passed away.

"If he wrote about DNA, why does he never understand what I'm saying?"

He met his fiancée while working at the Max Planck Institute, though she died a month before he published a second paper.

"Suspicious already."

Kali jumped. "Aren't you teaching a class?"

"It ended two hours ago." Cat smelled of alcohol, after-shave, and sex. In place of the sensible work outfit of this morning, she wore a filmy off-the-shoulder peasant blouse, skintight jeans and open-toed four-inch heels.

"My boyfriend told me Wyn highjacked the research of at least two grad students and then killed them. Why do you think I dropped him?"

"That's ridiculous, Cat. Why kill them?"

"Shut them up." Cat rummaged through her desk until she found a stick of gum and popped it into her mouth. "He built his reputation on the labor of these women. They became loose ends."

Kali shook her head. "You think I'm his new sacrifice."

Cat shrugged. "Gotta go. Gunner and I are taking his Gulfstream to Acapulco."

Her new boyfriend had a name.

Which reminded Kali that Sean hadn't called. He promised to contact her every few days. She dialed his cell, but got no answer. She opened her online address book and clicked 'Juilliard' for the name of his host family.

"Vitolska." Before she could dial, Eitan Sun buzzed. "Can you spare five minutes?"

She blew a calming breath, convincing herself Sean was fine by the time she reached Eitan's lab. She did a double take.

"Wow."

Sun wore an ivory tuxedo with gold buttons and satin lapels. A ruffled dress shirt spilled through a paisley vest cinched by a crimson cravat. Patent leather wingtips and diamond cuff links finished the outfit. She only recognized him by his signature posture. He always led with his head as though eager to get where he was going.

"I'm on my way to the Baltimore Society of Computer Generalists awards ceremony."

This was an eclectic association of professionals, one of the few groups able to pull Sun from his lab. Once a year, they feted the technical invention with the greatest impact on mankind. Sun's winning entry was a palm-sized device which detected the co-presence of saltpeter and charcoal, primary ingredients in gun power. Sun considered it essential for those who desired to avoid rather than confront conflict. Law enforcement bought it by the thousands to identify suicide bombers.

"You asked if Otto can find submarines. Yes," and he tossed her a dog-eared book with a dozen post-its.

Sun dumped half a cup of red M&M's into his mouth and

chewed, eyes roving the walls and ceiling of his lab. Kali waited, knowing he'd continue when ready.

"First, Einstein explains how Otto can *theoretically* use a magnetic signature to find the sub given sufficient time. He would act like the Navy's magnetic anomaly detectors, but vastly more sensitive and able to cover a much wider area than anything in existence today.

"The second part—tracking—is trickier. Earth's magnetic field decreases until midday, increases until late afternoon, and settles to a moderate night-time level. Deviations occur minute by minute, and vary depending upon latitude and longitude, more at the poles and less at the equator. These are predictable and measurable. We could program Otto to compare these expected deviations against real magnetosphere satellite data, and then sort the output for the Trident's size and mass over time." Sun swallowed another mouthful of M&Ms. "Again, theoretically possible, but complicated."

Sun hunched his shoulders and flexed his fingers, body language for insecurity, a trait Kali never associated with Eitan Sun.

"Why does this bother you?"

Sun paced, eyes unfocused as he crossed and recrossed his arms. "No MAD in existence can identify these infinitesimal changes. Only Otto. Statistically, this explains why you are being cyber-stalked."

Without another word, Sun left. Kali returned to her lab and buried herself in Einstein's theories as they relate to magnetism, trying to understand how relativity applied to submarines and magnetism.

Finally, Chantelle.

"Where have you been?" Fairgrove whined. He had called all day yesterday to schedule an emergency haircut.

"Hello, my friend. How was your dinner with Ms. Delamagente?" When Fairgrove sputtered, Al-Zahrawi chuckled. "She thought you were trying to get her drunk. Which no doubt is true."

Fairgrove didn't understand Al-Zahrawi's interest in Kalian, but it was significant enough that Al-Zahrawi had wormed his way into her confidence. She raved about him last night, said she trusted him and felt a loyalty to fulfill her promises to him.

Trust and loyalty—Fairgrove wished she felt those for him. She could be the most lucrative grad student Fairgrove had ever worked with. How best to respond to Salah? He needed to convince him that his email relationship with the woman was akin to looking at a painting through a straw. Only Fairgrove's broader lens of scientific connections could fulfill the man's greater needs.

Whatever those were.

Before he could mull that through, Al-Zahrawi continued, "I hope you found out more than her alcohol tolerance."

"In fact, I see hopeful signs. Why, only yesterday—"

"Skip the story, Doctor. I already know Otto theoretically can find and track magnetic signatures." Al-Zahrawi's voice quavered with anticipation. "She must make that a reality. Quickly."

Why did he want that? It didn't fit what Fairgrove knew of the man's plans. He started to ask, but Al-Zahrawi continued. "Is the Dr. Rowe problem solved?"

"I instructed Kalian to avoid him and informed Porter that Rowe will alienate Columbia's rich alumni. Administrators always drag their feet, but he'll see it my way."

Fairgrove paused to allow Al-Zahrawi to be impressed with his progress. When that didn't happen, he continued, "I even entered anonymous complaints." He saw that in a movie.

Into the growing silence, Fairgrove asked, "What do you have against him anyway?"

"He is smart. I dislike smart people."

Chapter 30

Friday

The woman placed her wedding ring in the car's cup holder and made sure her blouse was open one button too many. Her badge got her inside. The sexy was for the sailor who would take her to the Ethernet cables.

It had been a long day, but this was the last submarine. As a patriot, she was pleased America's Refit Facilities were well-guarded. Her employer had an emergency roll out of a network repair. She had been lucky to get this job and knew it had nothing to do with her engineering capability. She couldn't even change a lightbulb much less program a computer. All she did was deliver a cream that reminded her of orange Vaseline. When she asked about the goo—in case one of the sailors asked; she liked to be prepared—they told her it was need to know, Top Secret. She respected that, and wanted to do her part to protect America.

Still, she always took time to talk to the drooling seamen who helped her. She couldn't tell the difference between Ethernet or electricity so wasn't kidding when she gushed how much she admired their skill.

Two days ago, her boss gave her an upgraded goo for the submarines she'd visit today. He was pleased with her work and promised to use her to deliver the next update. She almost hugged him. $10,000 more—on top of the $14,000 she had already been paid. God surely blessed her. Her husband had been out of work for six months and then she'd been downsized right out of her lousy job. If she hadn't found this on Craig's List, they'd have lost their house.

As the sailor approached, she offered a shy smile. "Hi! I'm with General Dynamo, here to patch your network," and she showed him the Work Order.

"Oh. I haven't been told about this," he kept glancing between her face and her chest, as though the answer was there. That happened a lot.

She opened her jar and swiped a finger through the substance. "It's like the stuff you-all put on battery cables, but for networks, to keep them from cracking during long deployments. "

He scratched his head. "I don't know. I've been out twice. Never a problem."

She was surprised. Why would this—what was he, a Petty Officer?—question orders from his superiors?

She pasted a grin across her face. "You're lucky. The *USS Tennessee* and the *USS Tucson*," two subs she knew were at sea so couldn't be contacted, "They lost comms for a week because of a degraded cable. That's why this is such a rush. I'll show you how simple it is."

He led her through a dingy door into a small room with more electronics than space. She slipped by him, making sure her breasts rubbed against his chest, blushed demurely, and bent forward. "These?"

"Yes, but—" then gasped as she spread the goo across the wires.

"Done! Now it permeates the exterior and does its magic. Something to do with atoms and molecules. Within ten minutes, you won't even see anything on the cables." She purposefully forced a confused frown and swapped it for a grin. "When you're out there fighting our enemies, you'll thank me."

Before her dazzling smile had time to fade, the sailor slapped cuffs on her wrists. "You are under arrest for traitorous acts against America and aiding the enemy."

It was a long night, but James got everything from the young woman. She swore she loved the United States and yes she should have questioned a job too good to be true, but she needed the money. When queried how many cables she painted with the goo, she proudly announced eighteen—in half the time expected.

Why was she in trouble for helping the Navy? When she showed James the Work Order, he had to admit it was expertly forged with all required signatures.

They asked her to cooperate by not telling her boss about the arrest.

Eleven subs remained in danger.

Chapter 31

Annie had been a nanny pushing a baby carriage, a student returning from class, and a postal clerk making deliveries. The only strange activity was Mr. Winters checking his mailbox seven times and Zeke Rowe hiding in his car four houses down, like she wouldn't notice. She called it a night. When Delamagente got home around midnight, Annie pretended to be asleep. Kali got a glass of water, talked to Sandy as she checked windows Annie had already secured, and went to sleep.

"Wake up, silly, or you'll miss a yummy breakfast." Sandy snored in a dog-sized splotch of sun that spilled onto Kali's bed. "Did Annie wear you out yesterday?"

"No, I didn't!"

Kali inhaled the pungence of Kona coffee. Her mom used to make it, saying there was no reason to treat her like a child anymore. Mornings, before baby Sean awoke and it was just the two of them, were magic. They left the lights off and sat in the dark at the kitchen table. Mom always overfilled her cup and Kali could hear her slurp from the rim as they chatted about their youth, the existence of a God, and whatever else came to mind. Mom told Kali she saw a lot of herself in her daughter, but smarter and sturdier. Kali still missed her.

"I love roommates!" Kali shuffled out in worn slippers and an old robe, hair snagged loosely into a disheveled ponytail. Annie was dressed, showered, eyes lively, and Sandy's leash was circled around itself.

"Guess who got me out for a walk at 5 a.m." Annie glared kindly at Sandy as she filled two cups. "You know who I mean. The rare North American *Homo canine*."

She plunked a mug in front of Kali. "We already delivered coffee to Mr. Winters. Did you know he got the Navy Cross for saving ten Marines in Korea? Impressive."

Kali blinked. She didn't know that, or anything else about his time as a Marine. They never talked about it.

She inhaled the caffeine and put her feet up on a stool. "You hiking today?"

"My Timberland's? I got used to these in Africa. Now they're all I wear."

"I can't wait to hear your stories. I need some vicarious adventure."

"Tonight. Are we still on?"

"Unless my hamster wheel breaks."

"Or I win a spelling bee and turn into a dictionary."

"Or the Universe comes calling."

Annie laughed. "I knew a Russian who would say, 'Until the crayfish on the hill whistles'."

She bounced out the door, leaving Kali and Sandy deflated as though the party just left.

"Well, Pup, we have to entertain ourselves."

Kali poured a glass of Tang and toasted an English muffin before taking Sandy on a second walk. Then, she brushed his fur while reading about the Israeli dig at Gesher Benot Ya'aqov that inspired Rowe's work. Outside, trash cans clanged as they were emptied, police sirens howled, and a boom box played rap music with words she didn't even want to understand. After lunch, she cleaned the apartment to Francois Rabbath's string bass rendition of *Carmen* and then settled in to research while Sandy nestled between her feet.

When next she raised her head, the band of light from her window had moved an entire foot.

"I wonder what Lucy's typical day was."

Animals in Lucy's habitat rested when not hunting or eating. Only early man whittled tools, collected rocks for future use, planned, or simply thought. After months of watching, Kali decided the never-quiet human brain, using one in every four calories consumed, grew bigger because of constant exercise.

"Zeke hasn't told you about Paulette? Just like him."

The two women sat in the dim light of another restaurant Kali had never been to. The walk over was glorious as the last remnants of day shed a reddish glow on the skyscrapers silhouetted against the horizon. Kali wore black capris with a sleeveless pastel tunic, and Annie khakis and a green t-shirt. Kali liked Annie's image: strong, self-sufficient and oblivious to others.

The waitress poured house wine while Annie studied Kali as though trying to decide. A full ten seconds passed before she continued.

"He didn't tell me this. Bobby did, but I want you to understand how fragile he is. He almost got married twice. The first time was to a French woman named Paulette. He was living his dream, teaching at *Université de Paris* and engaged to the woman he thought would never find him. He was well-liked for his enlightened attitudes. He spent most nights in dusky Parisian coffee houses with his students, discussing the hypocrisy of the establishment.

"When riots exploded on campus, he rejoiced at the empowerment of the people. He didn't fear the violence of the crowds or the police's inability to control them. His armor was compassion, his weapons words."

Annie dipped her head and breathed in, then out. "One night, he and Paulette were walking home from class, comparing the marches around them to other historic socialist boycotts. A group of protesters sprang out of nowhere. Two immobilized him while the others threw Paulette to the ground." Annie spit out the last phrase.

"One was a student in Zeke's class, Zeke begged him to consider what he was doing as Paulette screamed and kicked until one of the attackers smashed her head against a rock. He smirked when she collapsed, finished his business, and the group left without looking back. Zeke couldn't revive her, so scooped her up and sprinted to the nearest hospital.

"As he cowered in the waiting room, knowing the outcome, Zeke realized how stupid he'd been to forget it wasn't just man's brilliance but his violent nature that shaped history. Zeke left the building and vanished into a life where those he loved couldn't be victimized."

The waitress approached, but Kali couldn't speak so Annie suggested the house special—rotisserie chicken with a mountain of caramelized onions.

"His next foray into love was equally doomed. His exploits in Iraq left him so physically damaged, he was told he could never walk again, much less shoot a gun, his fiancée visited once and two months later, married a banker. Trying a third time will take a massive leap of faith."

No wonder Zeke acted like two people.

Annie offered a wan smile. "I met Zeke between those two events, when academia and its memories were shadowy ghouls hiding in dark corners of his past and his next great disappointment was yet to come." Annie wadded her napkin into a tight spiral. "I lived with a Maasai tribe for six months so I could write an ethnograph on their culture. Such beautiful, straight-forward people. I grew up in foster homes so I know what it feels like to be an outsider. They accepted me as family, called me daughter."

She nibbled a pumpernickel roll as she traveled back in time.

"Our huts backed Ol Doinyo L'engai—"Mountain of the Black God" in Maa—along the Great African Rift. Many days, dense fumes and billowing smoke clouds exploded from its scarred maw and lava and poisonous gas crawled toward the shores of Lake Natron. The stench of sulfur and burned flesh permeated the land, but the Maasai never worried. They believed Enkai, their one god, would never endanger them.

"When it became clear an eruption was imminent, the American Embassy ordered me to leave, but I couldn't without the villagers, and they wouldn't go without their cattle."

"Finally, the volcano exploded, sending lava burning down the mountain. Dirty nimbus-like clouds clogged the air and buried the land in a blanket of ash. Acid rain burned everyone within the volcano's reach. The roof of my hut collapsed and dislocated my left shoulder and broke my arm. I wrapped a sling around it and fled with the Maasai to higher ground where I radioed a Mayday."

The waitress clunked their food noisily on the table. The spicy scent wafted up, but Kali's appetite had vanished.

"Zeke's SEAL Team answered. To the villagers and me, they were a miracle. Zeke said he could take only me, not the rest, because the helicopter couldn't carry that much weight. I said they would die and refused to go without them. I guess Zeke believed me because he loaded everyone into the chopper and we left. I don't know how the pilot did it, but he got us to safety. Afterwards, I realized the position I had put Zeke in. His decision to do what I asked could have cost his men their lives. He never blamed me, but hasn't spoken to me since."

Kali hung her head. While she had struggled through PTA meetings and felt sorry for herself every dateless Saturday night, Annie and Zeke had faced death. What was Wyn doing while Zeke decided the fate of a village? More than the quality of clothes separated the two men.

Annie's story broke the ice and they chatted through dinner like old friends.

As they paid the bill, Kali asked, "When will I get to meet the man worthy of you?"

Annie took a breath before answering, "He's a she." Kali froze as Annie waited, eyes hooded. "You never had a lesbian friend? Do you think we bite?"

Kali giggled. "What you see is relief you won't fight me for Zeke." She caught Annie's eye. "I guess I thought I'd know."

"I usually wear a sign. Seriously, Kal, I've never been

happier."

As they walked, Kali clopped along in clunky wedge sandals while Annie moved silently, eyes alert, body poised and ready. So much like Lucy.

Once home, they Kali went to bed and Annie settled into a chair with a book. Sandy flapped his ears in confusion and then sprinted toward Annie.

Chapter 32

Saturday

An alarm shrieked, fracturing Rowe's sleep. He palmed the phone from the nightstand almost knocking the lamp over. 3:30. It was still dark out so it must be AM. He read Fairgrove's papers last night until he passed out, as confused by this batch as the first. It was like a puzzle with no corner pieces. What he did know was something didn't fit, but two nights in a row without enough sleep didn't help his mental capacities.

"Bobby. You're better than an alarm."

"You awake?" James sounded fresh, but edgy. Too much coffee—already—which he confirmed by barreling past the answer. "We caught someone," and he told Rowe about the young woman who thought she was a patriot.

Rowe rubbed his eyes. They felt like sandpaper. "That's great news."

"Maybe. All she did was follow orders. I am surprised how fast they were able to manufacture the update. Either Stockbury was right—it is a simple weapon—or they're better than we think. We're analyzing the formula."

Rowe yawned, hoping James was done. He wasn't.

"I intercepted a call to Fairgrove. Listen:

Salah: "*Persuade her to discover faster. Have you solved the Rowe problem?*"
Fairgrove: "*I instructed Kalian to avoid him. What did he do to you, Salah?*"

Salah: *"He is smart. I dislike smart people."*

Suddenly, Rowe was wide awake.

"I'm running 'Salah' through NCIC as we speak." James punched through keystrokes, one-fingered judging by the speed.

"I like worried bad guys, Bobby. They make mistakes, but I don't like the reference to Kali."

"Annie won't let anything happen."

Rowe swung his feet to the floor and hunched into a sitting position on the edge of the bed and waited.

"Here we are. NCIC found 897 felons named Salah. Cross-checking them against our case gives me one match: 'Salah Al-Zahrawi', active with radical Islam. No contact info, no address."

Rowe had no doubt he was also looking at the generous Gegham Keregosian, "I'll follow Fairgrove. If they meet, I can compare his 'Salah' to the file image."

Rowe completed his morning workout, showered, donned old sweatpants and a cutoff t-shirt, ate a spoon of coffee crystals and two Tigers Milk bars, and caught Fairgrove as the scientist pulled out of the driveway. Rowe stayed well back, not because Fairgrove would catch him, but to see if anyone else was tailing him.

Fairgrove started at Nordstrom's, left two hours later empty handed, then took an aerobics class at his fitness club. Ten minutes into it, he stumbled to the sidelines where he mopped his brow and ogled the hard-bodied women. He exchanged a few hellos, but no one seemed interested in chatting with him. What a surprise.

He stopped for lunch at a bistro while Rowe founded a secluded spot to park. It was overcast, a perfect day for sitting in a car surveilling. Fairgrove flirted with the waitress and read the *New York Times* while he ate what might have been chicken salad, drank two glasses of white wine and pretended to be busy. Rowe munched through two more Tiger's Milk bars and a warm soda, acting the part of an office worker on his lunch break, always keeping Fairgrove in sight while basking in the breeze that drifted through his open window.

After eating, Fairgrove got a haircut and then glued his phone to his ear. From the dramatic expressions and expansive arm movements, he was trying to line up a date. When he stopped for carry-out, Rowe figured there were no takers. While Annie dined with Kali, Rowe staked out Fairgrove's home hoping Salah Al-Zahrawi or Gegham Keregosian would drop by. He gave up at 2 a.m. and went home to sleep.

But he couldn't shut his brain off. A mental clock ticked off the seconds, reminding him how much closer the terrorists were to their goal, whatever that was. He finally got up, splashed cold water on his face, ate two spoons of coffee crystals, and read more of Fairgrove's publications.

An hour later, he knew what bothered him. Fairgrove's writing style was all over the place. Sometimes it was clear and precise, other times flowery, and too often, muddled as though he didn't understand his topic. Rowe jotted down the differences, comparing where the man worked at the time and with whom, playing a hunch.

Frustrated, he shoved the pile aside. His shoulders were stiff, his knees creaky hinges, and his brain more like an overstuffed file cabinet than a finely-tuned machine. He rode the bike at level twelve hills, did six sets of pushups rotating between normal hand-width, wide stance and one-handed, and fifty pull-ups on a bar set high in a door frame. Then, he let his mind go blank so it could work on the clues.

Thirty minutes later, after a cold shower, he dressed in pleated chinos, a dark green polo and deck shoes with no socks. He'd eaten the last of the Tigers Milk bars yesterday so drank two power shakes. By four a.m., he was in the Lazy-boy in the living room sipping his second coffee and waiting.

A thread of Salah's conversation drifted back—*He's in the way.* How was he in the way?

Quarter after four, He jumped in his car. As he reached his lab, his phone buzzed. "Bobby. Three mornings in a row."

"We analyzed the goo that lady wiped on the cables. They

re-engineered Stockbury's virus, removed the backdoor."

Rowe froze. Stockbury had been sure no one could find her script. She made it simple and non-threatening to lull them into believing the virus was exactly as represented. Truth was, no one expected them to look.

"We underestimated them."

James grunted. "We caught two subs at the Refit Facility. We hope the others call in, but can't count on that. Our only real option is to stop Salah before he gives out the locations."

"The key is Otto, Bobby. Keregosian knows that."

The man was expert at manipulating people. He emailed Kali daily, encouraging without being pushy, inquisitive but not nosy. He asked her opinion about esoteric topics and always offered a thoughtful response to her ideas. Rowe thought, in Kali's shoes, he too would like the man pretending to be Keregosian.

What gave him away was the chronic asking about when Otto would be able to track and find. In their last exchange, Kali made it clear that even with funding, she could only work so fast.

At some point, Keregosian/Salah would stop being patient.

"But why Fairgrove's interest in Kali? You know him, Zeke. What's up?"

After reading much of Fairgrove's research, Rowe thought he'd figured out what was going on, but wasn't ready to commit. "Not sure yet. He may not even know Al-Zahrawi's plans."

"We found Devore and his cameraman, half eaten by rats in a deserted warehouse. A note was nailed to his chest."

Rowe sucked in a deep breath. "Like Zematis."

James grunted. "They're trying to panic us, force us to capitulate. When the press finds out civilians are being killed and mutilated over nuclear submarines, every crazy anti-war group in the country will be picketing the White House." He huffed. "What these terrorists want is impossible. Don't they know Tridents can't be reached with a telephone?"

Rowe didn't think this was an effort to build fear. Al-Zahrawi was buying time, keeping America occupied until the endgame was too close to prevent.

"I have a call to make," and James hung up.

Rowe needed coffee. He forgot to buy grounds for the pot he kept behind his desk so he unburied his mug hidden beneath a stack of research materials on the Dead Sea and re-traced his steps to an outside kiosk. It had ten vending machines, one with excellent brew at a reduced rate if you brought your own cup. Some green initiative that suited Rowe fine.

As he turned to go back to his lab, inhaling the piquant aroma, he almost ran over Fairgrove. The man wore a suit, jaunty scarf around his neck, shirt with French cuffs, and tasseled loafers. Did he ever work?

"I was coming to talk to you, Dr. Rowe. You need to do the honorable thing and leave Kalian Delamagente alone. You are hurting her chances for a professorship."

"What the hell are you talking about?"

"She's a great girl with a nice little future. Let those of us who know how to do so guide her."

Fairgrove's tone was surly, his eyes everywhere but Rowe's face. Rowe snapped his fingers. "Wyn, look at me," and Fairgrove jerked toward him, eyes wide and frightened. "You're no good at this. Get out while you still can."

"I-I don't understand?" Fairgrove smoothed his left eyebrow.

"Do you act this way with Salah Al-Zahrawi? Or should I call him Gegham Keregosian?" Fairgrove's face blanched, all Rowe needed to confirm he was right. "You can't be nervous and succeed as a sneaky lying bastard."

Fairgrove stuttered something unintelligible about connections he had that would do a lot more for Kali than Rowe, and then tipped his head as though hoping Rowe would agree.

"OK, Wyn, for the sake of argument, let's consider what you did for the women in your past. You usurped your high school girlfriend's work when she died. You took credit for your fiancée's research when she was killed in a car accident. And let's not forget your last live-in girlfriend. Is she still missing?"

Fairgrove's eyes widened and his mouth parted. Sweat beaded his upper lip and he rubbed his eyebrow again.

"This you want for Kali?"

Fairgrove brushed Rowe with a flimsy shove. "For once in your life, you should put someone else ahead of yourself!" and stomped away.

Rowe took a sip of coffee, breathed in Columbia's morning scent, and jumped in his car.

Chapter 33

Sunday

It was not even five a.m., too early for work, so Kali poured a coffee and settled onto her stoop. Night still clung to the road, lit only by streetlights and the white cones from the occasional car. When the sky turned from black velvet to gold, the joggers started on their early morning runs and the devout left for worship. For years, she had attended church as an example for Sean until he explained his faith required no building to legitimize.

Hearing Annie's stories about Zeke last night made him more puzzling than ever. He risked his life to save Annie, but now refused to speak to her so how did he know she needed a place to stay? And why reach out to Kali? It didn't add up. As much as she liked the two, it didn't take a mastermind to know they were hiding something.

"Let's go for a run, Sandy. We'll get donuts on the way back."

She changed into jogging clothes, donned the lanyard with her rape whistle and set out on a five-mile loop down Riverside Drive to the traffic circle, then North on Broadway to Harlem and Grant's tomb. An hour later, she jotted Annie a note and left for work, munching a donut as she walked.

Kali loved Sundays at Columbia. She could pad around barefoot with no interruptions from colleagues or students or administrators checking her progress. Today would be devoted to her thesis. The Dean was being uncharacteristically patient, but she knew that wouldn't last.

"Annie knows a lot about primitive people," she muttered. "Maybe she can help me understand Lucy."

"I'm sorry—I was walking by and missed what you said."

Wyn. Kali's good mood drained away. She smelled the cream and sugar in the cup he set next to her and ignored it, as she'd done the last two times he brought sweetened coffee for her.

"What's with you and Zeke?" She saw them argue, from her window. Wyn was frantic, but Rowe couldn't have been more laid back.

"He's a brute, but I've faced worse. Academia is no longer a cultured environment."

Kali let that go. "I'm surprised to see you on a Sunday."

"I work many Sundays. Science ignores temporal boundaries, and I did promise Porter to offer my assistance in completing your project." He relaxed into Cat's chair as though he owned it. "Any new pictures?" His face scrunched and he cocked his head. His lips smiled, but it didn't reach his eyes. "What the girl's name?"

Lucy. Kali felt herself relax. "Lucy is so much like me. I just watched her learning to use a spear. She balanced it above her shoulder, parallel to the ground, weight centered in her grasp, and hurled. It didn't clear her shadow. She retrieved it and tried again. She continued until her palms bled and she could no longer clasp the shaft."

Kali leaned toward Wyn. "Wyn, she's doing what we do—try, fail, try again—experiment. She's already human."

"Why would she do that?"

Kali pulled back. "You mean try to throw it or not quit?"

"Well, I suppose either." His head bobbed absently.

That did it. Kali swallowed the caustic reply that almost escaped her lips and spun her chair toward Otto.

"I'm stuck. What do you think of applying Einstein's Theory of Special Relativity to Otto's program?"

Fear filled Wyn's face. "You'll figure it out, my dear. I can't tell you everything." He pecked her cheek, flicked his finger across an eyebrow, and escaped.

"Don't worry, Wyn. I didn't expect an answer," she whispered.

Eitan Sun had been up all night, but he buzzed with energy. After playing Madden Football from 8pm until 2am, everything made sense. He spent the next eight hours digging, collecting, connecting, mulling, and steeping. Every step closer to the truth frightened him. For Kali.

And Rowe and Cat and Annie.

Something treacherous was brewing. The *How* eluded him, but if he was right, which he always was, not much longer. Rowe came by earlier to discuss how to make it look like Otto was stalking a submarine without actually doing it so they could fool Kali's spy. An hour later, Rowe left, a seed of a plan embedded in Sun's fertile brain.

Kali entered, but he couldn't stop. A stream of beautiful numbers flowed across the screen. An abundance of primes and the Golden Number... describing distance, length, count... Patterns jumped, shining and pulsing, from the erratic tumble of lovely integers.

Kali's lips moved, but he ignored her. He found twenty-three satellites—twenty-three, the first prime with numbers in ascending sequential order—with magnetic anomaly detection capabilities. Two could detect a three-inch delta in magnetic fluxes. One was operated by a friend. With a phone call, he secured permission to run its data through Otto's algorithm.

His eyes darted to the second screen, the blue one. A Fibonacci sequence whizzed by, Earth's own number used by traders to predict the market, Minoans to wage war, and musicians to compose music. How did he miss it earlier?

Kali's mouth moved again as she massaged a finger against her temple. The golden string, 1 0 1 1 0 1 0 1 1 0 1 1 0 1 0 1 ...

Six hours later, he sat back. "Done."

He smiled up at Kali, but she was gone. Only a whiff of her perfume remained. He knew why she dropped by. He'd call her. Soon.

He stuffed a handful of Cheez-its into his mouth and washed it down with orange soda. His screen glowed yellow, an irregular sequence of colors and shapes following a horizon of bulges and valleys. He dialed a friend, left an encrypted message, and then called Zeke Rowe. As he waited for a return call, he pushed play on his wife's photo.

"Hello, sweetie. I got Season Six of *Star Trek Voyager* on DVD. Get your work done and come home. I made popcorn. I love you!"

He listened a second and third time to the lilt in her voice and the lisp of her tongue thrust, before hunkering down to the mysteriosity of how much danger Kali was in.

And who would die before the week was up.

Chapter 34

Monday

Today, Kali had no concern about Wyn arriving uninvited. He had plans. She didn't know what nor did she care. She wanted the uninterrupted time to focus on magnetic signatures. With a few hours work, she could lay it out for DARPA. Not a prototype, but enough detail to garner funding and fulfill her promise to her son.

She'd sketched out the introduction when Cat arrived.

"Hey, Kali." Her voice was dull, emotionless.

Kali glanced up, fingers still typing, and froze. "What happened?" Her friend's eyes were rimmed in red, face flushed with sweat. She wore baggy chinos and a crop top, rarely-worn comfort clothes for a woman who spent thousands a month on her appearance.

"I couldn't drag him from the penthouse all weekend."

Kali rolled her eyes. "I can't believe you're in love."

Cat scoffed. "Nothing like that overrated emotion. He won't submit to me, nor I to him, which inspires mind-numbing sex."

"Got a picture?"

Cat frowned. "The man hates cameras." She grimaced and rubbed her chest. "Me with a hangover. When does that ever happen?"

Kali cast a skeptical eye. Hangovers didn't usually cause chest pains.

Cat dry swallowed four Tylenol and leaned back. "We're

taking the Gulfstream to Paris next weekend, Kali. Gourmet food, high-fashion, walking distance to the Eiffel Tower, all compliments of Gunner's company. He invited you to join us."

Kali's parents' took her to Paris one summer, a backyard picnic with French fries, grape juice, and a tape of Edith Piaf singing *La Vie En Rose*. She said nothing, hoping Cat would get the hint, but social cues were not part of her brilliance.

"He asks all sorts of questions about your research, said he can find funding overseas if you're interested."

Kali's fingers continued with the fury of a jackhammer. "I have to finish my dissertation." She wouldn't mention her new focus on magnetic signatures until she had something solid.

"Come on, Kali. Even Einstein had a social life. Take Wyn."

Kali flinched. Cat didn't know about her change of heart. "I should like him. He's established, rich, loves children…"

Cat offered the ghost of a smile. "I knew you were too smart for that nugatory misogynist. What about Zeke? He's mysterious with a dash of danger. If his feelings for you were purely lust, I'd seduce him." Cat laughed when Kali sputtered. "You can't tell he's in love?"

"He used to be a SEAL."

"A nonsequitur, but that explains his head on a swivel." She eyed Kali through half-closed lids. "When was the last time you did what you wanted, without considering the consequences?"

"Fifteen years, ten months and four days ago."

The jangle of Kali's phone interrupted them. "Ms. Delamagente. I'm receiving anonymous emails about your Dr. Rowe."

Kali bit back her first response and asked, "How are you, Dean?"

He exhaled into the receiver. "They accuse him of a personal agenda though his colleagues tell me he is professional and meticulous. Plus, his early man research brings Columbia acclaim in a field we were previously unremarkable."

Kali's call-waiting beeped. *Zeke*. She ignored it as she struggled to form a neutral response. "How can I help?"

"Every disagreement has two sides. What is Dr. Rowe's?"

The Dean saw everything as a verbal Mobius strip, where different opinions always arrived at his conclusion. "I've found him intelligent and unselfish with his time. Only Dr. Fairgrove complains, and I understand they suffer a history."

The Dean mumbled something like *No doubt* or *don't shout*, but continued before Kali could ask which it was. "Another item. You missed the deadline on your dissertation for the fifth time. Are you familiar with *economics*, Ms. Delamagente? While we altruistically support fledgling researchers in the search for truth, there must be hope they will *finish*, which I *question* in your case. Are you aware how much electricity your research requires? More than all grad students combined. If it was likely to conclude soon, I could extend my patience, but with this FBI interference..."

"The FBI is considering funding me," Kali lied. "They will pay for electrical consumption. I have made significant progress. Otto now integrates research from paleoanthropology's greatest researchers with logical guesses—"

"You're *guessing*?"

"I should use a different word. Otto uses events and circumstances, as the brain does when it makes decisions."

"You're making an *artificial* human brain, what *no one else* has accomplished?"

"Rather than commonalities in thinking, I seek out abnormalities. In fact—"

"Let me get this straight. You take the *research* of Ph.D.'s like Dr. *Fairgrove,* conjecture what they *left out,* based on your—what do you have? A *Masters* in Computer Science?"

By now, Cat could hear him across the room and popped

up two fingers.

Kali gave up trying to be reasonable. "Dr. Manfried. I know Lucy. I smell the sweat dripping from her body as we wander the African savanna. I taste the sulfur in the air from the volcanoes, always on the verge of exploding her world. I share her fear when a Sabertooth attacks and the excitement when—."

"You should transfer to the *English* department where they encourage storytelling. Your final deadline is Friday. Deliver your dissertation or lose Columbia's backing."

"—she survives," she pled into an empty line. "And I'm off campus till Thursday..." Kali settled the phone into its cradle and breathed. "How can I finish on that schedule?"

"Talk to Wyn."

Kali glared at Cat. "I don't want help from a man I'm beginning to despise."

"Screw help, Kal. This is about power. Ours will come, but use Wyn's now."

Rowe arrived, pencil spinning through his nimble fingers, as Cat left for a meeting and Kali completed a short conversation with Wyn's voicemail.

"Sorry, Zeke When you called—"

"You were chatting with the Dean."

"You were eavesdropping?" She wanted to snap his flipping pencil in two. "Never mind. What do you want?"

"Walk with me." When they were outside, he said, "Dr. Sun said Otto can shadow a submarine."

Kali tensed. "He told you?" Why would he do that? But if Eitan trusted Rowe, she should, too. "In theory, yes, but the practical application is more complicated. Otto would need access to a satellite with magnetosphere data for the entire planet. Those are all owned by the government and require top level clearance.

"Done."

Kali blinked. "OK. Next, the delta for change in magnetosphere fluxes is minuscule. Otto can find them, but the scripting required will be equivalent to coding Google

Chrome. I'm talking hundreds—thousands—of hours of work."

She studied him. She saw a mouth set in a tight line, eyes filled with intelligence, a slight nod that said he understood, and the iron will of a man who knew where he was going and nothing would stop him getting there. That trait no doubt served him well in his prior life.

"Let's say I got past that. Where would I get a magnetic signature to test the program? The Navy isn't likely to provide it to a researcher."

"I've almost figured that out."

Rowe struggled to keep his expression neutral, but the importance of what she just admitted couldn't be overstated. He spent the last two hours on a conference call with James' task force, trying to figure out how to warn the Tridents when they were intended to be unreachable. By design, only the sub's Captain knew where they were at any given moment.

While the members chewed on this, James shared an ELINT alert warning of veiled references to 'sale of US military resources'. When Rowe asked the Task Force members whether the sub's magnetic signature could be used as a homing device, he was met first with silence and then frantic claims that magnetic signatures were more secure than D.B. Cooper's whereabouts.

"They're on a SIPNet," an officious-sounding agent lectured. "That's the network that stores America's most confidential information. No one can upload to or download from it—or even sit there without top clearance."

"Truth is, I don't have time, Zeke. The Dean just read me the riot act. I have five days before he cuts me off." Kali's voice became soft, but firm. "You clearly think it's a big deal, Zeke. I'm sorry I can't help."

Her phone rang. He turned to wave goodbye and stopped. Her face was pale, eyes wide, mouth open as she stuttered into her phone.

Chapter 35

"It sounded like Wyn... He said Sean is in danger..."
Tears rolled down Kali's cheeks, the level-headed scientist
overwhelmed by the terrified mother.

Rowe stabbed *69 into Kali's phone. "Number's blocked.
Call Sean." He thrust it into her hands and speed dialed James
on his cell.

"Trace the last incoming to Delamagente's number,
Bobby, and check Fairgrove around the same time."

"What's going on?"

"Someone threatened her son." He hung up and punched
in another number.

"Operator."

"I'm looking for a student in your summer camp. He's
probably in a practice room."

"Please hold."

"Sean didn't answer, Zeke. I left a message." Kali's voice
cracked and then she pushed ten buttons, the last for her
speaker phone. Rowe heard a seductive, heavily accented,
Zdraz Vwitye.

"Mrs. Vitolska? This is Kalian Delamagente, Sean's m-
mom." She took a deep breath to steady herself.

"Ms. Delamagente! How nice of you to call! What a
pleasure is Sean. And his music—so beautiful. Of all students,
Sean is very very best. *Ochin Khorosho!*"

"Thank you—"

"Come to visit! We will love to entertain you, repay for
the joy of Sean's beautiful music."

Kali interrupted, "Thank you. Someone called me and said Sean was in trouble."

"Danger? *Nyet*. Hudson is beautiful. I treat him as I would my own son. He is very safe. He is always with group, and we never leave students home alone, even though this is very low crime. Local police confirm this for you."

"Ask if she's seen him today, and when." Rowe whispered. Kali repeated the question.

"*Konyeshnya*. Of course. We ate breakfast. Good healthy food, though Sean does not eat like other children. You must tell me what he like."

"Yes, I will. After breakfast?"

"*Da*. First, he leant me an arm with dishes. Such a good boy! Then he practice. He love practice. He will play same measure, same phrase over and over with different speed, different cadence. Very creative boy. He just left for lesson. I drove him to bus."

Rowe exhaled. What were the chances someone kidnapped Sean from public transportation?

"I am sure he is safe. What nasty hoax. I love this America, but some of people, such odd sense of humor. *Skazheetye Pozhalsta*. Why would someone want worry you? Sean speaks highly of you. How you would anger anyone? People do this in Russia, not here. What could they want from this boy? His genius is in his head and fingers."

Kali caught Rowe's eye and he shook his head. "Thank you, Mrs. Vitolska. I appreciate what you do for him."

"*Ne Mnozhka*. A burden of one's own choice is not felt."

"Would you ask him to call as soon as you see him?"

"*Da, da*. He should be home soon. I baking cookies for students, relax before more practice. The very moment he walk through door. I stick to him like leech. *Da Zvidanya*."

Kali hung up reassured, but Rowe's gut rolled. He needed to visit this summer camp. "Is she always blocked, Kali?"

"I never called her before," she answered as she opened an app on her phone, stared at a blinking light, and then tapped through a sequence of steps.

"What's that?"

"As student hosts for the summer camp, the Vitolska's are linked to a GPS locator. The call went to DC, but Ms. Vitolska said she was home, in Hudson, New York." She puckered her brow as her face lost more color. "The blue icon is Sean's phone."

"Can I help you?"

"I'm looking for Sean Delamagente."

"He's in a lesson. Do you want me to interrupt?" Deep, mellow scales reverberated in the background, then stopped when someone called Sean's name. Kali's eyes were on Rowe.

"No, I'll call later." He hung up and smiled. "This is a bad joke."

She threw her arms around him and spoke through tears, halting to blow her nose and rub her face.

"My grandparents took charge of Sean after my parents died. To me, he was a toy. All I did was kiss him goodbye over breakfast and peek in on him at night as he slept. When they passed also, this five-year-old became my responsibility and I was scared to death. If I had contact with Fletcher—his father—I would have asked him to take the boy."

She hung her head, face flushed with shame.

"I remember the day after the funeral. Sean's innocent eyes, a frightened but hopeful half-smile struggling to surface, arms stiff at his sides, chubby fists clenched as he fought tears. I wanted to ask him what he ate and did he need help getting ready for school or going to sleep at night. I had no idea what he did all day, the games he played, what he thought about. I always assumed it was nothing important. He'd just seen his grandma buried. Should I hug him? Feed him ice cream? In the end, I told him to go play and I returned to work."

Her eyes glistened with tears. She focused over Zeke's shoulder, breaths coming in short, shallow gasps.

"Over the next year, I let him do what he wanted as long as he didn't bother me. He was precociously smart, read any book he found around the apartment including my grad textbooks. He spent most evenings on the internet, pudgy fingers pounding through all manner of websites. I forbade adult sites—a check of his computer history said he obeyed. I was proud of him when I spared time to think about it, congratulating myself on my great parenting. My son would grow up to be independent and self-reliant. Soon, we had a perfect routine that rarely required we talk or even interact in any way. I thought he'd tell me if he needed help.

"He didn't.

"I found out from the school principal. *Ms. Delamagente—I'm sorry, we've never met. I'm Mr. Klecher. ... No, not new, I've been here three years... Well, we do organize meet-and-greets once a month, but Sean says you work a lot... Yes, I realize that and am sorry to bother you, but your son missed classes today, and yesterday, and twice last week. ... Well, I'm sure you did send him, but he didn't get here.*

"First, I was annoyed at the principal for questioning me, and then I was angry at Sean for disobeying our unspoken agreement. While I waited for him to get home that evening, I tried to remember the last time we talked about anything important, such as what he liked at school, who his friends were, his opinions on a book he read. I still cringed from memories of my parents nagging so much I'd wriggle in behind a dresser until they left. I refused to be that person, but more than that, to be honest, I wanted my own life. In the hour I paced, I couldn't come up with a single topic we'd said more than five words about.

"When he got home, he walked in without a greeting, face a mask, clothes rumpled, not even reacting to the oddity of Mom at the front door rather than pigeon-holed with her computer.

'How was your day, Sean?'

"He paused as though surprised by my voice, fixed me with the deadest eyes I'd ever seen on someone his age. Not a flicker of emotion crossed his face. *'Boring.'*

"Now I was frightened. When had my little boy changed? *'Do you want a snack?'*

He said nothing, ignored me as he went to his room, shoulders slumped, feet shuffling in unlaced shoes.

"Something broke inside of me.

"I sat at the little wood table grandma had set up for his homework and asked if I could see his science. After a third calm request, he dug it out of a dirty backpack, crumpled and smudged and incomplete.

'It's easy. I can do it in no time.' There was a quiver in his voice, the first sign of emotion since he entered the house.

"I asked him to demonstrate.

'Well, let me think about it.'

"I laughed and picked a leaf from his hair. *'I said that a lot in college.'*

"He tilted his head, tapped the table and said, *'You went to college?'*

"From then on, we did his homework together every evening. I was amazed how this seven-year-old connected information, paused to think, and stuck with a thread to its logical end. I started attending his music events and volunteered for field trips. We struggled at first with stilted discussions mostly about his classes, and then his day, and finally, I asked what was on his mind and shut my mouth. Gradually, I fell in love with this wonderful boy. Soon, he was my first sunny thought and last calming breath to every chaotic day."

Rowe made what he hoped were soothing sounds, but comforting anyone was well outside his skillset. He felt loyalty toward his SEAL brothers and vengeance for wrongdoing, but looking at the world through someone else's eyes felt like a wooden door warped shut, one he never thought worth opening.

Today, here, he wanted to do it.

When Kali calmed to an occasional sniffle, he asked, "You said Wyn's name when you answered the call. Did it sound like him?"

Her voice came out small and distant. "I thought so, but when I asked, he hung up."

He let that go. "Did Sean mention trouble with the Vitolska's? Or anyone?"

She shook her head. "He says Mr. Vitolska is great. Same with the camp students. He helps them with bowing and phrasing... Oh, Zeke, why is this happening? And why did he tell me Otto needed to track a submarine?"

Rowe froze just as his phone burped, saving him from answering. A text from Sun. *Come see me.*

He gently took her hand. "Everything's going to be OK." He needed to tell her about the tie-ins to Zematis, about the message pounded into Devore's chest, and his suspicions about Keregosian, but it would wait. "I'll be back to check on you."

Kali massaged her temples and didn't even look up.

Just as he arrived at Sun's lab, his phone chirped again. "What's going on, Zeke?"

Rowe checked that the encryption was turned on before recounting the last fifteen minutes to James.

"Does Keregosian know Sean is Kali's son?"

"He seems to know everything. I've always thought it was because he and Kali talk about everything, but this—Kali didn't even know it was possible until we walked through it together—"

He stopped, remembering yesterday's conversation with Sun. "I need to talk with Dr. Sun."

"Before you go, Keregosian is in communication with someone in Hudson. Isn't that where Sean is?"

Rowe clenched his fists. He needed to go up there yesterday. "Anything from Annie?"

James sighed. "If there's anything I should know, I'll hear from her. If not, I won't," and hung up.

Rowe settled into a chair between a ruined cardboard box and a shopping bag stuffed with snacks. Sun's eyes were bloodshot and his thinning hair stuck out like porcupine quills.

"Eitan. Kali's caller knew Otto might be able to track submarines. That could only be from us," he waved a hand indicating the two of them, "last night or Kali and I this morning."

Sun sat on his feet in his chair and bounced as his head bobbed, eyes fixed on his monitor, but all Rowe saw was a jumble of words against a black background. "What?"

"Keregosian sent audio files to Fairgrove of conversations between Kali and me and Kali and you."

"They're bugging her office, I'm sure of it. I just can't find the device—"

"They aren't always from there. Some are from your lab, the hallway, even outside. The earliest one I find is when you returned from Israel."

"Is it possible we were each tagged?"

Sun handed Rowe a palm-sized disk. "Let's find out. This is an electronic surveillance scanner. If you're within twenty feet of a recording device, it can find it."

Chapter 36

"She thought it was you."

Al-Zahrawi offered a rare chuckle on the other end of the line, but Fairgrove blanched. How could he earn Kalian's trust if she considered him a danger to her son?

"I told you to leave him alone." He squeaked through clenched teeth. "What did you say?"

"Her suspicions of you began long before today." Al-Zahrawi ignored Fairgrove's whining protest. "I gave her a good reason to focus on results, Wynton. Allah cares nothing about collateral damage—is this the term you Americans use?"

Fairgrove was furious. "Do you not see Otto is our money tree? With my paleoanthropologic connections, we will be modern-day Darwins, revealing the why and how to Nature's evolutionary pruning. Trust me, Salah. You will soon start a new life with your family in America."

Fairgrove paused, impressed with his impromptu speech. How could Al-Zahrawi resist its emotion?

"Why would I want to live in your depraved country, Wynton? My goal is revenge. Yours is fame. Otto gives us both what we want. Make Ms. Delamagente work faster."

Fairgrove tugged at his collar. "How? Brilliance works at its own perspicacious pace!" Fairgrove glowed at his latest epigram. He would repeat it to his students.

"Motivate her, Wynton, or I will."

Thanks to Ms. Delamagente and Dr. Rowe, Al-Zahrawi

now knew Otto could locate a sub at sea. No doubt Delamagente would make that her priority with her son's life at stake.

Al-Zahrawi had toyed with creating a duplicate of Otto, but his scientists said it would take too long; the auction was in two weeks. That left Delamagente. The longer she took, though, the more time Dr. Zeke Rowe had to stop her. If Fairgrove did not solve that soon, Al-Zahrawi would.

Al-Zahrawi was bone weary of Dr. Wynton Fairgrove. It would bring him joy to end the infidel's life. Yet Delamagente was like no woman he had ever met. The way she could connect the oddest pieces of information—it pained him he must kill her.

Chapter 37

Kali couldn't concentrate. A vision of Sean in baggy cargo shorts, backpack slung over a bony shoulder, string base strapped to his back like a refrigerator, quick wave as he raced for the bus that would deposit him at school kept rolling through her memories. She should use the hours remaining before her trip to Hudson either satisfying the Dean's demands or Zeke's requests.

She did neither.

Zeke declared the call a prank, but she disagreed. She massaged her temples, rolled her neck and glared at the tiny blue flag that was her son's mobile. It was exactly where it should be, unmoving outside the practice building. He ignored her calls and texts which was pretty much normal, so she did the math. He took an hour warm up on his string bass before a lesson, then ninety minutes with the instructor and an indeterminate amount of time reviewing.

She sipped water, chewed through two packets of pretzels, cleaned her inbox, and still no movement. Footsteps clattered past her door as students left for the day. Somewhere a phone chimed five times and stopped. Riverside Church's bells tolled the hour, and the next.

Nothing.

She straightened her desk drawers, dusted her shelves, scrubbed her monitor and picked dirt from her keyboard. She ran her fingers through her hair and then thrust them into her lap, laced together to keep them from shaking. Sean probably went to lunch and left the phone. He didn't take it everywhere like other teens.

Four and a half hours. He should have responded. She paced back and forth, checked the GPS app to be sure it was still working, and verified her internet connection. Everything worked, but the flag remained stationary. If this was Wyn's doing, he had sorely misjudged her. Using her research for personal reasons was amoral. Involving her son was unforgivable.

Or was he warning her? Was the real threat someone he worked with? She needed to find out.

Every digital device on Columbia's network required a password that must be changed each semester. Most people chose three related events or people. To determine Wyn's meant figuring out what he considered important.

It took seconds to break into Human Resources, rightly guessing the assistant's three children's names. A few clicks later, she was reading Wyn's file.

Interesting. He had a provisional contract, so they could let him go at any time.

"So much for high and mighty."

She browsed his records with an eye to passwords he would choose. No children, one wife. Too many girlfriends. More than three awards. One house. Forty-five minutes later, she found his curriculum vitae with an extensive list of publications. Only three had ISBN numbers. She input the first and crossed her fingers. She only had three attempts before the system shut her out and reported the intrusion.

"Oh, he's too much."

Wyn's face splashed across the desktop, complete with the cocky head tilt he loved, raffish grin, and an open shirt to display a rack of curly dark hair. She clicked Firefox and downloaded a sleuth program from a hacker website she frequented. While she browsed, it would copy his data and erase every trace of her presence.

She started with email. He communicated often with two online pharmacies, a girl named Lustybusty, and someone called 'Salah'.

Kali froze. Was this the 'Salah' who contacted her after Alfred Zematis' death? Surely 'Salah' was a common Muslim name? She shook it off, willing herself to move on.

This was odd. Why did Keregosian forward her emails to Wyn? Was Wyn responsible for her only financial supporter? Kali flinched at that thought.

She riffled through the 'Sent' and 'Deleted' files with no luck, and moved to internet searches. He googled Zeke and herself, but nothing else of interest. She'd check the browser History file. Lots of people emptied it, but few remembered to delete the cookies. There she found five sites, all other Universities.

One more place to visit before signing off. She opened 'My Documents'. No surprise he mommy-saved everything in a disorganized pile under the root folder. Lecture notes, class outlines, a scathing demand that Dean Manfried fire 'the imposter, Zeke Rowe', and a demeaning letter assuring the Dean Kali's youth and enthusiasm made her a valuable asset to the established researchers at Columbia. There were a few applications for guest lecturer positions and visiting professorships at the Universities he'd Googled. They all seemed to be unsolicited.

He also had shots of her computer, including her screensaver. According to the date stamp, he had them a week before their first meeting, plenty of time to decipher the 1's and 0's in the message. Without thinking, she massaged her thrumming temple.

What was this folder—'History'? Before she could open it, Wyn's offsite log-in activated. She had less than a minute to back out, verify no trace of her visit existed, and add a backdoor in case she wanted to return. She finished with two seconds to spare, just as Sean called.

"Mom! My teacher played for the President yesterday. How cool is that!"

Tears sprang to Kali's eyes. "You're OK? No problems?" Her breath came in shallow pants as she fought to control herself.

When Sean answered, his voice was confused. "Yeah, of course."

She forced a smile, though Sean couldn't see it. "You like the Vitolska's?"

"Sure. They're what I want to be." He sounded exasperated so she didn't mention the hoax. "Gotta go. My phrasing in *Pines of Rome* needs work. See you soon!"

Heat flared across Kali's face. She paced the tiny space of her lab, throat raw from emotion, heart pulling back from the brink of panic one shallow breath at a time.

"Are you alright?" How long had Eitan been there? He leaned quietly against the doorframe, fixing Kali with those deep, all-seeing eyes of his.

"A hoax, Eitan. Why are people so cruel?"

"They prey on the human propensity to believe what is easiest, not necessarily smartest. Isn't that your selling point for Otto? That he draws conclusions without emotion?"

Sun gazed at one of Kali's many Lucy pictures. In this one, Lucy and Raza hunted, what some scientists considered scavenging, awaiting the leftovers from a Scimitartooth's kill. Behind them, hidden in a dense patch of shoulder-high scrub, stood a male *Homo erectus*, spear canted, muscles rigid, eyes pinpricks, and mouth a tight gash across his weather-beaten face.

Behind him, upwind, oblivious to the two-legged predator, grazed an Hipparion.

Kali kept this as an example of early man's ability to weigh choices: a scrawny, bony primate who couldn't escape, or a fat, meaty fleet-of-foot mammal with a herd for protection.

A frown creased Sun's smooth forehead. He didn't have to say a word; Kali understand.

What Sun learned from a father who deserted his wife and four-year-old son to travel the world with a wealthy widow was to follow the path of least resistance.

In middle school, Sun analyzed what attracted girls and determined football stars had the best luck. He went out for the team and ended up the towel boy. That got hugs and kisses from the cheerleaders, but no dates. The closest he got was doing their math homework while they went out with the players.

In high school, a pretty girl asked for help preparing for a math competition, but Sun turned out to be a horrible tutor. He couldn't explain how the answers appeared to him, the magnificent patterns and shapes that pulsed from the page. The pretty girl's face lit up, but nothing this easy could impress her. When the instructor asked him to join the Mathletics, he agreed for two reasons: The pretty girl promised to drive with him and the teacher agreed to discuss all three volumes of *Tesla's Complete Works*.

By the time he graduated, he came to an epiphany: Most people didn't feel the beautiful numbers that called out to him in their pretty combinations. He got excited when the clock read 14:22 or the speedometer on his car shouted 36912 miles, or 112358. Or when his speed matched the tachometer. He used his favorite palindromic prime—134757431—for PINs.

He loved tables, spreading page after page with their sweet patterns waiting to be discovered. Graphs bored Sun. They drew conclusions about what was important, which usually wasn't. When he read, he didn't grab words one at a time, left to right, but gulped them in whole phrases and organized them. Patterns spoke so much more elegantly than a collection of syllables.

When the California Institute of Technology's Center for Advanced Research offered him a scholarship, he turned it down. He craved a challenge and theoretical calculus wasn't— until he met a professor in the computer science department. There, Sun discovered the quest to understand phenomena that couldn't be replicated.

He played his wife's picture one more time, for a total of three--the smallest Fibonacci prime and a good stopping point.

"Hello, sweetheart…"

Chapter 38

"Kali! I heard about your son."

Fairgrove elbowed his way past Rowe who was reviewing Kali's safety measures while traveling to Sean's concert. He asked Annie to tag along, but the agent was following a lead she hoped would unravel the case. He wanted to bring Duck's friends in, but Kali refused so Rowe settled for dropping a GPS tracker disguised as a pen into her purse and crossing his fingers she wouldn't lend it out.

"Is he OK?" Other than a five-o'clock shadow, Fairgrove looked fresh and crisp in a navy sport coat, baby blue shirt, and tasseled loafers. He'd even taken time to add a flower to his lapel.

Something unreadable flicked across Kali's face. "Yes, it was a hoax."

"How'd you hear, Wyn?" Rowe kept his tone casual, but narrowed his eyes.

Fairgrove's eyes fluttered. "From someone in the cafeteria, I think."

Wrong answer. No one was privy to the call except Kali, Rowe, and James. Fairgrove smoothed his eyebrow, adjusted his boutonnière and raised a finger. Rowe couldn't resist.

"You have a thought?"

"Why, yes." He turned is back to Rowe in an obvious effort to exclude him from the conversation. "Allow me to make a proposition, Kalian." He stepped closer and Kali cringed which Fairgrove didn't seem to notice. "Let's take Auto Otto—what a clever name for his portable identity. I just came up with it." Kali rolled her eyes and Rowe struggled to contain his laughter. "Let's take Auto Otto to Olduvai," East Africa, the Cradle of Mankind, considered the most prolific repository of hominid artifacts. "I have friends there interested in Otto's results." He lowered his voice. "If Otto confirms accepted beliefs, it will legitimize our research. If he contradicts it, you can rework his algorithms before you submit to Dean Manfried."

His use of the word 'our' rankled Rowe, but Kali ignored it. Rowe stepped in front of Fairgrove. "Is that always your goal, to ensure results agree with established wisdom?"

Kali glared at Rowe and turned to Fairgrove. "I'm not ready to show my work to the world—"

"I'll be with you, dear."

He shuffled into Kali's space, but she didn't waver. "Thank you, Wyn, but I'd feel terrible if I hurt your reputation." Before he could respond, she added, "I'm off," and fled.

"Kalian! Would you like company?" No answer. "I guess she didn't hear me."

"Kali needs your help like a submarine needs diesel fuel."

Fairgrove spasmed and stomped out without a backward glance.

Chapter 39

Tuesday

Rowe awoke moments before his alarm. He hadn't slept well, his dreams populated with images of Tomahawks reigning down on disbelieving citizens, their ravaged cries drowned out by the screaming whoosh and roar of cruise missiles. Trident submarines that should be America's last best defense were now her greatest enemy. His eyes felt sticky and his head like a jar of damp cotton.

He needed coffee.

James texted last night that two more subs called in. That made six. No one expected all the subs to make contact before Friday's deadline. The only hope to save those crews was for Rowe and James to stop Al-Zahrawi.

Fairgrove was the weak link. He saw himself as a disruptive force, but was more a malignant tumor. Yesterday's verbal sparring had been calculated to send him whining to his handlers. When he stormed out of Kali's lab, Rowe followed. He thought he got lucky when Fairgrove immediately placed a call, but James traced it to a sophomore anthropology major who apparently was unavailable for dinner with the renowned Dr. Fairgrove. He then drank his meal at a local bar and went to a movie—alone. Rowe stuck with him through an awful Hollywood conspiracy that attracted only a handful of viewers. He was thrilled when Fairgrove left half-way through and went home. When his lights winked out, Rowe joined James for a beer.

"Would you run Gunner through NCIC, Bobby?"

Moments later, they had a list of twelve hundred two names, mostly white supremacists and military journalists. Since Stockbury had no photo, Rowe spent the rest of the evening thumbing through bios while watching Kali's GPS tag on his phone and listening to James's take on fashion.

When James left for a date, Rowe went home. He was asleep by 1am.

Five hours later, he blew through his morning workout wondering if the sixth sense that had served him flawlessly as a SEAL was another casualty of the torture. Used to be, instinct pointed him true north. In this case, he was reacting to events, always a step behind.

He and James agreed to drop in on the Vitolska's. The man who attacked Rowe in Israel was Russian and Gunner's accent was Russian. Doubtless it wasn't a coincidence.

Rowe made instant coffee with hot tap water, gulped one mouthful and another, and felt the caffeine sizzle through his body. God he loved the first cup of the day. According to GPS, Kali remained exactly where she should be, which bumped his stress down a notch. Annie left him a text, but he couldn't reach her.

He scanned his email, but Griff—Dr. Josiah Griffin to United States Naval Academy Midshipmen—hadn't returned his call. He taught submarine warfare at USNA and knew more about magnetic anomaly detection than anyone on the planet. The six-week induction of first-time Midshipmen—called Plebe Summer—was a bad time to reach him, but too much hinged on sub magnetics to wait. If he didn't hear from Griff soon, Rowe would drive to Annapolis, Maryland and find him somewhere on the USNA yard.

No need to follow Fairgrove today. When Ajit hacked Fairgrove's OnStar, he was with a fellow paleoanthropologist on their way to the man's Harvard office. That would keep them busy all day. For the sake of redundancy, James was taping their conversation through Fairgrove's phone.

He took a two-minute shower, dressed in the same clothes as yesterday, and ate two stale English muffins with a thick spread of peanut butter. Ten minutes later, windows down, Trace Atkins blaring from the speakers, he cleared the George Washington Bridge and entered the Columbia campus. Birds serenaded the morning and a squirrel chattered shrilly to its mate.

At Kali's lab, he found Stockbury, arms crossed over her chest, head back. She grunted without moving. Her long sleeves, a high-collared shirt, and too much make-up shouted out what she wanted to hide. He cast a skeptical eye, but Stockbury ignored him.

Rowe looked across the room as though expecting Kali to poke her head from behind her monitor, and then settled wordlessly into her chair.

He leaned back, eyes closed, and balanced his feet on her trash can. The scent of her perfume wafting gently from her desk nearly broke him. The way she thought through choices, would never quit, how her internal beauty matched her physical—he couldn't go back to life before her, but had no idea how to go forward.

Something to think about when this was over.

"You're depressing," and Stockbury went back to sleep.

Rowe took a breath, then another. "How's your boyfriend—Gunner?"

"He's not abusing me. I fell."

Rowe pretended to accept that. As though remembering why he was here, he asked, "Kali says Gunner is interested in her research. Yours, too?"

He tried to sound innocent, but Stockbury saw right through him. "He's more into Otto than computer viruses."

After five more minutes of silence, he patted Stockbury's arm and left to meet James. She never moved.

Chapter 40

Rowe drove his Benz and James his government-issue Buick. In tandem, they slipped north, through the New York metropolis, past the rotten egg stench of the North River Sewage Treatment Plant, barely noticing as the Spuyten Duyvil Creek connected Harlem River to the mighty Hudson.

The Hudson River, *Muhheakantuck* or "great waters in constant motion" to the Iroquois, coursed through the heart of Eastern New York from its beginning in the Adirondack Mountains, past its juncture with the Erie Canal to its termination in New York Harbor and the Atlantic Ocean. Rowe loved its heady scent of fuel oil and fish. As a teen, Rowe spent much time outdoors fishing, hiking, camping, and thinking. It was there he found peace, regardless the turmoil that rolled through his life, and learned respect for life.

One January, he hunkered into the boughs of an old aspen by a beaver dam. They had to come out sometime, didn't they? He fell asleep and awoke the next morning to the *swish, plunk, slap* as an otter family slid down the dam into the water, over and over. When they tired of that game, they plunked a pebble into the pool, diving and catching it on their foreheads in playful abandon.

Soon, the road veered inland, across the Newburgh-Beacon Bridge and chugged through farmland and small towns, past West Point where thousands of cadets received a world-class education in return for five patriotic years defending the nation, to the hilly region where the air cleared and traffic thinned. And the tension melted from Rowe's body.

Two hours later, they reached Hudson New York, America's first chartered city and named for the explorer who spent the last years of his life searching for the Northwest Passage. It was once a bustling river port, but now best known for its antique shops. The two-car convoy wove through saltbox homes and ramblers until Rowe pulled up in front of the Vitolska's white clapboard house. It was indistinguishable from its neighbors—window boxes overflowing with seasonal flowers, freshly painted siding, well-tended lawn, and a brick sidewalk leading to a comfortable wood porch, which reminded Rowe he had to finish his.

"There's a van in the garage."

James texted the license to his assistant Tess and peeked in the mailbox. Classical music floated out the open front door.

"Anyone home?" Rowe shouted as he knocked.

A blonde mirage dressed in a pink halter and short white skirt glided toward them. China blue eyes flirted beneath black lashes and narrow sculpted brows. Her full lips tipped up with interest and parted to reveal perfect white-white teeth.

"*Shto vwi Hkotetye*. Can I assist you?"

The voice was more sultry in person than on the phone, but with the same deep accent and practiced innocence. Mrs. Vitolska was six feet, 140 pounds of well-toned vibrant femme-fatale, with nary an ounce of fat on the numerous exposed body parts. She moved with the feline grace of a panther stalking its next victim.

"You are Ms. Vitolska?"

"*Da*, this is me." She shifted her weight from one leg to the other and ping-ponged between them. "Which of you is Boss man?"

She moved a slender finger to her lips, the tip of her rosy tongue poking through, and fixed James with a wide-eyed bottomless gaze. "You, such stylish clothes, such elegant shoes, so beautiful. Like James Bond. You have girlfriend, yes? Or you," and the digit landed on Rowe, "What a bad boy with your seductive eyes, air of danger. You are heartbreaker."

Rowe pulled his tongue back into his mouth and was happy James responded.

"Mr. Brown and Mr. Black, from the FBI. May we take a minute of your time?"

She locked onto James as he showed his credentials. Her glistening red lips parted and her cheeks flushed. Rowe worried about Sean. No way a teenager could handle this predator.

"*Zdrazvwitye*, Mr. Brown and Mr. Black. I supervise students from Juilliard, one of America's great Universities for to train musicians. I learn at Moscow Conservatory. Also good school, but not so much since government changed, and not so good pay either."

She checked her watch, a diamond-studded Cartier. "I must to pick children up at twelve, but I am sure I can make a few minutes to talk. *Pozhalsta*, please, come in."

She broadened her smile and swept a loose hair from her forehead with a shake of her head.

"Please to be seated." She led them to a comfortable-looking sofa arrangement.

The room's decorations came right out of *Better Homes and Gardens*. Chintz curtains hung over the windows and photos of smiling faces from three to ninety-three covered one wall. The furniture shone with polish and the white carpet was streaked from recent vacuuming.

"Could I have a glass of water, Ms. Vitolska?" James stood as she uncrossed her sleek legs. "Stay seated, please. My wife taught me how to get around a kitchen."

"Your house is comfortable, Ms. Vitolska—"

"Call me Sam, Mr. Black." Her eyes were clear and steady.

"If you'll call me Zeke."

"Zeke. Is this nickname for Ezekiel?"

Rowe smiled with hooded eyes. "Sam must be short for Samantha?"

"You Americans with such brilliant nicknames—is this

what you call it? Always shorter than original. In Russia, this is not the case."

Rowe asked about her time in the United States and the students she shepherded for Juilliard, snapping pictures as he fiddled with his glasses.

"Your lenses, they do not fit? Or do I make you nervous?" She recrossed her tanned legs and leaned forward to hear his answer.

James saved him just in time with water for everyone.

"We received a missing student report earlier this week, Ms. Vitolska."

"Please. Sam—like Zeke. We are all friends here."

"Sam. His name's Sean Delamagente."

"Of course. His mother call me very worried. I try to reassure her. He came back in evening, as planned."

"Where is he now?" James sipped his water.

"This is very talented young man. Important people select him for Honor Orchestra. You are familiar with this group? They are best in country. I am lucky to enjoy his music."

"So he is where?" Rowe repeated.

"Washington DC. There is a concert at Constitution Hall. I study Constitution Hall for my citizen test. What a tribute to your wonderful country! Would you like address?"

"No, we can find it. Have you seen any strange activities, anyone out of place, or cars that don't belong in the neighborhood?" He took another sip of water.

She dropped her head. Full lashes brushed glowing healthy cheeks. Rowe felt the need to protect her.

"I have no knowledge of this. I do not want to forget something which could help. I ask my husband, Edik, when he returns." She tucked her hair behind an ear and her eyes fluttered toward Rowe. "Perhaps the Monroe's next door. They are more observant I think than I."

"Are you friends with them?"

"I would not call it friends. What I mean is they live here longer. They are familiar with what is normal."

James asked a few more questions and rose to leave. "We

appreciate your assistance, Ms. Vitolska. Every time pranksters make crazy calls, they run us through all sorts of paperwork. Me, I just want to be home in time for the baseball game." James caught her eye. "You like baseball, Ms. Vitolska?"

"*Konyeshna*. We like it for the children. America loves the team sports!"

"Thanks again."

Once out of earshot, Rowe whispered, "No way that antenna's for the kids."

James said. "The kitchen was unused—perfectly-ordered cupboards, empty dishwasher, and a spotless oven. Nothing like mine."

As they walked down the Monroe's driveway, a BMW pulled in. Rowe did a double-take. "Why it's Fred." Same disheveled hair and blank stare Rowe remembered from the photo. The hair rose on Rowe's neck and his senses went on alert.

When Fred got out of the car, James greeted him with his FBI badge, one hand hovering by his weapon, eyes dark pools. "Matt Monroe? My name is Special Agent Bobby James with the FBI and this is my associate. Do you have a minute?"

Fred's nose twitched as he tugged a nylon windbreaker over a pink collared shirt and yellow plaid trousers. Spikes clacked as he hurried up the sidewalk.

"I'm in a hurry."

"Or should we call you Fred?"

He flipped around and marched back toward James with a shake of his head. A sheen of sweat sprouted on his forehead. There was a faint whiff of alcohol on his breath.

"We have you on tape."

Now Monroe bolted forward with a quick backward glance. "My wife. She doesn't know. You got it on tape?"

James flipped through a small spiral notebook and read the guard's notes, "*I did my part. Leave the money where you always do.* Pretty incriminating, Matt. If you provide a full accounting of your dealings with Gegham Keregosian, it may be unnecessary to confirm your whereabouts with Mrs. Monroe."

Monroe's eyes clouded. "Who is Gegham Keregosian?"

"You may know him as Salah Al-Zahrawi."

Monroe shook his head. "He never gave me a name," and he told them everything. He got an email when his services were required. In this case, he was to chat with a Kalian Delamagente about anything he wanted, but look around her office while they talked. A camcorder in his glasses recorded everything and uploaded the files to a DropBox account that changed with every job.

His eyes narrowed. "Nothing illegal about talking."

"You broke into a secure building—"

"My contact gave me a key." He fumbled in his pocket. "Take it. I don't need it."

Rowe took it by the edges and dropped it into a baggy. "Can you describe this person?"

"I never see him. We communicate via email."

"What number did you call when you left Kali's lab?"

"I don't remember. He uses throw-away phones, different number each time."

"It's a 'he'?"

Monroe shrugged. "His emails sound male."

"What if you need to talk to him in between?"

"I don't. He always finds me."

"How many jobs have you done for him?"

"Two? Or three?"

Or twice as many. James reached into his pocket as he said, "Under Article 54 Section 582 Subsection 6 of the New York State Penal Law, I'm placing you under arrest for Conspiracy by association to cheat or defraud. Turn around, please."

"Wait!" His eyes went round with panic and he backed up a step, colliding with Rowe's stocky, unresisting body. "This can't happen!" Fear tugged at the fine lines of his face as Rowe slammed him against the hood of his BMW. Someone peeked out the front window.

James noisily pulled handcuffs from his pocket. "We want your contact, but will settle for you. If your story checks out and you help arrest him, I'll put in a good word with the judge."

"Yes! Of course I'll cooperate. I didn't know he was breaking the law!"

James crowded Monroe until he hovered an inch from the man's damp face. "Prove it. We'll skip this whole arrest thing if you call me next time you hear from him." He spoke softly, but there was no question of his intensity. "He wants to kill thousands of your fellow Americans. Help us put him behind bars."

Monroe's head bounced like a bobble-head doll, mouth open in an O, eyes so wide they were ringed by white. When James backed away and waved a dismissive hand, he sprinted into his house and slammed the door.

James waited, but the only sound was the lock snapping into place. "Think we'll ever hear from him?"

"Let's talk to the neighbors."

The woman across the street wanted to file a noise complaint about the constant music. James referred her to the local police. No one answered to the Vitolska's right, so James left his card. Several people mentioned visitors at the house. Descriptions ranged from Middle Eastern to Slavic to an American muscle man. After two hours, the duo stopped for coffee at a local McDonald's. Rowe downed his in three gulps and went for a refill while James skimmed his email.

"DropBox account and phone are inactive." He double-clicked a file. "Tess attached the lugs from Hemren's cell. A few local calls, pizza delivery, a Mosque." He stopped. "He dials Esfahan every week."

"That's where he told Kali he grew up."

James sat back, eyes looking inward. "Al-Zahrawi hijacks the subs with the virus, sells the locations to the highest bidder, and uses Otto to find them. The only tie in to the Vitolska's is Sean. But it's odd them living next door to Fred aka Matt Monroe. And how does any of this tie in to the threats?"

Rowe pulled his pencil out and started flipping it. "Friday is the deadline to withdraw the Tridents, according to Devore's murderers, or they murder someone else. If they expected the Navy to capitulate, they wouldn't pressure Delamagente. She certainly won't be done by Friday. She hasn't even started."

"Which Al-Zahrawi knows, like he knows everything else, so why the games?"

Something tickled Rowe's memory. "Why did he want Monroe to take a video of Kali? What was he looking for?"

Rowe turned the thought over in his brain, but got nothing.

"Have Agit compare the excerpts I sent you from Fairgrove's manuscripts. If I'm right, Fairgrove stole most of his ground-breaking research from girlfriends. We can use the threat of exposure to force him to talk."

James's jaw froze, staring at something in the distance, and then began chewing again. "Good idea. Something's going to happen Friday and we won't like it."

Rowe's phone chimed. Fairgrove was headed home earlier than Rowe expected.

Chapter 41

James stopped in at the Hudson police as Rowe hit the southbound Thruway going eighty. Fairgrove had abandoned a meeting with colleagues eager for his insights. There had to be a spectacular reason. As he merged into the fast lane, Rowe's phone rang.

"Griff!"

"Don't tell me you joined the FBI." It was good to hear his friend's voice.

"A long story. Ended up, I didn't have a choice."

Griff chortled. They caught up for a few minutes and then Rowe asked, "What can you tell me about magnetic anomaly detection and submarines?"

"Can the question be any broader?" He barked. "OK. Let's start with an overview. Magnetic Anomaly Detection—MAD—works by locating changes in the earth's magnetic field made as the sub moves through the water." He fell silent. Rowe imagined Griff trying to figure out the best way to explain this to a novice.

"Think of the Earth as a big magnet, fluxes spanning the planet from North Pole to South. Anything containing iron—like a submarine—interrupts the normalcy of those fluxes and can be tracked by its disruption to the magnetic field. The challenge for America is to dampen the sub's effect on the magnetosphere enough that it becomes so minute as to be invisible.

"That's harder than it sounds because a sub has two types of magnetism. 'Temporary' varies in proportion to the field around it and can be minimized by deperming—a process that removes excess magnetism collected by the sub's movement through the seas. 'Permanent' is locked into the hull at construction. Theoretically, MAD devices can be built that recognize both, but in reality, we're a long way from a device sensitive enough to notice the permanent.

"Regardless of the magnetism's source, even the best MAD devices are not the perfect discovery tool we wish they were. Range is limited so you need a tight search area. When you get that close to a sub, it will attack, evade, or hide below the thermocline until the threat disappears. Right now, we're better at hunting and evading than our enemies, but once some scientist invents an ultra-sensitive MAD, we're in trouble."

Rowe squirmed. He was pretty sure Griff would put Otto in that 'ultra-sensitive' category, but he couldn't tell him that.

"I know each submarine uniquely disrupts the magnetosphere, giving it a magnetic signature that identifies only itself, and I know that data is protected on a SIPNet." Griff started to say something, but Rowe barreled forward. "Can that server be hacked?" Rowe didn't trust the answer from James' Task Force. They had been flippant, even defensive in their denial. If there was a weakness, Griff would tell him.

"No." Nothing else. It was clear Griff was not comfortable talking about this topic.

Someone yelled in the background, followed by a swell of voices ending in 'Sir, yes sir!' What Plebe Summer cadre called a 'sir sandwich' and required of all new Mids.

Rowe prodded. "Could someone recreate them?"

Griff's answer was hesitant. "No, Zero, at least, no one ever has. What's up?"

Rowe's jaw ached. He'd been grinding his teeth, again. He breathed out slowly, relieved. Otto couldn't find the subs. Rowe swerved around a twenty-year-old Ford truck and then had to slam his breaks on to keep from rear-ending a Porsche.

"Just pulling a thread. If that changes, I'll call you."

He was about to say goodbye when he had another

thought. "One more question. How would I get ahold of a MAD device?"

Griff answered in a tone that told Rowe his friend was running out of patience. "You don't. They're the size of a torpedo and loaded on helicopters, fixed wing aircraft, or drones. Zeke, what aren't you telling me?"

Griff's chair squeaked and then the only noise was Griff's fingers tapping on his desk. When fifteen seconds passed and Rowe still said nothing, Griff continued.

"Let me be clear on the power of the Trident platform. Those boats can target thousands of locations and millions of people. The part they play in the nuclear triad—submarines, bombers, and land-based missiles—means no enemy will risk a first strike because they believe without a doubt America will fight back. That Mutually-Assured Destruction is the key to world peace."

Rowe tapped his brakes as taillights blinked red.

"These aren't idle questions about chatter that's 'probably nothing'." His voice was soft, concerned. "I heard about the virus that infected our sub off Florida. You're worried that next time, they'll not only infect the sub, but locate it using the magnetic signature. If there's any truth to that, I need to alert Command."

"Already done." He let that sit for a moment, knowing Griff would understand. "I appreciate the help."

Fairgrove couldn't remember ever being angrier. Al-Zahrawi had ordered him home—ordered! Now here he was, standing in his living room and no Al-Zahrawi. This had to end.

Up until Al-Zahrawi's call, it had been a spectacular day. Fairgrove once again was the scientific star, sharing insights that astonished his colleagues. Of course, he didn't tell them they came from Kalian. In fact, they may have thought she was working under his direction.

By the time he and Kalian published, he'd be as knowledgeable as she.

His phone beeped, a reminder to call Kalian, ask how her son was. Women liked a personal touch. As he punched through menus to his address book, he inhaled a whiff of her perfume lingering from last Friday. What an invigorating day that had been. She'd turned to him for advice and guidance, something no one did anymore.

When he raised his head, Al-Zahrawi stood in the foyer.

"I come to claim the Blood Debt."

"Blood Debt?" His eyes widened and darted away. "I don't remember anything about such a crass event."

But he did remember. During the halcyon days of youth, as he struggled to build a career, he made the deal, doubting it would be claimed. What could a paleoanthropologist offer a man like Al-Zahrawi?

Al-Zahrawi tossed him a photo album of a child Fairgrove thought was dead. He sucked in a breath, hands clammy as he paged through a chronicle of her growth. She had a dimple in her chin like her mother's and an innocence that evaporated before she graduated from high school.

"Now do you?"

The moment Fairgrove met Kalian Delamagente, he suspected the truth. There was a toughness about her beauty and a perpetual curiosity that filled her eyes—much like a woman in Fairgrove's past whom Al-Zahrawi had 'disappeared'.

He hadn't killed her though, instead used her as leverage.

He pretended to study the pictures as he collected himself. "What *is* a Blood Debt?" he finally asked.

Al-Zahrawi pulled a stiletto from his pocket and started cleaning his nails.

"It is similar to what you Americans call 'scratching back'—is this the phrase?"

"Yes! We help each other achieve our goals."

"But Muslims--we are a solemn people. We take our responsibilities with a seriousness no American understands." He looked up. "Get Delamagente's Otto or your blood will clear the debt."

Bile burned his throat. No doubt 'blood debt' was from that shari'a law he and Al-Zahrawi once discussed over aperitifs at the Club, but Salah had focused on a woman's inferiority and the dominance of church over state. Those topics bored Fairgrove, but now he wished he'd listened more closely. He started to speak, but Al-Zahrawi interrupted.

"Dr. Zeke Rowe has begun to interfere with my plans."

Fairgrove had a fascinating thought. "Let him be my Blood Debt, Salah."

"No. His death benefits you." Al-Zahrawi finished cleaning the dirt from under the nails of his right hand and moved to the left.

"I counseled him to change professions, but his meager mental capacities prevent him from acting in his best interests. He's proof God loves stupid people." When shock crossed Al-Zahrawi's face, he clarified, "My God. Not yours."

"Get rid of him or I will."

Fairgrove scratched his head. That would be OK, but Al-Zahrawi might set him up for the murder. No. Better to lodge more anonymous complaints.

Al-Zahrawi tossed the album onto the bookshelf by the door. "I need to use the khazi."

Fairgrove waved down the hall and turned away. When the toilet flushed and the front door slammed, he pulled the shades. The man was crazy. When this project ended, he'd cut his ties with Salah Mahmud Al-Zahrawi for good.

He checked his watch. It was too late to call Kalian.

What gave him away first was the new Nikes. Drunks didn't spend money on shoes. Annie attached a tracker to the one unfamiliar car on the street and then snapped a picture of Nike Man as he aimed a palm-sized device through Delamagente's back window. Minutes later, he climbed into the gray Volvo, gassed up at a Texaco and drove north with Annie in pursuit.

Chapter 42

Wednesday

Rowe arrived at the airport early. After confirming Kali boarded the plane and Sean was safely at camp, there was nothing to do but think, and he had a lot of that to do.

By the time Rowe had reached Fairgrove's house last night, the windows were dark. Rowe verified his car was in the garage, and then walked the perimeter, noting vehicles and unusual individuals. Ajit brought up traffic cams and local CCTV, ran everyone suspicious through facial recognition, but got nothing. That didn't mean much. Al-Zahrawi demonstrated a remarkable ability to elude surveillance.

Rowe found a seat with a good view of the arrival gate, and quietly, calmly, took the measure of his surroundings, looking for anyone out of place. He got more information from a person's actions and appearance than their words.

But no one seemed suspicious. One man, dressed in an expensive suit and shiny wingtips, paced back-and-forth by the far wall, one hand gripping a cell and the other crossed over his chest. His head hung and he banged into people without apology. By the time he got off the phone, his face was pale, eyes wet and he wandered off as though he had nowhere to go.

A professionally-dressed woman carried on an animated conversation with a child. They held hands, swinging their arms. She giggled at everything the boy said with a joy that stretched beyond her full lips to the fan of wrinkles around her eyes. The boy gazed up at her as she talked. They made Rowe happy.

He couldn't shake the growing dread that Friday would bring another death.

A swell of movement at the gate told Rowe American 4786 was deplaning. He waited through first class, business, and economy. When the pilot trundled out and still no Kali, Rowe's hands went cold. Where was she? Just as he took a step toward one of the agents, he felt a tug.

"Zeke! I didn't see you!"

Her face beamed as though backlit by a heavenly light. Hair spilled over her shoulders in shining waves, covering the narrow straps of a white tank dress. A shell necklace hugged her throat and he caught the hint of musk.

"I'm just glad you're back." He wanted to fold her into his arms, but settled for brushing his fingertips along her cheek. "How was it?"

"Sean got the Most Valuable Player award." Excitement danced across her face. "The concert mistress had a violin solo, *Carmen Fantasie*. Five measures into it, her E string popped."

The sum total of Rowe's knowledge about violins was they probably needed all their strings.

"Before anyone realized there was a problem, Sean picked up the melody. His strong full bow and dulcet tones, swelling and scooping, each phrase flowing over the audience like a wave—it saved the piece. I've never seen him so happy."

They walked through short-term parking chatting about Kali's trip and Rowe's research. Kali seemed recovered from the threatening phone call to her son. When pressed, she admitted when she brought it up, Sean rolled his eyes and said no one no way would get through the camp's security.

When they reached Rowe's 1974 Benz Diesel, Kali laughed. "Amazing this still runs."

"300,000 miles and counting. I change the oil every 3,000

miles and wax it once a month. Insurance is cheap, mileage is good. It goes zero to sixty in ninety seconds. What more do I need?"

She giggled. "Do you mind taking me to my lab? I need to make sure Otto's OK."

As they drove, Kali kept up a non-stop narrative about the concert, Sean's instructors, funny events that happened, and the other proud parents. Memories of relaxed weekends with Paulette and then Amanda poked through Rowe's mental cobwebs. It got harder each day to lie to Kali.

As he pulled into a handicap spot, the gray Volvo that had been following them for the last five miles sped past. Different license plates, but Rowe had no doubt it was the same vehicle in which Devore was last seen.

"I saw that car at the airport," Kali said.

"I'll meet you in your lab." His voice had turned hard, but he didn't care.

Rowe toyed with following the Volvo, but ultimately decided he couldn't leave Kali unprotected. When he hurried into her office, she arched an eyebrow. No better time to level with her.

"Kali—" Which was when his phone buzzed. "I have to go."

"What did you want to say to me?" Her eyelid twitched.

Rowe took a slow, even breath before answering, "I'm glad you're back. I missed you," and he left.

Kali turned on Yo-Yo Ma, pulled a DNA sample from her drawer and overlaid it with the one Zeke had analyzed for her. Her legs almost buckled, but she refused to cry. She placed the two samples in her drawer, fingered her mother's diamond earrings, and leaned back, losing herself in Mark O'Connor's *Appalachian Waltz*.

Al-Zahrawi read Delamagente's latest email with interest. Sun wanted to test Otto's ability to locate a sub's magnetic signature, but Kalian felt it would take hundreds of hours to complete the programming, time she did not have thanks to the Dean's deadline. Al-Zahrawi responded immediately. *You must pursue this wonderful opportunity. I posted additional funds to defray the costs of increasing your work pace. I will also reach out to your Dean to request his patience if you believe that is necessary.*

He smiled when Delamagente ended with, *I hope to someday express my appreciation in person, Mr. Keregosian.* He would make that happen. He forwarded the email to Wynton asking him to make contact with the Dean about this issue, to Aleksei Borodnoi, and to a third recipient who would never know he received it.

Next, he called Wynton. "Does Ms. Delamagente wish to move?" He didn't give Wynton time to respond. "The roommate—Annie?—took pictures of Mr. Monroe's house, even after he assured her he had no interest in selling."

"No. She'd tell me. Did she call someone afterwards?"

"Yes."

"There's your answer. Housing is expensive around here. People always want a cheaper place to live. She uploaded the pictures to a friend."

Al-Zahrawi disconnected in disgust.

"I get why he's stalking Kali, but what's Fairgrove's interest in Trident subs?" Rowe and Sun had spent the last hour reviewing the clues.

A ping drew Sun's attention to his desktop. "Keregosian forwarded Kali's last email to Fairgrove, a Russian mobster, and someone who will surprise you."

Chapter 43

Wednesday/Thursday

Sandy had been circling her since Kali walked in.

"Alright, boy. Let's go for a walk." She hid Otto, changed to running clothes, and they left. Mr. Winters was on the stoop, watering his container garden.

"Hi, Mr. Winters. Any visitors?"

"Not today, kitten."

"You're being extra vigilant, right?"

"Don't worry about me, kitten. Anyone who tries to better me is in for a five-star surprise. Five star." He rubbed his shoulder as he answered.

"How's the Arava working?" Mr. Winters had tried at least twenty medications on his psoriatic arthritis. Arava was the latest.

"Great. I'm glad to be done with those gold shots. I think the nurse was a sadist."

They chatted until Sandy dragged her to Riverside Park. She liked it here, with its winding trails and copious shady spots. They wandered the perimeter, past a church group serving food to the homeless, among the besotted undergrads holding hands and the masochists jogging in the muggy heat. Sandy bounced from bush to bush, marking some, sniffing others, engaging in doggy intrigue only he understood.

Until he growled, hackles up, tail stretched out behind.

"Find something, Sandy?" Kali tensed. Sandy's eyes were slits, ears flat. Another rumble vibrated deep in his chest. She gripped his neck as his head jutted toward a dark thicket of trees. Kali thrust her rape whistle into her mouth and searched the surroundings. "OK. We'll go home, boy. I'm nervous."

As soon as she got home, Kali locked her door and secured every window. She climbed into bed and stared at the ceiling, surprised how much safer yesterday felt when the unflappable Annie slept next door.

Five hours later, still wide awake, she got up.

With a plan.

She showered and donned clothing that would not distract her—loose linen slacks and a shapeless blouse. Otto in one hand, an apple in the other, she went to work. Instead of reading Wyn's History file as she had planned, she would complete her dissertation and include Otto's ability to track minute changes like magnetic fluxes. Completion would trigger the submittal of her research to professional journals which would legitimize her intellectual rights. At that point, if Wyn was behind the threats—in a clumsy effort to steal her work—they would be neutralized. Every grad student was familiar with the story of Charles Darwin. By publishing *On the Origin of Species* before Alfred Russell Wallace, he laid unassailable and historic claim to the Theory of Evolution.

If Kali knew the research community was this back-stabbing, she'd have become a librarian.

She downed three Tylenol, hoping to stay ahead of her headache, and went to work. Some days, the pain exhausted her so, her concentration—usually her greatest ally—skittered like a child on an icy sidewalk. Today was a good day. She put in four unbroken hours, completing the introduction and methodology, summary of steps, scientific principles, and problems encountered. Kali found the work calming. The editing, organizing, and data verification appealed to the clerk in her. She was vaguely aware of Cat coming and going, phones ringing, the footsteps of students passing by, and Riverside Church tolling the hours.

She paused only when Zeke called. She answered with, "I'm adopting your charming distrust of surroundings."

"Why would you do that?" His voice came from behind her. Kali swirled, sputtered about how long had he been there, and then launched into an overview of last night.

She ended triumphantly with, "Once I'm published, there'll be no reason to harass me."

Rowe's face was unreadable, but his eyes never left her face. "And what if they're faster than you can publish?"

Suddenly, she was tired of people assuming she couldn't manage her own life. "I can take out the trash if I need to, Zeke."

He smiled, eyes as hard as marbles, fixed on her but not seeing. She could see his brain posing and discarding options, adapting to new data as ideas were processed and questions resolved. With a blink, Zeke Rowe the Scientist returned, eyes like deep wells she could happily lose herself in. He took her hands and she tingled from fingertips to her toes. She didn't want him to let go.

"I've developed a great ... respect... for you over the past weeks. There are things I want to tell you." He breathed in deeply. "One is my background. My job with the SEALs was to unravel plots. I learned to distinguish them by characteristics and actions, by the people involved and how they made decisions, by their body language when dealing with others.

"That's how I know you're facing one now. Yours, though, is complicated. Instead of one person hell-bent on a goal, there are two, working together, on two goals. One may not even consider the other a terrorist. It could be expediency—the path they travel works for both."

His eyes locked onto hers with an intensity that frightened her. "When we find who they are, Fairgrove and Keregosian will be involved."

She pulled her hands from Rowe's grasp and folded them over her chest. "Wyn wouldn't help terrorists." Why was she defending him? "And Mr. Keregosian is always honest." Anger welled up and backstopped the tears that burned her eyes. "And who is the 'we' you refer to?"

Rowe quietly reclaimed her fingers. There was the electricity again. "Think about how Otto researches people. Everything you know about Fairgrove is superficial—what a search engine uncovers and what he chooses to tell you. It's not through his actions, personal relationships, or the trail left as he travels through time. I've worked with him, Kali. Every critical juncture in Fairgrove's life went his way. I don't believe that was luck, or because he's smart." Rowe smoothed her hair. "He's mixed up with bad people, probably thinks he can outmaneuver them, but he can't, and they'll do what is needed to accomplish their goals."

If Rowe wanted to frighten her, he'd already succeeded, but he continued. "Someone stole Cat's research and now wants yours, too."

"How can that be true?" she sputtered. "Cat understands what a breakthrough NEV is—light-years ahead of anything similar. She has the same security Otto uses!"

Rowe's answer surprised her. "She allowed it. She's helping Bobby James at the FBI. If that was all they wanted, it would be under control. But it isn't. They want Otto, too. They tried—"

"—and failed, and will continue to fail. No one gets through my firewalls."

"There are other ways, like threatening Sean. They won't stop until they get what they want. Or we beat them."

Her fear spiked. He made his point. Sean was her vulnerability. "What can I do?"

"Don't talk about Otto's potential skills with anyone."

"I'm about to submit my draft dissertation to the Dean."

"Can it wait?"

Kali didn't want to wait. What if Zeke and Eitan were wrong and this had less to do with terrorists than intellectual theft? Her solution—to publish—would solve it. The headache thumped. "The Dean gave me until tomorrow and then he pulls the plug."

Rowe's mouth tightened, but he said nothing. Kali popped two more Tylenol.

He called James on a secure line. "Any word from Annie?"

"Yeah. The guy she's tailing stopped at Matt Monroe's on his way north and she got pictures of two other men at the house. I'm running them through NCIC."

Rowe's shoulders tensed. "Anything on Monroe's key?"

"No prints other than his, although I just got his bank statements. Those are interesting." James hmphed. "We put a trap on Hemren's 'sister' calls. It might really be his sisters."

"How are we doing on call-ins?"

"Up to ten."

Not enough. That left hundreds of submariners in danger. Rowe was about to disconnect, but James stopped him. "Annie won't be back for at least another day."

"Got it." He needed to check on Mr. Winters anyway.

Chapter 44

Thursday

Kali trudged into her tiny apartment. Her eyes felt gritty and her mouth tasted like kibble—not that Sandy allowed her to eat it. Zeke's request still upset her, even five hours later. All she wanted was to lose herself in mindless television and fall asleep.

Before she could lock the door and drop her briefcase, Wyn called.

"You're home! Allow me to take you to dinner, to celebrate."

Kali washed back to memories of Fake Fred and his fake fiancée relaxing after a tiring day over a quiet meal. "Sure. Why not? Let me shower and get Sandy settled."

Where was Sandy? "Come here boy!" She chewed a vitamin C as she wandered through the Lab's favorite spots—the patch of sunlight by the window, Kali's bed, the cool darkness of the bathroom tile. "Hungry?"

The house remained silent and no sign of him in the yard, either.

"What's up, kitten?"

"Hi, Mr. Winters. Have you seen Sandy?"

"He went out once to do his business, and then whined at my door so I gave him a bone. He kept nuzzling me, putting his paw on my arm as though he wished he could talk. I checked for injuries, but he seemed OK and eventually went back in your apartment."

"I'm going to look for him. Grab him, please, if he comes home."

She started to leave a message for Wyn when he answered. "Sandy ... Your dog? We'll eat. I bet he's back by the time we return."

"I won't be hungry until I find him, Wyn," and hung up.

She walked the neighborhood first, then Riverside Park to Harlem in the north and the Pier at the south, past the Amsterdam bus stop where Sean caught his bus to school, and even the route they took around campus when she had time. She checked in with Mr. Winters several times, but no luck. She shouted Sandy's name and asked everyone she ran into, but no one had seen an eighty-pound three-legged yellow lab. One youngish Slavic-looking man thought a Labrador and a gangly teen had been jogging in Riverside Park. Something about his eyes made her uncomfortable, but she dutifully made a second tour of the area.

After two hours, she gave up, tired and discouraged. A call to the pound came up empty. If she posted signs or contacted the campus authorities, the landlord would find out. As she struggled with what to do next, her phone rang.

"Hi, Sean!" She forced an upbeat tone. "Are you still in DC?"

"Master Sgt. McClelland gave me etudes to practice. They're the hardest I've ever played!"

"And you've had some hard ones." Kali was having trouble concentrating.

"Yeah." He sounded confused. "A friend of yours asked me to call you. He said he's undercover. How cool you hang out with CIA types. He wants you to send him whatever it was you two discussed."

"Hmm. No name?"

"I forgot to ask, but I got a picture when he was down the block. I'll text it."

Her phone beeped. A shiver ran down her back. The photo was the young Slav she talked to while searching for Sandy. Was this a message? She remembered Rowe's words about what could pressure her to give up Otto.

In a heartbeat.

Her temples thrummed, but she forced her voice to remain calm.

"I recognize him. Thanks."

"Gotta go, Mom. Love you!" And he was gone.

Kali raced outside, but the sidewalk was empty.

Rowe sat in his car half a block away, hidden between two SUVs. Alarms had been clanging all day in his brain. Everywhere he went, he found himself glancing over his shoulder and checking the reflection in windows, sure he had a tail but finding none. James was watching Fairgrove while Rowe kept an eye on Kali. Rowe had gone through Annie's recent uploads, but uncovered nothing that rhymed with a clue. He'd have to wait until Al-Zahrawi made a mistake.

He took a picture of a middle-aged man with a blue scat bag walking a toy poodle, and another of a medium height dog walker with musculature typical of Special Forces. His German shepherd marked everything as though this was new terrain.

Kali arrived, looking exhausted, and disappeared inside. No one was following her. When she reappeared, she had on comfortable walking clothes and carried Sandy's leash but no Sandy. She stopped everyone she ran into, said something to which she always got a head shake—*No*. Why the hell was Military Man still here? A sneer painted his mouth even as he answered Kali's questions. Rowe took a picture and uploaded it to James.

As he was deciding whether she needed help, Sun called.

"Someone put a sniffer on Kali's computer. When she calls out or sends an email, the firewall will open a port and the sniffer will sneak through."

"Which means they aren't getting what they want. How'd you catch it?"

"Why would I miss it?"

Rowe breathed out. "Can you return the favor?"

The clack of keystrokes stuttered over the phone as Sun disconnected.

By the time Rowe hung up, Kali had reappeared, head hanging. She shuffled into her building and doused the lights. Rowe waited half an hour and was about to leave when one of the dog walkers re-appeared, this time alone. Rowe ignored him earlier, but now, dressed in black with a duffle bag, he caught Rowe's attention. The man surveyed his surroundings quickly and approached Kali's building.

"Hey! Can I help you?"

Rowe was halfway across the street when the man fled.

"Stop!" Rowe shouted and exploded after him. The would-be intruder was wiry, skinny and should be a high school sprinter. Rowe's running style was awkward, but fast enough to chase down most people. In fact, after a block, despite his throbbing knees, he was almost there.

Rowe speed dialed Bobby. "Get someone over to 112th and Broadway!" and then, "Stop! Federal agent!"

He'd have to stop. No way would the runner get across six lanes of nonstop headlights at full speed. The man peeked over his shoulder and then dove into the stream of cars.

Rowe yelled, but it was too late. A car slammed into him with a squeal of breaks and threw his limp body up and over the center divider. He was airborne for five seconds then bounced off a Chevy and crashed to earth with a sickening thump. Rowe just missed a car as it piled into two others, blocking all movement on the street, as he bobbed through stalled cars until he reached the body. The runner couldn't even be twenty, with peach fuzz for a beard, Middle Eastern bone structure, blue-black hair now streaked with red. His hands were smooth and manicured, his clothes expensive. His neck was twisted at an odd angle and blood dripped from his mouth. Rowe put a finger to his carotid and found nothing.

Rowe went through his pockets, but he carried no ID, just a half a stick of gum, a receipt from a bodega, two quarters, and Kali's address. He palmed that and slipped it into his pocket. When the police arrived, he told a whitewashed version of his involvement. Customers at Tom's Restaurant on the corner verified the man ran into traffic without slowing. A scientist from Goddard Institute for Space Studies out for a smoke said Rowe yelled at the runner to stop, but he ignored the warning.

Chapter 45

Friday

Without Sandy fighting for his piece of the bed, crawling up to cuddle on her pillow, his warm damp breath panting into her ear as morning approached, Kali gave up sleeping. She showered, threw on the first thing she put her hands on, and went to work. Sean was not due home for a week, Annie hadn't called, and now Sandy was missing. She couldn't remember ever feeling this lonely.

As she turned onto her hall, she found Zeke leaning against her doorjamb, holding two cups and wearing a crooked smile. She wanted to fold herself into his arms, hear him say everything would be OK, but settled for a scowl.

"I'm in a nasty mood." She unlocked the door and took one step, but stalled at the aroma of cinnamon coffee, no cream, no sugar. Perfect. "Thank you," she mumbled.

"You aren't wearing your earrings."

She fingered her ears distractedly. "I guess I forgot them." A gentleness in his voice made her wonder if he knew about Sandy. Had he talked to Mr. Winters? When she left this morning, her neighbor suggested she check at lunchtime because Sandy always came over then.

"Someone's been playing in your sandbox again."

Ah. This wasn't about her dog. "No one can get around my security, especially since you and Eitan made me paranoid."

She pressed her thumb against a pinprick-sized dot on the

desktop and squinted at the retinal scanner, then inspected the text scrolling down the screen. "One incursion attempted, from inside Columbia's network. Otto stopped it."

"We think Dean Manfried is involved," and Rowe explained the connection.

How could that be? Everything about him screamed bureaucrat from his button down shirts, pleated linen pants, and bland jackets to his dark socks and wingtips. Casual meant taking his jacket off. He socialized with academes, and subscribed to administrative magazines. In his time off, he schmoozed contributors.

On the other hand, nothing surprised her anymore.

"I hacked Wyn's computer," Kali offered while rubbing her temples.

Rowe smiled. "You've seen through his infamous charms."

"He's dumb and proud of it."

"You can lead a man to knowledge, but you can't make him think."

She offered a wan smile despite herself. Rowe always made her feel good would prevail. "That call about Sean, Zeke. Something strange." Before she could say more, Wyn entered.

"Wyn. Your conscience must be burning," but Rowe couldn't take his eyes off the image. It was one of last night's dog walkers.

Fairgrove ignored Rowe. His appearance was…contrived, like a report copy-pasted in pieces from the internet, everything there but nothing fit. He wore an open-collar shirt, seersucker jacket, cuffed white twill slacks and Top-Siders without socks. No one dressed this way except to offer firm manly handshakes to similarly-attired country club blokes.

"Kalian, my dear. The Dean said you had more computer break-ins."

Kali glared at Wyn. "A thwarted attack."

"You continue to be the pinnacle of Columbia's

information mountain, Wyn." This time, Kali scowled at Rowe and he changed his tone to one of polite inquiry. "The cafeteria again?"

"Porter and I often discuss strategic plans." He puffed out his chest, expecting acknowledgement of his importance. "In this case, Dr. Rowe was the topic."

Rowe rolled his eyes as Fairgrove slid in behind Kali and gulped.

"What—who's that?" Recognition flared which he covered it quickly. This was better than Rowe had hoped.

"My son took it in DC, but I saw him yesterday outside my apartment when Sandy disappeared." When she paused, Rowe took over.

"When I did Navy intel years ago, a truncated profile like this was a dead end, but today's facial recognition tools will identify him in a snap. You can save time and tell me who it is."

"I-I'm simply jealous. Is he an anthropologist?" Fairgrove didn't wait for an answer. "Are you tired, Kalian? Oh—your dog. What's his name? Rover? Did you find him?"

Kali shook her head and her face drooped.

"Dog's disappear all the time, darling. Does yours run away often?"

"Never." Kali's voice trembled as she exhaled the word.

Fairgrove rubbed his chin, and then crossed his arms. "To happier topics. Porter got another donation from your sponsor. No surprise now that we're together."

When Kali didn't respond, he waved and hurried out.

Rowe excused himself. "Hey, Wyn. Hold up."

Fairgrove never slowed, but his head dipped.

"That man in the picture—he's stalking Kali. She's in danger."

"What are you, an amateur detective?" Fairgrove's anger blasted through his meticulously-molded image.

"Is he Al-Zahrawi's henchman? That's right, I'm aware of your relationship with the terrorist, Salah Mahmud Al-Zahrawi. He gets rid of your women once you no longer need them."

Fairgrove pulled a ticket off his windshield and tossed it on the ground, banging his knee against the door as he jumped into his car.

"One of Al-Zahrawi's minions got himself killed last night by Kali's apartment. What did he want from Kali?"

Fairgrove swerved through traffic, and then turned onto W 120th and vanished.

Rowe's phone rang. "What did you find out, Bobby?"

"Dead boy was here on a student visa. He was active in the same Muslim group Hemren belongs to. And, the dog walker who is also Sean's stalker—also belongs to Hemren's mosque."

First Sean, now Sandy. Eventually, Kali would give up Otto. Rowe couldn't let that happen.

"One more thing. Annie missed her check-in."

Rowe found Kali in her lab. He was about to ask if she had heard from Annie when Stockbury arrived. A painful bruise surrounded her left eye and a raw bloody scratch stretched from cheek to swollen lip. Kali gasped and Rowe asked, "Did you fall again, Cat?"

She didn't answer, fluffing dull, limp hair over the damage without raising her head from a thorough study of her right hand. Two nails were cracked below the quick, but Stockbury didn't seem to care. She picked at the polish on the remaining fingers and dropped the flakes onto the floor. Rowe tried a distraction.

"What do you call ten millipedes?"

She paused for a second and answered, "A centipede." Not even a smirk. "Gunner wants to sail around the Mediterranean. He invited you, Kali. He was unhappy you didn't come to Paris."

Rowe knew an endgame when he heard it. Stockbury had outlived her usefulness and a cruise in international waters was a good way to get rid of her. "Don't go, Cat."

Stockbury wound a finger through a strand of lifeless hair

and swallowed.

Rowe eased onto a corner of Stockbury's desk. "Tell me what's going on, Cat."

Her face crumpled, dissolving into a look he'd seen on wives who couldn't escape abusive husbands. On women who realized their lives would never get better with the men and the religion they'd picked. Kali put her arms around her best friend and pulled her head to her shoulder. A tear rolled down Stockbury's damaged face.

"He had friends over last night. He came to bed angry," Stockbury pawed at her injuries. "I left before he woke up,"

"Do you have his picture?" Rowe's voice was calm, but hard as steel.

She reached beneath a paperweight and handed Rowe a blurred image of a tanned face surrounded by wavy blonde hair.

"I took this in Paris." A Patrician nose arched through bushy eyebrows to a vaulted forehead. He sported a flowered shirt over pleated pants. His appearance exuded confidence bordering on arrogance as he viewed his surroundings with piercing eyes and an irreverent smirk. On his arm was a Rolex Cellini Prince.

It was Sean's stalker.

"His last name is Goya."

Rowe uploaded it to James. "Gunner Goya, Stockbury's boyfriend and the guy following Sean."

As he hung up, Stockbury pulled him aside. "Gunner knows you're Special Forces. Last night, he asked where you lived. When I wouldn't answer, he slapped me. After I went to bed, he was talking to someone about you and Kali and something that was going to make him rich. Soon. Zeke, I'm scared." Her lower lip quivered.

"Did they mention the deadline?"

"No." She touched her swollen face. "We used to talk for hours, about Daddy, my research, our future plans. Now, he ignores me."

Rowe had known since the fight in Israel this group

would catch on to him. What he didn't want was Cat or Kali in the middle of it.

"Cat. I'll fix this. Until I do, stay away."

"I'll go to—"

"Write it down," he interrupted and circled his finger in the air. She jerked her head once, wrote with a hand that wouldn't stop shaking, and left. Kali stood, feet apart, brow furrowed.

Rowe caught her eye, and wrote, "If anyone calls, Cat's in the field." It was time to level with Kali. "Can I come over this evening? I still need—want—to talk."

"Uh, OK, but I'll be here a while."

"I'll bring dinner." Kali had the same bleak expression as Cat. "She'll be fine, Kali. She's smart. By the way, anything from Annie?"

When Kali shook her head, Rowe kissed her cheek and left. Back in his lab, he closed the blinds, posted 'Be Back Later', and sat in the dark. He needed to figure out how Fairgrove and now Gunner were privy to so much information and how to stop it. Did they bug Kali's clothes? Not likely. Was it in a necklace or ring, or glasses? Kali rarely wore jewelry.

Except those damned diamond chips. They were her mother's so she had them on nearly every day. He hit speed dial. "Eitan."

"What's bothering you, Zeke?" By now, Rowe was sure Sun had taken the voice version of a micro-expressions class.

"Could a bug—audio and video—be hidden in something as small as a stud earring?"

Two minutes after Rowe left, Kali's cell rang. It was blocked. She answered, but said nothing.

"Do you now believe I am your friend?" It wasn't a question. "The damage to Catherine, your son's reappearance, a missing dog—you are alive because I allow it."

Sweat broke out on Kali's upper lip and her hands became damp and clammy, but her voice was controlled and icy.

"Whatever your goal, you will fail if you hurt them. What is your name?"

"Call me Mr. Grant, after your famous president. We warned you, one a week will die. Who's missing this week, Kalian Delamagente? Whose death is on your conscience?"

Her thin veneer of control started to crack beneath the weight of his words. She tapped a program called Find My Friends that located people by their phone's GPS and watched Sean move across the Juilliard summer campus.

"What do you want?"

"Otto to do me a favor," and hung up.

Chapter 46

Kali wished she'd never met Lucy. Her strength in the face of adversity, her refusal to be defeated by circumstances set a daunting standard Kali couldn't live up to. When did that grit disappear from the female genome? Did Nature erase it in the name of civilization, or simply bury it, waiting for a need?

What would Lucy do, faced with a madman?

Kali pressed F5 and Lucy's world populated. Raza and a band of habilines squatted by a waterhole, one eye on an ancient rhinoceros, its body gouged and disfigured by healed wounds, the other supervising children playing at the pond's edge.

No one paid attention to *Crocodylus* until almost too late. It slithered so smoothly through the pond, only a rippling chevron showed in its wake. Inches from a youngster who splashed a hand through the murky lake, it rose like an apparition through the water's surface, jaw gaping, razor-edged teeth set into blood-red pulp. Raza flew to his feet, legs and arms pumping, snatching the astonished child from danger moments before the fetid mouth snapped shut.

"Crocodiles didn't live in this area."

Kali jerked at Wyn's voice. When did he get here? "Otto doesn't make mistakes."

"That's not what I meant, dear. If we find those bones, it will validate Otto's skill. I could go. A colleague in Africa extended an invitation…"

Kali allowed her face to express thanks, as though Wyn did her a favor.

"Well, then. I'll make the arrangements. An event of this magnitude, I'll clear my schedule."

As he hurried off, Kali called Mr. Winters. "Nothing yet, kitten, but our Sandy'll be home. A dog has to eat."

An hour later, *Sonata #3 in C Major* chirped. "Sean! How are you?"

"Thanks for the sweatshirt."

Kali felt a lump in her throat. Mr. Grant had left another message. Thankfully, Sean kept talking.

"I called to tell you I'll be out of contact for a few days at a retreat. No phones allowed."

"Sean." She had to tell him. "Something weird is going on. I received a call saying you're in danger."

"We already discussed this, Mom," but his normal buzz of moving body parts and tapping fingers stopped. "I talked with Edik about what you said. He's neat, spends lots of time with me. Says he's always wanted to hang out with a famous bass player. You'd like him."

"What's his advice?"

The tap-tap of fingers resumed. "Says he has my back." He chuckled. "This is Juilliard, Mom. People take their music way too seriously. A muffled voice interrupted. "Gotta go. Remember our code."

Their secret language—palindromes. Why he called her 'Mom' and she named her AI 'Otto'. Sean knew something was wrong.

Kali broke into tears.

Fairgrove ground his teeth, wondering the best way to tell Al-Zahrawi. The man had lost it when his cousin died last night. The boy was supposed to steal the portable Otto, but Zeke Rowe killed him. Al-Zahrawi had ranted for an hour about Allah's Will and infidels and the Cause.

Still, he must try or Al-Zahrawi would destroy everything.

"I understand your pain, Salah, but we must focus or your

cousin will have died in vain. Sean emailed Gunner's picture to Delamagente. Catherine Stockbury will recognize him."

Fairgrove breathed deeply and forced his shoulders to relax.

"Kalian asked me to go to Africa, to search for ancient bones Otto located. If they are there, it will prove Otto can find anything. That's what you want, isn't it—to use Otto to find… something…" though Fairgrove had no idea what. "I will persuade her to join me with her AI. Surely you have associates who can steal him once I complete my field study?" Fairgrove had no intention of losing Otto, but this gambit would buy time.

"And Dr. Rowe will also be there?"

"Of course not. Why would he?" Al-Zahrawi's obsession with Rowe was ridiculous.

"You have failed to get rid of Dr. Rowe." His voice was flat and steady, but filled with dark rage. "What should I do about that?"

"Luckily, I have no dog for you to kill!" Fairgrove retorted, realized how it sounded and tried to laugh, but it came out a high-pitched squeak.

"Dogs are effective hostages in America. My country eats them. You adopt them."

Fairgrove let it go. "Give me time, Salah. Please. Otto will soon be yours."

Al-Zahrawi didn't answer. He'd already disconnected.

New York's home for lost dogs had an institutional feel with its faded linoleum floors and layer upon layer of cages. The piteous yips from scores of forgotten pets bruised Kali's soul and each occupant wagged an eager tail, hoping she would rescue them, but Kali departed alone.

She put thoughts of Sandy and sweatshirts that appeared where they shouldn't be aside as she dressed for dinner and wondered what Zeke wanted to talk about. Four outfits later, she settled on a simple lace tank top over stretch jeans. She left her hair loose to frame her face, adding only a touch of translucent pink lipstick to offset a natural paleness.

The weather was terrible. A dense fog floated off the Hudson and a drizzly wind gusted down the streets and around the buildings. Maybe Zeke would cancel. When he knocked, she took a deep breath, squared her shoulders, and opened the door.

He stood like a boy on his first date, a bouquet of flowers in one hand and Chinese food in the other.

"I forgot to ask what you like, so I got one of each."

He wore an untucked black Polo over tan Chinos and well-worn boat shoes. She caught a trace of Old Spice as he cocked his head and offered a silly grin.

"You are beautiful. I mean, you always are, but, well… I like your jeans." His hand moved of its own volition to her hair.

"Is this silk?"

Kali giggled.

"And the earrings. You usually wear diamond studs."

Kali blushed as she touched the new gold hoops. "I got these at Nordy's, a gift to myself."

He seemed off-balance, too. She liked that.

"They're …delicate… perfect on you."

"Thanks." She bit her tongue to stop herself from admitting how special she wanted this evening to be.

Zeke explored her living room while Kali put the flowers in water and collected a bottle of screw top red wine and two glasses.

Kali popped open the food containers. "War wonton soup, egg rolls, orange chicken—my favorites."

The dying sun silhouetted his muscular form against the window as he browsed the room.

"Someone had fun." Zeke held a photo of her Grandpa, broad smile covering his weathered face, tanned arm rested comfortably on Sean's sunburned shoulder.

"Grandpa joined us for white river rafting. Sean loved him."

"Sean's a good looking kid." Zeke picked up the New

York All-State Orchestra photo. Only the principle string bass showed in full, with the rest of the bass line arrayed behind the cellos. Sean stood proud and tall, resplendent in a black tuxedo with long tails and ruffled dress shirt.

"There's a CD of his performance, if you can find it."

Zeke flipped through about twenty jewel cases, popped a disc labeled "All State" into the player and the spirited strains of Brian Setzer's *Rockabilly Riot* filled the room. Kali let the music wash over her as they ate right from the containers, passing them back and forth with satisfied grunts. Zeke seemed content in the silence, but Kali couldn't wait any longer.

"Annie promised to call last night. Should I be worried?"

Zeke put his carton down. "I need to talk with you. Annie's a good starting point."

A heaviness engulfed her. She knew she wouldn't like what he had to say.

"Annie works with the FBI like I do."

Kali masked her surprise. "You thought I didn't know?"

Rowe chuckled. "I'm not surprised you do." He shook his head with a wry smile. "Someone was outside your apartment a few days ago. She followed him. Since then, she missed four call-ins."

"But she can take care of herself?" Kali asked as fear squeezed her insides.

"Let me start from the beginning."

He told her about the intercepted chatter and why James focused on the two women. Kali interrupted every time it didn't make sense, which was often.

"Wyn I understand, to rejuvenate his career, but why anyone else?"

"NEV and Otto together make a weapon more advanced than anything out there. We think someone—Al Zahrawi—wants to sell them to raise millions for a *jihad*."

"But Otto is useless without my authentication, and I'll never give it."

Rowe jerked upright. "I didn't know that."

Kali flinched. "Do you think they know it, maybe Wyn said something? Is that why Sandy's gone a-and the hoax about Sean…"

Rowe dipped his head. "To ensure your assistance."

"They need Otto to prove he can find something." Kali's head began to pound. "Wyn's testing that now."

She thumbed through her phone and played Mr. Grant's message from yesterday and explained about the croc skeleton that persuaded Wyn to drop everything and head for Africa.

"He begged me to join him, with Otto, but I won't leave New York until Sean and Sandy are home."

A chill passed through her. Success would be pyrrhic if the people she loved were in danger, including Zeke and Annie.

Zeke placed a warm hand over hers, his eyes troubled. "Send me the file. Bobby can check for voiceprint matches.

"This brings me to Gunner Goya. His real name is Aleksei Borodnoi. He's bright, enigmatic, and resourceful. He's the new terrorist, a global citizen patient enough to await his opportunity. He communicates via public internet forums, shifts funds electronically and gathers information digitally. Gunner will sacrifice anyone to accomplish his target."

"Are you sure it's Gunner?"

"Open Interpol's website, their Most Wanted list, under Red Notice—"

"Red Notice?"

"Arrest and extradite, the highest authority for an international fugitive. Gunner stuffed his last girlfriend, the daughter of a Saudi prince, into a pipe in the sequined gown she wore on their final date. The rats ate her alive."

Kali sucked in a sharp breath. "No wonder you were suspicious of Cat's injuries."

She then told him about Sean's weekend retreat and Keregosian's latest donation. It was eleven by the time they finished. He took the trash out while Kali turned on the TV. She flipped through channels and settled on Fox. A frantic mob screamed about death to infidels. It looked like so many other barbarian mobs, Kali almost moved on when one image froze her in place. Her heart thudded and she tried to scream, but only one word came out.

"Annie…"

Suddenly, Zeke was at her side. "Close your eyes!" But Kali couldn't. Annie pawed at the bloody gash where her ear lobe should be and, in a calm voice, confessed to terrorism against the Islamic people and vowed to accept their justice. Zeke flung Kali onto the couch as a hooded savage slashed Annie's throat.

Chapter 47

Friday Evening/Saturday

When Paulette died, something fundamental in Rowe changed. He still heard the swell of conversation around him, the squeal of children, the happy yips of dogs at play, but nothing reached him. He was stronger but cold, smarter but numb.

He held Kali, wanting to say it would be alright, but unable to tell more lies. He ached for her, prayed Annie wouldn't be Kali's Paulette.

"She wanted to settle down and raise a family." Kali clung tighter. "Her mangled ear—it hurt her, Zeke."

That stopped Rowe. He saw it, but Kali noticed it. Annie would never allow her torturers to see her pain. She'd face it down as she had in Africa.

She was telling him something.

"Kali." He placed a finger to his lips. *Don't talk.* "I need to call Annie's girlfriend before she sees this." Rowe fumbled for paper. "You said you had her number." He scribbled as he spoke. *Show me your diamond studs.*

If Al-Zahrawi was listening. Rowe wanted him to think they were still oblivious.

Kali's expression was wretched. "It's in my room." She shambled to her dresser and opened an old wooden box. The earrings sparkled in a tiny bundle to the side. Rowe pulled a meter from his pocket and flipped a switch to silence the beep. Standing behind Kali, he waved it over her jewelry. The gauge bounced into the red every time it hit the diamonds. As they left the bedroom, Rowe shut the door and verified the signal didn't penetrate.

Kali wrapped her arms around her knees. "How long have they been spying on me, Zeke?" Her tone was weary.

"Probably since Israel. Was anything odd when you got back?"

She sniffed and stared into the distance. "I couldn't find my earrings, and when I did, they felt heavier. I figured it was because I hadn't worn them for so long."

Kali went to the kitchen to make coffee while Rowe dialed James. "This explains Monroe's visit to her lab, maybe even the stalker. Keregosian wanted to hide a bug on something she always had with her."

"They broke in not to plant bugs, but retrofit her earrings. I'll send a team over."

Kali returned with a tray holding a jar of instant coffee, packets of sugar and creamer, and earthenware mugs filled to the brim with hot water. They sat quietly, mixing their drinks, sipping while they awaited James's arrival. Kali broke the silence.

"I'm tired of being the victim, Zeke. Lucy would take control." Her face was pinched, her voice cracked and raw, but anger crept into her words. And resolution.

"Don't do anything, Kali. I'll find them. It's what I do." He couldn't erase what she saw, but this time he wouldn't fail.

When James arrived, he used a signal jammer to transfer the earrings to an FBI evidence box and Rowe carried a sleeping Kali to bed. Then, the two men sat down on the curb in front of Kali's apartment, drank cold coffee, and talked about what to do next.

Kali jerked upright, sweat plastering her body, hair damp and heart pounding. She was with Annie. The woman's face was battered and bloody, one eye swollen shut and the other locked onto Kali as she repeated the names. Kali didn't recognize them, so Annie repeated them, louder and louder, until her screams woke Kali.

Kali shook her head until the nightmare evaporated. An alarm screeched from her phone. Someone tried to hack Otto, again. She punched through a few buttons to confirm what she knew—that the intruder had failed. Zeke had said someone wanted Otto. If they couldn't hack the firewalls, they would try something else. What they wouldn't do was give up.

Where was Zeke? She felt safe with him last night, his reassuring words despite the pain he felt. Annie meant more to him than he'd admit.

When her breathing slowed, she padded around the apartment, checking doors and windows, peeking outside. All she saw was the glare of street lights. It was only 4:30 am.

Without Sandy, the house was too quiet. She missed his ecstatic greetings, how he bounded in at mealtime, how his ears alerted when she entered a room, how he leaned against her, tail wagging, when she most needed support.

She dressed and went to work. She slid into her chair, but instead of working, she sat, arms across her chest, eyes staring into the distance, with the dogged expression of an innocent on death row at a law library. A headache knocked inside her skull. Tylenol didn't help, but her resolve did. They threatened Sean, murdered Annie, and dognapped Sandy, but there it stopped. Last night, she'd been the prey. That ended today.

She tapped in her log-in, stared into the retinal scanner, and activated the video replay of the intruder.

Carl. Another betrayal. Was anything he told her true? He camouflaged his appearance with a watch cap and Coke-bottle glasses, but couldn't disguise the fervent sparkle in those close-set black eyes, the expression she mistook for anthropologic passion in Israel. The half-open lips under his thin nose, once endearing, now seemed stupid. The tweak of his ears when he concentrated used to intrigue her and now disgusted her. She didn't care anymore about his hardscrabble background. Rather than motivation to improve his life, it became the seedbed for treachery.

"What are you doing… Laslo?" Two could play this

game.

He wandered the false pages programmed with enough clandestine facts to be convincing, each new link rising organically from his previous selections. Five minutes passed and he logged out and then back in under Wyn's profile. He opened the scientist's email program, typed a note summarizing what he found, attached an audio file uploaded from a flash drive, and dead dropped it into the 'Draft Folder'. No electronic trail. No footprints.

"I can't believe I missed that."

Next, he loaded a worm onto Manfried's computer, one that would incriminate both Fairgrove and Manfried.

Kali stuck scotch tape over each key. She destroyed most of the fingerprints with her typing, but maybe he hit a few keys she didn't. She put the makeshift prints into an envelope and downloaded Laslo's keystrokes for the Dean's password to a flash drive as well as the dead-dropped email.

Then she logged remotely into Wyn's computer. This time, she activated a bot that would locate other bots, sniffers, and worms. It took only seconds to find one.

"Who's spying on you, Wyn?"

Next, she opened the audio file Laslo had attached. It was her conversation with Sun about magnetics. There was a second dead drop, this from someone named Salah, reminding Wyn he owed a Blood Debt. Was this the same Salah who wrote to him earlier? The one who killed Zematis and contacted her? Why the interest in Wyn?

Kali shivered. According to the date stamp, whatever it was expired yesterday. A chill sluiced through her body. Did Annie die because of Wyn?

She switched to the 'History' file she noticed last time. It included articles submitted to magazines, curriculum vitae, and letters of commendation, but nothing unusual. She had time for one more search. The Wyn she knew had no expertise at creating hidden files, but Laslo did. She logged off and back on under Admin. Like most tech newbies, he placed no password on this profile despite that it allowed complete access to his computer. A couple of clicks and she could see everything. He had a 'save' protocol that he used daily. A series of keystrokes unhid the properties and she gasped.

"Now why would that be here?"

Chapter 48

Saturday

Mr. Winters' lights were on when Rowe left Kali's. No surprise. Marines always woke early. Rowe showed him Hemren's snapshot. Yes, he recognized him, walking the street several times, always when Kali wasn't there. He also pegged one of the dog walkers as the utility man. The more they talked, the angrier the old man got. Rowe told him what he could, warning him without being explicit.

Finally, Mr. Winters said, "I tried to reenlist after 9-11. The sergeant I reached was real nice, professional. Took my name and called back sixty minutes later. Said he checked my records and I did some fine work with the Corps so they re-classified me 1600P. Well, I served in the Marines half my life and never heard of '1600P', so I asked him what the hell it was. Sarge said to relax. 1600P meant they'd call me after the women and children and right before the enemy got to 1600 Pennsylvania Avenue."

Mr. Winters chuckled and pulled out an aged Browning 45 from under his chair.

"This'll take care of me, son. You take care of Kali. I wish I could have done that for Sandy."

Rowe sat at his desk, arms crossed. When Kali entered, he cracked an eyelid, pushed a key, and his screen dissolved into an ancient pre-human map of the Middle East.

"If you know something about Sean, I want in."

He remained silent so long, she thought he fell asleep. As she moved to kick him, he continued. "OK, but stop me if it's too much."

Annie's vindictive words blasted from the speakers. "The United States occupies the land of Islam, plunders its riches, and humiliates its people. Many are dead—Ahraf, Olsal, Renug, Nyw, but not N—"

Her torturers slapped her so hard her lip split. "No names!"

Blood leaked from her cracked lips and shattered nose. One eye had puffed closed while the other burned crimson. "Praise be to God, who says, 'Slay the pagans wherever ye find them, seize them, beleaguer them, and lie in wait.' This is the duty of every Muslim. Whosoever denies his Islamic religion must be killed. I die proud to add my blood to their fight as my brothers redeem themselves by freeing me. "

"She's quoting Osama bin Laden's declaration of war against America, Kali, but I don't think her captors recognized it. She's telling us they aren't very smart."

The cadence of her phrasing was erratic, out-of-sync with the message. Zeke listened, repeating parts, stopped and started and replayed until Kali had it memorized.

She scratched her forearm and the back of her neck. "Why these names, Zeke? They aren't even Muslim."

"They may be code. We're running them by the cryptographers."

Something nagged at her. Annie couldn't doubt they were going to kill her, and this was her last chance to share what she learned those final horrible hours. She warned them of the earring recordings. She told them the enemy was more fervent than smart. No way were the names meaningless.

Kali stared into the middle distance, seeing nothing. Were they from her dream? She willed her thoughts back to last night, to Annie's blood red eye, her cracked lips as she spit out the same words over and over, taunting, like ducks in a shooting gallery. They danced, bounced... Something about the letters...

"They're backwards! Annie knows I like word codes. Play them again."

Rowe tossed Kali his pencil and texted the names she called out to James—Halas, Olsal, Renug, Nyw, and N... Salah, Laslo, Gunner, Wyn, and a name that ends in 'n'.

He turned to Kali. "You did well."

Not good enough for Annie. "Zeke. I met Salah."

Zeke jerked his head toward Kali. "What?"

"On the phone. He called me after the Zematis trial, offered to fund Otto. I refused. I also saw his name in emails to Wyn when I hacked into his computer."

"The man is dangerous, Kali. If he contacts you again, tell me." Rowe opened his mouth and snapped it shut, then said, "What else did you find about Wyn?"

She handed him a flash drive and an envelope. "Last night, Laslo tried to crack Otto. Of course, he failed, but these are the files Laslo looked at and his fingerprints if you can separate them from mine." She bit out the words, not trying to mask her contempt.

Rowe paused a moment before speaking. "Kali. I don't think Laslo believes like Salah does. He sends money to his sisters, talks about bringing them here 'when he's done'. I doubt he realizes the damage he's causing to the country he dreams of calling home."

Kali didn't care. Laslo had betrayed her trust. She wanted nothing more to do with him. "I'm going to meet with Al-Zahrawi. If he doesn't yet realize that Otto and I are a package, he soon will. You can catch him then."

"Don't do that, Kali. This man is more treacherous even than Gunner Goya." Rowe massaged the stump of his pointer. "Let me tell you a story. When Al-Zahrawi was a young man, five women from his village refused to honor arranged marriages. Al-Zahrawi raped all of them before slicing deep cuts into their skin, pouring honey in the wounds and leaving them to die chained to an anthill. No one helped the women and Al-Zahrawi's actions were applauded as retribution."

Kali swallowed her bile, walked in a circle, and turned

back to Rowe. "Al-Zahrawi thinks threatening my son will break me. He's wrong, but I won't shoot him. I'll outthink him."

The silence grew, broken only by phones ringing down the hall and muted voices. Kali said nothing. She wouldn't change her mind until Sean was safe, Sandy back, and Annie avenged.

He acquiesced. "Ok. We do this together, though. How long it takes to finish Otto's programming is how long we have to catch them."

Kali sniffed. "Zeke. Al-Zahrawi is calling in a debt Wyn owes, due yesterday. Was Annie killed because of Wyn?"

"A Blood Debt..." and then nothing. What was it about men? Couldn't they say something like, *Beat's me.* Or *Here's what I know.* No. They just stop talking.

Kali rubbed her temples. "Al-Zahrawi's setting Wyn up. When Wyn logs off, porn downloads to a hidden file. All Al-Zahrawi needs is a phone call to put him in jail."

She breathed in and out, eyes focused on her left foot. "That's not all. He has pictures of me." Her voice was as tight as the E string on a violin that's about to pop.

Rowe gently took her chin, tipping her face upward. His eyes were deep, angry, and caring in equal amounts. "The pieces are coming together. We'll get the bastard."

"I'm OK, Zeke. Just mad."

She swiped at her eyes and left, determined to finish her dissertation, which was when Mr. Grant called. "I'll send you a magnetic signature. Find the sub or your son dies."

Chapter 49

Sunday

Rowe's plan today was to visit every place where Annie used her credit card that final trip. Her GPS auto-loaded to an FBI cloud making it easy to follow her trail. Somewhere, something ended in her death. James wanted to join Rowe, but ended up in another FBI mandatory briefing.

Rowe finished up two Zone bars and a canned protein drink as he moved into the right lane, listening to James. "Even though Sean's at a retreat, I'm not discounting him as the N- name. A friend with the Park Rangers is checking on him."

Rowe exited the Thruway and wove his way to Old Niskayuna Road. "I'm at the Albany Airport General Aviation T-Hangars. According to Annie's GPS, she stopped here for 45 minutes. It has a good visual of the private planes. With the top down, in her low-slung Mini Cooper, she should have been invisible. Can you get a list of ALB 2:00ish arrivals?"

James grunted. "That's the Vitolska's local airport." Hunh. Coincidence? "OK. Here we go. There was only one departure, for Washington DC. A Cessna, Nellie-909-Major-Alpha, started in Los Angeles."

The twenty-something agent, Claude, remembered the Cessna. He squinted at the number through mascaraed lashes and tapped the page with a black tipped finger.

"The Eclipse 500 Luxury Edition. Navy-Bahama blue

striping. A beauty. I rode in one once with a … date. That Pratt and Whitney engine is so so smooth and quiet."

He blinked at Rowe and ran his fingers through longish bleached blonde hair. Rowe smiled.

"Any of these men on it, Claude?" Rowe showed him shots of Sean, Al-Zahrawi, and Matt Monroe. He still didn't have one of Edik Vitolska.

Claude cocked his head, touched his pale throat, and squinted again. After a few seconds, he huffed in exasperation and pulled reading glasses from under the counter.

"It sucks getting old. I just started using these. Nnh, unh. For sure not this sweet-looking boy. One guest was white, six foot, cute crew cut and muscles that could do anything." He paused, lost in his memories. Rowe prodded. "Anything else about him?"

Claude's brow puckered. "Hostile, and short tempered. I don't think he liked me."

Rowe flicked through his phone until he found Gunner. "Is this him?"

"Ooh, yes. That's the sneer, but I missed the Rolex. Is he rich?" Splotches of pink blossomed in Claude's cheeks.

"You mentioned a second man?"

"Yes. A Middle Eastern gentleman—short, dark hair. Charming and gentle. He made an effort to put me at ease when Mr. Muscle growled at me." He poked at the grainy image of Laslo. "That could be him."

"How about this woman?" Rowe showed him a photo of Annie. Wavy blonde hair framed a perfect face blooming with pink and white in all the right spots.

Claude shook his head. "I'm looking for a wife. I would have noticed her."

Rowe continued north, through a sparsely populated woodsy area, past a 410 million year old arthropod bed inexplicably named Fiddler's Green, to Hwy 9 and Schroon Lake until he pulled into the parking lot of Cap's Corner Motel, a cozy collection of eight rustic cabins, an office, and a serviceable picnic table dropped amidst a copse of trees. There sat Annie's Mini Cooper. He parked next to it, got out, and cautiously surveyed the empty vehicle as he called James. "I found her car. No obvious signs of trouble. Doors are locked."

Rowe discreetly searched the windows of the visible cottages as he crossed the nearly deserted pot-holed asphalt surface, past a sagging marquee that promised air-conditioned rooms and color TV's. Rowe guessed people came for the stunning view of the Adirondack Mountains and the high altitude forests, not creature comforts. He walked between chipped planters filled with hollyhocks, gladiolas and daisies, and ducked under a worn-but-clean American Flag with forty-eight stars.

The door squeaked open on a dingy 1950's lobby. It had scuffed off-white walls, two worn chairs, a cracked plastic table, and a rack for local maps and brochures. A reservation desk covered the far wall, in front of a door to what must be an office. A whip-thin girl, sixteen at best, poked her head out.

"May I help you?"

She wore a short-sleeved white blouse and salmon glasses over close-set blue eyes. Her shoulder length mouse-brown hair was wet or oily. Rowe couldn't tell which until he caught the odor of dirty socks.

"Hello." Rowe showed his badge as he read her name tag. "How are you, Kathy?"

"Fine, thank you. Things are a little slow so I'm reading. I like to read. Books take you places you couldn't go otherwise. I'd like to be a librarian, you know? This book's about England …" As she prattled on, she shuffled from one foot to the other and tugged at a clump of hair.

Finally, she wound down and stopped. Rowe guessed not many people listened to her for more than a few seconds. Now, she fumbled for what to do. He smiled and asked, "My friend's Mini is in your lot, but she's disappeared. Were you here last Thursday or Friday?"

Kathy's eyes went wide. "Last Thursday? You're here about those guys? Dad!" She backed away, but never took her eyes off Rowe. She started scratching a spot on her wrist that was already raw and chewing at the inside of her cheek.

A mountain of a man trundled in from the back office. His stained Cap's Corner t-shirt barely reached a pair of well-used jeans riding well-below his waist. He had shaggy salt and pepper hair and the spongy skin of someone who spent his nights indoors with a bottle. As he approached, he blew into a tired kerchief.

"He's here about the prossy." Scratch, scratch. A line of blood prickled up.

"Cap Barlow." He stuck out a leathery paw. "This here's my place. I knew those rag heads 're bad news. She tried t' say something, but they said she's drunk. I called th' police, but when they knocked, she said she's fine."

"Is this her?"

Rowe flicked forward on his phone to one of his favorite photos of Annie, in a cheery yellow cap-sleeved blouse over suntanned skin. Her head tilted to the side and a grin creased her heart-shaped face. Her eyes filled the frame with life.

"Yep. Pretty girl. She could've done better."

"Mr. Barlow—"

"Cap."

"Cap. Is this your motel room?"

Rowe showed him a shot from CNN. Sun had cleaned it up, but blurry hints of the violence remained.

"Yep, Cabin Eight, with th' new TV." He pointed to a ten-year-old seventeen-inch wood veneer set. "What's goin' on?"

"You hate TV, too, huh?"

"The last good show's *Bonanza*. They don't even play th' reruns anymore."

"Cap, can we see if my friend is OK? Leave Kathy at the desk."

Cap understood. "Work on the billin', Kath."

They walked in silence, feet crunching on dry pine needles and twigs. Shafts of sunshine broke through the canopy and dappled the earth with a mosaic of light. A squirrel family hustled across the path, collecting winter stores.

As the duo approached the cabin, Rowe picked up a distinctive low hum.

"No one checked out, but the car's gone," Cap swatted a cloud of flies that swarmed the door.

"Just crack it," Rowe said as Cap plugged the key into the lock. He didn't think the old guy could handle what was behind his door.

The buzz increased to a roar and a cloying sweetness squirted out, followed by fat green flies so gorged, they could barely get off the ground. Cap reared back like a spooked horse.

"Call the police. Tell them it's the place they visited before, but this time the girl's dead."

Cap backed up, fleshy hands at his sides and shaggy head bobbing. He made it as far as the bushes before he retched.

Rowe slammed the door and sprinted to his car where he kept a Sig Sauer 9mm. After Iraq, he thought he'd never fire a gun again, until he met Thomas Meier. Meier could adapt any weapon for any handicap. Missing fingers were no big deal. Hands were harder, but he'd done that, too. Rowe spent a week at Meier's 128-acre SigArms Academy. They adjusted the trigger and grip until he could fire faster and truer than at any point in his life.

As he pocketed an extra magazine, he took a picture of a white Honda two-door at the far end of the lot, then started a perimeter search of the cabin, searching out prints, trash, cigarette butts, and any foreign trace. His feet rolled heel to toe to tamp the sound of crunching twigs and leaves. A wren's lusty voice called and the chatter of sparrows. He silently searched for shadows, out-of-place noises, activity, all for naught when Cap huffed up to Rowe's side.

"The Police're on their way." He shoved a paper at Rowe. "They reserved two rooms."

Rowe caught Cap's eye and raised an eyebrow, silently asking, "*Where's this one?*"

Cap nodded toward a corner of the property and whispered, "I'll get m' rifle!"

Rowe shook his head, but Cap was already gone. No movement in the windows. The curtains were drawn, so he approached unseen. Footprints between the two cabins were sharply edged, the crushed vegetation green, making it less than a day old. He pressed his ear against the rough exterior, but got nothing. He moved behind the sturdy door frame and listened while a spider inched its way up the window. There was no sound except the breeze ruffling the treetops.

Rowe peered through a crack in the torn curtains. The bed was unmade. Old food containers and pizza boxes covered every flat surface. A light was on in what must be the bathroom. He edged the door open while flattening himself to the exterior wall. The room smelled sour and sweaty, but abandoned. He crouched and shuffled in, jerking his Sig corner to corner, then held it steady as he crab-walked toward the back room. He paused and then burst in swinging his weapon side to side.

Empty. If they were gone, why leave the luggage and car? That's when he got it. Cap owned the Honda. He started the process of reviewing the crime scene, but hands-off. He didn't want to interfere with the local police investigation.

Thirty minutes later, just as sirens arrived, he found fresh marks on the baseboard. They looked nothing like furniture scrapes, but Rowe had no idea what they were or if they were important. He snapped a picture. Ajit would figure it out.

Chapter 50

It took Rowe ninety minutes to explain the FBI's involvement to the local police, all the while avoiding submarines, DNA viruses and stolen military secrets. When he mentioned a terrorist connection and the broadcast of Annie's murder, the officer called it a Daniel Perl—death of an innocent at the hands of radicals. Rowe gave them his contact information as well as James's and asked to be kept in the loop.

He left them to their grisly task and stopped at the office. Cap trundled up, wide rheumy eyes fixed on Rowe.

"If they come back, call me at this number and hide." He handed Cap his business card. "I don't think they will now that the police are involved."

"Your friend dropped this," and he gave Rowe a candy bar wrapper with writing on one side. It was a maze of words, none of which made sense. Rowe uploaded a picture to James. "What about her car?"

"Someone will retrieve it. Until then, keep everyone outside the yellow crime scene tape."

"We never had nothin' like this b'fore. People come t' enjoy themselves, not get killed. How do I explain it t' Kath?"

After a moment, Rowe offered, "Tell her Annie was good and decent, and a Patriot. She died fighting the good fight." He patted Cap's shoulder and left, but a heaviness descended upon him as he sped from the lot. Even if they caught the thugs who killed Annie, they'd already won. And Rowe was losing. He felt like a hiker standing on a wooden bridge that hung by one tattered thread across a bottomless chasm.

He merged onto the thruway and called James.

"The landlord's shaken up. He wrote Annie off as a drunk prostitute getting more than she bargained for. He's kicking himself for not helping her. He has a daughter."

"Those tire tracks are less than a day old, but we know the kidnappers/murderers were there at least three days." James sounded efficient, but Rowe knew a rage simmered just below the surface, knew because he felt it too. Annie was like family. She wasn't supposed to die.

"Landlord says they rented one room and added another Saturday. Their original plan had nothing to do with Annie. What changed it?"

James' voice was tight. "She stumbled into them. Just bad luck, which she turned into an opportunity to give us clues." He coughed.

"I don't know if this is another clue, but it was scratched into the baseboard of the second cabin—" And then Rowe got it. "Kali."

"What about Kali?" James's voice notched up a tone.

"The scratches say 'Ilak'—Kali in reverse. It's her word games. I thought it was random marks…"

Rowe's hands went cold and his stomach tightened. "Sean's missing, isn't he?" That's why Annie shooed away the police. They threatened to kill Sean if she didn't.

There was whispering. When James spoke, it was with the voice that notified agent families of their death.

"When we called, the leaders couldn't find Sean. They hope he wandered off on a nature hike though the counselors say he never left his string bass except to eat. The Park Rangers are searching."

"Dammit!" He slammed a hand on the wheel. So much time and still he couldn't protect one boy. Maybe he *had* lost his edge. "Does Kali know?"

"Not yet."

"Where is it, Bobby?"

"At Smoke Rise Campsites on Schroon Lake, about a

mile from Cap's as the crow flies. I have agents up there, my best guys. You'd be in the way, Zeke."

Should he go to Schroon Lake or get back to NY to break the news to Kali in person? He breathed deeply. "I'll tell Kali. I'm an hour out."

Rowe bobbed around a threesome of sightseers and slipped back into his lane, narrowly avoiding an eighteen wheeler. The richness of nature flew by in a blur of wind and dirt. He had to ease off the gas as a VW Van appeared ahead of him. He honked and dodged around it.

"The kidnappers must have holed up at Cap's, waiting for the OK to take Sean, when Annie showed up. Once they figured out she knew too much, they got rid of her."

"Hold on, Bobby. Sun's calling," and he conferenced Sun into their call. "What's up, Eitan?"

"I wanted to see Manfried's reaction to the emails from Al-Zahrawi—"

"Eitan. Bobby's here, too. Can you cut to the chase?"

"I tapped into Columbia's security cams. The visible ones were incapacitated of course, but the one I hid worked fine. The Dean didn't open those messages. Al-Zahrawi/Keregosian made a mistake." Keys clattered. "I forwarded the images to your phones."

Rowe opened the email on his dashboard.

"Laslo Hemren, Zeke. Terrorist-to-be, young enough to slip up. He's on Columbia's roster as 'Jack Fay', night janitor, with keys to everything."

"That explains Matt Monroe's key." Rowe's neck burned. He'd made another mistake by not crossing the facial recognition program with the University database.

"There's more. Laslo forwarded emails from the Dean's computer to the same anonymous drop Keregosian uses."

"Which implicates the Dean in the conspiracy, as though he's trying to hide his trail."

"Right."

James huffed. "Good work, Dr. Sun." Whatever he said next was drowned out by background chatter.

"Say again, Bobby?"

"A note was hammered into Annie's chest. It says, 'Otto has seven days.'"

Chapter 51

Kali turned as Rowe barged into her office. His hair sprouted out at odd angles and dirt striped his face like war paint. There were grimy streaks on his arms and stains on his clothing.

And he was frightened, an emotion she didn't think he had. Before she could ask, he snapped, "You didn't answer your cell,"

"I turned my phone off to concentrate on my dissertation. Where have *you* been?"

He croaked out, "We need to talk."

Her phone buzzed. It was Sean. "Hold on."

Horror filled Rowe's face. "Kali, wait—"

"Sean!" Rowe pushed speaker.

"Mom. What's going on?" His words came out a hoarse whisper followed by a yelp and then the smooth voice of Mr. Grant.

"He is fine, which won't continue if you fail." His voice was friendly, a colleague talking to a friend.

"You haven't sent the magnetic signature! I can't do anything without it!" Her heart smacked so hard against her ribs, it hurt to breathe.

"Consider this a reminder of what is at stake—and put your earrings back on." The line went dead.

Kali crumpled, hands braced on her knees as her shoulders heaved. Rowe tried to pull her into his arms, but she resisted. "I'm alright, Zeke."

She wasn't alright. Not even close.

"I didn't get to tell you yet… Last night, he called… said he would be sending me a magnetic signature for Otto to find. … Zeke, I don't know if Otto can do that."

Her voice held no emotion, her face as flat as week-old soda. It broke his heart.

"Kali. I'll find him. I promise."

Kali wrapped her right arm across her belly, rested her left elbow on it, and chewed a cuticle that already bled. When her phone buzzed, she jumped, stabbed speaker and croaked, "Salah?" But it was Wyn, babbling about the excavation. Her face fell. "Wyn. I can't talk—"

He interrupted. "The skeleton was exactly where Otto specified. My crew will clean it up and ship it to Columbia." His voice was giddy. "What else has Otto found?"

"Someone kidnapped Sean."

Too quickly, Fairgrove said, "Do what they ask, Kali. They could kill you."

Kali's eyes narrowed and her face hardened. "How do you know, Wyn?"

"Well, I don't …"

"But you dealt with Al-Zahrawi before." As Fairgrove stuttered, Kali calmly activated an app on her phone.

"But not like this." His words stumbled over each other.

Rowe's cell rang. He eyed Kali as he answered. Her eyes were glassy, skin dry and pale. He was afraid she might go into shock. "What did you find out, Bobby?"

"A forest ranger saw Sean pounding on a car window. He thought it was a kid throwing a tantrum until he got the flier the camp put out. There aren't a lot of places that road leads. We could pick him up soon.

"More good news. IAFIS matched the fingerprints on Kali's keyboard to Hemren and gave us an address. His roommates say he's been missing a week which makes them happy. He scares them, attends anti-American meetings at all hours of the night."

Kali was massaging her temple. "Where is Sean, Wyn?"

"Salah wouldn't tell me! He's crazy!"

James barked. "Agit can track his emails--and he's motivated. When he broke Keregosian's code, it took him to a website. While he sorted through the pages, malware destroyed our system files." James grunted, "Ajit called it a Chernobyl Meltdown. You can use your imagination. These people are smart."

"Eitan's here. I'll call you back."

"I like you, Wyn. You're a good person, not evil. Help me stop them."

"I promise, Kali, they'll go through me before they get you."

"Do you hear my keyboard, Wyn? No? Ask Salah. He's bugging my lab." Well, only if she had her earrings on. "I'm putting your name on my research. I don't care about your past problems. I trust you."

"Sweetheart, thank you. Since I met you, I felt we were destined, and now you do, too. Please believe me: If I had his whereabouts, I'd tell you."

Kali stuck her finger in her mouth and pretended to calm down. "Of course, Wyn. Will you tell Sean I love him the next time you see him?"

"He's fine. I mean, I'm sure he's fine. You and I won't help Salah if he isn't."

Sun opened his laptop and caught Rowe's eye, but said nothing.

"Kalian, we are always together, late nights and weekends. We collaborate on a thrilling project. Who wouldn't be jealous of the emotional and intellectual bond we share. You see how it angers Rowe. It's my lifetime dream."

Kali sniffled for effect.

"Kalian, I hope when this is over, you'll see we belong together."

Sun pulled Kali's diamond studs from his pocket and fiddled with them. His eyes flicked from Kali to Otto and back.

"Here's what we'll do. We use Otto to find artifacts, like

the crocodile—"

"Wyn, I'm finding Sean first."

"We divide and conquer, like those military SEALs. I find the crocodile. You give Salah the proof he wants."

Kali ended the call. "I can't believe I was flattered by his attention. How stupid." Her eyes misted, but she said nothing more.

Rowe spoke gently, eyes locked onto hers, "Kali, can Otto find Sean?"

She cocked her head and squinted at him. "What do you mean?"

"In your DARPA presentation, you talked about Otto's ability to pick up on the tiniest bits of data and his sensitivity to minute changes. Could he find Sean?"

Kali put her hand out like a stop sign. "I know what you're thinking, that I was going to search for Angel's mom with Otto, but that was based on data. This would be Sean's *appearance*." She shook her head, but slowly, as though turning the idea around in her mind. "There are too many similarities between people—height, shape, mass. Even if I input exact specifications, Otto would come up with too many targets. I'd need visual, and I doubt there are cameras where he's being held." Her voice trailed off, lost in her own words.

"OK. I'm going to talk to the Vitolska's. This time, it won't be friendly."

She didn't seem to hear him.

Though Fairgrove disapproved of Al-Zahrawi's methods, they again worked. Kalian had just agreed to add his name to her research. When he rescued Sean, she might put 'Dr. Wynton Fairgrove' as primary when she published.

What Rowe wanted was still a mystery. If not money or fame, Fairgrove had no idea.

Chapter 52

Monday

"You need my help, Zeke. I know what's normal with my son."

Rowe ignored Kali as he hobbled toward his car. He came in early to get someone to cover his classes. He absolutely didn't want to see Kali.

"Aren't you working with Eitan? Never mind. Doesn't matter. Hudson is too dangerous." Al-Zahrawi's interest in Sean was Kali, so bringing her to what could be ground zero would play right into his hands.

"You won't understand Sean's puzzles." She blocked him, forcing him to stop.

He kept his eyes on the street. "You two use more than palindromes?"

"If he left a message, I'll find it."

Rowe considered her request and rejected it. "I can't risk Al-Zahrawi knowing where I'm going."

She fingered her ears. "No diamond studs. They're in my lab. Eitan programmed them to show a loop of me working. Al-Zahrawi will never see the difference."

Rowe scowled. "You two planned this." He scooted around her and hurried to his vehicle, Kali a step behind. "Any sign of danger, you're out." She jumped in.

As they sped north, Rowe asked, "What was that app you ran talking to Wyn yesterday?"

"Eitan created it. It records the conversation, compares

the voice to a baseline of the same person and determines if she or he is under stress, lying, or not telling the whole truth."

"What's the conclusion?"

She punched a few buttons and peered at the results. "A couple of interesting reads. First, the kidnapping didn't surprise him and he had little concern for Sean's plight." Her voice caught. "Second, he's annoyed at Al-Zahrawi, I don't know why. He knows Al-Zahrawi is hiding something from him and it makes him nervous."

That could be the edge Rowe needed.

The road took them through green hills and rolling valleys, but he was only dimly aware of the scenery. Sean was Kali's blind spot. She would do anything to protect her son. Rowe had to find the boy before Kali did something that couldn't be fixed. The Vitolska's—at least Sam—were involved, of that Rowe was sure. He just didn't know how.

They reached the Vitolska's in two hours. The lawn was mowed, curtains open, but newspapers cluttered the drive. Rowe checked the yards, garage, windows, but found no one.

"They left Friday night." The voice came from next door. An older man, lean and fit in a jeans shirt, stonewashed cargo shorts, and Birkenstock sandals, was resting on a rake. "Took a student with them, so must have been a concert."

"We're looking for a boy, Mr..."

"Dr. Joe Boyd. Call me Joe."

Rowe stuck his hand out and Joe shook it with a bony paw. His arms were pitted, and a scar ran from his wrist to elbow.

"Where'd you get the shrapnel?"

"Chosin Reservoir."

"My Granddad's got the same arm, but Leyte Gulf."

"Too crazy to stay away, huh?" Joe nodded toward Rowe's hands.

"Different war, same marching orders."

They chatted about warriors and battles, until finally Joe asked, "You must be the one who left the note. Bobby?"

"Bobby James is my partner. I'm Zeke Rowe." He passed

Joe his Columbia card. "This is Kalian Delamagente. Her son is one of the students."

"I almost called last night. Couldn't decide if there's a problem. One of the students—plays that big violin—he had a deep cut on his cheek, starting to scab over. I asked if he was alright, but Sam said he fell. Do they swordfight with the bows?" Joe started to chuckle, but stopped when Kali turned white. "Is something wrong? Did he miss the concert?"

Kali pulled up a photo of Sean playing his string bass on her phone. "Is this him?"

"Yep. Good kid. Always polite. He and Edik hang out a lot."

"Anything odd you could tell us about. He's missing."

"Damn, I'm sorry to hear that. No, everything looked legit or I would have done something. Talk to Connie and Matt, next door. They were friends."

"Thanks, Joe. Anything else, give me a call."

"Would a key to the house help? I'm the landlord."

Chapter 53

"Here's an invoice for $789, Zeke. It includes dozens of cleaning tasks, like 'bleach drains, clean air returns, vacuum under carpets'."

Surely for that kind of money, nothing was missed, but still he searched the rooms, cupboards, inside appliances, under carpeting, behind pictures, around the yards, and in every corner of the garage.

Two hours later, he was frustrated and needed a break. "I'll be next door. Do you want to come?" But Kali disappeared into one of the bedrooms.

One of the last places her son felt happy, with the belief Mom kept him safe, was in this eight-by-twelve room. Its gleaming windows sparkled, carpets bristled, the tiny closet bare and pristine. Kali inhaled the scent of rosin leftover from the raucous explosion in a vigorous musical selection. She picked out the rich fragrance of the wood polish Sean applied to his bass. She searched the shelves, between the furniture, behind curtains—everywhere for clues.

Nothing.

She collapsed onto the floor, back resting heavily against his bed. She could see him, earbuds in place, reviewing professional renditions of favorite pieces, matching his fingering and bowing to their interpretation, adjusting for *fortes* and *pianissimos*. She wriggled, trying to think like Sean. He wouldn't sleep in the bed because making it wasted time. He'd lean against it, using the natural light from the window.

But the bookcase had been moved. It blocked the window which Sean would never do. He loved nature's power, sun or rain, always wanted to add it to his music. She walked the cabinet side to side until it dropped back into its original place.

What was that? Faint marks were etched into the baseboard. She got her penlight and splashed a circle of light over the shallow contours. Random scratches, but new. She backed up to gain a perspective and saw it.

"I hear you, sweetheart. I'm coming."

Connie and Matt Monroe could be twins in their matching white yacht pants, deck shoes, and blue-and-white striped Polos. Connie had a jaunty red scarf tied around her plump neck, and her husband wore a ball cap with the logo of a local Little League team. Matt stared wide-eyed at Kali as she joined the group and then started sneezing violently.

"Hon, are you alright? Do you need some water?"

"No, pumpkin, I'll be fine." He put a protective arm around Connie and glared at Kali, as though daring her to out him.

"Like I was saying, Special Agent Rowe, Sam and Edik are cultured people. Our type."

Matt's fingers pinched into Connie's shoulder. She tried to shake him off as she continued. "They're well-regarded Russian musicians. We went to concerts at the Philharmonic together. They have box seats." Her nose edged up.

"Did they ever act suspiciously," Both heads started shaking before Zeke finished his question, "or invite people over you thought might be dangerous?"

"Of course not!" But concern clouded Connie's face and fright, Matt's. The man Kali knew as Fred by now must realize the job he did for Al-Zahrawi was bigger than a drop-in visit to a grad student. Zeke thumbed his glasses up, a nervous tick he developed in the last few days. Now that she thought about it, he didn't wear glasses. Well, except at the field study, in Israel.

"Is something wrong?" Connie's eyes darted from Rowe

to Matt.

"You better check the pie, precious. We have those kids on their way over."

"My goodness! Where's my head." She pressed her palms against her temples. "The Garden Club planned a children's day and we graciously offered our house. I have so much to do!"

As Connie hurried off, Rowe faced Matt. "Let's start with why you pay no rent." His voice was now all business.

Matt spread his feet and crossed his arms over his chest. "It's called a real estate exchange—I trade my Hudson property for this one."

"What's that address?"

Matt popped a Life Saver into his mouth. "What's this about? I don't have to talk to you."

Kali was seething. She wanted to slap the insipid smirk off his Botoxed face and demand he explain how a teenage boy was abducted outside his kitchen window. Was he preening for an evening at the theatre as the Vitolska's slashed her son so ruthlessly, an eighty-year-old man with bifocals saw the damage a hundred feet away?

Instead, she kept her face neutral.

"Last time we were here, you told us about your side job doing errands for Salah Mahmud Al-Zahrawi. What you didn't mention is how dependent you are on that income. Your paycheck falls far short of covering Connie's designer clothes, luncheons, the gentlemen's club, the golf membership, your girlfriends, and those other extra-curricular activities."

Matt's eyes widened and his mouth dropped open. "What gives you the right to hack into my finances?" His lip quivered. He tried for righteous and ended up frightened.

Kali couldn't stop herself this time. "My son's missing and a good friend gave her life trying to find him. Al-Zahrawi connects everything—"

"Which connects you to breaking and entering, conspiracy, and murder." Rowe caught Kali's eye and then moved back to Matt. "You're a small fish. Help us get Al-

Zahrawi, you could come out of this OK."

Matt glared at Kali and sputtered, "I'm just a guy trying to make ends meet."

Rowe clenched his jaw. "When Al-Zahrawi contacts you again, call me," and he handed Matt his card. "You could save a boy's life."

Matt shoved it in his pocket and sprinted into the house.

Rowe stared after his fleeing form. "Did you find anything in Sean's room?"

Kali's voice softened. "He scratched 'momom' into the baseboard. He calls me that when he needs help. I call him 'Shanayus'—spelled 'S-e-a-n-a-e-s'. He knew last Friday he was in trouble, but thought the camp was secure. What changed that?"

"I think Sean's kidnapping was unplanned, Kali. Whatever Annie said made them believe she could blow Al-Zahrawi's plan apart. Sean is insurance."

The sun had already set, but Rowe had one last stop before returning to New York. The phone call Matt placed after visiting Kali had terminated at a cell tower by the West Coxsackie Best Western. Probably a dead end, but Rowe turned over and pulverized every rock.

"You check us in while I talk to a few people." To Rowe's surprise, Kali didn't argue. In fact, she'd fallen asleep, head resting against the window.

Fifteen minutes later, they reached the rambling one-story Inn. Kali shuffled inside, more than half asleep. Rowe slipped his 9mm into the back of his pants, hidden by a loose jacket, and showed his picture collection around what passed for the local business district. When he retired from the SEALs, his parting gift had been a license to carry. Today, he was happy to have it. A gas station attendant knew Al-Zahrawi. The owner of a gun shop said Hemren bought 9mm rounds twice from him. A waitress at a diner had served Al-Zahrawi and Goya, but not Matt, and no one recognized the Vitolska's. Rowe was returning to the hotel when he got a call.

"Is this Zeke Rowe?"

"Matt. Change of heart?"

"Al-Zahrawi called. I'm supposed to distract the manager of the Best Western in West Coxsackie. He didn't tell me why. Like I said, nothing illegal about talking to a guy—"

Rowe bolted for the Inn in his limp-sprint version of running. As he neared the building, a slight male brandishing a handgun fled out the front door, followed closely by a blonde with Matt Monroe's build but the feline grace only military training bred.

"Gun!" Rowe bellowed and a round ricocheted off a trash can. Rowe returned fire, but over the gunman's head. He needed him to talk, not die. Gun Boy shot again, this time hitting a parked car. Two teenagers shrieked and crawled under the chassis.

Rowe knew Gun Boy.

"Mr. Hemren—Police! Stop!" It didn't slow Hemren and his friend, but did frighten citizens into diving for cover. Rowe's knees started to ache, but he charged on, past the parking lot to an open area maintained as a fire break between the hotel property and a sprawling industrial complex further north. If Hemren got into that maze, Rowe would never catch them.

"Laslo! Murder won't help your sisters!" Rowe shouted as the pair zagged across the 87 off-ramp.

Rowe's knees throbbed, mere moments from locking up. He slowed enough to put Laslo in his crosshairs and shot at the thick mass of his shoulders. The boy screamed and fell forward. When his partner turned to grab him, Rowe recognized the hawkish nose, domed forehead, and full sneering lips. Gunner Goya, aka Aleksei Borodnoi.

Rowe fired again, this time nicking Borodnoi's ear. The burly Russian twisted around to face Rowe as though making a decision.

"Give up, Borodnoi! There's nowhere to go!" He screamed as he speed dialed James.

"Bobby! Get a helicopter to the 9W north of the West

Coxsackie Best Western. I've got—"

Pow!

"Borodnoi shot Hemren!"

Laslo collapsed and Borodnoi disappeared into the warren of tilt-up concrete warehouses. Rowe panted to a halt next to a white-faced Laslo. The shoulder wound from Rowe's bullet was superficial, but Borodnoi struck the femoral artery, probably exactly where he intended. If Rowe didn't help, Laslo would bleed to death.

"And I need an ambulance!"

Rowe ripped a strip of fabric from the tail of his shirt and applied a tourniquet around Hemren's upper thigh. "What have you gotten yourself into, Laslo?" The boy's face contorted in pain, and his chest heaved up and down in shallow waves.

"Save me, Dr. Rowe! Aleksei is crazy!"

The bleeding from Hemren's leg slowed, but not enough. There was nothing Rowe could do other than put pressure on the wound. "I called for help. I'll stay until it arrives. Tell me where Sean is, Laslo."

The boy gripped Rowe's lapels with a fierceness belied by the spreading pool of blood under his body. "I know the Plan! I tell you, promise to bring my sisters here, to America, where they can be teachers. I never wanted anyone killed. You must believe me."

"Where's Sean?" But Laslo gasped and passed out.

Rowe found IDs for Hemren, Hamar, and Fay in Laslo's wallet, and a photo of three giggling teenage girls. Their eyes spoke of love and loyalty.

"You mistook terrorism for a game. Who will watch over your sisters now?"

By the time the ambulance reached Laslo Hemren, he was dead.

Rowe sprinted up the stairs to his room, the Inn's manager huffing after him, but no Kali. "Where is the woman I came with?"

Before he could punctuate his question with a persuasive grip, her voice stuttered from the bathroom, shaky but alive.

"Zeke, I'm here. Did you catch them?"

Her presence ran through him like a beam of sunshine. He grabbed her to his chest and buried his face in her hair. "No. Borodnoi got away by killing Hemren."

Kali sagged. "Laslo saved my life. He remembered I told him Otto would only work with my heartbeat and told Borodnoi. The Russian tried to grab me, but I locked myself in the bathroom. When you screamed, Borodnoi and Laslo fled."

Rowe didn't remember screaming, but was glad he had. He turned back to the still quivering manager and growled, "How did they get this room number?"

"We never give those out!" He blustered and wrapped a grease-stained tie around his fingers. "Someone did ask, so we called the room."

Rowe crowded him. "Was it one of the men I chased?"

"No! Someone else, but I never got his n-name."

"But if you saw his picture?"

"Yes! The desk clerk would recognize him!"

"Go collect everyone. Now!"

As he scurried away, Kali logged onto Rowe's laptop, drilled through to her online security program, and wiped Otto's drives.

"Now we find him." When Rowe looked confused, she explained, "GPS is embedded in the motherboard. Even if Borodnoi destroys the hard drive, we can still find it. There." A flag winked complete with a GPS tag.

"Tell James what happened, Kali. I'll find Otto."

Kali handed a card to the manager. "Call Special Agent James. Tell him what's going on and don't let anyone near these rooms." She caught up with Rowe. When he glowered, she responded simply, "It's my son."

Rowe rolled his eyes. Kali had become a lot like Annie the last few days. Twenty minutes later, they found Otto in a dumpster. Rowe scratched his head.

"They steal your AI, kill their own man, and abandon the

spoils. Why?" He reached into his pocket for a pencil but came up empty. "Someone tipped them off about the GPS."

They answered in unison, "Wyn."

Chapter 54

When Rowe got back to the Best Western, the manager was smiling and nodding to James as though a murder was a publicity event. He excused himself and walked briskly toward Rowe.

"Thank you for returning. I've explained the—the importance—of cooperation to my team." His voice trailed off as he waved an arm across the assembled group of dour-faced employees. "I think you'll find everyone… cooperative. Can I get you coffee?"

How did anyone trust this man with a multi-million dollar business? Rowe ignored him, turned to the bellhop.

"Do you remember these two men, Max?" He held out pictures of Borodnoi and Hemren.

"Yes, sir. This one," indicating Hemren, "was nervous. He kept fingering his jacket. I was in the Army, a sergeant, so recognized the concealed weapon immediately. I know what an undercover cop looks like and he wasn't one."

"How did you know?"

Max thought a minute. "He acted hinky. You know?" Rowe didn't know. He never used that word in SEAL intel, but Max didn't wait for an answer. "I was about to call the Village police—the Captain over there is a friend—see if anyone matching Hemren's description was on assignment when shots exploded."

Rowe thanked Max and turned to the maid who let the men into Kali's room. Before he could ask why, she blurted, "I didn't do anything wrong. They forgot their key," which brought a scowl to Max's face. She flushed and said, "Lots of guests lose keys," and then she broke down in tears. The manager glared at Rowe and rushed over to comfort her as Rowe approached the desk clerk. He picked Monroe out of a six pack as the one who distracted him so James dispatched an officer to pick the man up.

"He has a beautiful wife, a home in a nice neighborhood, and he throws it away? I don't get it."

Two hours later, FBI techs gone, James waved goodbye and Rowe went to his room. He hoped a handful of Bayer and a night's rest would dull his throbbing knees, but that all changed when he found Kali in his bed.

"I can keep an eye on you better if I see you."

The only clever retort Rowe could muster was, "I'll brush my teeth."

He scrubbed his teeth—twice—while reminding himself he was on a case and couldn't get involved, all the while knowing if she beckoned, he'd do stupid. She was gorgeous and brilliant with glorious prospects. He was damaged, grumpy, and shackled to his past. He had no patience, judged people too quickly, with skills better suited to national emergencies than wooing a soulmate. If his future were a person, it would be wearing tattered clothes, muttering to itself, where Kali's would be walking a red carpet.

He was more relieved than disappointed to find she'd fallen asleep.

He pulled a chair close enough to inhale her scent, his back pressed against the wall and a good view of the door. Her face showed none of the worry that must fill her thoughts. Finally, he fell into a light doze, just under the edge of awareness, hand on his weapon.

Tuesday

Kali awoke to the blare of her cell. She scrabbled blindly with one hand and finally answered, "What?"

"Dr. Rowe murdered one of my people, Ms.

Delamagente. That was a mistake." Mr. Grant's voice had the toneless quality of a man straining to cover true emotions. Traffic noises filled the background, a horn honking, someone cussing. He was in a city.

"Borodnoi killed Hemren, Mr. Grant, not Zeke, and he failed to steal Otto. That's what you want, not Dr. Rowe, so I'll make a deal with you."

Rowe kicked her. When she glared at him, his eyes were fiery, mouth a tight line bracketed by anger. Last night, she'd tried to put her son ahead of duty, but fell asleep. Rowe had been a gentleman and slept in the chair, which made her wonder what else she misjudged about him.

Part of her wished he'd awakened her. She ached to be held, to be told everything would be OK.

"Trade Sean for me. And Otto."

"An eye for an eye, Ms. Delamagente. Someone must die. Dr. Rowe? Catherine Stockbury? Your son?"

Kali's cool veneer cracked. "You already killed Annie—" she retorted, but he was gone.

"What the hell are you doing?" Rowe's posture was rigid, eyes drilling into her.

She didn't have time for his machismo. "Let's take what we have to Eitan."

As they drove south, neither said a word. What had been a comfortable silence on the way up, today was brittle. Each step forward moved them back and she was tired of it. To her, this was simple: Get Sean. No prioritizing, moral qualms, or academic politics.

She closed her eyes and let herself drift. Yesterday, she dismissed the possibility Otto could locate her son, but her subconscious had relentlessly worked on the question. Now, the world quiet save the old Benz's hum, the rumble of wheels over asphalt, and Rowe's warm confidence one foot away, she figured it out.

She opened her laptop and started programming.

Felix Whitetower had the prominent cheekbones of his

Native American ancestors and the leathery skin of an outdoor life. He was clean shaven, with an ebony ponytail that reached below his shoulder blades. His cousin the hairdresser cut it back to his collar whenever she visited, which had now been six months. He wore a rugged canvas shirt over blue Dickies and Timberland hiking boots. The Department covered part of the boots' cost and Felix the rest. He was on his feet all day and figured he should be comfortable.

Experience told him the boy was dead, but Felix had a sixteen-year-old son.

"Police. May I talk to the homeowner?" Felix studied the rundown building as he waited. Bowed front porch, dirty windows, chipped paint—the house looked unlivable. When he was greeted with silence, he went around to the backyard. It overflowed with junk and weeds. A falling-down shed filled the back corner, its tattered door falling off the hinges.

The new padlock was odd.

"Hi."

Felix started. A teenage boy stood four feet from him. He crossed long dirty arms over a ragged t-shirt. Mud and green slime streaked his pants. He wore socks, but no shoes. His eyes were frightened, darting around like a ping pong ball, and he tapped his fingers non-stop against his chest.

"You're trespassing, officer," a voice boomed from the back door of the house.

"I'm looking for a boy. He's about this age and size."

"That's my son. He's right where he should be."

Right. The boy's hands were soft, his eyes gentle. The haircut came from a barber and the clothes would never survive this rural country.

"Maybe he's seen the boy I'm after. What's your name, young man?" he asked.

"Shanayus."

"What an interesting name."

"He answered you. Go back to your chores, Shay-nus!"

Shanayus ran like a city boy.

"Thank you for your help, Mr.—

"Bill Clinton. I got work to do. We're hardworking folk out here. We ain't got time to chitchat. I've been as helpful as I can. Now let me raise my family!"

He pointed a rifle at Felix and motioned him to leave.

"I'm sure you have a permit for that, Mr. Clinton. What is it? A Browning LongTrac Semi-automatic? I bought one of those last year to hunt deer. Do much deer hunting around here?"

The man who called himself Clinton ignored the question and waved the shotgun toward the driveway. Felix tipped his hat, turned, and left. When he got out of sight, he radioed the station.

"Have Mary ready. I might have the boy."

The Department still used sketch artists, though they debated the pros and cons of cameras in the cars. He was going to buy one of those fancy phones that took pictures and videos and then his bosses could take as long as they wanted to decide.

Felix got to the office and described Shanayus to Mary Elder, a third cousin who'd been there longer than he had. He emailed her drawing along with the boy's name to the investigator who requested the surveillance and headed for the next stop on his list.

The sketch from Felix Whitetower and Mary Elder could be any teenage boy—dark shaggy hair, innocent eyes, arms folded around his chest. A photo would be better, but lots of rural police didn't have cameras in their vehicles. If it was Sean, why would the kidnappers allow the police to talk to him?

Where had Rowe heard that name before? The notes said the son pronounced it Sha-nay-us and the Dad, Shaynus.

An alarm thundered in Rowe's head. "Sha-nay-us—"

"—is Sean's palindrome." It was the first words Kali had said in an hour. "This is Sean. He always hugs himself, to protect his hands."

She stroked a finger over his face. Rowe turned the car

back north and contacted Whitetower. "He'll meet us at the cabin."

Rowe exited a couple off-ramps past Pottersville, wound his way down dirt roads barely more than trails, and approached an old Ford truck up parked on the shoulder. In front of it was a tall solid man in a worn shirt, his back to them.

"That must be Whitetower."

Whitetower turned as they parked. His eyes were calm as though nothing could surprise him and his shoulders squared against whatever life threw his way.

"Mr. Whitetower. I'm Zeke Rowe. This is Kalian Delamagente, Sean's mother."

"Call me Felix."

He smelled green and tan, like the landscape he roamed. His eyes never left the beat up house nestled in a dusty bowl of scrub bushes and stunted water-starved trees.

"Car's gone. I've been here since we talked and seen no one. I may have spooked them."

They descended together, weapons out but lowered. A crow cawed overhead and gophers scurried into their holes. Otherwise, the homestead squatted bleak and lonely.

"How did he look, Mr. Whitetower?" Kali's voice came out soft and hopeful.

"Healthy, Ms. Delamagente. You raised a fine, polite boy, nothing like Mr. Clinton. And smart."

They flattened themselves to the craggy wood siding and knocked. Whitetower pressed his ear to the rough unpainted door and Rowe peered in the grimy windows.

"There's only one room, empty."

Whitetower entered while Rowe and Kali slipped around the corner. They combed the yard in vain search of any evidence of Sean's presence before noticing the ruined shed.

"Felix thinks they kept Sean there."

The stench made Rowe gag. He swallowed quickly, took a deep breath, and edged inside. Kali didn't flinch, walked right in like it was home. Someone had sprinkled dirt over the commode, which did nothing to tamp down the flies crowding for space on the dense sludge.

"Sean's tough, Zeke. He would adopt this as a private place to think."

She examined the walls and ceiling, tearing at dense spider webs, some old, some still home to furry black creatures who didn't like her interference. "He's all I have. He trusts me to find whatever clue he leaves."

And she did—almost hidden by waste, eye level with the moldy baseboard, she dug her fingertips through the slimy crust. Each day, Sean scratched in his name and the date.

The last was today.

Chapter 55

Wednesday

"I'm done."

Kali squinted at her phone. "Eitan?" It was 6am. Zeke had given Sun Felix Whitetower's evidence late last night, actually, very early this morning. "You must have worked all night." Of course he did. "I'll be right there."

She threw on clothes, glad she showered last night though she had no choice. The sour reek of urine and feces overpowered her efforts to sleep.

She stuck a note on Mr. Winters' back door and sprinted to Eitan's lab. Rowe greeted her with a cup of coffee—no cream, no sugar. His shirt and jeans were fresh, but his face tense.

"Sam paid cash for the cleaning service." Judging by the body odor and piles of food wrappers, Sun hadn't left his geekosphere in days. "Joe Boyd's military record shows a decorated marine with a bad temper, honest to his detriment. Chain of command called him intractable because 'he always thinks he's right and usually is'. An *osculare pultem meam* guy."

He shot a glance over his glasses. "*Kiss my ass* sounds more cultured in Latin."

"My kind of warrior," Rowe responded absently.

Sun continued. "The Monroe's are two months from bankruptcy."

"What about the real estate exchange?"

"They bought the cabin where Sean was held for almost nothing and swapped it for the Hudson home, to an Eritrea-based conglomerate which has since gone bankrupt. I'm trying to trace the disposition of assets. Before you ask, James already pulled Monroe out of bed to ask who he arranged the trade with. He never saw them, all via email and messenger."

"A rundown shack for a manicured home? Why can't I make those deals?"

Sun ignored Rowe. "Cap's owned that motel his entire life, as did his Dad before him."

"Not surprised. My gut says Cap is a good guy in a bad place."

"The Best Western manager receives $1,000 a month as a consultant from the same black hole the emails go to. Whitetower's boss says the officer has no interest other than the safety of his hometown. He wants five more like him."

Rowe said, "I need to know where Gegham Keregosian and Salah Al-Zahrawi overlap."

Sun's fingers flew, eyes skittering over three of his seven screens. Rowe was about to ask if he heard him when Sun bounced twice, bumped his glasses up his nose, and gulped half a Styrofoam cup of red M&M's. "The search will take fifty-four minutes. Anyone hungry?"

They went to JJ's Place, one of Columbia's numerous cafeterias. Sun got coffee, sliced tomatoes, cherry pie, and seconds. Rowe devoured scrambled eggs, four slices of toast, two link sausages, and a chocolate shake. Kali ordered a salad which she ignored, choosing instead to shred her napkin and collect the pieces in a neat pile beside her fork. Her face had the passive expression of a spectator at a chess match, not a woman dying from the inside. But, her eyes were clear.

When Rowe tried to engage her in conversation, she interrupted, "I'm fine, Zeke. I just want to find Sean. How was your hamburger?"

Rowe smiled. "My eggs? Excellent."

When they got back to Sun's lab, a message was flashing.

Sun scooted into his chair and locked onto the monitor. "The auction's in twelve days. Invitation only," and Sun went to work while Kali offered suggestions Rowe didn't understand.

Rowe should have felt good about finding out the auction date, but instead felt like he was hanging by his fingers from a cliff, rimrocked, with no way to safety. Even if the Navy successfully wiped all the system files, which would eradicate NEV, they couldn't be sure Al-Zahrawi didn't have the magnetic signatures. With Otto, he could find America's Tridents a week from now or a year from now. The only way to stop that, and protect Kali and Sean, was to stop Al-Zahrawi.

Chapter 56

Wednesday

Kali and Eitan distilled the mishmash of ideas to one wobbly plan. Eitan calculated their chances of success at sixteen percent. Kali thought that was generous.

She pushed heavily to her feet, hoping to go home, pet Sandy, and get away from her worries for a few hours. Rowe had left long ago, on an errand he didn't share. Before she could rub the sleep from her exhausted eyes, Cat plopped into her chair.

"Cat, you're supposed to be hiding."

She winced, but said nothing. Her transformation the past week stunned Kali. Lank, oily hair stuck to her skull. Her skin was sallow and blotchy, and without make-up. She'd chewed her impeccably-manicured nails until they bled. Her clothes were mismatched, wrinkled, and hung on her frame

"He's a jerk. Hell if I'll run from him." The words tumbled out, almost the old Cat. Good.

Kali checked her email, hoping for but not getting a response from the Dean about her dissertation. "Do you want to talk, Cat?"

"I'm fine," but a tear escaped.

Kali rolled her eyes. "Right. You look fine." When that elicited no reply, she added, "We'll get through this—I promise."

Kali had to get some rest, but first she stopped in on Mr. Winters. He greeted her with a mournful head shake. "I miss our friend. Not many visitors for an old man, and dogs accept you even if your breath is bad."

They reassured each other it was just a question of time before Sandy showed up. She wouldn't tell her neighbor that Sean had been kidnapped until she had to. After hiding her briefcase under the couch, she crawled into bed.

"I will find you, Sean, and then we'll find Sandy. I swear on the graves of your grandparents, you will live out your dreams."

She fell asleep and dreamt she was Lucy.

A towering hunter materialized in front of her, a scowl on his hair-free face. He kicked a spear toward her and hefted one of his own. She matched his waist-high hold, bent elbow, and right-handed grip. More hunters appeared; together, they shadowed a mammoth herd.

"Our food. They are here for us." He strode forward with a feline grace, confidence in every step.

"They are Sabertooth's and Panther's also," Lucy motioned, but he turned away.

To her side, a frightened calf lowed, alone, without its mother. The hunters missed him in the shadows, but Lucy didn't. Her arm stretched back as power filled it. Her grip tightened, fingers adjusting. A foreign cry escaped her lips as she thrust the lance forward and released.

Suddenly, Kali became the calf. Terror froze her in place as the spear slammed into her throat and tore through her soft flesh like molten lava. She tried to scream, but the lance cut off her breath. The hunter reared back, a second spear cocked and ready to throw.

It's a dream, but it feels real.

She reached up, expecting a primitive lance but instead touched cold metal—a knife. A coarse palm crushed her mouth. She tried to pull away, but there was no place to go.

"I ask questions; you answer." Borodnoi straddled her tighter, his body granite, black eyes feral. "Where is Catherine

Stockbury?"

"Hiding, but I don't know where."

"You lie." Borodnoi smashed a fist into her cheek. Searing heat exploded behind her eye. She struggled, fighting off nausea. "Where is the portable Otto you always carry? Tell me, you live."

Her head swam, eyes tight against the pain. She thought her jaw must be fractured. Her face throbbed as she spoke slowly, deliberately. "Fuck you."

Borodnoi's voice hardened. "Wrong answer," and he hammered Kali's head, shoulders and chest. Her body screamed and her cheek burned as though scorched by fire. She tried to raise her arms, but they were pinned by his knees. She begged him to stop, but he seemed past reason. She felt herself slipping away. Sean needed her, but she cared less with every savage punch.

Somewhere far away, a door slammed, then the pounding of feet but they were too late. Her world had shrunk to the piercing pain in her ribs, the throb in her neck, the inferno where her face used to be. And the nausea, worse than her headaches, but she was afraid if she threw up, she'd choke.

"Kali! Are... ite?" The voice penetrated the pea soup of her thoughts moments after the weight on her chest lifted. A blurry figure crossed the room, quickly replaced by frightened eyes And the comforting scent of Zeke Rowe. She tried to point, but her arm didn't move.

"Gunner... after Cat." Darkness swallowed her words as she passed out.

Chapter 57

Thursday

"What happened?" Fairgrove grimaced at the welts on Kali's face, the raw bruises encircling her neck, and the ace bandage pulled snugly around her shoulder. He boosted himself onto her desk and ran a hand over his hair. He was perfectly turned out in a lemon yellow polo shirt and beige linen slacks, the rich scent of aftershave losing to the sour malodor of a drinking binge gone late.

"A car accident. I'm OK," though her body screamed otherwise. Any movement sent stabbing pain through her ribs. Her jaw throbbed nonstop and a pounding headache spiked waves of nausea through her body. At least she had all her teeth.

No surprise Fairgrove didn't ask how she got in a car accident when she didn't own a vehicle

Zeke said he happened to be in the area, which couldn't be true, but she wouldn't argue with the man who had saved her life. After ensuring Borodnoi was gone, he called James who called the campus police, checked for broken bones, and put ice on her face. When she refused to go to the hospital, he settled for aspirin and a bodyguard—himself. In the morning, he dropped her at the Columbia health center and promised to return after an errand.

She didn't see a doctor. She had too much to do. Five minutes with Otto confirmed her suspicions. Now she silently willed Wyn to leave so she could break the news to Zeke.

"Who's this, Wyn?" Rowe asked, though he had a good idea who the muscle-bound Russian was with the wide sloping shoulders and face pocked with bad attitude. He stood behind Fairgrove and eyed Rowe with a predator's unwavering attention. A too-small jacket bulged at the waist.

"A friend."

"You don't have friends, Wyn; you have accomplices. Does he call you Asshole, too?" Friend cracked his knuckles like a machine gun blast.

Fairgrove wrapped a paternal arm around Kali's bandaged shoulder. "You and Sean will be OK, dear."

Her face pinched.

"Wyn, she's not OK. Her dog disappeared. Her son's kidnapped. Her house was broken into three times. Now she's been attacked." Rowe jabbed a finger at Fairgrove's chest. "Time to talk to your buddy, Salah—"

"Back off." Friend stepped in between the two men, crossed his arms and spread his legs in a sturdy manly stance, probably intended to be menacing. Rowe chuckled.

"Friend of Fairgrove. I have no reason to dislike you. Keep it that way."

"Kali, I wanted to see you today—of course, I miss you, more each day—but also…" Fairgrove tried to muffle his next words. "I want you to marry me."

Kali's jaw dropped. Rowe roared with laughter and Fairgrove blinked, over and over. "I know it's sudden, but you'd make me so happy."

"I… I mean—"

"Fairgrove," Rowe fought for control. "This is a good time to shut up. Or apologize."

Fairgrove blanched and his hands shook. "This is a private conversation!"

Friend stepped closer to Rowe. He had at least fifty pounds and two inches on Rowe, which probably made him overconfident. Rowe widened his eyes and shivered. Friend smirked, giving Rowe the perfect opening.

He hit him first in the solar plexus and then the face, very fast and harder than Friend doubtless thought possible from a broken-down gimp. The thug stutter-stepped to catch his balance and Rowe slammed an elbow against his temple which dropped him like a felled tree.

"Outside," he snarled at Fairgrove. Weeks of rage blurred Rowe's vision, but he couldn't lose control. Yet. There was a bigger picture here. Destroying Fairgrove might be the right decision, but this was the wrong time.

Fairgrove trembled so violently he couldn't move, so Rowe pivoted him around, planted the sole of his shoe on Fairgrove's back and shoved. The man fell through the doorway and slammed into the opposite wall. He groaned as Rowe crimped his left arm up behind him until a loud pop and a scream told him Fairgrove's shoulder had been dislocated. Good start.

"I'd kill you, Wyn, but I need Sean. And Salah. Tell me where they are, you live."

Rowe twisted Fairgrove around and wrenched until the damaged joint popped back in place. "Here's another reason to help." He pulled out the information James faxed him that morning. "You didn't write your research papers and I can prove it."

Fairgrove squirmed, eyes darting from Rowe to Kali's door and back.

"This report goes public if I don't hear from you tonight." He shoved Fairgrove. "Take Friend and go."

As Fairgrove and the dazed bodyguard stumbled down the hall, Rowe smiled. Al-Zahrawi would see the beaten but living men and think Rowe weak. In war, deception was an honorable weapon.

Rowe turned to Kali, expecting disgust, even hatred for the Zeke Rowe he'd let out of the cage. He usually hid this warrior for fear of losing her, but today, the stakes were too high. Instead of revulsion, her eyes sparked with excitement. When had she changed? Was it when Joe Boyd told her about the gash on Sean's face or when she found Sean's desperate message in the rank outhouse? Rowe was happy for her new-found strength, but sorrowful for her lost innocence.

"Otto can find Sean."

He did a double-take. "What do you mean?"

"There are discrete differences in the human phenotype—height, weight, shape. They're tricky because unlike a... a submarine... they change when we move, carry items, or change clothes. Sean with a backpack is still Sean, but the algorithm can't find him.

"But I use that to find similar individuals and then narrow the search to Upper State New York—where we think Sean is--filtering hits from live feeds for Sean's picture. I bet the kidnappers send a live video stream to Al-Zahrawi wherever he is."

To Rowe, it sounded as good as any other idea. Find Sean, stop Al-Zahrawi. That made Rowe's most important job right now to guard Kali against Friend or Wyn's return while she worked her magic, so he settled into Cat's chair and took a nap.

Kali jerked upright, eyes wide. She checked the clock. Forty-five minutes lost. What had awakened her? She looked around the room. Zeke was motionless, head back, eyes closed. Her comm window to Eitan showed him tapping away, intent eyes reading, face benign.

Nothing unusual, so why was she awake?

The silence—that was it. Otto was quiet. He'd found something.

"Eitan!" The round boyish face turned to her. "Otto found a webcam in Finland with a profile that matches Sean. How can he be in Finland?"

Her fingers flew, oblivious to Eitan's answer. Otto was whizzing. A solid wall of letters and numbers and symbols dumped endlessly down the screen. Kali grunted, swore, scowled, but her gaze never moved from the display. The phone rang and she let it go to voice mail. Rowe said something, but she had no idea what.

Finally, she sat back and chewed a cuticle, eyes like lasers, face tense. Rowe rolled his chair over as a grainy picture formed, like a TV with bad reception. Minutes passed as it cleared until it became an image of Sean huddled in a corner as Fairgrove yelled at someone off-screen.

Chapter 58

"He's alive…"

Kali clawed at her bandages, glued to her son. Though tattered and filthy, he wore a striped t-shirt and beige chinos she purchased for his summer program. They'd fought that day because Sean wanted her to use the money for something important. His arms were bound in front and his head drooped. Stringy hair hung into his eyes, interleaved with some sort of plant waste. His legs bent gracelessly beneath him, but the sight of his muddy socks inside battered Nikes brought tears to her eyes.

"Where is he?"

Kali cried soundlessly, the hopelessness overwhelming her. "I don't know," she croaked.

"He didn't finish his dinner." Zeke referred to a burger abandoned to Sean's side.

"He doesn't like fast food." Kali hugged herself and rocked, eyes on the video stream. "His fingers—he's playing a bassline against his chest. He says it calms him."

Such a normal Sean action, one he did every day without a second thought, strumming the notes of a piece he was preparing, a virtual practice away from his bass.

"His surroundings have clues to where he is."

Her voice shook but held as she input a command string to compare details of Sean's prison against online photo databases, Instagram, Facebook postings, anything Otto could access in the public domain. She started with the window frame, flooring, wall coverings, and other interior minutiae, and then hunted for housing developments of similar age, construction and layout. Next, she tried to match the exterior slice she could see through the narrow, grimy window with web-based shots. Every few seconds, she reviewed Otto's findings and narrowed his field by eliminating the impossible.

But there were too many possibilities. She selected the vegetation in his hair and the mud on his socks and shoes, identified their habitats, and sent Otto on a hunt. When she compared this new data set against previous results, the pool of options shrank, but not enough.

The time required for Wyn to leave her lab and arrive at Sean's location extended the search area rather than narrowed it. Focusing on Pottersville, Kali launched web crawlers to find every camera tied to an internet or intranet. There were few; Pottersville was too rural. What about the house itself? Tax rolls might include a name she recognized so she searched the county assessor's files for small houses, townhouses, and condos which Otto would then analyze. If the kidnappers rented it recently, it might show up on the MLS, so she hunted through those databases. She ended up with such a massive list she had to write a script to auto-search the files.

Wyn yelled at someone Kali couldn't see. "I'm in charge. You do as I say!" The response was garbled, but the tone bored. Wyn pulled back, eyes slits. "I didn't approve a change of plan."

The same voice, but closer: "This was always the plan." Wyn moved out of the camera's range and then, there were only whispers.

Sean remained in the viewfinder, fingering his bassline on his chest, eyes down, face quiet.

Kali squirmed. "The food…" She hacked McDonalds, but the order was too common. In desperation, she accessed police blotters for service calls, hoping someone had seen a suspicious boy who matched Sean and called it in. Nothing.

Finally, she leaned back, tears glistening in her eyes. "I can't find him."

"Fairgrove will tell us." Rowe made a call and left.

Kali sat with Sean as he finger brushed his hair and tried to spit shine the dirt from his face. In between, his fingers played a silent song over and over, in a loop, a tiny smile dancing on his lips. She fell asleep with him and had her best night's rest in days.

Rowe talked Sun into a field trip to Fairgrove's palatial townhome. They sat quietly in the dark car, slumped down in their seats, until Rowe verified no one was home. Defeating the lock took Rowe half a minute. Once inside, Sun attacked the digital devices while Rowe searched the structure—back of drawers, under throw rugs, behind wall-hangings, down drains, in the freezer.

"Listen to this 'to do' list, Zeke—*Get visiting professor status revoked'*."

"I knew he was behind it."

"This spreadsheet's interesting. Fairgrove paid Al-Zahrawi after his—Fairgrove's—wife's death, his girlfriend's disappearance, and the publication of every one of his major articles."

Before Rowe had time to process that, an alarm sounded. "That's my phone. I friended Fairgrove on Bump. It alerts me when he's close."

"Bump?"

"It's a dating app Fairgrove belongs to. It lets him find other members nearby. He can chat with them or meet up." Sun stabbed a few buttons. "He thinks I'm a voluptuous vacuous blonde a block away interested in hooking up for the evening."

A phone beeped just outside the door and then footsteps hurried away.

"We better go. It won't take long for him to figure out he's been stood up."

As they snuck out, Rowe found an album by the front door with photos of a Columbia grad student he recognized.

Chapter 59

Friday

"Excuse me, Professor Delamagente?"

A student assistant stood in the doorway holding a bulky manila envelope. Rowe had just arrived after spending the night watching Sun analyze Wyn's computer—mostly worthless—and drinking coffee with James as they compared notes on what they knew and didn't know.

"Hold on, Kali." He pulled out his sat phone and activated an app that scanned for anything unusual. "OK, you can open it."

Kali pulled the zipper and removed a pliable bundle wrapped in brown waxed paper. A few snips exposed the contents—and she screamed.

Two ears, one human and the other the soft floppy size of a Labrador. As Kali wheezed, Rowe chased down the student who knew only that the guard asked him to deliver it. When confronted, the retired NYPD officer said it was waiting when he arrived. One call confirmed the courier had no record of the delivery.

As Rowe returned, he searched the faces of the students racing to classes and cataloged their backpacks, purses, and anything else that might be out of place. Nothing. Whoever had left this was long gone.

When he got back, Kali sat rigidly, eyes misted, face taut.

"We don't know they belong to Sean and Sandy, Kali."

He reached out, but she shook him off. "They don't. Sean

has both according to Otto's latest images, and Sandy's are whiter. Who pretends to hurt a boy and a dog and thinks that'll talk me into helping?"

"Al-Zahrawi." Rowe punched a few icons on his tablet and brought up a picture of a VW bug wrapped around a pole. The only visible part of the driver was a severed arm lying three feet from the wreckage. "This is what's left of Yaakov Demsky, the man Laslo Hemren replaced in Israel, on Fairgrove's recommendation. Yaakov was the first in his family to attend grad school. Friends considered him a gentle soul with a sharp sense of humor. He planned to marry when he received his doctoral degree."

Another gory scene burst onto the screen. "Salah Mahmud Al-Zahrawi was paid to kill a young Muslim woman. Her husband thought she was cheating on him because she spent two evenings away from home. 235 people died when an aircraft she was flying in exploded. Her remains were strapped into Seat 10A. After her death, a lawyer told the widower his wife had arranged for his parents to visit from Pakistan, as a surprise for his birthday."

Kali's shock gave way to the blank expression Rowe knew from battle-hardened soldiers. He pulled the scrapbook from his briefcase, the one he took last night from Fairgrove's house, and paged through pictures of an infant and mother, a toddler riding a pony, and a mother and preschooler on a peddle boat ride. Grins covered their faces as they waved to the camera. "Do you know this child?"

Whatever color remained in Kali's face vanished as though a drain had opened. "They're like the pictures on Wyn's computer..."

A kindergartner with her mom outside an elementary school, book bag in hand, a frightened but stalwart expression on her face. A seven-year-old Kali blowing out candles on a cake.

"The collection ends at Columbia."

"That's my mother. Did she give these to Wyn?"

"Were they friends?" Rowe countered.

Kali didn't answer, just kept turning pages. Rowe didn't tell her about the second album, of a striking woman with raven hair and porcelain skin with an eerie resemblance to Kali. She rested her head against a young Wynton Fairgrove who frowned into the camera. In another, the exquisite woman displayed a bulging stomach. She wore a flowered sundress and sat in a Queen Anne chair decorated with balloons. Her smile spilled warmth and friendship across everyone around her. In the next, and last, she held a baby.

To Rowe, only one scenario fit. Fairgrove contracted with Al-Zahrawi to get rid of Kali's birth mother when the relationship became inconvenient. For some reason, he spared the child. Kali didn't need to hear this.

Her jaw bunched as tears filled her eyes. Rowe gave her time. Finally her face hardened.

"Promise me you and Sean will live."

Rowe took her hands. "Sean won't die unless I do."

"Not good enough. No one else will die because of me. Annie, Alfred and his daughter, my m-mother. No more innocents."

Chapter 60

Friday

Last night's wind had blown itself out leaving a postcard perfect summer morning in New York. Kali showered and stood in front of her closet. There was a good chance she wouldn't be home for days so she wanted clothes that were comfortable, durable, and stain-resistant. She picked day-old jeans, layers of tank tops, a sweater, and the only sandals she could find.

She stuffed a handful of Tigers Milk bars in her purse and set out for Columbia. The pool down the street from the campus opened early today because of the heatwave and children were already lined up.

Would Sean's life ever be normal again?

As soon as she arrived at her lab, she called Eitan. He wore the same Hawaiian shirt as yesterday except more creases and bigger food stains. His eyes were bloodshot behind his backup frames.

"What happened to your glasses?"

"Glasses? I have them on." His fingers clicked nonstop as he talked.

"You ready?"

"I already started. I'm reconfiguring Otto's scripts to integrate the geologic landmarks…"

Saturday-Tuesday

When Rowe arrived each morning, Kali ignored him, and did Sun. Both were in a zone that had no room for flesh and blood or small talk. Didn't matter. This was where he had to be. He sat with an iPad full of Kindle books, feet on Stockbury's desk, lukewarm coffee at his elbow, head spinning from Kali's and Sun's geek-speak, hyperbole, and general mishmash of obfuscatory jargon. She hunched in her chair, trolled the room when Otto was rendering, popped Tylenol like candy and squirted Visine into her eyes. His grandma would call it *sitzfleisch,* the ability to do something for hours without stopping, something Rowe had never mastered except as a SEAL.

Kali didn't eat unless Rowe brought her something. He tried to bring the snacky foods he'd seen Sun eating—pizza, orange chicken, Cheetos, Twinkies, soda, juice, cashews, coffee, and pretty much every sort of junk food he could find. One day, Sun ignored all of that and Kali said in passing that he was eating white. Rowe went back out and loaded up on popcorn, burritos, white chocolate, milk, and cottage cheese, which Sun ate nonstop.

No one had died since Annie, and there were no more threats. James thought Al-Zahrawi understood a live Sean kept Kali working on the one item he must have to execute his plan: Otto. Rowe agreed. Interesting Al-Zahrawi hadn't sent the magnetic signature, hopefully because he couldn't get it.

Whatever the plan, it climaxed in ten days with the online auction.

James had agents tailing Fairgrove, but he hadn't left his house since the confrontation and the only visitors delivered food. Occasionally, James called with a clue which Rowe ran to ground. The warrant to search Hemren's room turned up a Qur'an, a prayer rug, and letters from his sisters begging him not to forget them. Hemren told the truth about the girls.

Borodnoi had disappeared. Matt Monroe was in custody, but refused to talk. James would hold him forty-eight hours as a person of interest in Hemren's death, and then release him with a covert tail. He figured Matt would find Al-Zahrawi once he was out because he needed his fee.

Ajit was tasked with finding the online auction. When James asked how it was going, Ajit responded, "Mumble, groan. Meh," which meant he had nothing. When James reminded him of the deadline, he whistled.

As the hours passed, Sean remained their only tangible lead to Al-Zahrawi so Rowe kept bringing food, watching Kali's digital clock tick off the minutes, and listening to her quiet mutterings.

Tuesday morning, the fifth day of the search, Kali sniffed her armpits, scrunched her nose, and then ignored the sour scent wafting from her body. The daily sponge bath consisting of soap squirted on a paper towel and a splash of baby powder hadn't worked for at least a day, but Rowe wasn't about to mention it. This was her only break that didn't involve falling asleep at her desk. Today, breakfast included her sixth Excedrin in three hours. Not that Rowe was counting, but didn't she worry about ulcers?

"Any estimate when you'll finish?"

She turned toward him, eyes angry red orbs surrounded by dark circles. Usually, they were filled with hope. Today, all he saw was despair.

"There isn't enough data. We need Al-Zahrawi to move Sean somewhere with cameras. How do we make that happen?"

Rowe left and reappeared an hour later, dragging a furious and frightened Fairgrove by the collar. Rowe threw him to the floor by Kali's desk. "Ask the world-famous paleoanthropologist, the embarrassment to my profession."

Kali eyed Fairgrove with the disdain reserved for a cockroach in the kitchen cabinet. "Tell me, Wyn. I'll do anything. Give you my research. I'll even marry you. Would that work?" Kali's voice was pleading and exhausted, but still she managed a kindness that might appeal to the man.

Fairgrove's eyes darted around the room, never settling anywhere for more than a second. "He won't listen to me anymore. He destroyed my 850,000-year-old English lance. Do you know what it was worth?" His voice held none of its usual superior condescension. He had become the emperor decloaked, standing in front of his subjects.

"Less than Sean and the millions of Americans Al-Zahrawi will kill if we don't stop him," Rowe growled and texted James about how somehow Al-Zahrawi got in to see Fairgrove.

Fairgrove stood frozen like a man in the path of a freight train. Finally, he reached into his jacket. Rowe snapped his gun into position and yelled, "Don't do that, Wyn."

"It's a note for Kalian, from Salah."

"I'll get it." Rowe pulled a folded paper from Fairgrove's pocket and handed it to Kali. Ten seconds passed before she spoke.

"This is the magnetic signature."

A chill rolled through Rowe's body. This was the endgame. Somehow, Al-Zahrawi stole highly-classified data from a top-secret SIPNet. Kali sat frozen, watching her monitor as a stranger with gentle hands who looked vaguely familiar put betadine on a gash across the boy's forehead. Sean seemed to trust him.

"I understand what this means, Zeke. I also understand that Sean will die if Otto doesn't find this sub." She turned to her videophone. "Do we have access to that satellite, Eitan?" He bobbed his head once, fingers still, eyes locked onto Kali. A silent message passed between them Rowe couldn't decipher. "I uploaded the scripts to Otto."

Otto panned out, scanning the world's oceans, stopping to focus on one interesting spot after another only to ultimately reject each. Over and over, he searched, analyzed, and discarded, until he reached the Sea of Japan. There, he zoomed in, inch by inch, evaluating, probing in concentric circles, calculating, moving on.

"The Seventh Fleet," Rowe whispered. Over forty ships, three carriers, two hundred aircraft, an undisclosed number of submarines, and 30,000 marines. What better proof of power than to incapacitate America's—the world's—most powerful collection of warships.

After one-hundred thirty-seven rejections, Otto plunged beneath the ocean until a murky black shape appeared in the water's depths. Before the '404' emblazoned on the conning tower even came into focus, Rowe recognized the distinctive tall rudder and the forward position of the fins.

"It's Chinese. The Han class." Rowe's voice came out a hoarse whisper. Relief flooded him. They didn't have the American signatures. "Al-Zahrawi tricked us." Kali had just proved Otto could do what Al-Zahrawi needed.

Rowe called James. "We have a problem." He explained what had happened. Silence greeted his words. "What?"

"You just made sense of a call from the SecNav who got one from the Chief of Naval Operations, who got one from the Commander of the Seventh Fleet. A buoy from a *Han* class Chinese sub popped up one hundred yards from one of our destroyers. We are mounting a rescue attempt with a deep diving submersible. Hold on."

James snapped at someone, his words muffled but not the crisp *Yes, Sir,* that answered him.

Rowe's throat tightened. "Bobby. They couldn't steal our magnetic signatures, but their point is the same: They just proved to anyone listening that Otto can find a submarine. That's all they need. We have to prevent them from using this."

James was silent for a breath, then, "How?"

"I'll figure it out."

Rowe glared at Fairgrove as he hung up. "The first step is preventing you from telling Salah his trick worked." When Fairgrove wouldn't meet his eyes, Rowe lost it. "You already reported." He wrenched the traitor forward, ripped the tiny transmitter from under Fairgrove's collar and crushed it beneath his heel. Fairgrove backed up, terror in his eyes, hands protecting his body. Rowe's world went red. He threw Fairgrove against the wall, smashing his head into the first aid kit. He would have collapsed, but Rowe held him by his hair and prepared for another strike.

"Stop! You need me. Please—I'm supposed to go see him right now!"

Rowe squeezed Fairgrove's shoulders until his fingers almost touched under the trapezius muscles, and then shoved him aside. "Get out of my sight."

When his steps died, Kali activated the GPS Rowe had planted.

"You track. I'll follow." It's what he should have done last time.

He was back in an hour, panting. "Following someone who's in a car is almost impossible if they know how to avoid a tail, and these guys did."

Several hours passed which gave Rowe time to read Griff in on the problem. They agreed the terrorists could have sabotaged the *Han*-class sub's electrical in ways that wouldn't work on an American sub and didn't prove it had been infected. Regardless, the nonstop news coverage it was getting, highlighting American humanitarian cooperation with China, would convince bidders Al-Zahrawi could deliver. Rowe promised to update Griff when he had more news.

"How many of the subs have we reached, Bobby?"

"All except one, the last out so the most likely to have the updated virus with the backdoor removed." James sighed. "In the hands of a madman, one submarine can destroy half the eastern seaboard or decimate our battleships who would view it as a friendly.

"Despite that, no one up the chain of command believes the magnetic signatures are vulnerable. The crisis will end once the final sub calls in."

Rowe disagreed.

"Zeke." Kali's voice trembled. "Wyn's with Sean."

Fairgrove's hair sprouted from his head like a desert shrub. Blood streaked his shirt and a painful bruise spread over his chin. He shoved a pile of money at the kidnappers which earned a derisive laugh.

Sean was curled into a fetal ball, his eyes slits and his

whole body shaking. Someone waved an assault rifle at Fairgrove and shouted in Persian, which Otto dutifully translated—*we no longer require either of your services.*

Fairgrove sneered at them. "You'll never get away with it."

The thug with the rifle tensed. His face turned red and he howled as he reared back, and aimed at Sean. Fairgrove leaped in front of the boy and a row of crimson exploded across his chest. Sean's eyes sprang open and he crawled toward Fairgrove as the kidnapper with the gentle hands snatched the rifle from his comrade, yelling that Sean was their only leverage. Sean cradled Fairgrove's head and bent to listen to the last words the world-famous scientist would ever speak. Otto translated:

Your mom can see you.

Chapter 61

Wednesday

"Send HRT to this address!" Rowe yelled into his phone and rattled off the GPS coordinates. "Al-Zahrawi has Sean there." If anyone could save Sean and capture Al-Zahrawi, it was the FBI's elite counterterrorism tactical team.

James stabbed at his keyboard. "It'll take thirty minutes. We only have one Hostage Rescue Team in the area. Keep Kali away—I mean it. She could make this worse," and he disconnected.

"I'll trade myself, Zeke," as though she heard James. "Otto and I can beat Al-Zahrawi."

Rowe bit his tongue, knowing there was no way to explain it so Kali would agree.

"What's going on, Kali?"

Kali jerked around. "Cat. You're supposed to be hiding. Go home!"

With a contemptuous wave, Stockbury sat down. "I have good news," she said to no one in particular, hugging herself, rocking forward and back, head hanging, feet pointed inward, eyes shut. For all her brilliance, she had no coping skills.

Rowe ignored Stockbury, turning back to Kali. "James will never let you trade yourself or Otto, now that he understands the AI's capabilities."

"It will work. When he logs on—or I do—Otto will hijack his network. Al-Zahrawi won't know what's happening."

Rowe shook his head. "You don't understand who you're dealing with, Kali. Al-Zahrawi will kill you and Sean and take Otto. No. We need a better solution."

Kali's eyes smoldered. "You're the one who doesn't understand. I'm not asking permission. I will get my son back. Your only decision is to help or move out of the way."

Rowe paused before holding his hands up, palms out, in defeat. She was right—he couldn't stop her. The best he could do was try to control things. "OK. We'll meet Bobby and the rescue team at the house, work it out together."

A beep announced the arrival of a fax just as Kali's phone rang. She stared at the number and pushed speaker.

"Get the fax, Ms. Delamagente." *Grant.*

Kali plucked the paper that dropped into the tray and read it for five quiet seconds before handing it to Rowe. Her hand shook, but her voice was calm.

"I can't do it, Salah. That last signature fried Otto's system. I have to rebuild his programming. I need at least a week."

Al-Zahrawi let out an exasperated grunt. "Always excuses. You have twenty-four hours or you will dislike the consequences. Oh—do not waste time going after your son. He is no longer there." The dial tone shut off further discussion.

"He didn't mention the earrings, Zeke."

Stockbury teetered to her feet. "Gunner will trade Sean for cash."

Rowe almost laughed, but stopped himself. Cat was serious. "Don't do that." She spent her entire life under Daddy's wallet, but money wouldn't fix a man like Borodnoi.

She ignored him and turned to leave, her path blocked by two dark-suited men. "Kalian Delamagente?"

"Behind me," and she slipped out.

Expensive haircuts, dark steely eyes, *FBI* ball caps. Rowe didn't have time for this.

"Ms. Delamagente. I'm Mr. Jones and this is Mr. Davis."

Kali seemed not to hear the man. "Zeke. They shut Sean's

feed down."

Rowe texted James, *They're running.*

"Who's Sean?" from Jones, and "What did you just hide?" from Davis.

"A proprietary video game." The only FBI Rowe trusted was Bobby James. He had no intention of telling these two anything. Their gaze darted between Kali and Rowe, trying to decide who the alpha was. "It uses avatars of real people. Do you think it'll sell?"

Jones' lips smiled. Davis' head bobbed from the clutter of food wrappers to Kali's ragged appearance. He rubbed a finger under his nose, maybe stopping a sneeze, and shook his head once, then stopped. Kali cocked her head, and then sniffed under her arm.

"We tracked a submarine ping here. What do you know about that?" From Jones.

Rowe kept his face neutral, but Kali gasped, which earned their attention. "Are you surprised we figured it out, Ms. Delamagente, or surprised we did it so fast?"

Kali looked at Rowe and then away. "They want to kill my son."

Both agents narrowed their eyes and asked in unison, "Who?"

"Call your colleague, Bobby James, gentlemen." Rowe handed over James's FBI card. "This is Top Secret. Questions go through him."

Jones dialed James's number. He spoke quietly into his cell, gaze shifting between Rowe to Kali. His tone became uncertain and he stuck a hand in his pocket.

Davis asked Rowe, "You in a hurry?"

Before Rowe could refuse to answer, Jones caught Davis' attention and jerked his head toward the door. "We'll call you."

They squirmed their way past a grandfatherly gray-haired man who eyed them with interest before turning to Kali.

"Ms. Delamagente? Your security guard does an excellent job. He checked my credentials and even called my boss. You must have had recent problems."

His voice carried an agreeable lilt. He had the broad honest face of an Irish sheepherder and the bushy eyebrows of steel wool. A smile played around his lips and eyes.

"You've met my F-B-I associates." He pulled a badge from the pocket of a corduroy sport jacket. "I'm Detective Cariole, NYPD. You're Kalian Delamagente, and you're…" he touched Rowe's arm as the former SEAL brushed past. Zeke glanced over without breaking stride. There was an alertness in Cariole's eyes, behind glasses that sat crookedly on his nose. "Dr. Zeke Rowe.

"You have a colleague, Ms. Delamagente. A Dr. Wynton Fairgrove?" The threesome hurried down the corridor, heels clicking, the sound echoing off the empty hallways. Without waiting for a response, Cariole asked, "When did you last see him?" His voice was weighted with a quiet authority.

"A few hours ago," Rowe answered for her as they exited the building. Cool night air blew against his face. When he took Kali's hand, the fingers were frigid.

"We found his body."

Kali blanched. "His body? What happened?"

"Shot to death. I was hoping you could provide context."

Kali turned green. "I just talked to him…" The cords in her neck bulged. She fumbled in her purse until she came up with a water bottle, gulped half of it, and spilled the rest down the front of her shirt.

Rowe stepped in. "Ms. Delamagente's son was kidnapped. Dr. Fairgrove is—was—trying to get him back."

Detective Cariole sized Rowe up and then jotted something into a notebook.

"Where did you find him, Detective?" They lost the GPS signal, probably when his body was moved.

"Behind Ms. Delamagente's apartment. Why would his killers dump him there?"

Kali barely made it to a trash can before she threw up. Rowe said nothing, knowing better than to speculate. Cariole waited, but all she did was shake her head.

"No opinion?" His pencil hung over his notebook. His first two fingers were stained with nicotine, but he didn't smell like a stale ashtray like most smokers Zeke knew. Maybe he was trying to quit.

"Anything else should be cleared through Special Agent Bobby James with the FBI. I'm sorry, but Ms. Delamagente and I have somewhere to be." He handed over James's card and hustled Kali to his car, the Detective's shrewd eyes following every movement. Rowe didn't rest easy until Cariole disappeared behind them, swallowed up by the dusk.

Twenty-five minutes later, they arrived at the GPS coordinates from the bug planted on Fairgrove. It was a falling-down unpainted wood shack with a tin roof, surrounded by dirt and scrub and three distinct sets of tire tracks. Rowe recognized the window from the video stream and the tree Kali had spent hours trying to place geographically with no success.

The HRT team declared the house empty with no sign anyone planned to return.

And no sign of Sean.

Chapter 62

Cariole was pacing in front of Kali's apartment building, puffing on a cigarette, when Rowe and Kali pulled up three hours later.

"Hello, Detective. What brings you here in the middle of the night?"

"Sorry to bother you. I forgot to ask about this," and he held out Kali's sweatshirt. "Dr. Fairgrove had it with him." She turned away to hide the tears that filled her eyes.

"That's mine."

Cariole exhaled a lungful of smoke into the night and then stomped out his cigarette. "Nasty habit. I'm trying to stop, but I've been at it too long." He fiddled in his pockets and pulled out a pack of gum. "Anyone? OK. Underneath him was this."

He dug a cracked gray bone from the inside pocket of his coat and handed it to Kali. The ball joint was directly over the outside of the knee, and though its dimensions were shorter and stouter than might be expected, it was unmistakably human. Kali's mouth dropped open and she sucked in a shallow breath.

"He found Lucy." Kali took it with reverence. "Where Otto predicted. I hoped for the skull, but the femur—of course. It's sturdy, robust, fossilizes well."

Cariole stared, mesmerized, and made no effort to stop Kali's rambling. When her words trailed off, he asked, "Who are Otto and Lucy?"

Rowe answered, "Kali's academic interest is *Homo*

habilis, man's earliest genus-specific relative. Dr. Fairgrove went to Africa to collect artifacts that Otto…an AI…said were there."

Cariole crossed his arms over his chest and raised his right eyebrow, so Kali gave him the abbreviated version of her paleo man research, Otto's reproductions, and Fairgrove's assistance.

"Assisting you?" Cariole checked his notebook. "He's a world-renowned scientist and you're a student. Are you two involved?"

Kali shook her head, face a mask. "I use mathematical algorithms as a modeling device. It intrigued him."

Rowe interrupted, "The rest is top secret, which needs to go through—"

"Special Agent Bobby James. Thank you for your time and my apologies again for the hour."

After Cariole drove off, Rowe suggested they stay at his safe house where they would be harder to find. Kali collected a duffle bag, stopped in to tell Mr. Winters what was going on, and they left.

"I'm sick of their messages, Zeke! They kidnap Sean and toss Wyn's b-body by my apartment. I said I'd help!"

Her hair was glistening from a shower, face flushed. She sat in the FBI version of an easy chair in sweat pants and a logo t-shirt Rowe didn't understand.

"What's 'WWMD'?" She twisted around and he read the flip side—'Dear God, I'm stuck in a snake pit'. "I get it—What Would MacGyver Do."

"They were giving them away when the show went off the air. I got four."

The microwave chirped. Rowe dumped a bag of popcorn in a bowl and set it between them with two bottles of Amstel.

"I'll destroy Otto so he can't be used." She shoved a handful into her mouth chased by a mouthful of beer.

"Al-Zahrawi will force you to make another."

"I'll refuse until he releases Sean," she said between

angry chews and another deep swallow of beer.

"And then tell him where the subs are? Could you live with that? Could Sean?"

Kali wilted, her eyes shiny. "What do I do?"

"If Otto shares military secrets, you become a traitor. You end up in jail and Sean spends the rest of his life blaming himself."

Kali looked like a woman clinging to a wall of soap. "Why me, Zeke?"

Rowe rested his forearms on his thighs and considered his working man's hands, scarred by too many near misses as a SEAL, nails permanently damaged from digging in the hardscrabble earth of ancient lands, calloused by the rough life he embraced. One Kali must never meet.

He answered gently. "People like me, I'm average and happy to be that, but you and Cat can make a difference in the world. The problem is, no one agrees what that is. Consider Robert Oppenheimer. Many credit his work on the atomic bomb as saving more lives than any other weapon in history. But he called himself 'the destroyer of worlds'. Personally, I like our geniuses conflicted as they move us forward."

The worry lines around Kali's eyes faded and her face turned resolute. "They can take anything I own, Zeke, even my life, but no one else's. Not Sean's. Not yours. They crossed the line killing Annie."

Rowe added Kali to that list. "We have two choices: outsmart Al-Zahrawi or kill him."

"Either is fine with me." She smiled at Rowe, eyes shining, as warm as he'd ever seen them. "Every day, you place country over self. You have no wife or children, no girlfriend. Is that the price of protecting our nation?"

Rowe swallowed. "Sometimes." He wanted to tell her how badly he needed a family, how every time he fell in love the Universe slapped him down, how desperately he feared involving her in his life.

But instead, he got himself another beer. By the time he returned, she was asleep. He tucked a blanket around her and went to call James.

"Hey. You heard yet from your FBI colleagues or a Detective Cariole with the NYPD?"

"Walk out front."

His safe house abutted the Flat Rock Brook Nature Preserve. At night, he was serenaded with a symphony of insects, grasshoppers clicking in the humid air, and coyotes calling to their mates. During the day, the creek babbled and dogs romped with their owners along the well-worn path. He could run until his lungs burned and still never reach another house. There was a spot off the hiking trail, a shaded stump where light filtered through the branches that met high overhead and shut out not only the sun, but the world. Rowe had never lived anywhere he loved more.

He handed James a beer. "Pleated chinos, a polka dot shirt with white buttons—"

"Australian pearl. I have a date. She gave me this after shave." James leaned toward Rowe. "Do you like it?"

Rowe sniffed gingerly and shrugged as he pulled the fax out of his pocket. "Are these the magnetic signatures for America's Tridents?"

James snapped a picture and forwarded it through a secure connection to a Navy contact. "Where'd you get this?"

"Grant, aka Al-Zahrawi. He wants Kali to locate them all in the next two days."

James humphed. "If these are legitimate, even if Otto can't find them, they expose every one of our submarines to extreme danger." His face was pinched and tight. "You know the Navy won't let Kali verify them."

"I'll come up with something. Just cover me."

James took one deep breath and another. "How'd you run into the Feeb's and locals in one night?"

When Rowe explained, James stared into the night. "I told Jones and Davis—clever names, huh?—you're on assignment, but they think you're stealing military secrets. Cariole considers you a person of interest in Fairgrove's death. He asked if you were the jealous type. Your alibi—Kali—

stinks."

"I can clear myself by giving up Otto's tape of the murder, but then your bosses are stuck explaining how the government spied on Americans. The fact Otto belongs to Kali will be irrelevant."

Rowe waited as James processed the implications. He had time to decide that the guy down the street playing his music loud enough to be heard in the next city was a jerk. He was about to shut him up when James started.

"It should have taken hours—not minutes—to track the ping to Otto." James rubbed his chin. "I reached out for background on Sam and Edik." He paged through his notes. "Interpol-UN has a Special Notice out on Samantha Vitolska for crimes involving everything from drugs to human trafficking. She's considered capable of anything. Edik—nothing. All filler. I think it has to do with Edik."

Chapter 63

Thursday

Rowe paced a slow circle and willed the answers to come to him. The only reason to dump Fairgrove behind Kali's apartment was distraction, to point the police at a jilted lover. Transparent, but it would delay Rowe a day. Or two. With the deadline only three days away, that might be enough.

Rowe awakened Kali early Thursday morning, made coffee, shared his limitless supply of Tigers Milk bars, and drove them to her lab. Now, as she worked, he mulled over the nugget of a plan that had surfaced last night, after James left and while Kali slept. It all relied on Otto.

For the fifth time in an hour, he asked how she was doing.

"I'm building an algorithm that directs Otto to filter for the Trident profile—size, shape, mass, protrusions, movement, and any other characteristics I can come up with."

Kali made locating fourteen cigar tubes each shorter than three football fields, in eighty million square miles of ocean— 70% of the earth's surface— sound as easy as picking sunflowers from a bed of pansies.

It took most of the day. When she finished, all she said was, "Now we wait on Otto."

While the AI analyzed and sorted, Kali studied Sean's jail. This new one was different but the same—rough-hewn walls, no windows, no furniture, and a plank floor encrusted with dirt. Sean looked defeated. The impish curiosity that always suffused his face had disappeared, leaving a forlorn waif with soiled clothes, greasy hair, and yellow teeth, strumming his chest. A rat bigger than his hand scurried over to his foot, sniffed, and scooted away only when a voice off-screen bellowed. Sean never reacted.

Something tugged at her subconscious. She blanked her mind, trying to force it to the surface.

"Kali?"

What was she missing? His fingers... "His fingers, Zeke. Sean's practicing the same notes over and over." Kali instructed Otto to display what the boy was playing. Sean's composition flowed across the monitor. "It's an unusual sequence." She uploaded it to a music composition program called Finale modified to respond to images rather than audio. When Sean's song played, it was discordant. The flats and sharps came at odd intervals. The phrasing was off, with measures ending at peculiar spots.

"I might have the key wrong." She tried all seventy-two keys, but it made no difference. What was familiar about this? She leaned back in her chair, stared into the middle distance for five seconds, and five more, mind working as her body went still, and then sat up. "Eitan?" His face appeared. "Can you decrypt this?"

Sun stabbed a few keys and announced, "It's *Musical Morse Code*—GDR and 7439." She should have thought of that. When Sean fingered his bass without bowing or plucking, he was sending a message. An eighth note was a dot and a quarter note a dash with a rest between each. "License plate for a Capri Blue S320."

Rowe called James with the number and car's description, and forwarded it to Cariole.

Her phone burred. Grant. She turned her back on Rowe, not wanting his input. "I located the subs," she lied, "but first I talk to my son."

Grant chuckled. "You are a fitting intellectual match, Kalian Delamagente. So we reach the endgame. I want the Tridents and you want your son. Whose desire is greater? I have no anger for Sean. He is polite. I would enjoy hearing him play the bass he so resolutely practices. I will contact you tomorrow."

The connection broke, but her phone jangled again.

"It's going to be OK, Kali. I know what Gunner really wants." Cat. "You're my dearest friend—I never wanted this to happen." Her tone was happy, but tinged with the weariness of someone teetering on the edge of a rooftop who's made the decision to jump.

Rowe grabbed the phone, "Don't do that, Cat. Where are you? I'll go—" but Cat hung up.

Two nights, and already Kali's presence felt right. Like a painting pulls the eclectic pieces of a room together, the fragmented parts of his spirit inched toward familiar territory.

"What color will your patio be, Zeke? At your real house?"

"What color are patios?"

"Grandpa kept ours white. It felt clean and comfortable. Sean drew a crayon family in the corner one year and Grandpa wouldn't paint over it until Sean promised to redraw it."

As she talked, she straightened pictures, put dishes away, fluffed pillows, and started a load of laundry. Her scent wafted over him. Her grace calmed him.

"What's for dinner?" She asked.

"I'm a bachelor. I eat take-out."

She chuckled. "Not tonight." She pulled out baking powder, butter, and flour, and mixed them in a large bowl.

"Knead this for five minutes. When you're done, roll it out with this…" she searched through his cupboards for a rolling pin, but found none. "…scotch bottle."

While Rowe flattened the dough to a half-inch-thick square, she shredded cheese, uncovered a can of chili, folded it all inside the bread and created one of the best *piroshky* he'd ever eaten. He added white wine and she ended the meal with instant pudding mixed with whipped cream, a poor man's mousse.

After dinner, he did the dishes while she showered, singing softly to herself. He didn't want to interrupt so went outside to update James. When he got back, she was gone. He listened, but nothing. All the doors and windows remained locked. He pulled his Sig from the back of his pants and checked each room, crouching as he entered and swinging the Sig corner to corner. He found her curled under his blankets, arms wrapped around a pillow, breathing soft and measured.

Friday

The lively aroma of cinnamon woke Rowe. He stretched, his neck cracking from being bent all night. The bed was empty.

When he shuffled to the kitchen, Kali grunted at the coffee maker, fingers never slowing on the keyboard. He poured a mug and found scrambled eggs, toast and sausage in the microwave, still warm.

"Where'd you get this?" He asked between mouthfuls.

"Sean and I would starve if the grocer didn't deliver," she said without taking her eyes off the screen, and then leaned back. "I'm done with the changes Eitan suggested. If Cat's plan doesn't work, we're ready."

Before Rowe could ask what the Hell she meant, her phone rang.

"Kali. Gunner lied…"

"Cat!" Rowe jabbed the speaker. "Get out of there! These people will kill you!"

"He can't. He's dead." Stockbury's voice faded in and out. "He laughed when I gave him the cash. Said Daddy and I throw money at problems. I told him what green stuff didn't solve, a 9mm did and I shot him."

Stockbury yelped, followed by a crash and a new voice came on. "Stupid bitch. Why she think I trust her?" Feral hatred filled Borodnoi's voice. "Bring Otto to my coordinates. Now."

"Leave Cat out of this or I quit." Kali's voice could have

frozen hydrogen.

"No you won't. I have your son." And a click.

"GPS shows he's at Cap's Corner. This must be a set-up, Kali."

"Cat needs help."

Chapter 64

Friday

"Is this Zeke Rowe?" The voice was a tense whisper.

"Cap, what's up?" Rowe stomped harder on the gas.

"You told me t' call if they came back. They broke int' cabin #8, down by th' black pines. Cap cleared his voice. "They got m-machine g-guns."

"Cap, listen to me: Hide. They killed at least nine people who got in the way. I'll be there in ten minutes."

"O-OK. I'll be in th' office."

"Are they in a blue Mercedes?"

"No, not this time. Somethin' gray."

As Rowe hung up, the phone burred in his hand. He would have skipped it except for the area code.

"Zeke? Joe Boyd."

"Joe. I'm a little busy."

"You're about to be busier. The Monroe's are fleeing, in a Mercedes, license GDR—"

"—7439. We've been looking for that car." Rowe added James to the call.

"I trailed them to a place called Cap's Corner. They met up with two guys carrying AK-47's, one a burly blonde Russian I've seen at the Monroe's."

"That guy's a mercenary. He's bad news. Stay away."

"They're leaving. I'll follow them."

"Don't do that, Joe. Bobby James has your coordinates. He'll find you. Stand down."

"The Bobby on the card? Good man? OK. Don't worry 'bout anything. Bobby and I got this covered."

"I said—" but Joe was gone. "God damn Marines."

"I'm calling the local police." From James.

Rowe clenched his teeth so hard he heard something crack. Five minutes later, he skidded into Cap's parking lot.

"Cat's here. I'll find her—"

"No." Rowe cut her off. "We don't know what's down there."

Kali chewed her lip, but didn't argue, which felt like a victory. He tried Cap's phone, but no answer. The office was dark.

"Do you have another gun, Zeke?"

He tapped the glove compartment. "If anyone comes, crouch down in the footwell."

"Right, like I'm going to do that," she muttered, but Rowe was already dashing toward the cabin, down the slope to a tight enclave of tall pines, stooping as he ran. Time slowed, his vision sharpened, and his breathing regularized. A lake breeze swished through the pine needles. Someone was boating, running their engine, enough white noise to hide his footsteps. The chronic ache in his knees receded as he snuck forward, stopping to listen, moving a few steps at a time until he reached the fire clearing surrounding the cabins.

There were three sets of fresh prints on the cabin's dirt patio. Two work boots and the third like a woman's flats. None matched Sean's Nikes. If this were a SEAL mission, Rowe would have an M4, an M60, grenades, and claymores. Today, he had the 9mm and a spare clip.

He gave the cabin a final once-over, took a step, and sensed rather than felt the trip wire. He dove behind a black pine as the building exploded, splinters of wood flying as far out as the lake, slamming him into the ground and knocking the breath out of his lungs. There was a scream and then nothing.

He checked his body for damage, found a deep gash on his arm and scrapes on his hands from dragging over the rough terrain. When he peered around the tree trunk, an inferno burned where Stockbury's phone had been. If she was there, she was dead.

As he considered what to do next, he felt a tap on his shoulder. One of James's men. His lips moved, but all Rowe heard was a muted, hollow tunnel of words. He touched his ears and shook his head. The guy motioned toward the parking lot. Rowe scrambled up the hill as Kali raced headlong down. He snagged her as she flew by. He didn't want her to see her best friend dead.

"Let James' guys clear this. There may be more bombs." She pulled up, eyes fixed on the rescue team. "Did you see anything?"

"A car left right after the explosion. Two people in it, I think."

"OK. I have to find Cap. "Stay here until I come back."

Rowe snuck up to Cap's administration building. Its window had been shattered by the blast, but the flag still proudly waved. He peered in at the ancient registration desk and the two wobbly chairs. His hearing was almost back—he caught the crackling fire and the shouts of the rescuers as they searched for survivors, but nothing else. He dialed Cap's phone and it rang inside, four times and went to voicemail. He elbowed open the heavy door and drew back at the sour stench of urine and excrement. He held his Sig in front as he snuck across the lobby to the desk and peaked around.

There, throats slit ear to ear, lay Cap and Kathy. Kathy's eyes were wide with fright, mouth hanging in an O. Cap had slashes on his hands as he tried to defend himself. Rowe rubbed his eyes and breathed deeply. Despite Annie's death steps away from his cabin, Cap had believed violence only happened to other people, not him and his young daughter. His arms reached toward Kathy trying to protect her one final time. Secured to his chest by a rusty nail pulled from one of the outdoor planters was a handwritten note: *Follow me or your son dies. Bring Otto.*

Rowe removed it and stuffed it into his pocket. This was

not a message James needed to see.

As he searched for clues, a voice boomed from the smoldering cabin. "We found someone!"

By the time he backed out of the building. Kali was halfway to the charred remains.

"Kali, wait!" She didn't even slow. One of James's team—*Jimenez* according to his tag—stopped her as Rowe caught up. "This is a crime scene."

"What happened?" Rowe flashed his badge and the agent scowled.

"We're supposed to keep you in the loop." His eyes turned away. "The woman was shot, stabbed and left to die, but managed to drag herself out of the cabin before it exploded."

"We can ID her," and Rowe raced toward three paramedics frantically working on a half-clothed, bloody body. He shouted back over his shoulder, "There're two dead up in the office, the owner Cap and his daughter Kathy."

Kali ran ahead. "Cat! Let me see her! I'm her friend!" She wrestled her way to Stockbury's side. Her face was a putty color and her chest moved in shallow tiny breaths. Deep gashes covered every visible part of her body.

"Move back. She needs a hospital." The paramedics lifted Stockbury into the ambulance, and then left with sirens screaming.

"We have to go, Kali. I'll explain later." He dragged her stumbling and numb up the hill to his car and they sped off moments ahead of the arrival of the fire trucks. Once on the highway, Rowe told her about the message. She twitched, but nothing more, eyes on her laptop.

"Cat will be fine, Zeke. She's a fighter. Now we find Sean." Her voice was disturbingly calm. "He's in a car." She added a dent between her eyes to the dark rings underneath. "See his fingers?"

Before Rowe could respond, Borodnoi pulled the boy from the vehicle. In moments, Otto switched feeds and focused in on the new surroundings.

Rowe dialed James. "They're at Albany Airport, trying to reach a Gulfstream, three stripes—baby blue between navy blue—Nellie 489 Golf Alpha"

"Joe and I are here. My guys surrounded them. OK. They're pinned down."

Al-Zahrawi, Borodnoi, and Sam Vitolska raced for the plane using a terrified Sean as a human shield. Al-Zahrawi sprayed someone off-screen with automatic rifle fire and boarded. As the Gulfstream took off, Rowe exited the freeway and wove his way past the sparse residential neighborhood that bordered Albany Airport.

"We got Edik and the Monroe's. Matt says Al-Zahrawi and Borodnoi plan to sell the Tridents to everyone who pays a minimum bid. Matt swears he had no hint the Vitolska's were criminals. He thought it was a custody fight. Sam said Kali used drugs and Edik wanted Sean away from her. Edik always spent a lot of time with Sean, so the Monroe's believed the story. Who else would treat someone else's kid with such kindness?"

Joe snorted. Marines hated how civilians turned a blind eye to evil, declaring themselves powerless to affect America's security.

"Edik—since his girlfriend tried to kill him, he's agreed to talk, but only to you."

"Me? How's he know me?"

"He says you'll understand."

By now, Rowe was on the airport property, in sight of the departed Gulfstream's hanger.

"I like Joe." James was now in sight, a strong upright figure in the distance, standing by an older but no less sturdy Joe. "He's you retired. When Matt started a rant about his innocence, Joe tripped him and knocked him out."

James handed off the phone to Joe. "Edik did a lousy job holding us off. I'd swear he shot at Sam. She sure aimed at him. Poor shmuck didn't know the escape plan included sacrificing him."

Rowe pulled up next to the group gathered around an

open T-hangar. He froze for a second then jumped out and shook his head.

"This schmuck used to be a pretty good SEAL. How'd you get caught up in this, Duck?" Rowe stuck a hand out.

"Someone's got to cover your ass, Zero." Duck's toothy grin spread across his face and into his eyes. Rowe got his nickname when Duck saw 'Z. Rowe' written on his SEAL duffle bag.

"Sam's a crummy shot if she missed your big target."

"She's a sharpshooter, but I swapped her rounds for blanks. Figured I was going to piss her off at some point." Duck chuckled. "Good to see you."

"I can't believe I didn't recognize you on the feed."

Duck had a lean Italian face all planes and angles, bulging calves, and a neck so thick it became part of his shoulders, but it was his warrior mindset that made him a dangerous foe. He never gave less than full throttle because second place could kill you. His job was the life of the guy next to him even if the price was his life. He tried a peacetime deployment—attaché to an Admiral—but got transferred back to a SEAL team when his boss tired of bailing him out of whatever trouble he got himself into.

All Duck really did—and he did it well—was fight. If not for the SEALs, he would have been in prison, but the Navy turned him into what his minister called 'God's pillar of the hood'.

"I disguised my appearance with cotton in my gums, colored contacts, put pebbles in my shoes to change my gait. I met Al-Zahrawi twenty years ago when he was starting out. He's a fanatic, kills for sport. Every time he came to the house, I ran errands."

Duck hadn't changed. His personality filled the area like sunshine on a cold day.

"Sorry I lost touch," and Rowe clapped his old partner on the shoulder.

Duck smiled as his eyes grew serious. "Al-Zahrawi hasn't done much since the Embassy bombings. We thought he was dead or in prison until we got chatter about a cyberweapon that hijacks submarines. Navy intel said it was theoretically possible, so assigned me to infiltrate. Sam made me babysit some kid. They were holding him hostage so his mom would cooperate."

"This is the mom—Kalian Delamagente."

Duck turned to Kali. "You invented a virus that infects subs?"

"That's Kali's office mate, Catherine Stockbury. Kali came up with a way to find the sub after the virus activates." Rowe could see Duck snap the pieces together.

Duck continued, "Something went wrong at the last minute because they're only auctioning one. Winners fill in a code which will deliver the sub to their home port of choice." He checked his watch. "It closes in 48 hours."

"Do you have the website address?"

Duck shook his head. "You don't either? Neither side trusted the other. Their goals aligned, but not the reasons. Sam wants money. Al-Zahrawi wants revenge."

Duck's voice softened. "They killed your friend, Cat."

"Tried. She's hanging on." Rowe explained her escape.

"I wanted to warn her, but we weren't around the same places. She was living on borrowed time the moment Borodnoi got what he wanted from her." His beefy face gentled. "Some guy close to you dead dropped regular updates on your progress."

A smile limped across Kali's face. "Not an issue any more."

James arrived, panting. "No flight plan. The only good news is they don't have Otto."

Kali's phone beeped—a text message. She read it and was about to share it when Rowe stopped her, "I told Porter you were busy all day," and guided her away from the group.

You have 48 hours to exchange Otto for your son. Bring Dr. Rowe so I can kill him.

"Bobby doesn't need to see this, Kali. If he does, he won't let you out of the country."

"I have a plan."
"So do I."

Chapter 65

Friday

"This baby has a cruising altitude of 36,000 feet at Mach .87. We can reach the Middle East or Africa before refueling." Ramey Giordano moved through the spotless G550 with the familiarity of a man who's exactly where he wants to be.

Kali had never met Cat's father, but when he called Thursday, she recognized his voice. In a voice filled with pain and guilt, he offered anything he owned if Kali and Zeke would make Cat's attackers pay. They settled on his Gulfstream G550, the pilot Ramey Giordano, and a planeload of whatever supplies Rowe needed. Rowe's only demand: The FBI couldn't know. The man agreed without question. The next day, Ramey Giordano, a fit-looking retired Marine aviator with shoulder-length silver hair pulled back in a ponytail, showed up at Kali's office and asked for a shopping list. Rowe scratched out two pages including military-grade weapons which didn't even make Giordano blink.

Kali had been feeding information to Otto for the last hour, searching for Al-Zahrawi. Finally, she pressed back into her chair and began chewing a cuticle that already looked raw. Before she could say anything, her cell rang.

"An international prefix. Kenya I think. I'll put it on speaker." She answered with a curt, "Delamagente."

"Hello! This is Dr. Xavier Blumenstein." The voice sounded like its owner should be teaching English literature at

Oxford. "Do I have the pleasure of speaking with Ms. Kalian Delamagente?"

"Yes, Dr. Blumenstein." She fought to control her emotion. "Dr. Fairgrove mentioned you. I'm here with a colleague, Dr. Zeke Rowe."

"It is so good to meet you, Ms. Delamagente, albeit telephonically. Dr. Fairgrove spoke of you often. He described your help with his research in smashing terms, called you a rising star." Kali winced that Fairgrove represented her work as his, but kept quiet. "I apologize for my tardiness, but I had to drive a hundred miles to make this call. It is critical I ring up the dear man, but I can't reach him. Do you have his current number?"

"I'm sorry, but Dr. Fairgrove died this week." Her voice was kind, but curt.

The Doctor sucked in a breath. "Gor Blimey… What happened?"

"The police haven't made a determination yet."

"Foul play, eh? Such a tawdry end for so magnificent a chap." Dr. Blumenstein sighed once, and then again. "Dr. Fairgrove made an incredible discovery, one which will return him to the forefront of paleoanthropology. A beautiful *Homo habilis* skull, and this on the heels of the autochthonous crocodile remains he found. He came into his own after too many dry years with the most remarkable ability to suss out our antecedents, as though he knew where their bones slept. An autumnal story."

Kali had no time for lionizing Fairgrove. "What can we help you with, sir?"

"Dr. Fairgrove was uneasy. When I asked why, he shook it off, but said if I didn't hear from him, to give you the bell. And so I am. He left artifacts here and coordinates to another location he led me to believe you would appreciate."

Fairgrove knew his plans were crumbling. Kali asked, "Where is this second dig?"

"In the hinterlands of Tanzania, by Ngorongoro and the East African Rift."

"Thank you. I do understand, Dr. Blumenstein. I'll get back to you in a few days."

"Take your time, Ms. Delamagente. I enjoy communing with these amazing artifacts. If you can't reach me, please keep trying," and he disconnected.

"It has to be the meeting." Kali mumbled as she added 'East African Rift' and 'Ngorongoro' to Otto's parameters. Like the Vulcan game Kal-toh, where one move transforms a mixed up jumble of sticks into a harmonious sphere, suddenly everything fit.

"The Great Rift Valley, a 3,700 mile crack in the earth's crust formed when violent forces tore east from west. It is literally the middle of nowhere." Edged by an archipelago of volcanoes and lakes, it extended through Lucy's homeland and included the foothills of Ol Doinyo L'engai where Zeke met Annie. It seemed to be the uniting force behind this case.

"Al-Zahrawi's going where he feels strongest."

Rowe deleted another message from Cariole. He would have to wait. Time had run out. The plane was loaded and ready to go, kitted out with three H&K submachine guns with infrared laser targeting mounts and sound suppressors, four Sig Sauer P226s with three spare magazines each, a Winchester 120-guage pump, one thousand rounds of additional ammo for each weapon, ten hand grenades, three stainless steel Super Tools, three CRKT Tanto folding tactical knives, and a bag of Tuff-Ties. It was enough to fight a small war if necessary. Support items included food for a week, twenty cases of water, a trauma kit with scissors, bandages, a couple of packs of clotting agents, disinfectant, lip balm, alcohol swabs, and prescription bottles of antibiotics and pain medicine.

Rowe and Kali jogged across the tarmac toward the sleek corporate jet. Both wore hiking boots, short-sleeved cotton shirts, jeans, and wide-brimmed hats. The weather was perfect with scattered clouds and a light wind.

Duck raced up as they neared the plane. "Get out of here!

James and Cariole are on the way. Kali received a deposit for a million dollars yesterday. James thinks she earned it by giving up Otto. Cariole—he says you lied to him."

Rowe hitched his bag up to his shoulder and started running. "Duck, Cariole's a good guy. Tell him we've been set up and are going to prove it. Tell Bobby I'm sorry."

Kali grabbed his arm as they ran. "That's why Hemren used my computer to send those messages and install the worm on the Dean's system."

"None of that matters. We either demonstrate your innocence or we're both dead."

Rowe took the stairs two at a time, Kali right behind, as sirens howled from the highway. Rowe shouted to Duck. "Find that website."

The steps clanked into place and Giordano expertly guided the Gulfstream down the runway as the lights of a police car raced toward the General Aviation hangers. The last thing Rowe saw as the plane lifted off was Duck saluting them and James flinging his thousand-dollar jacket to the tarmac.

Saturday

Eleven hours later, give or take, Giordano landed on an abandoned airstrip at the most likely confluence of Serengeti and Rift. From the air, the ground was etched with winding blue streams and studded with water holes, but once on the ground, Kali saw only miles of yellow-brown savanna shimmering under the scorching heat.

Giordano dropped the stairs and a blast furnace hit Kali. She struggled to breathe as the weight of hot, humid air pressed against her chest. Sweat poured off her head and down her legs, soaking her socks and leaving her hair stringy and limp.

Rowe seemed unfazed. He told Giordano to leave if they weren't back in thirty hours and then trotted North through the tall tussock grasses and brittle scrub, not pausing until he reached the protection of a boulder field. Kali staggering after him.

"We'll find their trail from there," and he indicated the craggy top of the lone hillock.

Kali jerked her head once. After the stifling heat in Israel, she thought Africa would be fine, but the thick humidity and brutal sun left her faint and nauseous.

"How does anyone—"

Before Kali could finish, there was a whoosh overhead and an explosion shook the ground. Rowe dragged her behind a boulder where they hunched until the noise subsided. When she peered back toward the plane, the acrid stench of petroleum assaulted Kali's senses and her skin reddened from the heat rolling off the plane's smoldering carcass.

"Ramey!" Kali lunged forward, but Rowe stopped her.

"He couldn't survive, Kali! You're only going to give Al-Zahrawi another target." Rowe searched for the launch site. "That weapon is accurate only a short distance which means Al-Zahrawi is close… There." Rowe pointed southwest to a cut between two hilltops. "That overlook. It's the only landmark high enough."

A shape moved against Nature's browns and yellows. "He's not even hiding. He wants us to follow."

So much death and violence. How would the world survive if this was how it solved problems? Clearly, Al-Zahrawi thought it effective, which was why he kidnapped Sean, tortured Annie, and blew up Ramey. He expected Kali to capitulate.

She wouldn't. She had her own favorite method of problem-solving.

When she turned to Rowe, he was watching her. There was a sadness to his posture, pain in his expression, replaced quickly by resolution.

"We can still do this, Kali. We'll find food and water off the land. Everything else we need is in our backpacks and our heads."

"Of course we can. Let's go."

Duck took the seat next to James that Cariole vacated. "How bad is it?"

"The Detective insists we stake out all airports in the Gulfstream's range and arrest Zeke and Kali when they land."

"Come on, Bobby. Zeke will never give a weapon like Otto to our enemies. Trust him to do his part. He won't quit until he's done what needs doing. You and I need to find that auction or whatever he does won't be good enough."

James scowled, but said nothing, engrossed in his laptop. "What's that?"

"I'm replaying video of Al-Zahrawi's arrival at the airport. We picked it up through OnStar and a computer Sean had in the backseat."

Sam sat in the front, breasts pushing against the thin fabric of her tank top, blonde hair flowing over her shoulders and down her chest. Al-Zahrawi was in the back, his dark molasses face shining, pleated slacks and striped silk shirt not even wrinkled. He and Sam argued over something. Sean huddled next to Al-Zahrawi, but as far into the corner as possible. One hand played a rhythm against his chest while the other scratched up and down his leg. His eyes were wide and frightened.

I'm trying to find a reflection, or angle, that gives up the website they're fighting over."

Duck jerked upright. "Stop! Play it again, Bobby."

"See something, Duck?"

"Sean's fingers. Rewind it."

"Yeah. He's telling us the car's license plate, but they're airborne." James rewound anyway.

Duck leaned in. "The boy told me about the code. Type this into the computer. W, w, w—it's the URL."

James entered the rest of the sequence into the browser's address bar.

A splash of color crystallized into a stark collage of destruction underlaid with the American flag. A log-in box appeared with a countdown clock on the right side.

"It's the auction. Forty-two hours, twenty-one minutes

and fourteen seconds."

"Now all we need is the username and password."

"Clever. The web page has no metatags, which makes it invisible in the virtual world. I wouldn't find it for months. You need the address and an invitation."

"You can crack it, though?" A nub of doubt entered James's voice.

"We need to know who has an account and break their log-in."

Duck rose. "Matty will tell me."

"Hold up. I'll walk you out."

Before Kali and Rowe took off, each came to Eitan Sun with a plan. Each had a 23% chance of success. Both were one-way tickets. Rowe's was easy, but Kali's more complicated. When Duck and James left, he picked up the phone to call his buddy, the Secretary of Defense. Sun got his agreement to Kali's idea with the condition that the Chief of Naval Operations agreed.

"How the hell—"

"We're past the point of blame, Sir, but after this, I'll fix it."

"You think this will work?"

"Simple."

Simple, like the Riemann Hypothesis.

"How's it going?" Duck sidled up to Matt Monroe for the mandated ten-minute exercise break.

"They got you too. My attorney says I'll be out tomorrow."

"Yeah, they got nothing. They want to scare us so we talk." Duck circled a conspiratorial finger between the two of them. "I'll make a deal for what I know, maybe even win me a finder's fee. But nothing about Sam. No way. She'll be back for us."

Matt refused to make eye contact, his lips in a tight line.

"I helped her escape, you know. She'll be back for me.

She loves me. I'll make sure she takes you, too. And Connie if you want. Or not—start over."

Matt shook his head. "Yeah. You got it all planned out, but they're accusing me of stuff I didn't do. I don't even know anything—except about that Dean."

"They already know that, if it's what I'm thinking. You got something else?" When Matt didn't answer, he leaned in and lowered his voice, "Of course you do. What d'you have?"

"He's a biggy. He could sell us both out!"

Duck painted a worried expression across his face and scratched his cheek. "Yeah, that's a problem. They'll see all the phone calls between him and Al-Zahrawi and arrest him I bet before tomorrow. He'll give us up for a deal, so we gotta move first."

"He's got everything on his computer, even access to the website."

"Yeah, the website. The one with the auction."

"Yeah. I wish I could give them that!" Matt's eyes skittered around the yard and he wiggled closer to Duck. "Hemren told me Porter's log-in when I promised to sponsor his sisters, but the only access is behind some hidden partition on his computer. Really hidden, in an Easter Egg. That's one of those coding tricks programmers use, but we need an address."

"Yeah, I got that too. He uses that name…" Duck let his voice trail off.

After a moment, Matt chimed in, "His kids, yeah and his wife."

"Yeah. They have that already. You gotta have more."

"No—not real kids. He calls his bank accounts his kids. You know, the numbers."

"I know and they know. We need something else."

"There is nothing else! Why would I think I needed something for trade? I figured this was a scam when Al-Zahrawi paid me so much." He rubbed his hand over his mouth and murmured into his palm, "D'you think this espionage stuff is real?"

Duck scrunched his brows together. "Doesn't matter if the police believe it. And the FBI! Then Salah goes killing people. We're on the chopping block for that. I didn't sign on for murder. Did you?" A frantic head shake from Monroe and Duck continued, "We gotta close our deal before Porter or we go to jail."

"Time's up, ladies. Back to your cells."

Duck clapped Matt on the back. "Don't talk to anyone, Matty. Everything's gonna work out." He liked the despair that enveloped Matt's face as he did the zipper move across his clamped lips. "I like your uniform, Jerry. Makes you look important. Hey, you don't believe this stuff do you? My buddy and me would never endanger our country. He's not smart enough, and me, I just liked Sam. You saw her, didn't you?"

The guard leered and Duck winked at Matt.

In seconds, they were in. A clock ticked down from thirty-six hours, twenty-seven minutes. To the right was a list of the current bidders—both US friends and enemies—and a satellite photo titled 'Proof'. Duck clicked on it, and it panned to the outed Chinese sub.

James' call to Rowe went straight to voicemail.

Chapter 66

Saturday

The sun was high and heat cracked the hard savanna earth. A cheetah shadowed a summer-thin herd of gazelle. A flock of hopping, bobbing raptors clutched shreds of meat from a carcass nothing more than bones and hooves.

With less than thirty hours left, Rowe and Kali chased Al-Zahrawi deep into the hinterlands. The ground baked under their feet, the grasses scratched exposed skin, and insects bit mercilessly to drink their blood. The duo avoided the populated animal routes in favor of dense, harder-to-penetrate-and-therefore-safer scrub. They eased over humps and trenches, up and down steep eroded banks. Dust was everywhere—on leaves and branches, in their teeth and throats. They struggled through calf-high vegetation, past rocky outcroppings, resting where possible under the humid shade of an acacia where the temperature silenced even the birds. An elephant herd three hundred strong wandered in aimless abandon. A gazelle whinnied, elegant head bouncing high as she accompanied a male with sweeping horns. A sow with five hoglets rushed single file across their path. A stately waterbuck watched, alert but unafraid.

Kali and Zeke divided up duties. Zeke stalked their human prey while Kali gathered food. She knew how because Lucy did this often—insects lived under rocks and grubs in the deadwood of old tree limbs. Hyraxes and lizards were nutritious, but almost impossible to catch.

Finally, panting and dripping sweat, the pair took a break under a euphorbia and Rowe explained his plan. When he finished, Kali stared at him.

"That's not a very good plan."

"Probably not, but it's what we have."

Kali bit back her next comment and rose to continue on the trail left by Al-Zahrawi and Sean.

Hours later, as the sun burned orange just over the jagged horizon, they collapsed at the foot of a hill by a craggy old baobab. Its gigantic gnarled spirals thicker than a man's body joined the main trunk about head high. Lucy would vault into the arms of a baobab when chased by a Sabertooth. Rowe picked a rough-skinned frog from the cracked and lined bark, bit the head off, offered the rest to Kali, and downed it himself when she gagged. They rested until full dark, and then Rowe disappeared into the velvety night.

Kali relieved herself downwind and started to build a tree nest, high enough for safety but low enough for escape. She crouched in the fork of two branches and wove slender fronds into a springy platform. Next, she braided leafy foliage into a circular bed and cushioned it with grass. It took her an hour.

Lucy did it in three minutes.

The evening shadows turned the landscape into a city of ghosts, sparse tree limbs limned against a gray background. Tall grasses swayed to the rhythm of the nocturnal hunt. Indigenous canines, eyes sparkling, wondered if she were prey or predator. An owl rose smoothly from the ground carrying a writhing snake. Not far in the distance, a young bull elephant stood silhouetted against the horizon, testing the air with its trunk, calling to its herd. In Africa's pure skies, sound carried for miles.

Kali felt close to Lucy here.

A twig cracked. She froze, slitting her eyes to hide their reflection.

"Any room for me?"

"Zeke, dammit. You scared me!"

He scampered up and into the nest. "This has been your

goal all along, to get me into a comfy bed and take advantage of me." Kali giggled. "It won't work on a man of my strong morals."

Kali snuggled in. "It's been a long time since I went to bed the same day I woke up."

Through the canopy was a brilliant display of crisp stars, accompanied by the glowing swath of the Milky Way. She absorbed the cacophony of African life—the trill of insects, the distant hoots and hollers, and the rustle of wind. It was hard to accept that this overpowering beauty hid such danger.

She fell asleep, dreaming Lucy found Sean.

Sunday

Rowe shook Kali awake. "Time to go." They licked dew from the leaves to quench their thirst and Kali used the latrine while Rowe prepared a breakfast of raw rabbit and ptarmigan. Between bites, he recounted the night's recon. Al-Zahrawi and Sean traveled alone, armed with a submachine gun. No sign of Sam or Borodnoi.

James had heard nothing since Giordano radioed they were landing. Rowe might have insisted on silence. That probably explained it, but only fifteen hours remained. One sub still hadn't called in and that wasn't the worst of it. Rowe had to stop Al-Zahrawi transmitting those magnetic signatures. Failure meant America lost her military dominance.

"Any indication Otto's in Al-Zahrawi's hands, Eitan?"

Sun shook his head.

"Which means Rowe is alive." As long as Rowe lived, nothing would stop him.

But James didn't know Kali, not really, so he asked Sun, "If Al-Zahrawi captured Kali, is she strong enough to commit suicide or allow her son to be killed to save her nation?"

Sun stuffed Twinkies into his mouth before responding. "She knows right from wrong."

James had never worked with Eitan Sun before, but had heard a lot about him, everything from quirky to genius to annoying. James would add 'loyal' and 'patriot' to the list. Sun had a personal courage that had nothing to do with physical strength, military weapons, or political power. It came from the man's moral core. Eitan Sun could stand on James' shoulders anytime.

"I can get you some of whatever color you're eating today, Eitan."

"No thanks. I just ate," and he leaned into his monitor.

"What?" James asked as Sun gobbled down another Twinkie and grinned like he won the lottery.

"I found a corner piece."

"What?" James repeated, brow furrowed in confusion.

"Of the puzzle."

Before James could demand an explanation, his secure phone rang. An unknown number was highly unusual. He connected, but said nothing.

"Special Agent Robert James? This is the USS *West Virginia*. Captain Actual Desmond Hilgrave. Can you confirm a high priority message we received?"

It took James a moment to pull the name from memory. "Captain Hilgrave." He was a friend of Rowe's. "Why are you calling on this line?"

"Before I continue, for security reasons, please verify the last three places we saw each other."

James took his time, wanting to be entirely accurate. "There's only one, Captain, last August at Arlington National Cemetery, your Dad's grave, with another Officer Zeke Rowe calls Griff."

"Affirmative, Bobby James. Thank you. I received an order to call in. You are my UCV"—unexpected contact verification.

"Yes, Sir, there is an urgent message. Code Purple."
Reinstall from back-ups. Primary network compromised.

"Roger that," and he disconnected.

James smiled half-heartedly. "All subs are now virus-free."

"A pyrrhic victory if Al-Zahrawi can find the entire fleet at will." Sun spoke with a quiet intensity.

A hollowness grew inside James. "Let's give Zeke a few more hours. I do not want to make that phone call to the CNO, explaining how billions of dollars' worth of warships must be replaced. Our Naval strength will be decimated for years to come."

"Don't underestimate Zeke. He won't return until all signatures are secured, all individuals with knowledge eliminated, and Sean is safe."

"What do you make of these footprints, Zeke?"

"Al-Zahrawi is speeding up. He wants us tired when he springs his trap. To him, you're a pencil pushing academe and I'm a cripple. We're close to the end."

Kali bent over. "But something's wrong. The right side— it's always deeper than the left."

"Those are Sean's. He weighs less so his impression's shallower. He's limping."

A pack of wild dogs materialized, first one and then its brothers and sisters. Kali coated herself in the elephant dung they had collected, as did Rowe, which turned the predator's attention to Al-Zahrawi and Sean. For the first time since they landed, Kali was glad Al-Zahrawi had a gun.

Kali and Zeke finally reached the uncrossable East African Rift. Craggy walls, thousands of years of horizon layers painted brown-red to humus-black, plummeted downward. When Kali peered over, she imagined she could see the prints of a long-gone mammoth etched into the rock-hard valley floor. Far beyond this primal landscape, fumaroles from one of the most active volcanic regions in the world billowed smoke and gas into the unspoiled air.

"Thirty-seven minutes left."

The whop-whop of a helicopter came out of nowhere. Kali threw a horrified glance at Zeke, but his face remained calm. Maybe it was Bobby James or Zeke's SEAL friend Duck Peters--and then a spray of bullets spewed shards of rocks into the air, the rat-a-tat burying all other noise. Clouds of dust choked her as she zig-zagged, trying to escape, every moment expecting a sharp explosion of pain in her back.

And then she heard a wet grunt. She jerked toward the sound and found Zeke in a crumpled heap under a jutting stone ledge, a red mist floating above him. His eyes glazed as blood pumped from the rich red holes stitched across his chest. Kali screamed and raced to his side, covering him with her body. Her ears rang, nostrils stung with the reek of cordite. He winced, tried to sit up, and collapsed to the ground. Her hands trembled so, she couldn't keep pressure on all the bullet holes.

"I can't do this without you, Zeke. Please, you must live!"

He smiled, eyes hooded, arms relaxed. "Kali... won't... make it." His voice sounded hollow, agonized. "Go. You can..."

He fell silent. Tears spilled from her eyes, but she swiped them away with bloody hands and stepped into the meadow.

Chapter 67

Sunday

"I'm here, as requested," she shouted. "Let my son go."

The chopper hovered, like a raptor over carrion, and then landed on a flat expanse of scrub the size of a football field. She marched to a spot halfway between the body of Zeke Rowe and the helo, carrying a briefcase, her only weapon her brain.

Out from a narrow rocky defile stumbled a grubby, ragged creature more animal than human. His hands were tied behind his back, head bowed, feet bleeding, but his eyes lit up with hope and love as their eyes met. The torn shirt and dirty trousers, new a month ago, now nothing but rags from trekking across the hinterlands, bagged on his gaunt frame. It was all she could do not to race forward and wrap her arms around her son's grimy emaciated blood-streaked body.

In the nanosecond their eyes connected, she told him everything would be alright and he told his mom he believed in her.

Heart thumping, throat rough and dry, a visceral dread threatening to overwhelm her senses, she fixed on a tall, regal figure approaching from Sean's left. Al-Zahrawi's head was high, eyes shrouded in long lashes, a beautiful face marred only by a three-inch scar. He had the relaxed assurance of a man who's won. He was armed with a boxy gun, the one carried by every terrorist on every news feed. He shoved Sean. The boy stumbled, unable to break his fall, collapsing painfully onto his right shoulder. He kneeled clumsily, cricked his neck and gave Kali a brilliant smile until Al-Zahrawi kicked him, throwing him face-first in the dirt. Kali turned a dead-eyed stare on the man she once considered a friend, a label she didn't give to many.

"Don't hurt him, Al-Zahrawi —or shall I call you Gegham Keregosian." His eyes widened. She'd surprised him. Good. "Your jihad depends upon his safety."

She quashed her anger. Emotion caused mistakes, and that could cost Sean his life. She breathed in and out, gaze steady as she absorbed her surroundings. In the open door of the copter stood Aleksei Borodnoi, grinning, holding another deadly-looking weapon with a curved handle. To his side, a lissome vision with corn silk hair and sculpted features—the venerable Sam.

The day waned, bathed in the humid light of a sinking sun. A web of clouds promised rain, but delivered not even a slight breeze. At a distance, frightened off by the copter's arrival, paced the wild dogs, the pack growing by the minute, heads raised, ears and tails erect, yellow eyes fixed on their human prey. The aroma of danger and desperation wafted in equal parts from their bodies.

Overall a good place for a clandestine meeting: too camouflaged to be easily spotted and far enough from the original landing site to challenge even Sun's skills.

A headache flared, her first since arriving on this continent, but she turned her attention to Sean. "Are you alright?" Her voice to her ears sounded strong and steady.

Sean tried to answer, but Al-Zahrawi stepped his head into the dirt. A deep weariness threatened to unravel the tenuous marriage Kali had cobbled together between what she wanted to and must do. She squared her shoulders, jutted out her chin, and studied her prey.

On another day, if she didn't know about Al-Zahrawi, she would consider him attractive, but today, eyes bright with passion, muscles bulging, gun's barrel stabbed into the neck of an unarmed teenager, Al-Zahrawi was nothing more than a demented fanatic. Kali waited through a lengthy silence, wordlessly thanking legions of male colleagues for teaching her the intimidation game. When Al-Zahrawi opened his mouth to speak, she interrupted.

"You're tired, Salah. You lost weight. You're painfully sunburned—you forgot the mud mask. Here," and she tossed a plant root toward him. "Spread this on the worst parts. Didn't you learn anything from Lucy—other than, of course, how to destroy?"

Sweat trickled down his forehead and wet circles marked his shirt. His eyes darted between Kali's eyes and what she held in her hands. She felt his excitement like the beating pulse of disco music, tasted it like a fine French wine. His goal was so close. Zeke's words seeped through her sensibilities, *Play to his ego. You can't miss it. Look for his largest feature.*

"We're here for one reason: To trade Sean for Otto." She gripped the briefcase with both hands to hide their shaking. "You understand Sean's importance to me, Salah. Family is the bedrock of Islam." Her accent on *Islam's* second syllable earned a slight smile from Al-Zahrawi. "Raising Sean is my priority." She fought to keep her tone reasonable, unhurried. It took almost more effort than she had. "At our core, you and I are alike—responsible to God's law over man's. Today, I must care for my child."

Al-Zahrawi never removed his eyes from her, lips in a tight line, vein throbbing against his left temple. Kali breathed slowly, stretching out the silence, headache thrumming against the front of her skull. A buzzard rasped, calling his mate. The wild dogs panted, saliva drooling from their open mouths, yellow teeth glistening.

"You are here at your request, Ms. Delamagente. You wished to thank me in person."

Of course—her email to Mr. Keregosian. Kali adopted a faint smile, ignoring the sweat dripping down her body and tickling her skin. "I hope you got your money's worth."

As she spoke, she placed the briefcase at her feet and moved her arms behind her back.

Al-Zahrawi scowled. "Your American moxie is distasteful. Islam teaches a woman to earn her children with obedience. Are you obedient, Kalian?"

"Let's skip the pleasantries, Salah. I'll trade Otto for Sean. With my AI, you can fulfill your prophet's words—slay the pagans wherever you find them, seize them, beleaguer them.

"Otto is the means to your end." With that, she brought her hands forward. In the right was Zeke's seven-inch Ka-Bar. Borodnoi aimed his weapon at Kali's head as she pressed the blade to her own throat. "Take Otto, but understand: If my son or I die, Otto dies too." A cloud of confusion filled Al-Zahrawi's eyes. "Otto must find me or he stops working." She tapped a welt on her arm. "If I'm dead, he dies too."

That wasn't quite true, but Al-Zahrawi wouldn't find that out until too late.

"If you kill my son, I kill myself. If you take me with you, I kill myself. The only way you get Otto is to leave me here and hope I survive long enough for you to complete your auction."

As though on cue, one of the wild dogs uttered a soft growl and fixed the humans with malevolent yellow eyes, teeth bared, tail stretched behind skinny bodies, hackles raised in menace. The pack leader bounced forward, hissed and snapped and withdrew, testing the courage of his prey. Borodnoi sprayed them with a submachine gun, grinning. Bullets tore into two of the animals and the pack skittered back, but didn't flee. The Alpha growled, drooling white saliva.

Kali stepped forward. Al-Zahrawi pulled back.

"My apologies, Salah. I covered myself in feces to confuse the predators," and she indicated the wild dogs, feral eyes fixed not on Kali but Al-Zahrawi and Sean. "I saw Lucy do it so often, it seemed right, but I forgot your predilection toward hygiene. It is half your deen."

While most people considered cleanliness desirable, Muslims believed it central to Islam. Worse, being around animal dung was a gross defilement. Kali denigrated Al-Zahrawi, his religion, and his *jihad* by standing so close to him.

Al-Zahrawi wrinkled his nose in disgust. "You are dumb for a smart woman. With Zeke Rowe dead, I am your only escape."

"You are my prison, Salah." Her words were harsh and clipped. "I choose the freedom to die on my own terms. Surely you respect that. Is this not the choice your mujahedeen make?" She shrugged. "But do not concern yourself. It will take me days to starve to death, plenty of time for you to complete your mission."

She chose her next words carefully, intended to demand action. "Taking this opportunity to stop your enemy is your duty. *Maa shaa Allah.* Sean is the price of my help. When he is out of danger, I give you Otto."

She planted her feet in the ground, bumped her chin up a notch and cocked her head as if to say, *What's there to think about?* Before Al-Zahrawi could respond, Borodnoi tapped his watch. "Time to go!"

Al-Zahrawi ignored Borodnoi, eyes fixed on Kali. "Prove your Otto works."

Kali stooped, snapped open the latch on the briefcase, and activated the AI. "Normally, he requires my fingerprint and geomagnetic signature to start, but to speed things up, I eliminated the former and programmed in the latter."

Otto gave an audible 'Ready' and Kali punched in a set of digits. Otto telescoped out and across the Pacific Ocean to somewhere between Japan and Hawaii, then panned in until a murky shape appeared. It was long and narrow with the identifiable conning tower and sonar array of an American submarine. She flipped the laptop to face Al-Zahrawi. "There. Satisfied?"

"How do I know you are not tricking me?"

She waved him forward. "Come. Enter any location, as long as it's one I received. I assume you trust the agents you got them from?"

Al-Zahrawi took a step closer and gagged. "You do it. Use the Chinese sub's signature."

Kali had racked her brain for how this part of the negotiations would work. Al-Zahrawi would not select any of the Tridents because he couldn't prove Otto had located them, but the man probably had the exact coordinates of the *Han*-class sub, which made it a logical choice to confirm Otto's skills. Now everything depended upon Eitan Sun, whether he had done as she asked. If not, well, she didn't intend to live out this day anyway.

Otto flew up into the stratosphere, past the 7th Fleet, north to Jianggezhuang Submarine Base in Shandong province, and focused in on one dock.

Al-Zahrawi smiled.

"Hurry up!" Borodnoi barked. "Two minutes!"

Al-Zahrawi motioned Sean forward, gun trained on Kali. When Sean reached her, she whispered, "Hide in the boulder bed," without turning away from Al-Zahrawi.

"But—"

"I'll be OK." She spoke gently, but firmly. Sean scuttled out of sight.

"Good decision, Salah. Otto is yours." As she approached, he gagged, but held his ground. "If you bother my son anymore, or me, or force me on that copter, I'll kill myself and you end up with nothing. Pray I live long enough for you to reverse engineer Otto. It took me only a few months, but surely, you're faster than one infidel female.

Aleksei shouted as the helicopter's rotors started. "Salah, we have what we need. Let us go!" His tone was strident and anxious.

Al-Zahrawi didn't turn, eyes glued to Kali. "You are worthy of your namesake."

Kali didn't understand. She wasn't named for her mother. As though he read her mind, he continued.

"Not your family, Ms. Delamagente. You do not know your name's history? No wonder you pronounce 'Kali' wrong." He used a long 'a'. "In Sanskrit, it means 'she who devours time'. The goddess *Kali* possessed four arms. Two held a sword and a severed head. Two were elevated in prayer to guide initiates into the hereafter."

He cackled like a maniac. "I never intended you die, just Zeke Rowe. I transferred one million dollars into your account and released your name as the genius behind this attack. When you go to prison, your FBI will think justice is done and leave me to organize my next attack, protected by western social democracies who allow Islam to rule itself."

Al-Zahrawi gave a courtly bow and tumbled into the helicopter as it took off.

Kali's plan was simple: Free Sean. Transmit his location to Eitan to be rescued. Destroy Otto by destroying herself.

It was true, what she said about Otto requiring proof of life. What she didn't say was he not only stopped working, he blew up. And Al-Zahrawi couldn't guess that she had no fear of dying.

But for her plan to work, she had to stop him after he sent the locations to the successful bidders and before he landed.

Zeke tried to tell him he had a better solution, but Kali wouldn't listen. Under his plans, she told him, Annie had been slaughtered, her son kidnapped, and Sandy died. This time, she'd do it her way.

As the chopper lifted off, Kali sprinted up the scree slope to keep the helicopter in sight, give Otto a few more seconds to transmit the data to a waiting Eitan. Zeke yelled at Sean to stay behind the boulders and then raced after her. How Zeke survived being gunned down and left for dead would be a conversation for later. Zeke caught up with her at the top of the hill where she stood, eyes locked onto the chopper. There it hung, inches above the horizon.

And then, before she could end her life, there was a puff of smoke and a muted explosion.

Chapter 68

Kali felt Sean's ribs through the thin fabric of his shirt as she crushed him to her chest. She hadn't trusted herself to hold him before, fearing it would melt her resolve. Now she would never let him go. When he rasped out he was choking, she released him. When she couldn't stop her tears, Sean rested his head on her trembling shoulder.

It took several minutes before either of them could speak. It was Sean who recovered first. "I thought you were dead, Dr. Rowe."

He ruffled Sean's hair. "We only had one Kevlar vest. I wanted your mom to wear it, but she insisted they would never kill her. Guts seem to run in your family."

Sean fingered the embedded rounds. "Where's all the blood from?"

"That's animal blood. I exploded a bladder of it when the helo started spraying us with bullets. They needed to think they killed me."

Sean was flushed, his body steaming in the late afternoon heat. Rowe dragged him to an overhang, the only shade available.

"How did you stop Salah?"

"Have you met your mom's friend, Dr. Eitan Sun?" When Sean nodded, Rowe continued. "He persuaded the Navy to implant holographic digital files in buoys around the ocean, programmed to mimic a Trident sub right down to the magnetic signature. It's experimental technology, but Dr. Sun is overseeing the work. The real subs hid in spots like

Norway's fjords where Earth's natural magnetism overpowers anything coming from the boats.

"I implanted explosives onto Otto's motherboard which blew up after the chopper hit a pre-determined altitude. I gambled on the fact that he'd transmit the locations immediately after take-off. That gave Eitan time to grab the signals and find us before Otto destroyed himself."

Sean smiled. "I read about those fjords. They saved the Allies during WWII."

"So the holograms succeeded?"

Sun bounced three times. "The lucky auction winners happily pinged the fake subs which activated a virus that swarmed their networks—including Al-Zahrawi's—and gave us their locations and data. Each bidder was eager to be first among the many and most didn't encrypt their communication, which made it even easier. We rounded them all up in hours."

Duck whistled. "Good. That's good," and then asked the million dollar question. "Where are Zero and Kali?"

Sun hiccupped. "The helicopter exploded before Otto transmitted. All I have is a fifty-mile radius."

Duck sighed. "OK," and left. SEALs never expected a plan to survive activation.

Chapter 69

"I couldn't believe it, Mom!"

Kali dabbed at Sean's wounds with antiseptic from the first aid kit while Sean told his story. The gash on his forehead was healing with only a slight red ring around the jagged edges, thanks to Duck Peters aka Edik Vitolska. She owed him a lot for looking after her son.

Sean was pasty despite the sunburn, but the tension had melted from his face—and then he remembered Sandy.

"Sandy found me. He traveled over two hundred miles!" The boy's eyes teared. "When they came to move me, Sandy started barking and growling. They clubbed him until he passed out."

Tears rolled down Sean's cheeks. Kali hoped instead of vestal virgins, Muslims who beat a dog got the Gates of Hell.

"He couldn't walk after that, so he dragged himself after the car. Mom, do you think anyone found him? We can look for him, can't we?"

Kali nodded. "If any dog can make it, Sandy will."

Time for happier thoughts. "We wouldn't have solved this without you, Sean." Kali tried to finger-comb the boy's hair, but it was matted and sticky with filth.

Sean's eyes met Kali's in a shared understanding. "I knew you'd remember our code."

As they talked, the rain began, the drops sizzling as they hit the overheated ground. They used the downpour as a shower to wash the grime and dung from their bodies. When clean, Rowe picked out a smudge in the outcrop, partially hidden by brush.

"Let's shelter in that den."

When they arrived, Rowe blocked the way with his arm. "Those are wolf prints." He bent closer, studying them. "They're old. See the silt over them?" He waved everyone inside.

The air was dusky, the ground littered with bone shards and piles of molted fur, but it was dry. The dense smell of urine and decay made Kali gag. She hurried to the rear where she found several tunnels, one pitch dark, but the other with a patch of light at the end. This would be the wolf's escape route. Here, too, insects and rodent prints overlaid the canine's. When she returned, Rowe had a fire going and Sean was building a briar barrier to keep out predators. The group hunched around the blaze as the storm turned the Rift canyon into a roaring river.

They ate food Kali had scavenged, drank rainwater, and talked. Everywhere, life sought protection from Nature's power. A row of birds crowded wing-to-sodden-wing in a euphorbia. An elephant herd huddled, heads together, as the rain poured in rivulets off their bodies. A wild dog scampered along the plateau's edge, tail heavy with water and tucked between its legs, carrying a sodden rat in its mouth.

"Put your head in my lap, Sean, and I'll tell you how Lucy's story ends. She escaped her own terrorists."

Across the Rift stood Lucy's band, strong of body, heads high, faces expectant. She must warn them. She picked up her enemy's spear, walked to the edge of the precipice, and lifted her arm. She felt the weight in her hand, the balance over her shoulder, the even placement of her feet, and flung the weapon forward into the abyss.

It sailed through the air like Eagle. Her band watched, their faces following its arc until it crashed into the rocky scree below.

They understood.

Lucy drank in their shapes and burned them into her

memory as one by one, they melted into the landscape. Now it was Lucy's turn. Boah and Garv led, with Lucy behind. Voi placed a tiny trusting hand in hers. Ump leaned in to her side as though knowing she needed his support. Their steps turned northward.

There, Lucy was sure, they would find safety.

Epilogue

True to his word, Al-Zahrawi left a trail that implicated Kali in his ruthless plot. When Duck found them two days later, the FBI arrested her for aiding and abetting terrorists. Rowe played the tape of Kali's negotiations with Al-Zahrawi, but even James wasn't convinced.

Experts dug through the accusations. She spent hours with the investigators explaining every step of her involvement. Despite their acrimony, she insisted Dr. Wynton Fairgrove was not in league with Al-Zahrawi, simply misguided. His only crime was trying to highjack Kali's research. As proof, she turned over Otto's video of the scientist's death.

That brought them to a discussion of Otto. Kali went over DNA, geomagnetism, Special Relativity, in detail and multiple times, but lost every expert who tried to debrief her. Finally, James called Sun.

"Kali may end up in prison because she can't explain what happened in a language the interrogators understand."

By the time Sun finished explaining what Kali and Otto had done, they applauded her for her creativity in exposing a web of terrorists bent on destroying America.

Cariole escorted her from the building. He'd become a staunch supporter of her innocence, and she appreciated his logic among the sometimes vicious investigators.

As they stepped outside, he said, "The Monroe's got ten years for their part in this."

Kali shook her head in confusion. "What makes a couple go off the deep end?"

Cariole shrugged. "I have lots of answers, but never for that question."

Rowe's phone interrupted them. "Mr. Whitetower?" He poked speaker.

"Yes, Dr. Rowe. I don't know if you remember me—"

"Of course I do. I don't think we could have found Sean without you."

"I think I have his dog, at least I rescued a badly injured Lab who responds to 'Sandy'."

Kali gasped. "He's alive?"

"Very much so. He's a great dog. You're lucky to have him in your family."

"How did you find him?" Kali struggled to control her voice.

"I went to the cabin, see if I missed anything. I found a blood trail that led me to what I first thought was a dead coyote. Until he shivered.

"Most dogs are mean when they're injured, but Sandy wagged his tail and licked my hand like he trusted me. He possesses the warrior spirit."

Kali's throat closed and her eyes welled with tears. "I'll come get him—"

"No." Felix cut her off. "I know you're worried." Whitetower paused and said, 'Good boy, Sandy'. "Give me a week to get him healthy enough to travel, then we'll negotiate my visitation rights. Oh, and thank you for the cameras. They will be put to good use."

As she hung up, she looked at Zeke, waiting.

"The FBI shares camera phones with local police to build better relationships. Bobby shipped five to Whitetower."

Cariole tapped her on the shoulder. "Before I forget. When we went through Dr. Fairgrove's home, we found this."

He handed her a white rag envelope sealed with wax. *Kali* was penned in ornate script on the front. According to the date, it was over twenty years old. Kali slipped it into her pocket.

He patted her arm. "There remain several details I must wrap up. I may call you."

He smiled and walked across the street, hands in his pockets, whistling, like a man without a care in the world.

Kali and Zeke got only five minutes with Sean before the

nurse threw them out. *The patient is dehydrated and sun sick. If you expect him home soon, he needs rest.* Next, they went to intensive care where Cat remained in a coma. There, they sat for an hour, updating her, telling funny stories, and then just holding her cool, dry hand.

James was waiting outside when they left. He had wrinkles that hadn't been there a month ago.

"Do you want to join us for a snack, Bobby?"

"I'm going home. Just need a minute with Kali." He glanced over their heads at the glorious evening. The sun had dipped below the horizon, leaving a golden afterglow behind the buildings. Red and orange wisps of clouds clung to the dusky sky with the first scattering of stars twinkling in their midst.

"The FBI would like a closer look at Otto, when you recover."

"Bobby, I decided to destroy Otto. How do I protect my family and others from terrorists who want him for their own nefarious reasons?"

"Top secret projects go on all the time without endangering participants. You've been working with one of the contractors for quite some time."

Rowe jumped in. "Speaking of Dr. Sun, I was hoping to thank him, maybe meet his wife. We could all have coffee." Kali gasped and Zeke asked, "What? Does she have two heads?"

Kali started and stopped and finally spit out, "She died a year ago. In childbirth. I don't know if I should be the one telling you this, but every time Eitan has to answer well-meaning questions, it sets him back."

Kali licked her lips and uncrossed then recrossed her arms over her chest. "There were complications. The doctors told Eitan they could save either the mother or children. Sun begged his wife, said they could have more babies, but she refused. They fought—the first time in their marriage—and then it was too late. All three died and Eitan's never been the same.

"The truth is, I was scared to death Eitan wouldn't survive. He missed two months of work, rarely ate or changed clothes. He slept on a couch because he couldn't stand waking up in the bed they'd shared. The thought of living paralyzed him. I'd find him standing in the hallway or the back yard and he couldn't remember how he got there or why. He'd be in the kitchen and not know if he ate. He was afraid to turn the stove on for fear he'd burn his house down."

Rowe grimaced. He should have caught that—the chronic ache that had nothing to do with physical pain and everything to do with a shattered spirit, knowing it couldn't be fixed. It made sense now—the talking picture, never wanting to go home, burying himself in his work.

At another time, that was Rowe.

The corners of Kali's mouth tugged up in a wan smile. "I wish you'd known Eitan before—not better, just different. Something fundamental in him changed after her death."

"Is he seeing anyone?" Rowe had been sure he never would until Kali stumbled through that conference room door.

"That's one more failure he can't come to terms with. His wife made him promise to find someone new, but he says he can't, and it tears him apart to lie to her."

"How did he get himself back to work?"

Kali looked through Rowe. "One morning, two months ago, he woke up and declared it over. He took a few steps outside and the world didn't close in on him. He spoke a question and didn't hear his wife's voice. He spent five whole days watching the sun rise in the east and set in the west, and decided it was similar to what used to be. He replaced all his furniture and realized he could keep living if no one expected much. Since then, he takes life a day at a time. I think helping you, Zeke, did Eitan a lot of good."

James cleared his throat. "Anyway, if your Navy gig doesn't work out, just wanted you to know you had options." He shook her hand and left.

Rowe gave her a quizzical look. "What was that?"

"The Navy asked me to work with their people to add DNA security to the system firewalls so NEV or its cousins will no longer be a problem. They're naming the project after Cat."

Rowe drove Kali home, but he didn't turn the car off when they reached her building. He might as well ask, even though he was pretty sure what both the Navy and James offered were better choices. Still, if he learned anything these last weeks, it was not to make decisions for her.

"In my write-up on the Israeli dig, I want to include a theoretic but evidence-based conclusion of what brought descendants of the three species out of Africa. I could use your help."

She didn't even take time to think. "Yes, if you add my name when you publish. It's time I started looking after myself. I have a son to put through college."

She sat in the car, glancing between her front door and Rowe.

"I can't believe how much I miss Annie. How did she get inside me so fast?" She leaned into his shoulder. "Can I stay with you until Sean comes home? I don't want to be alone when I figure out if Wyn was my father."

"That second DNA sample I ran."

Kali hung her head. "How could he ask me to marry him? He must have known."

Without waiting, she raced into her apartment, returning in five minutes with a duffle bag and an envelope.

"I got a response from the Berkeley Geochronology Center." She tore the letter open. "The age of the bone Cariole found under Wyn is 1.8 million years old. They want to meet me."

Rowe left shortly after they arrived, something about talking to Bobby James, and Kali used the time to think through everything that happened the last months. It came to one surprising conclusion: She didn't want to get rid of Otto, not because of his intellectual powers or because he had become what she proposed to DARPA. The real reason was personal. How could she say good-bye to Lucy? Lucy's life experiences, how she cared for her family and solved her problems, had taught Kali more than any other person in Kali's life. Lucy was a best friend who didn't judge or use others. Kali had no one to fill those giant shoes.

The front door opened. Rowe smiled a greeting but had his phone glued to his ear.

"Hello? I'm calling from the United States. I was hoping to talk to the sisters of Laslo Hemren..."

As Rowe talked, Kali reached into her purse and pulled out the letter Detective Cariole had given her. The brittle adhesive cracked open to reveal three sheets of linen paper. Kali curled into Rowe's couch and began to read.

Dear Kali. I have much to tell you...

Want More?

Read the next in the Rowe-Delamagente series, *Twenty-four Days*:
https://www.amazon.com/dp/B072NZF8N8/

Find out more about Lucy (from *To Hunt a Sub*) in the spin-off novel, *Born in a Treacherous Time*:

Preview of *Twenty-four Days*

Monday, August 7th
HMNB Devonport England

Until last month, Eyad Obeid considered himself a devout Muslim. He prayed five times a day, proclaimed God's glory in every conversation, and performed the required ablutions when confronted with uncleanliness. When his brother was executed by Israeli gunman five years ago, Obeid swore retribution. No nobler purpose could he imagine for his worthless life than dying for Allah.

But instead of a suicide vest and the promise of seventy-two virgins, the village imam enrolled him in college to learn nuclear physics, thermodynamics, chemistry, and math so complex its sole application was theoretical. Much to Obeid's surprise, he thrived on the cerebral smorgasbord. In fact, with little effort, he attained all the skills required by the Imam.

By the time he earned his PhD in Nuclear Physics, he had learned two lessons. First, he was much smarter than most people around him, and second, the western world was not what he had been told.

Now, just weeks after graduation, Eyad Obeid approached the dingy Devonport pub on the frigid southern shore of England and wondered how to explain to the man responsible for giving Eyad Obeid this amazing future that he would fulfill his obligation, but then, wanted out.

He squared his shoulders and entered the pub.

His stomach lurched. Rather than his mentor Salah Mahmud al-Zahrawi, he found the Kenyan and his three henchmen. He had first met these thugs in San Diego California where he learned to run a nuclear submarine under the friendly tutelage of British submariners. When Obeid finished his studies, the Kenyan slaughtered the Brits. No warning. No discussion, just slash, slice and everyone died.

As did Obeid's belief in the purity of Allah.

The nuclear physicist jammed his hands into his pockets, hunched his shoulders, and approached the table. The Kenyan had never introduced himself and Eyad Obeid lacked the courage to ask.

"I was expecting Salah al-Zahrawi," Obeid offered as he slipped into the booth.

The Kenyan stared past Obeid, eyes as desolate as the Iranian desert, thick sloping shoulders still, ebony skin glistening under the fluorescent lights. Danger radiated from him like the hum of a power plant. He had three new fight scars since their last encounter, like angry welts but otherwise, he looked rested, clearly losing no sleep over the slaughter of innocents.

"You have one more job before you are released." In a quiet, toneless voice, the man without a soul explained the new plan, finishing with, "If you fail, you die."

Obeid was stunned. His gut said *Run!* He risked his future—his life—staying a moment longer with this crazed zealot, but Obeid did little more than croak a strangled, "If I succeed, I will also die!" His University friends called it a Sophie's Choice.

The Kenyan shrugged. "But less painfully."

Obeid twitched as heat washed his face. As he sought an appropriate response, the waitress arrived with tea. She poured a cup for each of them, chattering to no one in particular about how she had forgotten her blarmy slicker because her boyfriend kept her up the whole bloody night, di'n he, and she was frightfully knackered. No one responded.

"Shall I tell you the specials on offer?"

The Kenyan slowly ratcheted his head toward her. "Go."

The waitress backed away, almost knocking over another server and his steaming tray of eggs, bacon, black pudding, and baked beans. "Well, aren't we in a bloody mood," and she left.

The Kenyan did not seem to notice, his flat dead eyes back on Obeid. The physicist squirmed. He was but one man. His only hope was to quietly warn the authorities. He folded his hands into his lap to hide their shaking.

"*Insha Allah,* I will help. What do you require?"

"Do you remember the training you received from the Parishers?"

The British submariners you butchered? Obeid nodded.

"You must ensure the sailors perform their duties after we hijack the sub."

With no further explanation, the Kenyan tossed a fistful of notes onto the table and left. As Obeid hurried after him, he surreptitiously thumbed a message into his phone and pushed send.

There was no signal.

The Kenyan parked in the crew lot outside Her Majesty's Devonport Plymouth Naval Base. Obeid changed into a uniform and emerged from the car carrying a loaded gun in a prayer rug. *Maa shaa Allah.*

The storm broke and quickly turned the parking lot slick and shiny. Obeid shivered despite the heavy pea coat with the warm fur-lined collar. How did the British stand the weather? When this ended, he would never again leave the sparkling sun and cloudless skies of his beloved Iran.

"Eyad!" It was Tariq Khosrov, with two other friends from Obeid's graduate program, all with PhDs in nuclear physics. Tariq was one of the smartest boys Obeid had ever met and the most naïve. "Are we going to steal a nuclear submarine?"

Obeid hissed, "Quiet!" and the Kenyan nudged him toward the base's thick metal gates. They had been designed to stop an AK-47 or a firebomb, even an RPG, but not the weapon Salah al-Zahrawi would use. Faithful Muslims who worked for naval personnel had replaced pictures of the dead

San Diego Parishers with Obeid and the rest of the hijackers. By the time the Royal Navy realized something was wrong, *HMS Triumph* would be gone and missing.

"Next!"

The man in front of Obeid passed his ID to the bored security. He checked the man's face, his computer screen, and waved him through.

It was Obeid's turn. "ID, please."

Obeid's chest tightened as the stern-looking sentry, blonde hair trimmed close to his scalp, collar turned up against the wind, fingers like thick sausages on powerful hands, turned a flint-eyed glare to Obeid. The nuclear physicist froze and the guard's boredom became suspicion. He read the name stitched on the right breast of Obeid's uniform. "*Haim* is it?"

He looked Obeid up and down, as though to determine if the name matched the slight figure in front of him with wire-rimmed glasses and the thatch of black hair dripping rain down his forehead. True, he couldn't tell Obeid's stomach lacked the six-pack of muscles the real Haim had been so proud of, but he could see Obeid's slender hands and they were those of a scientist, not a sailor. Surely, the guard would say something.

Obeid fumbled, almost dropping the ID before shoving it forward.

"Anything to declare?" The guard's gaze flicked to the prayer rug.

Sweat broke out under Obeid's arms. Should he tell the guard there was an AK-47 in his prayer rug or would he shoot before listening to Obeid's explanation? No, better to deal with the problem onboard. Besides, the Kenyans claimed they were simply leveraging demands against Britain backed by the threat posed by the sub's weapons. They would never use them.

He bit his lip hard, tasting blood, and forced anger into his voice. "You suspect me because I am Muslim? Do you want to examine my prayer rug?" His voice dripped with righteous indignation as he had practiced and he extended the tightly-bound bundle, taking care to keep the ends turned away from the soldier. "Maybe I am carrying an A... K." He purposely stumbled over the name.

The sentry flushed and stepped back as though burned.

"Now I didn't mean that mate, did I? O' course you're fine," and waved Obeid through.

Across the yard, limned against the grey sky, towered the domed shape of the *HMS Triumph*, its deck slick with rain, sail glistening in the early morning light. The warheads it carried could reach the vast majority of the planet but the bustling sailors, some in oil-stained uniforms, others nattily dressed in white with jaunty officer caps, greeted each other, oblivious to the danger approaching them in the uniform of shipmates.

What had he done?

"Keep going," the scar-faced Kenyan hissed between clenched teeth.

Obeid balled his fists to stop their shaking and forced his steps to be slow and measured as if in no rush to start what would be a three-month deployment.

When the group reached the *Triumph*, they were greeted by a cherub-faced seaman. "You the Parisher blokes?" He stuck his hand out. "Name's McEwen. We're the Second crew. First came down with food poisoning." He chuckled, eyes crinkling with merriment, brows like gray steel wool. "Brill, you think? Who wants to play hide and seek with a Diesel?"

McEwen poked the Kenyan in jovial familiarity while Obeid combed through his training for what a 'diesel' might be.

"Enough yakking. Get sorted, blokes. We leave in an hour."

About the Author

Jacqui Murray lives in California with her spouse and the world's greatest dog. She *has been writing fiction and nonfiction for 30 years and an adjunct professor in technology-in-education.*

You can find Jacqui Murray on her blog:
https://worddreams.wordpress.com

Twitter:
https://twitter.com/WordDreams

LinkedIn:
https://www.linkedin.com/in/jacquimurray

www.ingramcontent.com/pod-product-compliance
Lightning Source LLC
Chambersburg PA
CBHW031116210626
46816CB00016B/1470